Neon Dreams

Marilyn Mufson

Dedication

For Rebecca Kanter Abrams and Sara Abrams Sharnik

Acknowledgements

My heartfelt thanks to Christopher Sawyer-Laucanno, who gave me permission to write; Phyllis Hatfield, who polished my diamond in the rough; Jeanne Martinet, who helped me master the art of plotting; and the late Joyce Engelson, whose brilliant insights made Neon Drams sing! I would also like thank the legendary literary agent, Roslyn Targ, for believing in me. Many thanks to Sean Dazet, I couldn't have asked for a better business manager. Finally, I could have never written this book without the love and support of my husband Mike, and my children, David, Ariana and Zachary.

Las Vegas, Nevada
October, 1962

I splashed cold water on my face and held onto the rim of the sink to steady myself. Why did I have three martinis on an empty stomach? There was a jar of Safeway Instant on the counter next to the sink—a red kettle on the stove. I opened the cupboard. Three white mugs. A sugar bowl. I'd be fine after coffee. Lots of coffee.

Until now, I hadn't paid much attention to the interior of the house. The kitchen was shades of boring brown—not much bigger than the one in my parents' apartment. The living room had a standard beige wall-to-wall carpet and drapes. I half-walked, half-staggered around the room, holding onto knotty-pine furniture when necessary, snickering at various desert-motif knickknacks including an over sized turquoise ashtray with three grooves for cigarettes, and a cowboy riding a horse on a burlap lampshade. Hardly the dream house advertised in last Sunday's paper.

I felt much steadier after my second coffee. There was a phone on the bar that separated the kitchen from the living room. I'd call the police; tell them I was almost raped. They'd take me home. What if they said it was my fault for getting drunk? What if they thought I'd led him on? The hell with the police. I'd call a cab. I had ten dollars. But, how could I tell the cabbie where to pick me up when I didn't know where I was? I went over to the window and peeked out between the drapes to make sure the bastard was really gone. The street was deserted. I opened them all the way. It was dark, but I could see a street sign on the corner. I looked for my shoes. Damn! They were in his jacket. Big deal. The heels were so high I could barely walk in them anyway.

My teeth chattered when I went outside. I should have worn my coat. I vaguely remembered it slipping off while he was lowering me onto the couch. Thinking about him made me shudder. A rock dug into my heel. My knees buckled in pain. I felt it all the way up my leg. At least it sobered me up. I limped to the sidewalk and turned in a circle, trying to get my bearings. No roads off in the distance. No neon glittering from the Strip. It was so dark out I could barely read the street name. *Stormy Road*. Funny. In Las Vegas, where it rains once a year. Hurrying to get back in the house I tore holes in my nylons.

I looked up Red Cab. Picked up the receiver. No dial tone. My stomach plunged. I fiddled with the phone, shook it, banged it, checked the other rooms. No working phones. What now? Spend the night in hopes that somebody nice would show up tomorrow and rescue me? No way. If Mr. Big-shot had a key, his pals probably had them, too. I had to get out of this house—the sooner the better. Stormy Road had to lead somewhere. I'd walk home, even if it took all night. But I'd need shoes.

The twin beds had quilted brown-and-white checked bedspreads with no sheets or pillowcases underneath. I ripped one up with a carving knife from the kitchen, wrapped the two hand towels from the bathroom around my feet, added three layers of bedspread and tied them on with my nylons and cord I cut off the drapes. I sealed it all with Saran Wrap.

I peeled off my girdle, kissed it for saving my honor earlier and stuffed it in my purse. It would be easier to move without it, especially if I had to run from a coyote. I found a flashlight in the cabinet under the sink. Stuck it in my coat pocket. My empty stomach growled. The refrigerator contained a six-pack of Budweiser, three slices of lunchmeat with pimento, a jar of French's mustard, a Snickers bar, and moldy cheese. "For God's sake, Beck, put it back. It's got fur growing on it!" I dropped the cheese, ate the pimento out of the lunch meat, gobbled half the Snickers and stashed the rest in my pocket. Passed up the Budweiser. I'd heard beer has nutritional value, but I'd had it with alcohol.

By now it was pitch-black out. No moon to speak of. I left the door unlocked in case I lost my nerve. The newly paved road was easy on my homemade shoes, which were far more comfortable than my heels, but clumsy. And noisy. The Saran Wrap crunched as I walked. One hand clutched the flashlight; the other was in my pocket with the knife, my purse tucked under my arm. At least I had ten bucks. Walking-home money, as my mother would say. *Oh, Mama Sadie, if you could see me now! I'll call the minute I get home. I won't say a thing about the man who almost raped me. Why add to your pain?*

A coyote howled. Coyotes don't attack humans unless they're provoked, do they? I'd grown up here, but I didn't know. At least I didn't hear anything growling. With the flashlight, I could see about twenty feet. Could they see me? My teeth chattered.

Sadie's voice said, "You only have yourself to blame." I know, I know. I shouldn't have had three martinis. I should have insisted on eating something. But I'd trusted him completely. It was all an act. He led me on. He was worse than my father.

I pointed my flashlight as far as it would go. Still no lights in the distance, no signs of life. Concrete foundations at either side of the road. Stacks of lumber. With all those houses going up, you'd think there would be a Seven-Eleven or a Shell station. Something flitted across the road. A lizard. Don't be such a coward, Beck. Lizards are harmless. Then I remembered: "Always carry a snakebite kit when walking in the desert." Where'd I read that? Same place I read about a kid who had his leg amputated after a snake bit his foot. Sarah Bernhardt only had one leg when she played Hamlet, but she was an established actress. I was still unknown. I'd never get a foot in the door. Bad joke, Beck. You deserve to be bitten.

Something else could be lurking out there, more dangerous than a snake. My hand gripped the knife. Last week the police had found a headless body in a ditch off the road between Pop's Oasis and Baker. Review Journal. Front page. This would be a perfect spot for a murder. I could scream and scream. Nobody would hear. If something happened to me, my would-be rapist would be overjoyed. My father wouldn't lose any sleep—my ex-boyfriend either. I had to stay alive to spite them.

"I'm not afraid! You hear me? I'm not the chickenshit you think I am!"

I took out my knife, stabbing at the sky. You're tough, Beck. This little trek in the desert isn't going to bring you down. How long had I been walking anyway? An hour, at least. Probably more. My feet hurt. The Saran Wrap was in shreds. The wind blew dust in my eyes and pricked my face like tiny needles. My flashlight hand felt numb. On the positive side, I felt thinner. I'd read somewhere you have to walk thirty-six miles to lose one lousy pound. My God, Beck, how can you think of weight at a time like this?

I stopped, heart pounding. Were those lights up ahead? Yellow flashes, shimmering in the distance. What else could they be? I ignored my aching feet and ran. Lights! A good omen. A sign of life. I slowed down to a walk. Stopped. Flashing lights illuminated a yellow sign: CAUTION. PAVED ROAD ENDS. PASS AT YOUR OWN RISK. I pointed my flashlight. About twenty feet ahead, Stormy Road ended, turned to rocks.

No wonder there weren't any cars. Construction crews were probably the only ones who had a reason to drive out here. I knew I had to keep going. Nobody would find me out here, except a rattlesnake, or a murderer. But my knees refused to hold me. I collapsed in the middle of the road.

For the longest time, I lay with my cheek resting on the gritty surface of the road, my teeth coated with dirt. I felt heavy, weighed down, drained. I'd been through a war. Not just tonight. My family. Yelling, screaming. Like being shelled, over and over. Now all I wanted was to avoid pain, even though it meant giving up. Professor Milligan had said my life was full of brilliant starts that went nowhere. They led here. The future was a yellow sign that said DEAD END.

Sorry, Mom. It's not your fault I ended up here. You tried to protect me. My father didn't give a damn, but you cared too much. Sorry, Grandma Rosie, for letting you down. You were my best friend. Is that your hand, Grandma Rosie, stroking my forehead?

C'mon, Rebecca! Get up! You've got half a Snickers bar in your pocket. Eat it, darling. It's like Popeye and spinach.

I sat up. "That's not Grandma Rosie. It's me. The ventriloquist." I wiped my mouth on my sleeve, reached in my pocket and pulled out the Snickers. Flat as a fast-food burger and covered with lint. Wrapper half-gone.

"Hey, Milligan! You asked what it would take for me to believe in myself? A Snickers that's been through hell." I licked my fingers and stared at a sky full of stars. Millions of them. So beautiful and hopeful they almost made me cry.

My heart pounding, I picked up my purse, found my flashlight, and shuffled to the end of the road. Big rocks, little rocks, smooth, rough, sharp. If I chose my path carefully I could minimize the pain. I checked my "shoes." The left one had worn down to the towel. The right still had two layers of bedspread. Don't think about it, Beck. Do it!

I led off with my right foot, followed by my left toe. The shoes helped cushion the blow, except for the sharp ones. Go ahead. Yell. Nobody will hear. If I ever get out of this, I'll never drink another martini. That's right, Beck. Bargain. Lie. Whatever it takes to get going. How about, I'll never trust another man? Or, I'll dedicate my life to worthy causes? "Ow!" I bet if Lucille Ball were in my shoes she'd turn it into a sketch for The Lucy Show.

The goddam flashlight was fading. But I was making progress. Looking back, I couldn't see the "road closed" sign. My left foot was cramping from walking on the toe. I let down my heel. "Ow!" It felt as if I'd stepped on a nail. I stood on one foot to look, but almost fell. It seemed like a bad idea to sit on the rocks. I got my girdle out of my purse, dropped it behind me, hiked up my dress and plied all the way down, placed my other hand on the girdle and gently lowered myself.

Sitting almost made up for the pain in my heel. I

held my foot under the fading flashlight. Oh, God. Glass. My hand shook as I picked it out. The cut wasn't deep, but the sight of blood made me shiver all over. I stopped the bleeding with a Kleenex and waved my flashlight. Up ahead, broken beer bottles, cans. Everywhere. Jesus. Hadn't I suffered enough? C'mon, Beck. Get up. Don't chicken out. Keep going. That's a girl. One step at a time. "Ouch! Oh, God. Oh, fuck! This is not fun. It's hard. It's painful. It sucks!" The flashlight flickered wildly. "Oh, God. Now, I've really had it."

I needed something to cheer me up, keep my mind off the pain. Movies. Gene Kelly with his umbrella and a shit-eating grin, tapping his heart out in *Singing in the Rain*... Hepburn and Bogart picking leeches off each other in that rickety old *African Queen*. "Ouch! Damn!" God were they good. The best! Judy Garland in *The Wizard of Oz*... And Margaret Hamilton with her green face. "Who killed my sister? Was it you, my pretty?" Peter Lorre as Joel Cairo in *The Maltese Falcon*. "Ow! Shit, that hurts!" Lorre put sniveling on the map. And Sydney Greenstreet as Gutman, the fat man. Nobody was ever more sinister. Bogart as Sam Spade, Private Eye, bullshitting in Greenstreet's hotel room. The essence of cool. When life throws you a curve, pretend you're Sam Spade.

Oh, my God—a road! I could see it—about half a block in front of me. And a bench. It had to be a bus stop! A goddam bus stop in the middle of nowhere! I couldn't see any headlights, but it was just a matter of time. In a twenty-four hour town, busses run all night. "I'm saved," I said, laughing, crying, hobbling to the bench. "I'm saved!"

There was a cardboard sign taped to the

window of the bus: BEEN ROBBED TOO MANY TIMES. EXACT CHANGE ONLY. There weren't any passengers. The driver would make an exception when he saw how pitiful I was. The bottoms of my shoes were in bloody shreds. My God, he'd probably rush me to an emergency ward. I hobbled up the steps on the sides of my feet and held onto the pole by the door.

"Um, excuse me. Where does this bus go?"

Poor guy looked like he hadn't slept in weeks.

"McCaren Airport to Fremont. Next stop, Nevada Southern."

Thin, haggard, zombie-eyed.

"I need to get to Paradise Road."

"Transfer at Flamingo."

A gash throbbed under the big toe of my right foot.

"That's not going to get me home."

"Make up your mind. Ain't got all night."

I let go of the pole and staggered toward him.

"You don't understand. I can't walk. My feet are cut up. All I have's a ten."

He stared straight ahead with his living-dead eyes.

"Couldn't you... couldn't you just drop me at a gas station or something?" I was shaking, almost crying. "So I can call a cab? Please? Look, I've been through hell the last two days."

He sneered at me! "That's your problem, lady, not mine."

"I'm not about to give up ten bucks for a fifteen cent ride that won't even take me home!"

"Then get off the fucking bus!"

I lurched over to him, on the sides of my feet.

"Where's your heart? I know you've been robbed, but that doesn't give you the right to rob me!"

"Jesus fucking Christ! You got blood on the floor!"

"I can't help it! I told you my feet were bleeding."

"Give me the ten, or get off the bus."

"That's it! I've had it!" I pulled out the knife and waved it in his face. "I'm not taking shit from you or anybody else. Not anymore."

His eyes bulged. "Jesus fucking Christ!"

I backed toward the door, grabbed the pole with one arm, brandished my weapon with the other.

"I could rob you, if I wanted. I could make you do anything. I could steal your fucking bus."

His face was all contorted. "Put that thing away!"

"I said, if I *wanted to*, which I don't, but you…"

He practically sobbed. "Why me? I don't deserve this!" He banged his head on the steering wheel. "Not again!"

"You think bad luck comes because we deserve it? Hah!" I hobbled to the front window, jabbing the air. "It's random. Completely random."

He started punching change out of the tubes. It fell on the floor. "Take it." He slid it toward me. "Take it. Take it all."

"You're as bad as them, you know that. The people who robbed you. You're…"

He got out his wallet. "Take it all." Threw it at me. "I don't care anymore."

I threw it back. "Weren't you listening? I said I didn't want to rob you."

He pulled the lever that closed the door and started driving. Fast.

"What are you doing?" I held onto the pole.

"Just don't talk to me. That's all I ask. Just don't

talk."

"But I was just…"

"Jesus fucking Christ! Shut up!"

The bus was weaving back and forth. I wished he would slow down. I almost dropped the knife. I wrapped my arm around the pole to steady myself"

"Hey! It's Nevada Southern. Aren't you supposed to stop? Somebody's on the bench."

"I know there's a fucking bench."

"You better go back. They could report you. And you're speeding. You could get a ticket."

"I could get a ticket." He was laughing, but it wasn't laughing. "That's rich. I could get a ticket."

"On top of everything else! A ticket could push you right over the edge. Believe me. It's the little things."

"Please, lady. Don't talk."

"Don't make it worse for yourself."

"Shut the fuck up!"

He almost drove off the road!

"Sunrise Hospital. There's Sunrise Hospital. Great cafeteria. You can eat for a dollar. Not just a snack. A real meal. Why are you turning? Is this a stop?" He pulled into the circle driveway, nearly wiping out a row of little green shrubs. "Do people get on here?"

He pulled a lever. The door opened. He looked at me.

"Oh, I get it. You want me to get off. This was really nice of you. I take back all I said." I giggled, uncontrollably. "When I first got on, I thought, he'll probably take me to the hospital. And here we are!"

2.

August, 1962
Two Months Earlier

"Becky?"

Sadie's voice rang out over the tap water. I'd taken to calling my parents by their first names in my head; that way, it seemed like they were just people who happened to be related to me. She banged on the door. Since there was nothing we could talk about without hurting each other I tried to avoid her as much as possible.

"You're turning into your cousin Dorothy with the genius I.Q. She wasted her life on the toilet with the door locked."

I opened the door to probing eyes behind cat-woman glasses with rhinestones at the corners. Sadie's hairdo, by operator Forty-six at the Las Vegas College of Beauty, stood straight up from her head, a blonde tidal wave. For a woman of sixty-something, her skin was remarkably smooth. She could still be attractive if she ditched the glasses, fired Forty-six and stopped selecting her wardrobe from the bargain table at Payless Drugs. That yellow sleeveless sheath with the giant cactus in the middle didn't do a thing for her.

"I'm almost twenty-three, Mother. I have a right to privacy." I dropped my towel and climbed back in the tub, instinctively hugging my knees. Sadie was the kind of mother who stares at your crotch when she's talking to you because it's the part of you she hates most.

"Not in my house. You've been home almost three months, you still don't have a job and you refuse to let me fix you up with anybody. You're going nowhere fast."

"I'm not ready for another job. As you love to remind me, I went through five jobs in four months in Scottsdale. Worst experience of my life. I came home to recover." I turned away from her and resumed shaving my legs. "Besides, I don't want to face my public until I've lost another five pounds."

"I told you you were crazy to stay in Arizona, but you wouldn't listen. How could you expect to get anywhere without shorthand and typing?"

"Don't start with the typing, Mom." In her day, Sadie had been a crack typist. Legend had it she'd clocked in at a hundred and fifty words-per-minute. I was lucky to make forty. "Being a secretary is not my goal in life." I covered my shin with Ivory soap. "As I've told you several million times, I am an actress."

"That's not a job, it's a dream."

A bitchy little voice said, *she's right*, but I told it to shut up. "Thanks for the encouragement, Mom. It's because of you that I'm where I am today."

"It's because of me you went to college. Every penny my mother left I gave to you. Ten thousand dollars down the toilet."

"What do you mean, toilet? I graduated last January. Class of '61, remember?"

"By the skin of your teeth!" She closed the toilet lid and sat, leaning so close I could smell the Spraynet. "Education means nothing unless it pays the rent. If you couldn't find a husband, at least you could have gotten a teaching degree. Your problem," she pointed her finger, "is you think some director will discover you walking down the street and hand you a movie contract like Lana Turner. You're a good-looking girl, but Lana Turner you're not. Furthermore, actresses are fanatics about their figures. You've never been able to stick to a diet. No self- discipline. That's your problem."

"How many times do I have to tell you real actors don't go to Hollywood? Hollywood is about money. New York is about Art." Yeah, right—but, if I convinced her, maybe I could convince myself. "Furthermore, I've been living on cottage cheese and lettuce since I came home. You've been too busy stuffing your face with Sara Lee coffee cake to notice."

"Your other biggest problem is your mouth. That's why you can't keep a job."

"I get my mouth from you. You should be proud I have the guts to speak up." I turned my back on her. "I knew I shouldn't come home. I knew it, I knew it, I knew it!"

"You're lucky you still have a home to come to. That Christmas you told me you weren't a virgin, I thought I would die."

"Why?" I stared at a drop of water clinging to the lip of the faucet. "I was the one who was sleeping around, not you."

"Everything you do reflects on me." The drop made ripples in the water. "Since you can't keep a job, your only hope is to find a husband to support you. Not like that actor—that beatnik from Jersey who never took a bath the whole time he was here. Somebody respectable with both feet on the ground."

Sadie was referring to Joey Goldman. I'd told her he was out of the picture, but he was waiting for me in New York. I'd been putting him off for months.

"Unlike you, I could never marry for security." Her cheeks flushed as I gave her the same snotty look she was giving me. "Anyway, after all these years of watching you and my father tear each other to shreds, I'm not that anxious to join the club."

Sadie stared at the floor. I finished shaving my armpits. I'd nicked my legs several times. The little wedges of toilet paper I'd used to stop the blood were turning crimson. Finally, she looked up.

"You say you're afraid to get married because of your father and me. You complain you grew up without culture—Las Vegas held you back. Well, let me tell you something. My father worked fourteen hours a day at a factory. I shared a room with my four brothers. We couldn't afford beds so we slept on rags. When my mother was sick, and there was nobody to take care of us, my father put us in an orphanage. In spite of all that, my brothers put themselves through college, and law school, and medical school and graduated at the top of the class. They would have paid my way through college, but I didn't have the guts to go. I didn't have *drive*. You're worse than me. You can't even get out of the bathtub!"

That did it. "You're right, Mom. It's time for me to show some initiative and get a job." In a few months I could save enough money for a one-way ticket to New York and my share of the food and rent.

"I think you should apply at the Atomic Energy Commission."

"They make bombs!"

"That's at the test-site. Fanny Sweet's niece works at the one in town and all she does is type forms, which even you can do. With a college education you could work your way up."

"Doesn't matter if it's at the test-site, or here.

They are still engaged in the manufacture of nuclear bombs. You know how I feel about ..."

She put out her hand and smiled down at me like a sweet-little-old-Jewish grandmother. "I don't want to fight. All I want is for you to be happy. Before I forget, Fanny has a nephew who has a big job at the Sands. He's tired of going out with shiksas and wants to meet a respectable Jewish girl."

If I refused, I would never get her out of the bathroom. "Here I am."

"Good. I'll call her."

"Thanks, Mom. Before you leave, could you hand me some toilet paper?"

I peeked out the door. Sadie's nightgown, and the net cap she wore to preserve her hairdo, lay like a pile of pink flesh on the twin bed next to mine. Joined by a rosewood headboard, the beds were part of a suite she'd bought the day she'd moved into my bedroom. We'd been roommates since I was fourteen, after my father went on a two-week gambling binge and she decided she didn't want to sleep with him any more. He became "the Boarder." In the beginning, I liked the company. We giggled over boys and dirty jokes. But the first time I came home with my dress inside out she lost her sense of humor.

On the way to the dresser, I left a trail of wet footprints on the wall-to-wall carpet. I dropped my towel and reached in my underwear drawer for my 32-D Maidenform long-line strapless bra.

The clothes in my half of the walk-in closet were divided into slim, zaftig and fat. Since I'd been home, I had lost fifteen of the twenty pounds I had gained in Scottsdale. I was ready for a size nine with a full skirt. Even if I ate cottage cheese forever I would never look like Audrey Hepburn; I'd been all boobs and butt since my first period. I chose a dress with a high neck and plunging back for my employment interview. Respectable without being boring.

While Sadie was on the phone with Fanny Sweet, I sat at the kitchen table eating a Lender's frozen bagel. Great diet food. They take forever to eat and make your jaw ache from chewing. Like a full meal. It was impossible not to overhear Sadie's end of the conversation. As usual, she and Fanny were exchanging sob stories about their husbands. Sadie claimed her Izzy was worse than Fanny's Moe.

"I can't even afford a cleaning lady. The goddam s.o.b. owes every joint in town. Some day, they'll come after him with a gun and I'll push him out the door."

I could see it: Izzy, dying on the sidewalk. Sadie, watching *The Untouchables*.

"He's out of town, her nephew." Sadie joined me at the table with her coffeecake. "His name is Milton Sweet. He'll call you next week."

"I can't wait." He would probably be bald, broad and boring like all of the Sweet men. Big deal. I only had to go out with him once. "Now all I need is a job." The mere thought of which depressed me, but there had to be something out there that wouldn't require selling my soul. Maybe I could be a receptionist at a doctor's office, or a hostess at a restaurant. "Maybe I could be a showgirl."

"Oy!"

"For your information, not all showgirls are sluts—they're dancers. Fannie's neighbor, the one who taught me that Charleston routine for the Senior Assembly, used to be with the Ballet Russe. She moved to Vegas because she's married so she doesn't want to go on tour all the time. It's the same with musicians. They can work year-round here."

"My life is over—I might as well blow my brains out."

"Alright, alright! I won't be a showgirl." I finished the rest of my bagel and washed it down with Maxwell House. "Not with my plentiful thighs. I'll go to the employment office and see what they have. Anyway, it doesn't matter where I work, since I'll be leaving."

"What do you mean, leaving?"

"I'm an actress, Mom. And all my friends have married and moved away. There's nothing here for me."

"In the bathroom, you said you'd forget about acting and look for a husband." She smacked her forehead. "Talking to you is like talking to the wall."

"I'll go out with whatsisname, but that's it." I crumpled my napkin and stood. "And I won't ever forget about acting. Everybody says I have talent—everybody but you. Soon as I have the money I'm going to New York."

Sadie closed her eyes. "Go ahead. Ruin your life. What do I care?" Her face was a Jewish Mt. Rushmore.

"Thanks for your blessing, Mom. Can I have the car keys?" Sadie opened her eyes.

"The employment office? Remember?"

She dragged herself to the kitchen and reached into her pocketbook. "Be home in time for me to pick up your father."

"I will."

"Know who you remind me of?" She asked my back. "Natalie Wood in *Marjorie Morningstar*. The one where she's a nice Jewish girl who thinks she wants to be an actress but she really wants to be a housewife."

"I hated that movie."

Driving to the employment office, all I could think about was Joey Goldman, my boyfriend in New York. It wasn't just that I missed him. The first time we ever talked, it was mostly about jobs. That was three years ago. I was nineteen, a second semester sophomore at Arizona State. Joey was just a freshman, but we were both in Intermediate Acting. I could tell he was attracted to me from day one. I wasn't the least bit interested. Younger men were much too unsophisticated. Plus the khaki uniform he wore twice a week for ROTC made his swarthy complexion look green. Even in regular clothes, something about him said "outsider." Then, Dr. Rogers said we had great chemistry and cast us in *The Moon Is Blue*.

"Can you believe the movie of *The Moon Is Blue* was banned?" I asked Joey after rehearsal. We were sitting in a booth at the Varsity Café. "Just for having words like *virgin* and *seduce*? Our society is so conservative." I ordered another iced tea and smiled back at a guy I knew from Introduction to Mass Communication.

"Yeah." Joey bit into his burger. He had dark, thick hair and big, sensual, Burt Lancaster lips. I hated Burt Lancaster. "But it was a hit on Broadway before they made it into a movie. I guess New York's more liberal."

"You're from the East Coast, aren't you?"

"How can you tell?" Instead of his ROTC uniform, he wore brand new Levi's, a plaid shirt and cowboy boots that must have cost a mint.

"Your vowels." I added sugar to my iced tea. He smiled. I stirred.

"I grew up in Jersey City." His eyes were sad-dog brown. "Transferred from Rutgers."

"Jersey. That's so neat! I've never been east of Cincinnati, where my mom's from. I'm dying to go to New York."

"The best thing about Jersey was leaving it."

"Yeah, well, you didn't grow up in Las Vegas." I poured some more sugar in my tea. "Actually, I was born in Hollywood, but my parents didn't think it was a proper environment for their precious only child, so they whisked me off to Las Vegas when I was five." He smiled. I stirred my tea. "That's not what really happened, but it always gets a laugh. Why'd you come all the way out here for college?"

"I'd never been west of Chicago." He shrugged and grinned which made him look even younger than eighteen. "I thought it would be cool to be a cowboy."

How naïve. "I know all about cowboys. Vegas is full of them. You should have stayed in Jersey, believe me."

"I love it out here!" Arms wide on *here*. "People are so real. Nobody cares what college you go to, or where you buy your clothes."

"I hate to tell you this, but cowboys are mostly bullies and drunks." I leaned across the table and lowered my voice. "And dumb. I read somewhere the average IQ in New York is ten to twenty points higher just from living there."

"You should transfer to NYU." He pushed his plate away with a bite and a half of hamburger left. "They have a great theater major."

"My mother's still getting used to my being this far away. Freshman year, she'd call every night and say, 'I'm standing in front of your room, crying, but don't mind me. Go out and have fun.' Can you imagine if I was in New York?" I was dying to eat his leftover hamburger, but I forced myself to stick to my diet.

"Plus, I'm an English major. She disapproves of theater— says I'll never make a living at it. Plus, NYU would probably cost more." I gave him a look. "We're not exactly rich, so I've learned to scale down my ambitions."

He flushed. "We're not rich, either. But, I guess you could call us well-off. My dad has his own business. He sells millions of plain black neckties to civil servants, funeral directors—people like that. My mom sings and plays piano, but just for fun. She was in a band before she had me. She's an artist at heart. Guess I take after her."

He was trying to get me to like him. Not a chance. I waved at a cute guy from Advanced Composition.

"Sorry, what were you saying?"

"My dad wants me to take over his business when he retires."

He looked gloomy. Was it my flirting, or his dad?

"I loved it, in class, when you did that routine where the son tells the father he wants to be an actor."

His face lit up. "Shelley Berman. I memorized all his albums." He cupped his hand and talked into it. "Hello? Hello, operator? You don't know me—I work in the office building across the street. Uh, there's a woman, hanging from a window on your tenth floor...'"

I couldn't help laughing. "You're funny."

"Talk about funny, your Gracie Allen routine was brilliant. You have to be born with that kind of timing."

"Yeah, well, if it weren't for my sense of humor I'd probably be a basket-case."

He gave me an I-see-inside-your-soul look. "It must have been weird, growing up in Las Vegas."

"Yeah, but I didn't realize it until I left. I mean,

when you live there it seems normal for people to have names like Three Fingers and Bugsy."

"Three Fingers." He grinned. "That's wild."

"Only thing I like about Vegas is the shows. I've seen all the greats: Danny Kaye, Martin and Lewis, Sinatra, Milton Berle, but there's no culture. I've never been to a real play." I sucked the last of the sugar out of my glass, folded my straw into triangles and flicked it off the table. "If I ever get to New York, I'm gonna devour everything. Theater, museums, Carnegie Hall. Everything!"

"Yeah. New York's the greatest. Last summer I shared an apartment with two other guys in the Village. Waited tables, took acting at the New School. I'd still be there, but my parents thought I should go to college."

He had lived in the Village? Right out of high school? I tried to act like I wasn't impressed. "I—I've always dreamed of being a serious actress—you know, in New York. I love acting more than anything. But I'm scared I won't make it and I'll starve to death." I stared at his leftover hamburger and bread-and-butter pickle slices on a lettuce leaf. "I can't type. I'm a lousy waitress. My first day at Pancake Heaven in Scottsdale I got fired for dropping seven plates and being slow. You're lucky. You can always work for your dad while you're waiting for your big break."

"I can't do anything I don't believe in. I could never sell ties. Nobody really needs ties." He shrugged, brown eyes wistful.

"After high school, I was an information operator at the Telephone Company." I stared at his pickles. He passed me his plate. "The woman next to me was turning into a phone. Always wore black, with little telephone earrings." I shivered. Ate a pickle and passed back his plate. "I could never go back there."

His eyes went from sad to depressed. Talking about jobs depressed me, too. I checked my lipstick in the little mirror from my purse and put on some more. Lipstick always cheered me up.

"You know who you remind me of?" he asked. "Julia Meade, from Ed Sullivan. When you read from *Caesar and Cleopatra* in class I said, 'It's her.'"

"But she's boring."

"Oh, no. She's classic. A legend. The quintessential TV goddess. Nobody's as cool as Julia Meade."

"I am not cool. I fall a lot. I always miss the armhole when somebody holds my coat. I spill things. You gonna eat that?"

He passed me the rest of his hamburger.

"Anyway, I'd rather do radio than TV, but radio is dead. It kills me; if I'd been born ten years earlier I could have been a great radio actress. I can do all kinds of voices—young, old, dialects. I sing. I even do birdcalls." I demonstrated.

"Wow. That's great. How do you do that?"

"It's a gift. You gonna eat those?"

He passed me the bag of chips that came with his burger.

"I also tap dance," I added, "but that's dead, too."

His face lit up. "Hey, maybe we could be an act? I do sound effects. Trains, creaking doors, a toilet flushing. I hold my breath and explode. It's very authentic-sounding."

"We'd need a lot more than birdcalls and toilets." I finished the potato chips.

"I play piano. We both sing. We could do improvisations, like Nichols and May."

"Oh, God, I love them!" I turned the chips bag upside down, shook it into my palm and licked up the tiny fragments. "We could never be that good."

"C'mon! We could try it out in class, for our final. See how it goes." He looked a little too eager. "Dr. Rogers says we have great chemistry."

"This is strictly platonic, right? I mean, you don't want to get involved or anything?"

"It would only get in the way."

I licked away the last of the salt and wiped my hands on my skirt. "You really think we could make a living?"

His eyes gleamed. "I think you'll never have to waitress, and I'll never have to sell ties."

3.

At the Nevada State Employment office, a receptionist with a pencil behind her ear gave me a form to complete and said she'd call me when my turn came. She directed me to a small waiting area with folding chairs. I refused to sit near the middle-aged woman in the pink sleeveless dress with baby powder showing under her arms. Instead, I sat next to a girl in sunglasses and white shorts. I smiled. She popped her gum and looked away.

I filled out my form, trying not to feel like a criminal for leaving out the jobs I'd lost in Arizona. Out of boredom, I perused the room. The State of Nevada hadn't invested much in their employment office. Shabby Venetian blinds. Walls, badly in need of paint. Four rows of gray desks. No pictures. No plants. I felt sorry for the employees, but I didn't trust them. Why should they care about finding us good jobs when they were stuck in a dump like this?

Across the room, a female employee sat on a platform like a bingo caller, eating a powder doughnut at a table piled high with folders. She was plump, with stringy brown hair and no makeup. Her bra strap showed. I couldn't stop looking at her. Her downcast eyes and dull expression made me think she was about forty, but her skin was firm. Poor thing was probably closer to my age. She yelled for coffee. A moment later I recognized her. My God! Libby Coleman.

Libby had been two years ahead of me at Vegas High. The one time she said "Hi," I ran home and recorded it in my diary with red ink. I made Sadie buy me a powder-blue Jantzen sweater, like Libby's, and penny loafers. I dreamed of trading places. I could be head cheerleader, homecoming queen, prom queen, and wear Lash Farley's ring on a silver chain. He was the sexiest boy in school. Every night, freshman year, I whispered, "Lash" as I kissed my pillow.

Once, I saw the two of them making out in the front row of the El Portal. They didn't come up for air until the lights came on. They missed Pat Boone in *Bernardine*. Libby got pregnant her senior year and quit school. Lash disappeared. I heard he joined the merchant marines.

"Wake up," said the girl in white shorts, "They just called us."

The man at the desk was so pale he appeared to have been embalmed. His eyebrows went up and down as he looked over my employment history. I tried not to stare at Libby.

"I need a job where I don't have to type," I said, before he had a chance to speak. He continued to inspect my credentials.

"Well, you say here you worked at the Telephone Company for two summers. Why not go back there?"

"I can't stand phones!"

"I see." He tapped his pencil on his ink blotter. "Do you like filing?"

"I don't think it's possible to like filing." I stared at my chewed off fingernails. If I hadn't been so repressed in high school I might have ended up pregnant, like Libby. "You can hate it, but you can't like it. It's just something you do to get paid."

"Well, how do you expect me to place you with an attitude like that?" I barely heard him. I was thinking of Libby's radiant face the night she was crowned homecoming queen. "We all have to start at the bottom, Miss Plotnik, even with a college degree."

A tear trickled down my cheek—then another. I sniffed. He offered me a Kleenex.

"Look, Miss Plotnik, you refuse to type. You don't like filing. You can't stand telephones. It's obvious you don't want a job."

The tears kept coming.

"Nobody has ever cried during one of my interviews."

He looked insulted. How could I tell him I was crying because of Libby getting fat and dumpy and wasting her life?

"I have to get out of here." I grabbed my purse, resisting the urge to grab Libby and take her with me. "It's too depressing."

People stared as if I were deranged. My interviewer shook his head and shrugged. As I ran for the door, I glanced toward Libby. She was gone.

Outside, I was assaulted by 110 degrees of dry heat. In the car, I turned on the air- conditioner and gazed in the mirror. Chewed-off lipstick. Puffy eyes with mascara smudged underneath. Shit! No Kleenex. I wiped my eyes on the hem of my skirt. "Dammit, Beck," I said, emptying all the junk in my purse on the passenger seat, "why did you have to cry?" I found my Persian Mellon lipstick and Sea Green Mist eye shadow. "She wasn't even a friend for God's sake!" Going home jobless was out of the question. I was close to the department stores and specialty shops on Fremont, but it was too late in the day to ask for a job. There was nothing else downtown except Glitter Gulch, two blocks worth of gaudy gambling joints down by the Union Pacific Depot. Working there wasn't an option. Not only did I abhor gambling, I'd never done it in my life.

I took after Sadie's side of the family. The Cohen's occasionally played the slots when they were in town, and dabbled at bingo, but they were more interested in getting a tan and seeing the floorshows. Sadie had played the slots when she first moved to Vegas, but that was before television. Now she watched soap operas and played canasta with her Hadassah group. The Plotniks were a different breed. Even my cousin Mark, who graduated with honors from Yale, had to be dragged from the blackjack tables. Sadie would die if her only child, a college graduate, ended up working in a gambling joint.

While driving to Glitter Gulch, I pondered this. Working in a casino would be like studying a foreign culture while pretending to be one of the natives. Maybe I could be a change girl—wear one of those belts with tubes full of quarters, nickels and dimes. It had to be more fun than filing.

I parked in front of the Horseshoe, two blocks from Sammy's Race Book where Izzy worked. He probably love it if I got a job at a joint. We'd finally have something in common. I called Sadie from a pay phone, said I'd take Izzy home, and hung up before she had a chance to speak.

Of all the clubs on the street, The Mint had the tackiest sign. Bubblegum pink, with bright yellow letters. There were no doors. Everything was wide open. I stood under an awning that blew cool air, staring at rows and rows of slot machines. Six hundred, according to a sign. I'd passed through the casino once, with my parents, on our way to the restaurant for the weekend spaghetti special. After midnight the place would be packed, but that afternoon, only about a dozen gamblers were glued to a machine or playing the field.

I walked up to a man wearing a tiny green apron and a matching eyeshade with "The Mint" printed in gold letters.

"I want to be a change girl."

Without indicating that he'd even heard me, he tilted his head toward a door that said "Stairs."

On the second floor, a middle-aged woman with thick glasses, sat behind a desk. She wore a name tag that said: Mrs. Bertha Fox, Receptionist. She handed me a form that I filled out on a green Naugahyde couch with masking tape criss-crossed over a tear. Bertha Fox perused my application.

"Oh, a Lantzman," she crooned, shaking my hand like a long-lost relative. Her fake fingernails matched her tomato-red lips. I stared at the gold cross around her neck. "I'm not Jewish, myself, but I'm married to one." She pulled out a cigarette holder and stuck in a Chesterfield.

"Want a smoke?"

"Thanks, but I don't smoke."

"So, what's a nice Jewish college girl like you doing in a joint like this?"

I almost preferred the interviewer at the employment office.

"I want to be a change girl."

"You gotta be kidding. That's not for you. Tell you what, honey. I'll inquire if they need another secretary. It's more your speed."

"I hate office work!"

"Okay," she said, "Don't say I didn't warn you.

Wear a black skirt and a white blouse. We'll start you Friday on the night shift. Eleven to four, with a fifteen-minute coffee break and a twenty-minute lunch at 2:15."

"Fine." I loved the concept of lunch at 2:l5 in the morning. A middle-aged man in a suit stepped out of a room down the hall. His face looked familiar. It was Marty Glassman. He'd lived next door to us on Thirteenth Street when I was in high school.

"Hi, Mr. Glassman. I forgot you worked here."

"My, God, have you grown up gorgeous," he said, shaking my hand. "Like a movie star. Why are you here, sweetheart?"

"I just got a job as a change girl."

From his face, you'd have thought I said a hooker. "Your parents will kill me."

Bertha Fox waved her cigarette. "I told her, Marty, I said to her, a nice girl like you should be doing something respectable, but she got huffy."

"Look," I said, "I appreciate your concern but I don't want any favors. You have no right to tell me I can't be a change girl."

"Calm down, honey," Marty said, putting his arm around me. "Tell you what. How's about I put you up in the change booth. It's a lot better than wearing one of those heavy belts, and being on your feet all the time. Do me a favor. So I can face your parents in shul."

"It's better pay," added Bertha.

"Can I still do the night shift?"

Marty shrugged. "Sure, but tell your mother I said it's meshuga."

It was late so I gave in.

"I hate like hell to see you kids around here," Marty said, taking my arm as he guided me down the stairs, "but it's none of my business, so I'll keep my mouth shut. If you change your mind about the night shift, call. I'm here till seven."

"Thanks, Mr. Glassman, but I don't think so."

"Okay. At least, I tried. Say hello to your folks." He patted my shoulder good-bye.

I stood in the middle of the slot machines staring at the change booth. Sitting up high appealed to me. Private. Like a lifeguard. Marty was right—it made more sense than being a change girl. And he'd let me keep the night shift!

4.

In the old days, Sadie would take me along when she picked Izzy up from work at the California Club, the Savoy, the Pioneer, the Nugget, and casinos whose names I couldn't remember. They had a routine. She'd double park and beep three times. After five minutes, she'd beep twice. If he still didn't show, it meant he was playing poker. She'd go from club to club until she found him. I'd wait in the car because I was under age. Fine with me. I liked watching the tourists in their Hawaiian shirts and Bermuda shorts. But I hated the fights on the way home.

I beeped three times outside Sammy's Race Book. Unlike Sadie, I refused to play waiting games. Five minutes, then the hell with him; let him take a cab. If he had any money left. I switched on the radio. Fats Domino sang: ... *ain't had no lovin' since you know when* ... Izzy'd had no lovin' for close to ten years. Alone at night, in the back bedroom, with the door closed. In spite of everything, he still loved her. Bragged about her looks. Laughed at her jokes. For as long as I could remember she had never even called him by his first name. He was hardly an ideal husband, but after ten years of solitary confinement the guy deserved a break. I lay on the horn.

Out he came, all smiles as if happy to see me instead of her.

"Park the car. I want you to meet the gang."

I pictured convicts breaking up rocks. Izzy had worked in some sleazy places, but Sammy's was the worst. No neon lights. Not even a sign. Just the name scribbled over a door.

"C'mon." He waved his arms. I hadn't seen him this excited since he won five hundred bucks at blackout bingo.

Inside, Sammy's was even more depressing. A dark hall, a scoreboard, a few stools for patrons, and a counter where three pickle-faced old men sat discussing the news: I*t was in the papers…Yeah, I seen it too… fuckin' head in the desert. Police dug it up last night…Think it was the Greek? I ain't seen him around lately … Me neither--*

"Want to see a good looking girl?" Izzy interrupted, squeezing my arm. In heels, I towered above him.

Three pairs of used-up eyes gave me the once-over.

"My daughter," he beamed. It must have occurred to him that I could be some sweet young thing he grabbed off the street.

"She's lucky she don't look like you," said the fat one with the cigar. I figured he was Sammy.

"She's a looker," said Izzy, smiling so hard I could see the top of his false teeth. "Like her old lady."

He was showing me off like a prize horse. All the same, I was touched.

"My name's Rebecca."

Izzy always forgot to mention it.

"What did you say, girlie?" asked the man I figured was Sammy, and the others echoed, "Whadshesay?"

"REBECCA."

"Pleased to meetcha," said Sammy, ogling me

with his empty eyes.

"Nice meeting you, too. All of you." I felt like a stripper in a graveyard.

"Well, see youse tamara," Izzy said, ushering me out the door. "Gimmie the keys." As usual, he walked ahead while I poked along in my heels. He slid behind the wheel, reached over and unlocked my door. "So, where's your mother?"

I thought I detected anxiety. Even fear. He started the car, turned off the radio and made a right onto Fremont. Neither he nor Sadie listened to music while driving; it might interfere with their depression.

"She's home," I said. "I borrowed the car to look for work."

"Yeah?"

"I got a job at The Mint, Dad. In the change booth."

"Yeah?"

Izzy wasn't a talker, which had been an advantage in the old days when he was a bookkeeper for the mob, but was definitely a drag where conversation was concerned.

"I start Friday. The night shift."

His face was expressionless. In the forties, Collier's magazine had photographed Izzy at the Nugget dealing cards, for the article, "Sin City USA." The caption read: "The empty face of Las Vegas." The Cohen side of the family was horrified. Izzy considered it a compliment.

"It's not easy, making change," he said.

"Yeah?"

"You gotta have a head for numbers."

Numbers were Izzy's passion. He could do any kind of complicated math problems in his head. That was how we related when I was a kid. I'd feed him problems, he'd spit out answers, I'd double-check them on paper. He never made a mistake. At his last job as a cashier, it had broken his heart when he was replaced by an adding machine.

"So it's okay with you if I work there? Around the gambling, I mean."

"Up to you."

Unlike Sadie, he'd probably have approved if I got a job as a topless dealer. We stopped for a light by the Golden Nugget, the most popular club on Fremont. Diagonally across the street, the fifteen-story Hotel Fremont stuck out like a sore thumb in a town where most places stopped at two.

"Hey, Dad, remember when Mom was a sky-watcher on the Fremont roof?" I giggled. "She thought it was her duty to defend our town against the Reds, remember?"

"I told her she was nuts," Izzy said, his face reddening. He didn't crack a smile. But, he never laughed much.

"She took that stupid course at the high school on identifying enemy planes, but when she showed up for her shift there was nobody on the roof. The other sky-watchers were down in the casino playing the slots. Boy was she mad, remember?"

"Goddam fool. Up there all day by herself."

"That whole civil defense thing was a farce. Sophomore year I did a term paper on nuclear testing. The bomb tests were a hundred times more dangerous than the Russians." This was a chance to show him I'd learned something in college. "Remember how they said there wasn't enough radiation to kill a fly? Utah's Leukemia rate went way up. If the wind had been blowing toward us, we'd probably be dead by now."

Izzy frowned. For once, he was listening to me.

"Of course, Mom thinks anybody who doesn't love the bomb is a commie. She says the Atomic Energy Commission is the best thing that ever happened to this town. Our first respectable industry. Can you imagine?"

"She's nuts."

"You're right, Dad. I'm so glad we agree. Really! Thank God Kennedy finally made the tests underground. I wish he'd stopped them completely. I still have nightmares about fallout."

"Goddam Kennedy shoulda minded his own business. The tourists stopped coming. We lost our goddam shirts!" He gripped the steering wheel so hard his knuckles turned white. "Goddam sonovabitch!"

I was stunned. At least Sadie's passion for explosives came from a misguided sense of patriotism. Izzy didn't give a damn about his country. The A-bomb was a fucking floorshow. He cursed Kennedy under his breath as we passed Rex Bell's Quality Western Wear. Maybe I had expected too much. This was a guy with a third-grade education. The only legitimate job he ever had was making baseballs for the Cincinnati Redlegs. After that, it was racetracks, casinos, cops breathing down his neck. Nevada was the only state where he could be a law-abiding citizen. No wonder he loved it, bombs and all.

He seemed calmer by the time we reached the "respectable" part of town, where locals out-numbered tourists. Most of the stores were closed for the day, the sidewalks empty except for a few stragglers. There was Ronzone's Department Store, where I'd bought my first bra. I felt a twinge of nostalgia. Izzy made a right at The National Dollar Store. We were on Fifth Street, heading towards the Strip.

"Seems like a hundred years since I went to Fifth Street School," I said. Izzy grunted. "There's the

White Bunny. You took me there for ice cream, once. Remember?" His face was a blank. "Seventh grade, you picked me up from school when Mom fell off the porch and broke her leg. She had that big cast on her leg all summer."

"What bunny? What are you talking about?"
"Never mind."

His head was full of chips and dice. I stared at places I'd seen a million times but never noticed—24-hour cleaners, a hardware store.

"So how are things at Sammy's?" I asked, watching some tourists take pictures of the cardboard camels on the Sahara Hotel lawn. Grandma Plotnik had played the slots at the Sahara three days before she died of heart failure. She was so weak, my Aunt Rhoda from Miami had to help her pull the handle.

"Lousy. It's all these goddam hotels. They built too many, and downtown we're starving." He waved at the Stardust. "Look at that dump. Who needs it? If Benny was alive, it wouldn't of happened. He wouldn't of let these new guys in."

Benny was Bugsy Siegel, who'd been Izzy's boss when I was little. He'd built the Flamingo, Vegas' first luxury hotel. Nobody called him Bugsy in those days, if they wanted to live; but I called him Uncle Bugsy and he called me Gorgeous. I was in third grade when Benny died. The papers said, "shot full of holes by an unknown assailant." Izzy lost his job at the Flamingo and had to work downtown for less money. A lot less.

"If Benny was around," Izzy continued, "he'd show them. Goddam crooks. That's what they are."

I felt like saying his Benny was the biggest crook of all, but the only time I'd ever seen Izzy cry was when Siegel died.

"If you ask me," he said, as we neared the

Flamingo, "Benny's hotel is still the classiest joint in town."

"Oh, come on, Dad. What about the plastic flamingos? And that sign? Pink neon bubbles in a gigantic highball glass. How tacky can you get? You want class, go to San Francisco. The Mark Hopkins, the Fairmont. Those hotels have class."

He screeched on the brakes, made a U-turn, and pulled into the Flamingo entrance.

"What the hell are you talking about?" Not only was he red in the face, his baldhead was turning pink. "This is a goddam beautiful hotel!"

"Okay, okay," I said. "It's beautiful. Let's go home."

"We're going in."

I knew better than to argue. Izzy had a terrible temper. Even Sadie was afraid to push him too far. Once I had a boyfriend over for dinner, and Izzy got into a fight with Sadie about what type of steak we were eating. He grabbed my friend's steak off his plate, along with some mashed potatoes, and waved it around, screaming, "This is a goddam rib steak!" We all said, "You're right! It's a rib steak."

Izzy parked. We went inside. "Now this is a lobby," he said.

"You're right. It's a lobby. Now can we go home?"

I felt faint. I hadn't eaten anything since that frozen bagel, and my heels were killing me. He led me to the gambling tables. The casino was dead, but to our left the lounge was thriving. Happy hour.

"Benny spent millions on this place," he said. "Before the Flamingo, there were only two hotels in the whole goddam town. The El Rancho, and the Last Frontier. Dumps. Benny wanted to buy into the El

Rancho, but they wouldn't let him in. I was there when they pistol-whipped him by the El Rancho pool. Right in front of everybody; blood all over the place. Me and Mel Grossman helped him up. And Benny said to me, 'I'm going to build my own goddam hotel, Izz.'"

"You told me that story already, Dad."

His gaze fixed on a card game at the far end of the room. "Wait here." He took out his wallet. I didn't try to stop him. That was Sadie's role, not mine.

If he doesn't take me home soon, I thought, I'm going to pass out, right here on Uncle Bugsy's million-dollar rug. I hobbled over to an empty table, and slipped off my shoes. I never should have let him stop at the Flamingo. He was just looking for an excuse to gamble. I would have called Sadie to tell her we'd be late, but I didn't have a dime and my purse was in the car. I stared at the recessed interior of the table. Green felt, white rectangles with numbers in them, red and white chips. I'd never gambled in my life; I had no idea what any of it meant. I was tempted to climb over the side and stretch out. Instead, I leaned against the mahogany rim and closed my eyes. I thought I was dreaming when I heard Izzy's voice behind me, saying: "I want you to meet my daughter."

Oh, Jesus. Here we go again. I turned, expecting to see another creepy old geezer.

Standing next to my father was a tall, slim, handsome man with the scariest smile I had ever seen. One corner of his mouth turned up, like a hook. He wore a white-on-white shirt with diamond cufflinks. His pants were tight. Silvery gray, the color of his hair. His tan so even it looked like makeup. He had three rings on his right hand. All diamonds.

"My pleasure," he said.

In my entire life, I had never met anybody so

suave. A run started in my left stocking and crept up the inside of my leg to my garter belt. I felt kind of stupid with my shoes off, but there was no way I could slip them on without his noticing, and I didn't want him to think I was doing it for him.

"Frankie and me used to work together at the Savoy," Izzy said. He looked up at Frankie, then at me. "Now, he's one of the bosses here."

"Izzy was the best cashier around." Frankie put an arm around my father. "They never should have let him go."

"They treated me like shit," Izzy added.

Frankie patted Izzy's back and checked his watch. "I'd buy you a drink," he said, shifting his gaze to my breasts, "but I have to meet somebody."

I felt like saying *they* weren't thirsty. I didn't want a drink, but I'd have done anything for some peanuts or a maraschino cherry.

"Thanks," I said, "but we have to get home anyway. Mom's probably wondering what happened to us."

"What could happen?" said Izzy. "You're here with me."

"Next time you're here," Frankie said, smiling his hooked smile and handing me a card, "ask for me."

Real people don't give out cards, I thought. But my hand trembled.

"And by the way," Frankie said, flashing his rings in my face as he turned to go, "don't forget your shoes."

Izzy moved next to me and squeezed my arm.

"Now, he's got class."

I looked at the card. Frank E. Pierce, Esq. With a tiny pink flamingo in one corner.

"How old is he?" I asked, when we were driving

home.

"He's young. Not even forty. He's got what they call premature hair."

"That's not so young."

Izzy's head was turning pink again. I couldn't believe my own father would try to fix me up with Frank E. All those diamonds. Probably murdered somebody to get them.

"A good-looking man like him can have anybody he wants," Izzy said.

"So why isn't he married?"

"He's been married two times already!"

"Jesus!"

"What the hell does that mean?"

"Nothing. I'm just tired."

He turned right at Paradise Road. "What the hell are you tired about? You haven't worked in three months."

I resisted talking back and took in the scenery, if you could call it that. Beer cans, broken bottles, used Trojans, endless dirt. We passed my favorite landmark: an abandoned sofa with springs sticking out, a black rocking-chair and a TV on an orange crate—they had been there since before I left for college. But if you looked up instead of down, the sky was spectacular. No trees, houses, or hills to obstruct the view—just uninterrupted blue. The Sons of the Pioneers strummed their guitars in my head ... *and the skies are not cloudy all day*...

"Mom will probably have a fit when I tell her about The Mint."

Izzy's head wasn't pink any more. His eyes had a faraway look. I wondered if he'd lost a lot of money and was scared to go home.

"It's not like I'm going to work there forever.

Just until I save enough money to go to New York. Mom says I should give up acting. Who was it that dragged me to MGM when I was little? I can still see her face when they said I was too short for the part. She's more of a dreamer than I am. Why all the dancing lessons and elocution if she didn't want me to act? She pushes with one hand and holds back with the other."

Izzy sniffed and wrinkled his nose. I had the feeling that he sympathized but couldn't show it, out of habit.

"You know what her problem is, Dad? She lives through other people. First, her brothers, now me."

I could tell from the way he wiped his nose with the back of his hand that he agreed. "I wish she'd live her own life and stay out of mine."

My stomach turned at the sight of our apartment house—a two-story stucco, the same pink as a French poodle I'd seen at the Hacienda pool, dyed to match its owner's bikini. The building was set back from the road to show off the tasteful landscaping: squares of fresh, green lawn bordered by Cinderlite blocks, bordered by miles of empty desert. Paved roads connecting to unpaved roads connecting to nothing.

"I'm going to New York, no matter what she says," I said, more to myself than him.

"I could have bought land on the Strip at twenty-five bucks an acre," he said, eyes glazed and on the road, as if he longed to drive forever. "She said it would never be anything but dirt. Now it's worth twenty-five grand."

He parked, leaving the keys in. Sadie stood on the wrought-iron balcony, waving for us to come up. Izzy opened his door. I opened mine. But we stayed where we were. Father and daughter. Sitting there in the car, its front doors wide open, like wings.

5.

"Dinner is ruined."

Sadie stood in the doorway holding an orange potholder with a giant hole where she'd burned it. Izzy rushed past her to the TV and changed the channel.

"Where the hell have you been?" Sadie looked from him to me.

I moved between them. "We stopped at Sammy's and the Flamingo," I said, and to help his case, "he wanted his friends to meet me."

"Fuck'n Cubs! C'mon, Banks. Hit the goddam ball!"

"How much did you lose, Plotnik?" She turned off the TV.

"None of your goddam business." He sat on the couch, opening the paper to the sports section like he'd been home for hours.

She tried to take it away. "You goddam sonovabitch!" It ripped in half. "How the hell am I supposed to pay the rent?"

"Goddam you, gimme my paper!"

There was nothing I could do for him. Or her. I went into the smoky kitchen. Burnt pot roast. These people aren't real, Beck, I told myself. Ignore them and they'll go back in the TV. I grabbed a box of Kellogg's Corn Flakes, some cottage cheese, honey, and a soup spoon and said, "Don't bother making dinner for me," as I passed, unnoticed, on my way to the bedroom. Izzy was on his feet, clutching what was left of the paper.

"You're not a man. A real man supports his family." Sadie swung. Missed.

"Shut your goddam mouth or I'll ..." He raised a hand. It froze. He backed toward the kitchen.

Saddie grabbed a Chinese lady with a hollow head full of plastic flowers. "Scum!"

Izzy ducked. Pieces of Chinese lady flew everywhere. Half my childhood had been spent cowering in closets, waiting for them to kill each other until I realized the boring truth. He would never lay a hand on her, and her aim was bad.

I closed the bedroom door behind me and turned on the radio full blast. Dean Martin, Vegas' favorite lush, sang, *Money, burns a hole in my pocket* ... right on cue. I sprawled on the bed, poured honey on my cottage cheese and ate from the carton with handfuls of cornflakes.

I heard a crash. Probably a candy dish. Poor Izzy. Candy was the only food he really liked. Peanut M&M's, Hershey Kisses, Paydays. He didn't have to worry about cavities; none of his teeth were real. I finished the last cornflake and licked honey off my fingers. You'd think, after thirty years they'd get a divorce. Not my parents. I'd stopped feeling sorry for her long ago. She could go to her brothers in Cincinnati. He loved her too much to leave. *You know, Beck, twenty-two years of exposure to Sadie and Izzy is hardly ideal for an impressionable young woman. No wonder you're single.* I went to my half of the dresser, took Joey Goldman's picture from its hiding place in my underwear drawer, kissed it, and drifted back to Arizona.

As a bribe for staying in school, Joey's parents

had bought him a shiny, new '59 Ford. After acting class we would drive to a secluded spot off Camelback Road and perform for an audience of saguaros. I did my birdcalls and my Ethel Merman imitation. He did his toilet. I laughed so hard I almost believed it when he said we'd be famous overnight. I taught him tap; he taught me the tango. Plotnik and Goldman. I hated "Plotnik," but Joey said, "Always go with the real thing." I couldn't believe he wanted my name to come first when it should have been G before P.

It felt like we'd known each other forever instead of a few weeks. We had long talks. We read poetry to each other. I was big on Whitman. He liked e.e. cummings. We both thought Salinger was the greatest writer of our time. Joey had even named his dog J.D. He lent me <u>Franny and Zooey</u>, and I agreed with everything he'd underlined. He was more sophisticated than I'd thought. For someone his age.

"What was high school like in Jersey?" I asked, taking a swig of warm Coke and passing it back to him. We were in the desert—surrounded by cactus, sitting next to the car on his sleeping bag.

"Wasn't in Jersey. Massachusetts. Prep school."

He passed back the Coke. I took a swallow. "What's prep school?"

He went crazy. "Yahhhhh! I love it. You're great."

"Why?" I handed back the coke and stared at a bent saguaro. The Arizona desert was full of color. The mountains were purple; the ground was tinged with red. Unlike Las Vegas, it wasn't just dirt. It was scenery. "What'd I do?"

"Back east, that's all they care about. What prep school did you attend young man? Which Ivy League college? It's such crap, but out here? You never even heard of it!"

"Oh! I get it. Boarding school! Like Holden Caulfield went to. I just never heard it called that. I don't think they have them in Nevada. Oh, God! How can I go to New York? I'm such a hick."

"You're incredibly talented. That counts. The rest is bullshit." His face was so serious it looked ten years older, especially his eyes. We finished off the Coke. He reached in his Army surplus bag and handed me some Fleer's Double Bubblegum. "What was high school like in Las Vegas?"

"Weird." The wind was picking up. I read my gum cartoon, crumpled it, and got my sweater from the car. "Mormons and hoods."

"You were a hood, right?"

"Funny!" I punched his shoulder. "My crowd was two Mormons, an Episcopalian, a Methodist, a Catholic and me. We didn't drink, smoke or swear, and we were all prudes except for GiGi Marshall, the Catholic. Senior year, she went all the way with Alex Harmon while her parents were out of town. I was jealous." I popped a huge bubble with my fingernail. "I had a crush on Alex, but I was too shy to let him know. Besides, he liked GiGi."

Joey usually looked grumpy when I talked about other guys, but this time he seemed intrigued.

"Alex was this incredible artist, but cynical—the type of person who could throw his talent away. I used to fantasize that only I could save him. My mom says I have a need to save people. She says my idealism will do me in some day."

"The world needs more idealists."

I shook my head. "Oh, no. Not like me! I honestly believed Elvis Presley was distracting the youth of America from achieving world peace and curing cancer, and I said so in this stupid debate in front of the whole school. I'll never live it down."

He laughed. "You're great."

"Oh, yeah. Great. Even my Mormon friends loved Elvis. My best friend, Leanne, has an autographed picture of him over her bed—*To Leanne, with love, from Elvis.*"

Joey lay on his side, pulling at a loose string on the sleeping bag. "Would you say you've changed since high school?"

"Oh,yeah." I stretched out and found my own string. "Would you believe I never even swore before last year? My first week here, I locked myself in the bathroom and said fuck 300 times."

"You counted?"

"Yeah. I still haven't done it but at least I can say it. Have you? Done it, I mean?"

He sat up, so I couldn't see his face. "Yeah."

Was he embarrassed? Or ashamed?

"Why is it you're a year younger but you've done all these things, like living on your own and sex? It's not fair."

"It's the East Coast. We mature faster."

I loved his timing.

"Something in the water."

And his deadpan.

"I was so repressed, I didn't even know about..." I was too embarrassed to finish the sentence.

"About what?" Joey asked.

"Masturbation." I covered my face with my hands and talked through my fingers. "Some guy had to teach me. That's how repressed I was."

"Anybody'd be repressed with their mother for a roommate," Joey said.

He was so sweet, and understanding. I could tell him anything. I moved close to him.

"The thing is, at the beginning she was so much fun. She'd tell me dirty jokes and dirty songs—she even lent me her Harold Robbins books, and Frank Yerby, and pointed out the dirty parts. She was the best mother!"

"Wow. I had a totally different impression of her."

"She can be the biggest prude, but other times she's incredibly liberal and, oh God, is she funny! My friends used to come over just to hear her tell stories. But, you never know when she's going to turn on you. I'd walk in from a date and she'd look me up and down and say, 'Don't you feel filthy?' The most I did back then was French kiss." I smirked. "So I took a lot of baths."

Our shoulders touched, but I didn't mind.

"My dad's unpredictable, too," Joey said. "He'll start yelling for no reason. I think he's pissed that I don't want to sell his damn ties."

"My dad's only said about thirty or forty words to me my whole life including 'Shaddup, and eat your goddam dinner.'" Usually, I played that line for laughs, but right now it wasn't funny. I threw my gum at the bent saguaro.

"He moved away, right? When you were little?"

"Yeah. We stayed in LA with my grandmother. My mom was really depressed. I thought it was my fault. She was always criticizing me. Four years old, I felt like a failure." My eyes started to fill. I blinked, and turned away. "Good thing I loved movies. If it hadn't been for movies, and Grandma Rosie, I probably wouldn't have survived."

"Tell me about Grandma Rosie." Joey rubbed my back. It felt strange—his touching me—nicer than I had thought, which confused me because I didn't think I was attracted to him. "She was my best friend. Wise.

47

Dignified. Never raised her voice. Money didn't impress her. She'd say, 'We never own anything in this life. We only borrow.'"

Joey smiled. "Words to live by."

"The whole family worshiped her—especially my mom. But Grandma Rosie loved her sons more than her only daughter. My mom used to cry about it. She said she was the stupid one, with all these brilliant brothers. Now that I'm older, I've realized it wasn't me my mother was depressed about. It was her life."

He put his hand on mine. Comforting. Warm. "Maybe she was jealous because Grandma Rosie gave you all the love she wanted."

"Grandma Rosie was always protecting me. She'd say, 'You should be ashamed, Sadie, treating a child like that.'" My eyes filled up, again, but I didn't care. "It was really hard when she died. But, every night after her funeral, she'd float in before I went to sleep— an angel in wire glasses and a navy blue dress with tiny white polka dots, and black lace-up shoes. She'd tell me not to be afraid." I wiped my eyes with my sweater sleeve and moved away from him. "This is getting maudlin. Let's talk about your family."

Joey leaned back on his elbows. His eyes had that sad dog look, like at the Varsity Café. "My parents fought a lot, but not in front of me. They'd wait until they thought I was asleep, but their bedroom was next to mine. If I put a glass against the wall, I could hear everything. My mom wanted more kids. Not him. He was too busy making money. Money's all he cares about."

"God, I hate money! It brings out the worst in people, especially in Las Vegas. My parents are always fighting about it. My aunts and uncles from Cincinnati lord it over us because they're well off and we're not.

God, I hate rich people!" I didn't mean him, exactly, but wanted him to know I wasn't impressed with his car and his well-off family.

"I don't give a damn about money," he insisted. "It's the American dream, but it's not my dream."

"Come on. You want to be famous—you know you do."

"Sure, I want to see my name in lights. I want to walk down the street and hear somebody whisper, 'Hey, Mabel, it's him, the guy from the play.' But money? All I want is enough to get by." He grinned. "Well, maybe a little extra for books and movies."

"It's easy to say you don't care about money when you have it." He stopped grinning. "When your father is a gambler, you care about money. I used to count my change over and over when I was a kid, to make sure I could pay for my cherry coke and fries at Fremont Drugs."

All of a sudden, he got this sappy, love-struck look. "You know, for a beautiful leading lady type, you're incredibly real. I don't think I've ever met anybody as real as you."

"I'm not beautiful."

My jaw tensed up so hard it hurt. I'd thought he was my friend, but he had no idea who I was.

"C'mon, Beck. You know you are. All those guys drooling over you at the Varsity Café."

"Beauty is just how other people see you. It comes and goes." I ripped a loose thread off the sleeping bag and threw it. "Those guys at the Varsity Café are good-looking and popular. I know you don't approve, but guys like that never noticed me before. I've waited a long time for this, and I'm not giving it up. Guess I'm not as real as you think."

"It's not that I don't approve. I just happen to

think they're jerks. You're way too good for them."

Suddenly, I was fighting back tears and hating him for it. I jerked my shoulder away from his hand. "When I was little, everybody said I was beautiful. They used to beg me to sing and dance—they couldn't get enough. Then, around seven or eight, I lost my looks— poof, gone. All the relatives said, 'She used to be so pretty. What happened?' Nobody wanted me to perform any more. Everything fell apart. My friends deserted me—even Leanne. My teacher used to throw erasers at me for not paying attention. I was so miserable, I would hide in the bathroom for hours with the door locked." Joey had such a long face I couldn't stand it. "Don't look so morose. Things got better in eighth grade. Leanne and I were friends again. Once I got to high school, boys started asking me out. Until the Elvis thing." I smirked. "Seems like every time my life gets better I fuck it up."

For the longest time, Joey just stared. "You have no idea how incredible you are."

I stood up. Stomped around the sleeping bag kicking dirt. "I am <u>not</u> incredible! If I were incredible, I wouldn't spend hours primping in front of the mirror and never feeling I look good enough. And I <u>still</u> hide in the bathroom, when people get me down—even though I know they're assholes! If I weren't such a wimp, I'd tell them to shove it."

His face glowed. "Do it!"

"What?"

"Tell them to shove it." He stood up and faced me. "See that big saguaro? It's that teacher —the one who threw erasers. Go over there and let her have it."

"This is stupid." I approached the big saguaro. Very slowly.

"Think of it as an acting exercise."

I took in the saguaro's nasty needles, trembling

like I was nine again. "Don't you ever yell at me again, Mrs. Bunker. Or shake me, or call me a dreamer."

"Too soft, Beck.

I took a deep breath and closed my eyes. "Bitch!"

He clapped and whistled. "Wow. They heard that in Scottsdale. Now, what's your mom's name?"

"Sadie." I backed off. "Oh, no. Not my mom. I can't. Really, I can't."

Joey took my hand, pulling me along. "You are going to feel so good after this. I promise." He stopped at a huge cactus—taller than both of us. Very green

"Oh, God. I can't do this. I can't, I can't."

"Yes, you can." He wasn't smiling.

"Shove it, Sadie!"

"One more time," Joey said.

I pictured cold cream and curlers. "Shove it!"

Joey hugged me. He lifted me up. "You're the greatest!" We spun around, laughing. "Nobody can push you around, Beck. Say it."

"Nobody can push me around!"

Spinning, laughing, falling all over each other, collapsing on the sleeping bag. Arms around each other. Lips touching. Joey on top of me. His mouth warm and so soft. I never imagined how soft, or how much I would love kissing him. Long drowning kisses. Mouths open. Tongues, like flames.

"Wow!" I snuggled my head on his shirt. "I never thought that we—I mean, you're a whole year younger."

He stroked my hair. "Officer, arrest this woman for taking advantage of a minor."

"It's just that we said we wouldn't get involved and I thought you were naïve and I'd made up my mind to have millions of admirers—but you're right. I don't need those jerks to make me feel good. All I need is you." I squeezed him so hard it took my breath away. "Jesus. I feel like we're engaged or something." I sat up so I could look at him. "Do you think marriage ever works?"

"I have this aunt and uncle, married forty years, but still madly in love—it's in their eyes. He pulls out her chair and helps her with her coat. She calls him 'Dearest.' They're devoted to each other."

"*Devoted.* Oh, God, I'm so glad I've never gone all the way, because I want it to be with you."

Joey gave me a look that sent shivers through me. "Not here!" I said. "It has to be special."

"How about an apartment in the Village with black walls and one orange dot in the living room and no furniture expect for a stool in front of the dot?"

I grabbed him and kissed him all over his face. "And a mattress. We have to have a mattress." A very long kiss. "Do you think your mom will like me?"

"What's not to like?" His face turned gloomy. "What about *your* mom?"

"She wants me to marry a doctor and stop dreaming about New York, but I don't give a shit because I want to live in the black apartment and be devoted the rest of our lives." I lay down beside him, put his hand between my legs, and squeezed my thighs.

6.

Izzy's door slammed. The fight was over. Sadie would be picking up glass, tidying the living room. I looked at the mess in our bedroom: cottage cheese on the rug, cornflakes on Sadie's side of the bedspread, honey on Joey's picture. I had a sudden urge to lick it off. I got on my knees and bent over, when Sadie opened the door. I froze. On all fours. With my tongue hanging out.

"You look like a dog."

"I was a dog." I sat up and put the picture in my skirt pocket; hands shaking so hard I had to sit on them. "I was doing this acting thing where you become a dog. Actually, it doesn't have to be a dog; you can be a kangaroo, a canary, anything, as long as it's an animal. It releases your inhibitions."

Sadie looked suspicious, but since that was her natural expression it was hard to tell whether she bought it.

"It's very big in New York."

"What's in your pocket?" She pointed with her green sponge.

OK, Beck, you're an actress, so act! "A bone."

She wasn't impressed.

"God, Mom, do I have to explain everything? It's a piece of paper. I was pretending it was a bone. Why else would I have been licking it?"

"Oy, gevalt."

"You should have knocked before you came in. You ruined my concentration."

She moved toward the bed. I crawled away.

"What's on my bedspread?"

"Cereal."

"What in the hell were you eating?"

"Cottage cheese, cornflakes and honey. I'm trying to lose five pounds in a hurry." I had a terrific urge to pee. "Don't worry. I'll clean up after I go to the bathroom."

Beck, I said to myself, as I locked the door and lunged for the toilet, sometimes I really love you. The dog routine was brilliant. Maybe you can't always think on your feet, but you're dynamite on your hands and knees. Jesus! Sadie'd probably think licking Joey's picture was worse than oral sex.

I peeled Joey's picture from my pocket, licked his face, and his dog JD's face. Oh, baby, if you were really here, I'd lick every inch of you like ice cream. She doesn't know that I'm going to live with you in the black apartment. Soon as I have enough money. If she knew, she'd do her best to ruin it. Don't worry, my love, you'll be back safe in my underwear drawer soon as she's asleep.

I opened the door. Sadie was on the bed, wringing her sponge, staring at a spot of cottage cheese on the rug. "You look tired, Mom. Why don't you watch TV? I'll clean up."

"I don't want to watch TV. I want to die."

I'd heard that a million times, but she looked so depressed it scared me.

"You'll feel better in the morning." I patted her shoulder. "You always do."

"Why should I? I'm married to a no-good sonofabitch, and my only daughter is wasting her life."

"As I've said many times, Mother, you don't have to stay with him. You could get a divorce and move back to Cincinnati. Your brothers would support you."

"He'd die in a week with nobody to take care of him."

"What do you care? He's the boarder."

"I don't want to talk about it." Flashing me an injured look, she started cleaning—dabbing at the dresser with the sponge, shaking cereal off the bed. "When you're older, you'll understand."

"Oh, come on, Mother, who are you kidding?" I grabbed the wastebasket and followed her around, collecting garbage. "You make jokes about giving him the wrong pills so you can get his life insurance. He knows you're waiting for him to die. I think he keeps going to spite you."

"If it wasn't for me, he'd gamble twenty-four hours a day."

"He gambles because you treat him like a nobody. You don't sleep with him. Why should he come home? This isn't a home. It's jail." I hadn't realized how angry I was.

"Why the hell do you care about him all of a sudden?" Her whole face was trembling. "I'm the one you should feel sorry for. I'm all you've got."

I clung to the wastebasket like a life preserver. "You married him so you could quit your job and leave home. He loved you. How could you use him like that? He's a human being. You treat him like he's shit."

"You're a goddam fool. He doesn't give a damn about you. He didn't want to have you. He hates children. He used to push you away when you were little."

"It's your fault he was never a father. You

wanted me all to yourself so you could live through me. Devour me!"

I let go of the wastebasket. It fell on its side. The cottage cheese carton rolled out. We stared at it.

"I wanted a baby more than anything in the world. I left him. Went home. My brothers, everyone I knew, had children. I was almost forty. He was my only chance. I only went back to that sonofabitch to get pregnant."

"Jesus! You used him!"

Tears poured from her eyes. "I almost died having you. I had a fibroid tumor. The doctor said I never should have gotten pregnant. But I wanted a child—a daughter—more than anything in the world." She began to sob, holding her stomach where my birth scar was. "You were my only reason for living."

My gut felt like there was a knife stuck in it.

She screamed out, "If it wasn't for you I would have blown my brains out a long time ago."

"Oh, Jesus, Mom. I'm sorry. I shouldn't have said what I did." She backed away.

"I didn't mean it. I was just ..."

"He didn't want a baby," she said, sitting on the bed. "He only cared about the sex."

I reached out to comfort her. She swung. Hit me. Just my hand, but the pain ripped me.

"Get away from me, you goddam fool." Moaning. Hugging herself. Rocking.

"I didn't mean it, Mom. I didn't mean it."

"Who sent you to college. Who gave you dancing lessons?"

"You, Mom. Only you."

I sat on the floor between the bed and the dresser and cried like a baby. Between the two of us, we went through a box of Kleenex. I asked her if she wanted me to get her nightgown. I knew if I didn't get up I'd stay on the floor all night.

"Don't do me any favors."

Any other time, she would have said: "Why are you so embarrassed? We're two women." Tonight, she didn't even look up when I came out of the bathroom. She was naked, by her side of the dresser with her nightgown in one hand. I could see the scar from her C-section, an ugly, jagged, stitch- marked line down her belly.

"I'm sorry I hurt you, Mom."

"What good is sorry?"

I got in bed first, closed my eyes, exhausted, knowing I wouldn't sleep. Sadie made a lot of noise in the bathroom, slammed the toilet lid, the medicine cabinet door. She switched off the light and got in bed. For a long time I lay smelling cold cream, wondering which of us would speak first.

"Mom?"

No answer.

"I tried to tell you before, but you wouldn't listen—I didn't mean to hurt you. It's just awful when the two of you fight. I can't stand it. It would be better for everybody if you'd get a divorce."

I wasn't sure, but I thought I heard her sob into her pillow.

"Mom? I know you won't believe this, but I wish I could pay you back for all you've done for me. If I ever make a lot of money, I'd like to buy you a house with really nice furniture and..."

"You live in a dream. Always have. Always will."

"Jesus, Mother, I'm trying to make up, and you say that. *Always have always will.* That's the worst thing you can say to somebody. I feel like I'm doomed. I might as well dig a hole and jump in."

"Your only hope is to get married."

I sat up. "You wouldn't let me! He was the nicest boy in the world, the only one I've ever loved, but you said I'd ruin his life."

"Who was the nicest boy?" Sadie said, sitting up beside me. "You mean that goofy actor from New Jersey? Him?"

"Him."

"You're out of your mind."

Godammit, Beck, why did you do that? You were supposed to keep him safe in your underwear drawer. Now he's out there, right in front of her so she can chop him up.

"He'll never make a living," she said. "You'll end up like me."

"I don't want to talk about it."

I lay back and closed my eyes. I'm sorry, Joey. I blew it.

"Two years ago, you said you were through with him. He was too immature, you told me."

"He was the best thing that ever happened to me, but it's over. Go to sleep."

"I can't sleep. I'll never sleep again. Joey Goldman. My stomach is a mess."

"Take some Pepto Bismol," I said, putting my pillow over my head.

I heard her get up and go to the bathroom, talking the whole time. "You think you're so special, you and him? And you can go to New York and be famous, one-two-three, just like that? Well, I've got news for you. The people of New York are sophisticated. They are not going to stand in line to hear your birdcalls and his toilet."

"How many times do I have to tell you, it's <u>over</u> Mom!" She can't hurt us, Joey. Be my pillow. Lie on top

58

of me. I'm not afraid to want you deep, deep inside of me where no one has ever been. I'm not afraid to be happy. Oh, my God, Joey, I want you.

"My stomach is killing me," Sadie said as she got back into bed. She moaned and cried, and said "Oy!" a million times.

I didn't care. I was back at Arizona State, with Joey.

7.

When spring break came, Joey and I kissed goodbye until our lips went numb. His first letter to me consisted of one typed line in the middle of a sheet of thin white paper. *She is all states, and all princes, I. Nothing else is.* John Donne. I told Sadie I had fallen in love with an actor. I probably should have left it at that, instead of going on about Plotnik and Goldman and the black apartment with one orange dot in the living room and no furniture.

"He sounds like a mental patient." Sadie stopped eating her cucumbers and radishes in sour cream. "One dreamer's bad enough. Two are a disaster area."

"But, Mom, he's the nicest boy. He's brilliant, and talented. He plays the piano without any sheet music, he sings, he's funny—he's even Jewish!"

"So what if he's Jewish? He's crazy! Only a rodent would want to live in a black apartment. I'd rather you'd marry a goy!"

"I'll do what I want. I'm over eighteen."

I was proud of myself for standing up to her, but for all my bravado I feared she was right. The black apartment seemed stupid and childish—a dream. So did Plotnik & Goldman. But my hopes soared again when Joey's second letter arrived. Like me, he'd told his mom everything. Not only had she approved, she'd offered to help us financially. Which was wonderful, but

I couldn't help resenting that, unlike Sadie, she was so approving. And rich. Other than that, I loved his letter. I could hear his voice in my head as I read it over and over:

> Don't let Sadie crush you, Beck. Remember the saguaros. Fight back with everything you've got. Don't be afraid to be happy. I found a great line in <u>Steppenwolf,</u> by Herman Hesse. "Learn what is to be taken seriously and laugh at the rest." I think we should add it to Grandma Rosie's words to live by—with your permission, of course. I've been thinking about how our choices define who we are. You have to do what you believe or life is meaningless. The act defines the actor. Hey, that's not bad. Maybe we should include it on the list? Only nine more days before we see each other again. J.D. barks hello. Love (with a giant L)

Grandma Rosie used to say that happiness is hard to come by, and harder to keep. Toward the end of the semester, Joey wrote the dean that he could no longer participate in ROTC because he didn't believe in war. "I can't believe they're threatening to suspend me because of fucking ROTC," he said. He stopped going to all his classes but acting. While I struggled to stay awake in biology and Spanish, Joey bussed tables at the student union cafeteria and read <u>Lady Chatterley's Lover</u> under a tree. Every day we rehearsed our act, after which we read each other juicy passages about Constance Chatterley and Mellors, the gamekeeper who won her love by leading her astray. I convinced him we should put off discussing our future until after the performance—it might interfere with our concentration. But, I was secretly worried that we'd bomb and we wouldn't have a future.

It turned out, Plotnik & Goldman knocked 'em dead. Joey improvised on the piano. We sang show tunes. He told sick jokes. I did my birdcall while singing *She's Only a Bird in a Gilded Cage*, which Joey insisted was the high point of the show. I thought his toilet got more laughs. We received three curtain calls during which we tapped and tangoed and did improvisations on request. Dr. Rogers said we managed to combine slapstick with existential ennui, and we'd be a hit in New York—he even offered to recommend us to an agent he knew from his acting career. The next day, in the middle of clearing dishes at the student union, Joey climbed on a table, threw off his apron and said, "I've had it. I'm going to New York to be an actor." People applauded as he ran out of the dining hall and leapt over the patio wall. He wanted us to leave right away.

"I can't," I said. "Not until after I get my diploma."

And he said, "It's only a piece of paper."

"God, Joey, you're such a dreamer! Nobody gets famous overnight. How are we going to support ourselves in the meantime?"

"We'll get jobs. Big deal."

"You're forgetting I'm a lousy waitress and I can't type, which limits my options, especially without a college degree. You've got your dad. I've got nothing."

"Bullshit! You've got incredible talent and intelligence, and my mom said she'd help us."

"Jesus, Joey! Don't you have any pride?" I'd never seen him look so ashamed. "Why should anybody pay our way? It's not like we're trying to save the world or cure cancer. We're just actors. Who the hell cares if we succeed? It won't make any difference."

"Yes, it will, Beck. Theater isn't mindless entertainment, it's Art. It's a gift to be able to make people think, and laugh—to make them feel. You have that gift. You can't just throw it away. You should be proud of being an artist."

"I am proud. Too proud to accept money from your mother."

"Okay, okay. I won't go to New York. I'll go back to Jersey and work for my dad and save enough money for six month's rent. I promise."

I threw my arms around him. "And, soon as I get home, I'll ask my mom about transferring to NYU."

Being home was hard. First, there was life without Joey. Then, there was my boring summer job in under-garments at J.C. Penny's. Then, there was Sadie. I told her about Joey quitting Arizona State because of ROTC. Before she had a chance to react, I laid it on thick about Plotnik & Goldman—how we were the biggest hit of the year, and people called us the next Nichols and May, and Dr. Rogers' friend was this famous agent—so can I transfer to NYU?

"Over my dead body. New York is very expensive. And nobody gets famous over-night. It takes years, no matter how talented you are. And what kind of a person throws away his education because of ROTC? Only communists refuse to serve their country."

"Joey's not a communist. He's an idealist."

"Same thing. You'll end up electrocuted, like the Rosenbergs."

"Oh, for God's sake! Joey's not the least bit political. He's just an actor who happens to believe that war is immoral."

"What does an actor know about morality? And while we're on the subject, what if you get pregnant?

He'll have to give up acting to support you. He'll end up hating you. Eddie Tannenbaum was a violin prodigy. He married Ethel Schwarz. They had six boys. He worked twelve hours a day in a factory. He used to cry on my Brother Jake's shoulder. 'If it wasn't for her and the kids I'd be playing the violin.'"

"I'll have an abortion!"

As the word left my mouth and Sadie ran for her Maalox, I remembered a movie Dee Dee Walton's mother took a bunch of us to see at a drive-in when we turned thirteen about a teenager who died in an alley after leaving this creepy boarding house where a doctor with a missing front tooth and a fat nurse with a hairy chin terminated the girl's pregnancy. And her life! I worried about that when I was trying to sleep. I worried even more about being a burden to Joey. An albatross.

He'll end up hating you.

Joey talked his dad into giving him two weeks off in August, and I persuaded Sadie to let him visit, so she could look him over. She didn't exactly give him a warm welcome when he arrived at our door with a green duffle bag over his shoulder. She refused to let him sleep on our couch, because she didn't want him to think she approved of the match, so he slept on the lawn of the Catholic school across the street. He didn't mind; he liked the smell of the grass. After he performed the routine about the son who tells his disapproving dad he wants to be an actor, Izzy giggled and said, "He's funny." Sadie didn't crack a smile. Not even when he did his toilet.

While I sold brassieres and underpants at Penny's, Joey read <u>War and Peace</u> at the library. After work, we hung out with my friends. We took him to all our favorite places—Mt. Charleston, Lake Mead, the bumper cars at the Frontier Village, Sill's Drive-In— they loved it when he ordered a *Danish* instead of a sweet-roll. They squealed and jumped up and down when we performed Plotnik and Goldman on the front steps of Vegas High. Leanne was positive we were meant for each other, but we'd never have a chance without Sadie's approval. "You've got to win Mrs. Plotnik over," she said. "Even if you have to lie." Gigi agreed. "Tell her you've changed your mind about acting. Say you've decided to go to medical school. Or law school."

Joey and I were silent. We knew they were right, but we couldn't admit it. Especially to each other.

Joey did try to win Sadie over. He poured on the charm, and it almost worked. She seemed to be having a hard time hating him. Until one morning near the end of his stay. The three of us were eating breakfast at the kitchen table. Out of the blue, she started picking on me.

"Becky was so slow—in school they used to call her 'the pokey little puppy,' after that children's book. Always the last to finish her work, if she finished at all. And she hasn't changed a bit. Never sticks to anything. Always dreaming. I'm amazed she's still in college." She laughed. "I guess, in Arizona, the standards aren't so high." Expecting Joey to be on her side, she gave him her sweet-old-Jewish-lady smile and winked. "But we love her anyway, don't we?"

"Your daughter is amazingly intelligent and talented, Mrs. Plotnik. All she needs is confidence."

Sadie was still smiling, but I could feel her getting furious. I prayed he would stop.

"Too bad she can't get it at home."

The smile, and all the color left Sadie's face. She left the table without looking back. Why the hell couldn't he have kept his mouth shut and pretended to go along with her? Now, Plotnik & Goldman could become the most famous comedy team in the world, but it wouldn't matter. She would still hate him, and do everything she could to keep us apart.

The day before Joey left, we were in his car reading to each other from *Lady Chatterley*. On page 282, Mellors tells Constance, "...And if you're in Scotland and I'm in the Midlands, and I can't put my arms around you, and wrap my legs round you, yet I've got something of you." I took Joey's face in my hands and kissed him, and said, "I want something of you— tonight."

I waited until Sadie was asleep and snuck out of the apartment, wearing only my nightie and a bra. We decided doing it in Joey's car lacked originality. Joey suggested the lawn of the Catholic school.

"But what if somebody sees us?"

"We'll go behind the bushes. Losing your virginity is a once in a lifetime thing, Beck. A true, religious experience. All that Catholic repression and hypocrisy and us, rolling in the dirt. Purifying it. We're morally obligated. This is our chance to make a statement, Beck. It'll be the best thing that ever happened to that school."

"Well, okay, if you put it that way."

"How about under the cross?" Joey asked, grinning.

The school had a white brick wall around it with a wooden gate in the middle. There was an arch over the gate, with a cross on top. All white. The gate was directly across from my parents' apartment.

"No! Behind the bushes or the whole thing's

off."

We crawled behind the oleanders at the side of the gate. He wanted to make a bed of leaves. I nixed it; too many bugs. I told him to get his sleeping bag from the car. While he was gone, I repeated: "Something of you no one can take away. No one can take away. Not even Sadie." My teeth were chattering.

"Let's pray," Joey said, as he spread the sleeping bag.

I bowed my head. "Dear God, please don't let the police arrest us."

"C'mon, Beck. Not like that. On our knees, facing each other." He opened Lady Chatterley to his bookmark and read: 'We fucked a flame into being. Even the flowers are fucked into being between the sun and the earth.'" He bent over and kissed my neck. "Beautiful and holy, don't you think? And sexy."

"Yes, but I can't deal with defiling the Catholic school, maybe the entire religion, and me in my cousin Suzie's Lanz nightie and a Star of David around my neck." Tears ran down my cheeks, ruining my makeup.

"Hey," he hugged me and stroked my hair, "don't cry. It's okay if you change your mind. It just seemed like a neat idea, but it can wait until New York. We can do it on Broadway, or in Times Square, at Schraft's, or the Empire State Building. Or in the black apartment with the door locked and the shades down, just you and me."

"Godammit!" I pushed him away, pulled my nightie over my head, undid my bra and threw it, hard as I could, "I'm tired of being a chicken-shit!"

Joey pulled off his tee shirt and his pants. We grabbed each other. Feeling him naked was like tasting chocolate with my whole body. Our kisses were deep, slow, soft, hard. He held my breasts, kissed my nipples, his mouth warm and open. I caressed his hair, the back of his neck. He was burning. He held me tight—tighter. I could hardly breathe. We fell back on the sleeping bag.

"Wrap your legs around me."

He's said that before, to other women. Oh, God, Beck, don't ruin it. Think only of his fingers between your legs. Warm lips on lips. Tongues dancing.

I closed my eyes. Sadie's face, white as the cross above the gate, looked down at us, saying, *don't you feel filthy?*

"Atta girl," Joey said. His penis pressing, pushing, hurting. "C'mon, baby."

He's not talking to me; he's talking to some tramp he picked up. Some filthy tramp. If he really loved me, he'd be gentle, slow, instead of a grunting pig animal. Fast, faster, harder, harder.

I'm ten years old. I hear Mommy and him through the wall. Take off your pants. No you're too big. Go back to sleep. Take them off! No, not tonight. C'mon, he says. Open up. I run to the kitchen and get the butcher knife. I'm coming, Mommy. I'll save you. Listen at their door. Nothing but the bed creaking. In the morning I ask her: You didn't do it, did you, Mommy? Please say you didn't. She says, Mommy wouldn't do something like that. Mommy is clean and good and clean and good and filthy, filthy, don't you feel filthy?

"Stop! Get off." I screamed. I hit him, over and over. "Please, please get off or I'll kill you."

"What's wrong?" Joey sat back on his knees.

I was sobbing. "I'm sorry. I'm so sorry. I can't. Not with them. Not with my parents across the street. I'm so so sorry."

"Poor Beck. They've really done a job on you."

We dressed without talking. When he walked me home I said I was sorry again. He said it was the wrong time, the wrong place. I didn't believe it. We could have had something that no one could take away, but I blew it.

Sadie was snoring when I peeked into our room. I went to Izzy's candy drawer in the living room and ate a whole bag of peanut M&Ms. In the morning, my stomach was killing me, but Sadie was in a fine mood. She actually made Joey her special French toast, and sent him off with a bag of cookies and fruit. "Good luck with your acting career," she hollered, as we waved goodbye. The minute his car was out of sight, she said he would ruin my life and thank God he wasn't going back to school.

I ran to our bedroom and slammed the door.

8.

Sadie doubled up over the kitchen table as if in pain. "My daughter, a college graduate, working in a gambling joint."

I paced between the fridge and sink, eating Wonder Bread out of the bag. "I've told you a hundred times, it's temporary. In a few months I'll have enough money to go to New York."

"You'll fall in with the wrong kind of people. Coarse, uneducated." I tossed the Wonder Bread back in the fridge and headed for Izzy's candy drawer in the living room. She followed, babbling while I shoveled M&M's into my mouth. "And why in God's name did you ask for the night shift? It's dangerous!"

"Can't we discuss one thing at a time? You keep jumping around."

"You don't believe me, read the paper." She grabbed the <u>Morning Sun</u>; waved it in my face. "Every day they find another body in the desert. Not just riff-raff. Respectable people."

"This is a tourist town, Mother. If there were that many murders nobody would come." Chocolate dribbled out of my mouth and onto my blouse. I ran to the kitchen for a paper towel. She followed as far as the fridge. "Las Vegas can't afford bad publicity." I spat in the sink. "Like Dad says, when the mob runs the show, everybody behaves."

Sadie reached in the fridge and took out an

unopened Sara Lee chocolate cake. "I'll never forget how they murdered poor Sally and Saul Stein." She tore open the box and crammed a handful of cake in her mouth. "Why her? She was president of Hadassah."

"She was a gangster's wife." I poured myself a glass of water and gulped it. "There are more people downtown at two in the morning than during the day. And millions of neon lights. So how can you say it's not safe?"

She sat at the kitchen table, eating cake with her hands. "They went to services every Friday night, the two of them. He was such a mench. President of the temple. Everybody loved him and still they killed him." She stood up and yelled: "Call the Mint. Tell them your mother won't let you work at a gambling joint."

I shook my head.

"Then I'll call. Marty Glassman will listen to me."

We both rushed to the wall phone. She grabbed the receiver.

I held her wrist. "I'm twenty-two years old. It's my decision."

She tried to dial. I wouldn't let her.

"If you don't stop, I'll walk out the door and never come back. I will, Mother. I swear."

"What's the difference if it's now or three months?"

"Goddamit, give me the phone." We struggled. I got it away from her. It was sticky with chocolate cake.

"I give up." She turned her back on me. "You're hopeless, just like your father." She sat down. Sulked. Ate a handful of cake.

I went to the sink. Poured water in the kettle. "Want some coffee?"

"Tea. Lipton's. The Red Rose is stale."

I waited for the water to boil. She read <u>The Morning Sun</u>. I served her tea in a mug with a puppy decal.

"Why should I worry?" she smiled up at me. "You won't last more than a couple days. You don't have a head for numbers."

By the time I left for work, my black skirt was so tight I couldn't zip it more than half up. I had to wear a giant safety pin and a wide patent leather belt that cut into my hips.

"You'll be sorry," Sadie said, handing me the car keys.

"Be careful with the car," Izzy said, without looking up from his racing form.

Anybody with half a brain can make change, I thought, driving down Fifth Street.

"You Plotnik?" asked the woman in the change booth, opening the little door in back. There were two steep steps. "C'mon in."

She was short and stocky, with a butch haircut, and two tiny Band-Aids criss-crossed on her chin. She grabbed her purse and a pack of cigarettes.

"Weekends are hell. My totals are there." She pointed to a black book on the counter. "The bosses checked them. Don't let the customers hassle you or you'll come out short. They don't like that." We sidestepped to avoid each other. She paused on the bottom step, her hand on the doorknob. "And keep an eye on the silver. People steal left and right."

"Wait," I called after her, "aren't you going to break me in?"

How was I supposed to know what to do? At least, she could have introduced me to the other employees. I felt like Rapunzel, locked in the tower. The black book was in front of me. Silver dollars in stacks of ten were lined up on one side. On the other were bunches of empty paper rolls held together with rubberbands. A sheet of paper taped to the counter said:

Job Description - Cashier

1.) Give coin in rolls to changegirls on request.

2.) Don't give coin to customers. That's what changegirls are for.

3.) Change coin to cash for customers in the event of a jackpot.

4.) COUNT THE COIN. Roll loose coin when you have time. Left over coin goes in the bags.

5.) Try to use the facilities during your break. If you have to leave get someone from floor to replace you.

A man in a pink fluorescent baseball cap handed me a ten and asked for silver. I gave him a stack.

"I said five, not ten," he yelled.

I tried several drawers before finding cash. "Sorry, I'm new … couldn't hear … slot machines."

He gave me the finger. A change girl demanded five rolls of quarters. "Hurry up. Haven't got all night." Another moved in after her, followed by a long line of scowling customers. I couldn't believe how rude people were, especially my fellow employees. My eyes stung from the florescent lights and the smoke. I'd never seen so many cigarettes. And the noise was giving me a headache… grinding, belching, grating… A woman with tiny slot machines hanging from her ears demanded change.

"Ask the change girls," I snapped. "That's what they're for." I had a feeling none of the change people liked me.

"Gimme twenty bucks in dimes," a changegirl said. "Hey, didn't you go to Vegas High?"

"Class of '57."

She looked about forty. "Becky—something, right? You sat behind me in Family Life. My hair was brown then." Her crooked teeth rang a bell. She'd lost a lot of weight. She was now the kind of thin that makes you grateful your clothes are tight.

"Darlene?"

"Yeah. Wanna take a break together?"

"Sure. I'm supposed to get fifteen minutes at 12:30, but I don't have a watch."

"No sweat." She showed me her watch. "I'll get Francie to cover."

"How long you been working here?" I asked, staring at my smudged mascara in the mirror behind the counter. I dipped a corner of my napkin in my water and fixed it. Darlene kicked off her shoes and rubbed her feet.

"Eight months." Her eyes were empty, her face haggard. Sadie was right. This was no place for a young girl. "I work a double shift."

"How can you stand it?"

"Got three kids to support. My ex was a dealer at the Nugget. He skipped when I got knocked up the third time."

"Wow, that's too bad." I hated myself for sounding so juvenile.

"Floyd Beatty." She lit up a Lucky Strike. "Class of '56."

I vaguely remembered a boy with greasy blond

hair and pimples.

"How can you work, with all those kids?"

"My mom takes them part of the day. She's a bingo caller at the Showboat. She's divorced too. Three times."

The waitress came with our coffee. I added sugar. Darlene took hers straight.

"Half of our class is working down here," she said. "Tommy Ferris deals blackjack at the Horseshoe. Moose Romero's at the Fremont."

"But Tommy went to Stanford."

"Maybe he did, but he's back. Most everybody ends up coming back. Look at you." She looked at me. "In high school we used to call you the virgin queen. You and those goody-goody Mormon girls you ran around with. You still see them?"

"No. They're married with kids."

Darlene took a long drag on her cigarette and stared in the mirror. Sadie would consider her "the wrong kind of people." But what happened to Darlene could happen to anybody. If I hadn't gone to college, I might have fallen for somebody like Floyd Beatty.

"That's the weird thing about Vegas," she said. "It's full of Mormons and whores. Not much in between." She poked me in the ribs. "Except you and me."

Her choice of words, and our new-found intimacy caught me completely off-guard, as did her shit-eating grin. I coughed into a napkin.

"You okay?" She touched my arm.

"Yeah. Went down the wrong hole. How can you stand the slot machines? Doesn't the noise drive you crazy?"

"Oh, yeah. You work here long enough you lose your hearing. One woman who's been here three years, she's practically deaf."

"My God! That's awful."

"You think that's bad? C'mere." I scooted toward her until our shoulders touched. "Two of the change girls who've been here a couple of years had to have little operations, if you know what I mean."

"Operations?"

"Jeez, don't you know anything?" She moved away, as if I'd offended her. "I mean the one where they cut out your sex organs." She pressed under her belt to illustrate. "Women just weren't made to carry a lot of weight below the waist."

"Oh, my God, I'm glad I got the change booth."

"A lot of people are pissed at you, you know." She ground her cigarette in the ashtray.

"Nobody gets the booth right off unless they know somebody."

"I asked to be a change girl. It's not my fault!"

Darlene shrugged, lit up another Lucky. "Like I said, you know somebody. No big deal. Everybody's out for themselves. Only reason I work here is the money." She lowered her voice. "You can make lots of money around here, once you know how. Lots of money."

"Really?" I pretended to be interested.

"C'mere." I scooted over again. "Nobody counts the change once they get the rolls. So we just help ourselves. A dime here, a quarter there. It adds up."

"But that's stealing!"

"Everybody does it. After a couple weeks, you will too." She spoke so softly I had to strain to hear. "Better be careful, though. They're watching you. It's easier for us because we move around."

"Who's watching me?"

"The goons. The old guys in suits that act like they own the place. Murder, Incorporated. Their job is to make sure nobody steals, especially employees. They can bump off anybody and get away with it."

I remembered a creepy old man eyeing me from the slots. I heard Sadie ... *Every day they find a new body in the desert* ... I heard Izzy's gang at Sammy's ... *They dug up a head ... A fuckin' head*!

"We better get back. They don't like it if you're late."

I had to pee, but the ladies room had a line. My next break was in two hours. It would be better to wet my pants than mess with Murder, Inc.

Back at the booth, things were even busier than before. Whenever somebody hit a jackpot I had to count the money and put it in little burlap bags. In the middle of counting, somebody'd interrupt, and I'd have to start over. I still had to pee. Couldn't cross my legs. I had change on my lap. At least the changegirls weren't as snotty. Darlene must have put in a good word.

Finally there was a lull. An old woman in pink toreador pants was talking to herself by the dollar machines. She carried an oversized straw bag with "Miami Beach" on it in red yarn. Poor thing. She reminded me of Grandma Plotnik, who loved slot machines. I wondered if she had anybody to take care of her. She must have caught me staring. She shuffled over.

"I got to pee," she moaned. "Where is it, the ladies room?"

Oh, how I longed to take her there. "There's one in the restaurant." I turned to point. A bag of change fell off my lap, spilling coins. "If it's too crowded," I yelled from the floor, "there's another one by the exit sign."

When I stood she was gone, along with two stacks of silver. My stomach plunged. Maybe I was paranoid. I counted the stacks. Twenty dollars short.

She must have grabbed the silver while I had my head down. No sign of her. Oh, God. They'll think I stole it.

Truth was out of the question. A little old lady? Disappeared into thin air? I could hardly believe it myself. I went through my purse. Eight dollars and thirty cents. If I added that in, I'd only be $11.65 short. For such a small amount they wouldn't waste their bullets. I remembered the Band-Aids on the cashier's chin. Maybe they wouldn't kill me but they might work me over.

C'mon, Beck. Think! There's got to be a way out. Your twenty- minute lunch break's coming up... I know! I'll call home and ask Sadie to take a cab and bring the money... No, you'll never live it down ... Maybe I should just quit. Tell them to forget about paying me... And give Sadie the satisfaction of saying I told you so? No way! ... What if I try the slots? I know, it's gambling, but it's not like I want to hit a jackpot. All I need's eleven bucks and some change. It'll be easy... But not with the goons watching. Go some place close. But not too close. Like two casinos down.

The ladies' room at Benny Binion's Horseshoe Club was out of toilet paper. I had to use an old Kleenex. The casino attempted to be different from the Mint. Instead of pink bubbles and champagne, it was western motifs and beer. For my trial run, I asked a change girl for thirty cents in nickels, and picked a machine in the back.

Close your eyes and pull. Cherries are good. Think cherries. The machine churned. Click. Coins crashed into the cup. I opened my eyes. Two cherries and an orange. Thirty- five cents. From the noise I'd expected more. Still, I was ahead. Stay with the machine, Beck. Eyes open, this time. Pull! Oranges and lemons. Nothing. The next two times I alternated eyes closed, eyes open. Nothing.

A man in a ten-gallon hat and spurs walked away from a machine down the row holding a paper cup full of change. It made sense to try a machine that was already primed. I moved in. The handle was still warm. An orange. A banana. Grapes. Nothing.

C'mon, Beck. You're not concentrating. Remember the first time? Think cherries. Now pull. Cherries! But in the wrong place. You didn't win, but it worked. Again. Concentrate. Pull. Lemons. Damn!

I was still fifteen cents ahead. I scanned the other people in my row to see how they were doing. A woman with a bald spot sat at my old machine. She wasn't winning. I was right. It was a dud. Two machines down, another woman, hair in pincurls, cigarette in mouth, pink chenille bathrobe, sat on a high stool, scooping nickels into a paper cup. Like Izzy used to tell the relatives, "Some got it. Some don't." He also said, "Stay away from the slots." I put that out of my mind.

I waved at a change girl and asked for eight dollars in nickels. At first I didn't win. Then I won a handful, and another. I fed my winnings back. Stopped thinking about the people in my row, whether they were winning or losing. Forgot about little old ladies in toreador pants, and goons with tommy guns. Just me and my machine. Juicy red cherries, brilliant bananas, succulent oranges, luscious purple grapes.

Seven nickels left. Seven sacrificial virgins, waiting to plunge into the pit. I chose one and pulled. A tiny victim in a hula skirt fell into the abyss. So what? There were six more where she came from. Everybody knows seven is a lucky number, so when four, five and six fell to their deaths, I didn't flinch. Seven was special. She wore a red sarong with a lei of white carnations, like Debra Padget in that movie where she gets rescued from the volcano at the last minute. *Bird of Paradise*. I closed my eyes. Come on, Paradise!

Eight dollars in nickels seems to last forever. When you reach over to the side of your machine for another roll and there's nothing, you refuse to believe it. You get down on the floor. You shake out your purse. Not even a penny. You know what it's like to be Izzy Plotnik on his way home with empty pockets.

"You look like shit," Darlene said. "You get your period or something?"

"Lost all my money at the slots."

"Dummy. You should have asked one of the change girls which machines were hitting."

"What do you mean?"

"C'mere."

I leaned so far forward the wires from my bra dug into my ribcage.

" Do I have to spell it out? You slip her a five. She tells you which machines are hitting. If you hit a jackpot, she gets part of the take."

I should have known there was more to winning than luck. "Listen, Darlene. One of my customers ran off with two stacks of silver. I'm twenty dollars short. What'll they do?"

"They'll fire you. Big deal."

She hurried off to a customer. I began putting loose change in rolls.

Dammit! I hated to go home unemployed! I'd rather beg, borrow or... Why not? Darlene said nobody counts the change in the rolls. A nickel here, a quarter there. It wouldn't really be stealing because I have no intention of keeping the money.

A couple of men in suits stood just outside the entrance, smoking cigars. Big. Old. Ugly, like at Sammy's, except these guys were built like bouncers. Another, fat, bald head, leaned against the wall by the STAIRS sign, clipping his nails. Two more in back, talking to the dealers. Nobody seemed interested in me. Even if they were, how could they tell what I was doing? I opened a roll and took out a quarter. It gave me a funny feeling, like getting drunk the first time. My fingers trembled. C'mon, Beck! Don't lose your nerve. Remember, it's not really stealing. Think of it as expanding—making what you have seem like more.

A customer asked for dollar bills. I was so flustered I gave him a roll of quarters. How much time did I have before check out? I tried to get Darlene's attention. Damn! She was with a customer. I finished my second roll, placing it on the counter next to the first, when I heard: "Okay, toots. Checkout time."

I almost jumped out of my seat. It was the fat man with the bald head from the STAIRS sign.

"You got twenty minutes to total your coin and put your figures in the book. Do cash and silver separate. Take it to the floor man to get weighed." He handed me some plastic trays and put a CLOSED sign in front of me. I expected him to go back to his post, but he leaned against the booth and got out his clippers. I resigned myself to getting the ax.

It took far too long to count the coin. Each time I looked at Baldy he was looking at his watch. Twenty dollars short. Actually, $19.50 because of the two quarters. I would have put them back but I'd forgotten which rolls they were from.

"Sorry to bother you, but I can't carry all the money at once, and I don't want to leave the rest because somebody might steal it."

"Don't worry, toots. I ain't going nowhere." He called a security guard. "He'll show you where to go."

We made our way through the tables to a kind of podium with an old-fashioned scale on top. I assumed the guy behind it must be the floor man.

"Put her on the floor."

For a second I thought he meant me.

"There's more," I said. "She was too heavy to carry in one trip."

It took me several trips to deliver the money. The security guard could have done it in one.

"I'll take the coin first," the floor man said.

I knelt on the floor and began sorting out change when I noticed a man's shoe. Then another. I counted five pairs of polyester pants. Thick legs, like tree trunks. I looked up and saw cigar smoke where leaves should have been. It was the goon squad. They had appeared out of nowhere. Oh, God. They're not going to shoot me. They're going to step on me!

But they ignored me, smoking their cigars while I struggled to get the damn money off the floor. At least they could have offered to help. Even if they were planning on finishing me off.

"Okay, now give me the silver and the bills." The floor man frowned at the figures in the black book.

When I knelt down for the rest of the money, the shoes walked off. At first I was relieved. Then I wondered if they were behind me, guns cocked, waiting for somebody to yell, "Fire!"

"You're twenty dollars short," said the floor man, as I handed him the bills.

"A customer ran off with it." My teeth began to chatter. "He was about twenty-five, wearing sunglasses."

"Why didn't you call security?"

My teeth were going a hundred miles an hour.

"I was afraid I'd get fired because I didn't stop him."

He looked disgusted. "I'll let it go, since you're a friend of Glassman's and it's your first night."

I was stunned. When I got back to the booth, Baldy was in it with the CLOSED sign in front of him. Before I could say a word he handed me my purse. I couldn't wait to tell Darlene I still had a job. She was standing outside, smoking a cigarette, her pale face drawn, her hair copper under the neon.

"They didn't fire me."

"Hey, that's great." She squeezed my shoulder. "Wish I could stick around to celebrate." She kept her hand where it was and closed her eyes; for a moment, I thought she'd fall into me. "Gotta catch some sleep before the kids wake up."

"Want a ride? I have a car."

"Nope. I live close. Near the train station." She checked her watch. "Better get going or I'll never make it through another shift."

I watched her thin body grow thinner, and disappear. Washed-up at twenty-two. It wasn't fair. I was doing this to go to New York. Darlene was doing it to live.

9.

Standing in front of the Mint, under the cold air vents at four in the morning, was like being in a science fiction world with artificial air, light, and people. The sidewalks teemed. As I walked past the Horseshoe, a quartet of glassy-eyed tourists with drinks in their hands nearly mowed me down. Zombies. Was I real, or one of them? Go home, Beck. Sleep ten hours. You'll be fine.

Once I turned onto Third Street, I was alone. There, at the end of the block, was my getaway car. I had survived the night shift—eight bucks poorer, but I still had a job, and gambling had brought me closer to Izzy. I'd never forget how desperate I was when I stole those quarters. I could use that as an actress.

Suddenly, I heard someone behind me. Oh, my God! Following me. My heart pounded in my throat. The car was half a block away. Should I run? Too late. I felt his breath on my neck.

"Freeze!"

"I don't have the twenty. Please believe me. I've never stolen anything in my life!"

"Turn around."

Something about his voice... "Oh, Jesus, Billy! God, Billy, you scared me. Jesus!"

He laughed. "Didn't anybody tell you, little girls don't belong on the streets after midnight?" I'd forgotten how sexy he was. Those ice blue eyes. Those chiseled cheekbones. That mouth. He was standing so close, I could feel his warm breath on my face. "Big bad wolf might get you."

Billy Roberts, a.k.a. Loverboy, Vegas High, Class of '56, traced my chin with his finger. I knew those fingers well. The summer after I graduated from high school, it was he who taught me to masturbate in the back seat of his car.

"You scared the shit out of me! It was my first night at the Mint. I was twenty dollars short."

He chuckled. "You're the last person I ever expected to see down here." He wore a white shirt, black pants, and a green apron. I'd always thought those little aprons looked dumb. But on Billy? A loincloth.

"It's just until I save enough money to go to New York. I thought you were in Reno at the U of N."

"Came back after I graduated. Got a job at the Nugget." His eyes focused on my hips. I imagined his fingers unbuttoning my blouse.

"How about a drink?"

"Can't. My mother's expecting me."

He grinned. "She still your roommate? Some things never change."

"Do they still call you Mr. One-Night Stand?"

"Touché. Rumor has it you're not a virgin anymore."

Billy had to be pissed that in three whole months we'd never gone all the way. On our first date, he had told me he had no interest in getting to know me in other than the biblical sense. But we actually became sort-of friends; he'd even told me about his parents' divorce—how sad he'd felt when his dad moved out.

"If I hadn't resisted you," I said, smiling, "I never

would have gotten to know you."

He stopped smiling.

"You didn't get to know me. How about tomorrow night?"

"I don't know." I knew I should tell him I had a boyfriend, but my body ignored my head.

"You don't know?" He laughed, reached back, undid his apron, rolled it, stuck it in his back pocket. With his hair slicked back forties-style, and a wicked gleam in his eyes, he owned the night. "You're even sexier than you were at eighteen."

So are you—oh my God so are you. "I look awful in this."

"You'd look better without it."

I felt like ripping my clothes off. "I'd better get home."

"What are you afraid of?"

"Nothing. It's just—it's my first week. I don't get time off till next Wednesday."

"Okay. Wednesday, after work."

I reminded myself that I loved Joey, but a little voice whispered, *He'll never know*. "Okay. I guess."

"You guess?" He smirked while running his finger around the buckle of my black patent leather belt. "See you Wednesday."

He stepped off the curb into the street. Halfway across he turned on his heel, made his fingers into a gun, and pulled the trigger.

10.

Two weeks after Joey went back to Jersey, and a week before fall semester in Arizona, I had dinner with Sadie and Izzy at the Silver Slipper. I had thought that as long as I loved Joey I couldn't be attracted to anybody else. On the way out of the restaurant, I ran into Frosty Ryan. He'd been voted best-looking senior when I was a freshman at Vegas High.

"Say, don't I know you?" he asked, blonder than ever in a white cowboy hat and boots. His flashy blue shirt said: "Junior Chamber of Commerce."

"We worked on the Wildcat Echo together at Vegas High," I said. "I was a lowly freshman."

"I can't believe we never went out."

I gave him my name and phone number. On the way home, Sadie asked me all about that handsome young man in the cowboy suit. I said even if he called, which was unlikely, I wouldn't go out with him. She said, "You'd be crazy to pass up somebody like him. Don't worry. Whatsisname will never know."

When Frosty Ryan called for me Saturday night, Sadie whispered: *He looks like a movie-star.* He took me to the Pair-a-Dice Lounge. "Can't believe we never went out," he said, and after my second or third drink, he kept repeating, "Jesus, you're beautiful." I stared at myself in the mirror behind the bar. I was beautiful, just like he said. I thought I heard him tell the bartender to keep filling my Manhattans, but his voice sounded far away. I woke up in a motel. On a bed. Frosty was taking off my panties.

"No," I said, trying to grab his hands, but I was weak from drinking. "Don't. Please, don't." He got on top of me. The room was spinning. "Please don't. I've never done it before." His body: thick, heavy, suffocating. My hands, useless. "Please," I begged him. "I don't want to. Not like this."

"You'll thank me when it's over."

"Stop!" I tried to punch him but I didn't have the strength. "No!" I screamed.

He put his hand over my mouth. I bit it. He laughed.

"You want to play rough?"

The headboard banged against the wall.

"You're hurting me. Stop hurting me." I was crying. "Please stop. Please stop hurting me."

"If you relax it won't hurt as much."

"You sonofabitch! You're raping me. Stop, goddam you. Stop!"

"You're the best-looking Jewish chick I've ever seen," he said, in the car. "You want to do it again sometime?"

I slapped his face.

"Guess that means no."

The next day, I stayed in bed until after dinner. I told Sadie I was too sick to eat. It wasn't just a hangover. I wanted to die of remorse. If I hadn't been so drunk, maybe I could have stopped him, instead of lying there like I wanted it. I heard what he said to the bartender. I knew he was setting me up but I kept right on drinking and drinking. I deserved what I got.

Later that night, as we were packing my clothes for college, Sadie went on about what a nice boy Frosty

Ryan was. So polite—for a *goy.*

"Why the long face? Are you thinking about that goof ball from Jersey? Don't be so depressed. You'll go back to Arizona, meet other boys. You'll forget about him in no time."

Before I left for Arizona, I told Leanne about Frosty. It turned out she had lost her virginity months ago, to a football star she'd had a crush on in high school. She'd been afraid to tell me because she'd thought I was still a virgin, and I'd lose respect for her. They'd slept together several times. But he was good-looking and popular, and he'd stopped calling.

"I'm not sorry I did it," she said. "Just wish he loved me back, that's all."

We hugged. She wasn't the girl-next-door any more. Her breath smelled of beer and cigarettes.

"I could never tell my mom about Frosty," I said, rolling down the car window. "She wouldn't understand."

"Neither would mine," Leanne said. "I don't care what the church thinks, but I'd die before I'd let my parents know. They'd think it was their fault I didn't turn out right." She put her arm around me and rubbed my shoulder. "Now that I know how good it feels, I'd do it again in a minute. I wish it could have been that way for you. Frosty Ryan is a jerk."

"The thing is, Leanne, none of the guys I went out with tried to rape me—not even when I was drunk. They stopped when I said *no*—they always stopped. Why did he make me do it when I was crying, and begging him to stop?"

Leanne lit up a Lucky Strike. "Guys like that don't think they're raping you, Becky. They think they're doing you a favor."

When I got back to school, I was even more depressed. I had trouble sleeping, couldn't concentrate in class. No appetite, even for chocolate. I kept thinking about Frosty, and hearing the bed bang against the wall. It took two weeks to write Joey three lines*. I haven't answered your letters because I can't deal with us right now. I need some time to figure things out. Please be patient, and don't write or call. B.* If I'd thought he would hate me, I'd probably have told him about Frosty right off. But I knew he'd make excuses for me, and I'd hate myself even more. Deep down, I knew Frosty wouldn't have happened if I'd made love with Joey that night at the Catholic school. I could still see Sadie's giant face looking down at us. If only I'd had the guts to defy her. Instead, I let her talk me into going out with a dumb cowboy.

I couldn't bear to think about Joey, and what a bitch I was for betraying him. So, I pretended he didn't exist, and tried out for the fall play. Then, I received a letter from Student Health. I figured somebody in my dorm had reported me for being depressed. A pretty, middle-aged woman with kind eyes led me to her office and closed the door. She told me that a man whose name she could not disclose had been diagnosed with syphilis, and had listed me as a sexual contact. It felt like I'd been punched in the gut. The government had tracked me down. People I didn't even know knew all about me. The woman with kind eyes patted my hand while I cried through two boxes of Kleenex and told her about Frosty Ryan.

The man who gave me the Wasserman test tried to make small talk, but stopped short after blurting out that he had a daughter my age. But the doctor who gave me the pelvic exam didn't attempt to hide his disgust. I told him he was hurting me. "You're used to it," he said.

I knew the doctor had more reason to be ashamed of his behavior than I did. But on some level I felt I deserved it. He was Sadie in disguise. *Yes, Mother, I feel filthy*. That night, I forced myself to go to a callback at the Little Theater and gave the audition of my life. Amazing what despair can do for your concentration.

I told Terry, my roommate, everything—mostly because we shared a bathroom and I was afraid she might use my towels and get infected. Terry confided that she had lost her virginity over the summer and had gone through two and a half weeks of hell waiting for her period. "What I went through is nothing compared to being raped and getting syphilis," she said, squeezing my hand. She invited me to go home to San Francisco with her over Thanksgiving break so I wouldn't have to face Sadie until Christmas. Two days later, the doctor called me in. I had tested negative. He still looked disgusted. I was beginning to hate men.

That was when Joey drove all the way from Jersey to Arizona to see me. There he was, sitting in the lobby of my dorm. At first, all the love flew back as if nothing had happened. But when we hugged, I remembered Frosty, and pulled away. Joey suggested going outside to talk. It was twenty minutes before lock-out, so we sat in his car.

"What's wrong, Beck? You can tell me."

How could I tell him that I had lost my virginity because I let some jerk get me drunk because he told me I looked beautiful? I started to cry. Joey tried to comfort me.

"Don't!"

"What is it, Beck? What's wrong?" He put his hand on my arm.

"Don't touch me!"

We both jumped at the warning buzzer. Joey

held my wrist. I broke away and ran from the car. I may have hit him—I don't remember. The whole time, my housemother stood at the door, watching.

"Not a moment too soon, Miss Plotnik," she said, shaking her silver key ring as I approached. She didn't care that I was breathless and crying, or that Joey was pleading with me to talk to him. "And you, young man, had best be on your merry way."

Joey stuck around for a week. I kept telling him he would be better off without me, but he wouldn't listen. He followed me to class and sat in at play rehearsals. I told him I'd changed my mind, and I didn't love him anymore. I believed it! I couldn't bear the thought of being touched, fondled, caressed, fucked. I hated sex. I hated doctors, and cowboys with VD. I wanted them all to leave me alone, including Joey. I was glad when he ran out of money and had to go back to Jersey. I refused to talk to him when he called. I didn't even read his letters. I tied them together with red ribbon, and hid them with the others in a shoebox in my dorm closet.

Over Christmas vacation, I told Sadie I wasn't a virgin. She had been nagging me about not going out on dates. She thought Joey was the reason I was depressed. She said I would never get over him if I didn't give somebody else a chance.

"I did give somebody else a chance. That goy in the cowboy suit, the one you said was so polite and looked like a movie star. You said I'd be a fool to pass up somebody like him, and guess what? I'm not a virgin anymore."

For a moment, she seemed contrite. Then she looked at me. I will never forget the heartbreak and disgust on her face. And she didn't even know that her daughter had been tested for VD.

By the end of vacation, Sadie seemed resigned to my fall from grace. Now, she was determined to marry me off before I could disgrace her more. I assured her I had no interest in sex. I meant it. But, back at school, my friends nagged me to start going out again, to get over being raped. So, toward the end of junior year, I met a guy I liked, and another, and gradually discovered I still enjoyed the hors d'oeuvres—it was the main course that gave me indigestion. I also discovered that, once you've lost your virginity, red-blooded American males consider it an insult if you don't have sex with them, even if you explain that you were raped. It's amazing how many guys think sex with them is the only way to get over a traumatic experience. Sex didn't solve any of my problems, it added to them. I was convinced I would never have an orgasm until I found true love. Until then, sex would be disappointing, the way it was for Lady Chatterley until she found Mellors. D.H. Lawrence really knew what he was talking about when he wrote that book.

My roommate, Terry, summed it up brilliantly: "Even if the sex is great, which most of the time it isn't, we can't forget our mothers raised us to be like Doris Day in *Pillow Talk*." We counted to three and yelled: "I hate Doris Day!" But, Terry had had three orgasms out of twenty attempts, so at least she had some incentive to keep going.

Other than Dr. Rogers' advanced acting class, Terry was the best thing about Arizona State. Then, second week of senior year, she got pinned to a Sigma Chi and I barely saw her. When I did, all she could talk about was him. They eloped over Thanksgiving break. About that time, GiGi wrote that she'd fallen in love with a grad student at the U of N and had moved to Reno. To make matters worse, Leanne met a nice Mormon boy from Provo, Utah, swore off drinking and smoking, and returned all of my subversive books. She even threw away her Elvis picture. She'd be happier married—I knew that. But, I also knew it was the end of our friendship. At Leanne's wedding reception, when the newlyweds announced they had decided to settle in Provo and start a family right away so they could grow up with their kids, I gagged, spilling fruit punch on the tight-in-all-the-wrong-places bridesmaid's dress that Mrs. Larson had made on her sewing machine.

"Next time, it'll be your wedding, honeybunch," Mrs. Larson said, dabbing at my bosom with a wet paper napkin.

Mr. Larson patted my back. "We thought you'd get hitched before Leanne. What happened to that actor from New Jersey? You were perfect for each other."

"Yeah," I said. "I blew it."

I didn't confess that, after attending my friends' weddings—three in Vegas over the summer, two in Arizona, and now Leanne's—I had no intention of getting hitched. I wasn't going to waste my life making tuna casseroles. That's all my friends talked about. But the main reason I was never getting married, at least not until forty, is nobody really knows who they are at twenty-one. Thank God, I had more sense than my friends. But, being without them sucked. I ended up celebrating my twenty-first birthday eating Chinese food at Fong's Garden with my parents.

"College is almost over," Sadie reminded me over Chop Suey. "You'd better find a husband while you're still in Arizona. In Las Vegas, the pickings are slim."

My last semester in college, my grades plunged. My weight fluctuated wildly. Whenever I had sex I would think of a hundred and fifty things I would rather be doing, including cleaning the toilet. I knew I should talk to a shrink about my binge eating, and sex, and my parents, but even if I were dying, I would never go near Student Health again, and I didn't have the money for anything else.

I didn't graduate with the Class of '6l. Too many incompletes. I had succeeded in putting off graduation, but I'd spent practically all of Sadie's money with nothing to show for it. So I registered for fall semester. To help with tuition, I worked all summer as a supervisor at the Telephone Company in Las Vegas, and part-time at the admissions office after returning to school in September. In January '62, I received a diploma. A piece of paper, as Joey had called it.

Joey. Nobody had come close to replacing him in my heart. After that impulsive trip from Jersey to Arizona he'd continued to write me for over a year, despite the fact that I'd only answered once. *Please don't write any more. I'm too messed up for somebody as nice as you.* His last letter came in February of '61; he had saved enough money to move to New York. *It's not too late for you to join me, Beck. Think about it*. A few weeks before graduation, I did think about it, but even in the unlikely event that Joey still loved me, I only had thirty dollars and seventy-five cents in the bank. How could I go to New York? Soon, Sadie would be driving to Tempe in her Buick Le Sabre to move me back home. We'd be roommates again. Shit! I couldn't let that happen.

I found a job as a receptionist in a doctor's office, answered an ad to share an apartment in Scottsdale with two other girls, and told Sadie I was staying in Arizona. She said I was nuts. I didn't tell her that as soon as I had saved five hundred dollars I planned to join Joey in New York. More than ever, I was convinced Joey was the love of my life and I wanted to be an actress. Of course, there was one minor detail I hadn't addressed: Joey wasn't in on the plan. I hadn't heard from him in a year. Maybe he wasn't even in New York? Jesus! He could be married! I tried not to think about it.

As it turned out, Joey's whereabouts, and even his marital status, were the least of my worries. I hated my first job, but not as much as the next three. I loved my five days as hostess at The Sugar Bowl Ice Cream Shoppe in Scottsdale, and hated to quit, but jobs like that barely pay the rent, and the whole point of working was to save money for New York. Worst of all, I didn't get along with my roommates. It was hell coming home from a crappy job to a cramped apartment with one bathroom and two roommates who loathed me, but I couldn't afford to live on my own. Sadie pleaded with me to give up on Arizona. Once, she even showed up at our door and tried to drag me to her car. I agreed with my roommates that I should move out by June first, when it would be easier for them to find a replacement.

One night, when my roommates were out avoiding me, I drank a bottle of Ripple and dialed Joey's number in Jersey. His mom gave me his new address. I wrote him that I wouldn't blame him if he didn't want anything to do with me. I confessed I still had his copy of <u>Frannie and Zooey</u> and hugged it like a teddy bear every night before I went to sleep. I didn't expect, or deserve, an answer.

Dear Beck, Funny you should write. You've been

coming into my head lately, like an old movie. Great beginning, but the ending sucked. I'm living in the Village and studying acting with Stella Adler. You have to audition to get in. Just for the hell of it, after my Pinter piece I threw in my toilet. She cracked up. She told all the guys they had to wear a tie. I brought in a dozen from my dad's warehouse. Seconds. Sold them for half price. It paid for the class. I figured it was a means to an end. Hope you don't think I've sold out. Other than playing games with my draft board—they think I'm obliged to bear arms, like those assholes at Arizona State—life is good and my career seems to be heading in the right direction. When it comes to theater, Phoenix is a dead-end, Beck. If you really want to act, and I know you do, you have to move here. New York is the most exciting city in the world. Forget about me, you owe it to yourself!

Apartments on Bank St. and W. 49th go for as low as fifty-eight bucks. And lots of actresses live at the Barbizon Hotel for Women—it's cheap and you make great contacts. Temporary Talents specializes in jobs for people like us who need flexible hours. When you're working to support your art like everybody you know, you can put up with boring jobs. For extra dough, I wait tables at Gerde's Folk City. Been catching Bob Dylan. Remember that name! You asked whether I think we could ever pick up where we left off. I think Plotnik & Goldman can still knock 'em dead, but it's your decision, Beck, not mine. Just like with New York, you're going to have to stop worrying and dive in. No net. No parachute, no guarantee. Just love, J. P.S.

I painted the apartment black. I'm a sucker for happy endings.

We wrote many letters and Joey spent way too much on phone calls. He was more optimistic than ever. He'd been cast in an off-Broadway play—he'd be making money <u>and</u> getting his Equity card, <u>and</u> he'd talked to Dr. Rogers' agent friend about an audition as soon as I moved to New York. So, I put aside all my misgivings and promised to meet him in four months at Grand Central Station. He said I might not recognize him because he had a beard, but he'd be standing by the information booth with a rabbi and two witnesses.

But the bride didn't show. She gained twenty pounds and went home to her mother.

11.

I'm in a bedroom. Mirrors on the walls and ceiling. Round bed. I sit on the edge. The pink quilted bedspread reminds me of Sadie's bathrobe. I'm wearing panties and a bra.

"Room service." It's Frankie Pierce, in a silver jumpsuit, holding a silver tray with silver dollars on it. "Nice bra. Maidenform?"

"No." I hug my knees and scoot to the middle of the bed. "It's a Bali."

He places the tray on the floor, dances around admiring himself in the mirrors, grabs a microphone off a stand. *Take one tender night of bliss...* He sounds exactly like Dean Martin.

"I hate that song. It's corny." "What are you afraid of?"

It's Billy Roberts in a green apron and nothing else. I turn away, but he's in all the mirrors, including the one on the ceiling. He reaches back, unties his apron –

"Wake up!" Sadie shook me. "You talked in your sleep. You screamed: 'Joey, Joey!' Even your subconscious agrees with me. He's a nightmare."

It wasn't just nightmares that kept me from sleeping more than three or four hours between shifts. I couldn't get used to day-sleeping, even with foil on the windows. Tuesday morning, I tossed and turned in bed, thinking about Billy Roberts. Our date was less than forty-eight hours away. This wasn't just about betraying Joey yet again, or being ambivalent about sex. My instincts told me Billy was more dangerous than the goons at the Mint. Four years ago he was a bad boy with a heart, but now he had become a predator. In my sleep-and sex-deprived state I'd be lamb stew. By the time Sadie left to take Izzy to work, I'd decided to use Joey as an excuse. I'd tell Billy my fiancé would kill us. I looked up Billy's number, hung up after one ring.

I took Joey's letters down from the closet shelf. I'd moved them from the shoebox to a Kotex box because Sadie would never look there. Hadn't heard from him since I left Phoenix nearly two months ago. He was probably pissed at my last letter. I'd begged him to understand that I couldn't come to New York and I had to go home to Vegas because I'd gone through so many jobs my confidence was at an all-time low. I didn't tell him that I'd washed down a packet of pills with castor oil to bring on my period after a one-night stand. I didn't tell him I'd gained twenty pounds; I'd never let him see me like that. I made a very big point of telling him not to call or use the blue envelopes with his Jersey address when he wrote me at home, because of Sadie.

I undid the red ribbon. The thin paper crackled as I unfolded the top letter and pressed it flat. His typewriter was missing the letter g. "Rehearsals for the play are reat and class is oin well. In class, I'm doin Biff in <u>Death of a Salesman</u>. The uy playin Willy is only ei hteen, but he's incredible. Everybody, includin Stella, thinks he'll make it bi . Bobby DeNiro. Remember that name. Saw Truffaut's *Jules and Jim*. Wish you'd been with me. It was hard sleepin alone afterwards."

I crumpled the letter and threw it. "Dammit,

Joey! You're such a fucking saint!" It hit the dresser mirror, landing to the side of Sadie's perfume tray. "You don't know me, Joey! You don't have the least idea who I am." I stared at the pale face, the empty eyes in the dresser mirror. "Neither do I."

A car door slammed. Sadie was back.

"Jesus!" I rushed to the dresser, smoothed the letter, folded it. "I'm sorry, Joey. I didn't mean it." I stuffed the letters back in the box. "I'm just so fucking tired I can't think." I slid the box to the back of the shelf, sweaters in front. The red ribbon was still on the bed. I slipped it in my underwear drawer as I heard Sadie open the front door.

"Milton Sweet's back in town," Sadie said, as I drank my fourth cup of instant Maxwell House.

"Who?"

It was three o'clock. I was sitting at the kitchen table in my robe, trying to build up the courage to call Billy again.

"Fanny Sweet's nephew. The one who works at the Sands. You said you'd go out with him"

Shit! I'd forgotten about him.

"I can't. Working nights, remember?"

"You have Wednesday night off."

"All I plan to do Wednesday is sleep."

"Quit the goddam job."

"No."

"Do me a favor at least," she said, chewing some Maalox tablets. "Let me ask Marty to switch you to days."

"No." I got up and snatched a box of Oreos from the cupboard above the stove. I ate half a row and came up with a plan.

"You win, Mother. Tell Mr. Glassman I can't sleep

and want to switch to days. If he says okay, I'll go out with Fanny's nephew tomorrow night."

She jumped at the chance. Working days, I would never run into Billy again.

"Marty says it's fine," Sadie said, when she got off the phone. "He said he told you not to work nights, but you insisted. What are you, crazy? I'll call Fanny."

12.

I had expected to see a light in the kitchen when I got home but the apartment was completely dark. Thank God she's asleep. I would have gone straight to bed, but I was starving. Oreos. I deserved them for subjecting myself to Milton Sweet.

"Becky? Is that you?" Sadie hollered from somewhere near the bedroom.

She switched on the living-room light. I stuffed three Oreos in my mouth before she reached the kitchen.

"Why didn't you turn on the lights? I thought somebody broke in."

"Didn't want to wake you."

"You know I never sleep." She settled into a chair at the kitchen table. "So? How was it?"

"Terrible." I ate another Oreo. "I left him at the Stardust. I took a cab."

"Why?"

"He was so sleazy! After the show, we're standing in the lobby and he says, 'Go into the lingerie shop, honey.' Then he leers at me, with the eyebrows going up and down, and says, 'Buy anything you like.'"

From the look on Sadie's face, it was clear she didn't get it. Then it hit her. "You must have led him on."

"Goddamit, Mother," I said, heading for the bedroom, "I've had it."

"In my experience" she said, following me, "a

Jewish man doesn't say a thing like that without provocation."

"That creep has the gall to make a pass at me, and you say I led him on? Great. Fine." I kicked off my heels and unzipped my skirt. "My own mother defends him instead of me."

"Fanny said he was a terrific guy. Even your father liked him."

"Well, you're all crazy." I pulled off my sweater and threw it at the dresser. "First of all, he totally ignored me in the car. Then he drooled over every other woman he saw. He took me to this horrible show at the Stardust. Naked gold women coming out of the ceiling. Naked ice skaters."

"You mean the Lido de Paris?" She folded my sweater, put it away. "Everybody raves about it."

I threw my skirt over a wire hanger and grabbed my nightie. "It was disgusting! At least the men got to wear bikinis. Hairy legs in ice skates! Ugh!"

She switched my skirt to a plastic hanger with clips. "They come from all over the world to see that show."

"Well maybe *they* enjoy seeing gold women tied to posts, but I don't. I was tempted to cut them loose with my steak knife." I went into the bathroom and began removing my eye makeup with toilet paper.

She poked her head in. "He bought you steak?"

"Ringside seats, filet mignon, wine in a bucket, the whole schmere."

"What a mensch!"

"He looked like Milton Berle. Without the sense of humor." I brushed my teeth. "I told you about the lingerie," I pointed the toothbrush at her. Toothpaste dripped on the rug. "And you call him a mensch? What does it take, Mother?"

"Maybe you misinterpreted."

I spat in the sink. "He was a letch, goddamit! You and your friend fixed me up with a letch." I wiped my face on a hand towel.

"That's an expensive show. Hard to get into. Ringside seats. He must have tipped the maitre d' plenty."

"Yeah, and he expected me to be grateful."

"Since when are you such a prude?" Her face glowed with revenge.

"Jesus, Mother!" My knees gave out. I sunk into the bed. "I can't believe you said that."

"Why? You keep telling me I'm behind the times."

"I don't care if you are my mother. You have no right to say what you did. I'm getting out of here. Soon as I get my paycheck I'm going to New York."

"Is that so?" Her arms, folded across her chest, her chin goading me. "How the hell will you survive without a penny to your name?"

"Joey's there already. Waiting for me."

Her face drained of color. "But you said it was over."

"I lied. I was supposed to meet him there in June, but I came home. Biggest mistake I ever made."

She staggered. I thought she would fall, but she caught herself. "Go! What do I care? I'm sick from worrying about you." She went into the bathroom. Slammed the door. "I'm sick. I'm sick. I'm sick!"

I slept on the couch with the plastic slipcover.

13.

In the morning, after Sadie left to take Izzy to work, I called the Union Pacific Railway. I would have to borrow money from Joey at first, but he was right. I'd get a job, like everybody else, and we'd audition for the guy at the Village Gate. It would take five days to get to New York. Five days of lettuce and coffee. I'd be thin as a rail. A bumpy rail. I dialed Joey's number. *Guess what? I'm coming. Diving right in. I get paid in two days. Enough for a one-way ticket. Meet me at Grand Central.* It rang four times. *What if he's met somebody? What if she's there?* Five. I hung up. Waited ten minutes. Called again. "Hello?" The voice on the other end sounded very sleepy. And very female. I stared at the phone like it was from outer space. "Hello?" she repeated. I hung up. I was still in a state of shock when Sadie came back. The phone rang. She answered.

"Marty Glassman wants to talk to you."

"Do me a favor, honey," Marty said. "Take the night-shift the rest of the week. I can't get anybody else. Next Monday, you'll start days. It's the best I can do."

"Sure, Mr. Glassman," I said, in a monotone. "I'll be there."

"Hear you're switching to days," said the cashier with the Band-Aids.

"Couldn't get any sleep."

"Days. Nights. They're all the same to me."

Yeah, me too, I thought. Nothing mattered. Joey had finally wised-up and found somebody else. So what difference would it make if I allowed myself to sink lower than ever and had a one-night stand with Billy? Since I had already ruined my life I might as well ruin it some more.

When Billy sauntered in after my lunch break I stood by the change booth waiting for the inevitable. He grinned as he walked toward me, stopping when his shoe touched mine.

"That wasn't nice the other night, standing me up."

"I was sick."

"Poor baby."

"Tried to call. Couldn't find your number in the book."

"There's only one Billy Roberts." He sucked his bottom lip until it hissed. "You still don't know how to handle men, do you?"

"Can't talk," I said, moving away from him. "Have to check out."

"I'll wait."

He had a black Oldsmobile convertible with power steering. On the way to his place, he put the top down. It was still dark out. And warm.

"How was Arizona?"

"Okay. Probably should have stayed there instead of coming home." I leaned against the car door.

He grinned. "C'mere."

The seat cover squeaked as I scooted next to him. He put his arm around me. "Why'd you come back?" His hand gripped my shoulder.

"I hated my job. I was getting fat. I didn't have the money to go to New York."

He ran his fingers along the side of my neck.

"I want to move to New York. Keep losing my nerve."

"That's one of your things, isn't it?" His fingers were inside my ear. "Losing your nerve."

"Yeah. I guess."

"I don't think I've ever been stood up before, you know that?"

By now his hand was inside my blouse, on my breast. He squeezed. I went limp. I didn't care about Joey, New York, past, future. All I wanted was the sinking, swirling, burning in my breasts, my crotch, my thighs. He pulled up in front of a small duplex near where I used to live on Thirteenth Street. I closed my eyes and let his tongue go wild in my mouth.

"I was really disappointed in you. Thought you had more class."

"Please don't talk. Just kiss me. Please."

"How long have we known each other, anyway?" He unbuttoned my blouse, his mouth and tongue on mine.

"Three—three years."

He undid my bra. Fondled my breasts.

I'm gone. Lost. "You didn't notice me until the summer after I graduated high school, but I always noticed you. You reminded me of James Dean."

He ran the tip of his tongue around my lips.

"Especially your mouth." I'll die if he stops. I'll die.

He pulled up my skirt, his hand on my thigh, between my legs.

"I used to fantasize about you."

"Tell me about it. But not here." He opened the door and got out, offering me his hand. "We're too old to be making out in cars."

He turned on the air-conditioner but not the lights. I couldn't see anything but shadows, shapes. The hot, helpless desire I'd felt in the car was beginning to fade.

"Unfortunately, we can't use the bedroom," he said, "my roommate's in there."

"What if he comes out?"

"Don't worry," he said, clearing off the couch, "he sleeps like a rock."

"I don't know."

"Too late to change your mind," he said, slipping my blouse off and kissing my shoulder. "If he comes out, I'll tell him to beat it. He's cool." He started fiddling with my belt.

I held his wrists. "I can't." I shook my head, avoiding his eyes. "I can't do this."

"Yes you can. You were mine the minute you got in the car."

"The act defines the actor," I said, under my breath. "Words to live by."

"What?"

"Nothing." I let go of his wrists.

He pulled me against him. His teeth burned my lips. "No more games."

I didn't want him to know about the safety pin that was holding my skirt together. I asked him to turn his back while I undressed.

"You're too much," he said, taking off his clothes with his back to me. "I can never quite figure you out."

"That makes two of us."

He laughed. I piled my clothes on a chair, underwear on the bottom. "Can I turn around now?"

"I guess so."

"Why are you shy? Most women would die for

tits like yours." He took my hand. "Your problem is you've been brain-washed into thinking that sex is wrong." He led me to the couch. "You're conflicted. You want it so much you're all over the guy, but the minute he shows his cock you close down." He stretched out on the couch and pulled me down beside him. "Don't worry, my dear. You're about to be cured." He put his hand between my legs. "God are you wet. A fucking river." Slid his finger in and out of me.

I grabbed his hand. "Stop. This isn't going to work."

I could hear Sadie, saying, *Since when are you such a prude*?

"You know what? I put up with your bullshit a whole summer. Not anymore." He handed me a Trojan. "Want to put it on me? Most chicks really dig that. Okay. Give it back. I'll do it myself. I hope you know how lucky you are. Most guys think it's the girl's responsibility to be prepared. Jesus, you're soft. Like butter. My roommate would go nuts if he knew I had somebody like you out here. Maybe we should ask him to join us?"

"You're not depressed, are you?" He asked, afterwards. "Some girls get depressed after sex."

"Not me. I don't feel anything."

14.

A few days after I slept with Billy, I quit the Mint. Marty Glassman smiled when I said I couldn't stand to work in a casino another minute. "Sweetheart, to tell you the truth, I was hoping you wouldn't last." And Bertha Fox offered words of encouragement as she handed me my paycheck. "You don't belong in a casino, dear. You belong in an office."

I turned onto the Strip and drove past the Flamingo. The receptionist job would probably be boring, but it was the best the Review Journal want ads had had to offer, and the architect had sounded nice on the phone. Plus he'd promised there wouldn't be much typing. I smiled at the Riviera marquee: Eddie Fisher and the Doodletown Pipers. Marquees always cheered me up. I'd used my Mint paycheck to pay for an English class that started tonight at the university. It required a writing sample, so I'd written passionately about why I loved to read. The professor must have liked it, because I got in. Though I might have to drop it when, (and if!), I left for New York. I needed to be around books, again. I had to do something to get the sleaze of the Mint, and Billy Roberts, out of my system.

I pulled into a parking lot behind a two-story office building. Only half-painted. White with aqua trim, like one of those tacky motels past the Tropicana. Three lonely cars in a lot with space for a hundred. You'd think an architect would have a little more class. Grow up, Beck. It's just a job. A means to an end, as Joey would say. One thing was certain—I was not going to give up on myself the way I had in Scottsdale. I hadn't had the nerve to call Joey yet, but I'd promised myself *tomorrow*. Just because a woman answered didn't mean he'd stopped loving me. I'd do anything to win him back. But deep down I had a feeling it was too late. I blotted my lips on a crumbled candy wrapper I found on the floor of the car and combed my hair with my fingers*. Look at it this way, Beck. You got out of the Mint with your ovaries and your hearing intact. Think of Darlene!*

The architect had told me to use the back entrance to get to the second floor. The door at the top of the stairs said WET PAINT. Inside, the hallway was strewn with packing crates. Shoe prints covered the dusty floor. At least the air conditioning worked.

"Hello? Anybody?"

A tall, trim, silver-haired man of about fifty, with a deep tan, stepped out of a door at the far end of the hall and bounded toward me.

"Rebecca?" In a pale blue cotton suit and white tennies, he looked elegant and hip at the same time. "Quent De Remis." He squeezed my hand, chatting as he led me down the hall. "Please call me Quent. Excuse the mess. We've only been here a month. There's a souvenir shop opening downstairs, and a dry cleaners... A real estate bunch up here. It's a bit hectic. Here's the office, such as it is."

It was a small room with a wooden desk in front of the window, a water cooler in one corner and a stack of folding chairs in the other. On the wall by the desk, diplomas in fancy frames looked out of place. In an adjoining room, a blonde girl—pixie haircut, hoop earrings, black cowboy boots—bent over an art table. She was talking to a guy I couldn't see. Herb Alpert and the Tijuana Brass blared from a radio. The invisible man turned it down.

"Please don't judge us by our appearance," Quent said, gesturing with his long arms and unfolding a chair for me. He moved a stack of blueprints and sat on the desk. "We're moving once we have an established clientele. At the rate things are going, that should be any minute now." The phone rang. Quent put his hand over the receiver and whispered: "One moment, Rebecca." He was very classy on the phone. Yes, he would have the preliminary sketches ready today. He'd hand-deliver them. No, it wasn't out of his way. Kept smiling at me, to let me know I wasn't forgotten. I took a close look at the diplomas. Stanford. UCLA. An award from the Chicago Art Institute. Wow. The girl in the other room stuck her head out and wiggled two fingers. This job might be fun. "I have more clients than I can handle, but I can't afford to turn anyone away," Quent said, hanging up the phone, "at least at this point." It rang again. "Nina! Could you answer the phone?" Nina sauntered in, pencil behind her ear. Annoyed. "Thanks, my dear. Ten…"

"Minutes at the most. I promise." Nina said, mocking him. He didn't seem to mind—in fact he laughed. Nina answered the phone. She had the neatest British accent.

"I might as well be honest, Rebecca," Quent said, turning his attention back to me, "I'm desperate. I don't know how many girls I've interviewed by now—twenty, twenty-five. And every one massacred the English language. Most hadn't even completed high school. You were so articulate when we spoke, and when you mentioned your college degree I was tempted to offer you the job on the phone." He smiled. The lines around his eyes deepened. Kind, twinkling eyes. "I need a 'girl Friday.' Someone to take phone calls, make appointments, do my banking, errands, but above all I need someone who will make a good impression on clients. I know it might not sound challenging to someone like you, but it could lead to a lucrative career in real estate."

Real estate. Ugh. "It sounds perfect. Just the other day, my father and I were discussing real estate when I was driving him home from work. To be honest, I'm looking for something away from the casinos. I detest gambling." He smiled, approvingly. "And architecture fascinates me." I hesitated before saying, "Senior year in high school, I had a huge crush on Philip Bosinney, the architect in <u>A Man of Property</u>."

"<u>The Forsyte Saga</u>." His eyes gleamed. "Been years since I've read it."

He seemed so refined I felt intimidated. "I-I didn't read all three books—only the one about Soames. But it sort of gave me an idea of what architects are like. I think designing a house would be similar to composing a symphony."

From the look in his eyes, I knew I'd charmed him.

"Lovely analogy, Rebecca, but I'm afraid our little enterprise is more mundane."

"Oh, but still, to be able to dream up a hotel, or design a restaurant ..." My empty stomach growled. I coughed to cover it up.

"Water?" He gestured toward the water cooler.

"No, no, really. I'm fine." Growl. I cleared my throat. "Must be the dust."

"I'm so sorry. I've been meaning to call a janitorial service." The phone rang again. Nina answered. "You can see why I haven't." He whispered to Nina. "Just a few more minutes. There's a dear." She made a face. He laughed, and turned back to me. "I value a sense of humor—sure sign of intelligence. And Rebecca, there is nothing I value more than intelligence." Finally a job where I wouldn't get fired for being sarcastic. He reached across the desk for a yellow lined pad and a pen, handing them to me. "If you take the job, no more dust, you have my word. Just put down the usual—education, social security, significant employment, three local references. Hours are nine to five."

I started writing, omitting all employment but the Telephone Company.

"On the phone, you mentioned your BA from Arizona State. I lectured there one summer. What did you think of Phoenix?"

"It's more scenic than Las Vegas, but I prefer a real city. Like San Francisco. I visited my roommate there, and fell in love with it."

"Next to Paris, San Francisco is my favorite city."

"Mine, too."

"You've been to Paris, then?"

"Me? Oh, no. I've never even been to New York. I mean San Francisco's my favorite so far." Great. Now he knew what a hick I was.

"I admire your honesty, Rebecca. A breath of fresh air in a city of con artists. How long have you lived in Las Vegas?"

"Since 1944. My mother and I moved here from LA."

"So you were here around the first big growth spurt." Quent shook his head, clicked his tongue. "Your mother had spirit, I must say. And courage." He paused, lowering his voice. "Did she come for a divorce?"

I knew I shouldn't blab personal stuff at an interview, but it seemed rude not to answer. "Just the opposite. My dad moved here a year after I was born, but my mother didn't like it, so we stayed in LA with my grandmother. After she passed away, my dad begged my mother to join him. He was making a lot of money in those days, working for Bugsy Siegel."

Quent's eyes lit up. "Your father worked for Siegel?

"Quent," Nina said, handing over the receiver. "Your lawyer. Says it's important."

"Thanks, Nina. You can go back to work." He smiled at me, but his demeanor was all business.

I asked Nina for a telephone book to look up my references. She winked as she went back to her drawing table. Jesus! I really wanted this job. I listed my favorite high school teachers and a school principal. Quent talked at length to his lawyer about contracts, royalties. He sounded so knowledgeable and intelligent. For an older man, he was quite attractive. Pale blue eyes. Chiseled features. He came around to the front of the desk and sat on his spot.

"Nice young fellow, my lawyer. Harvard Law School. Went to Las Vegas High. Perhaps you know him. Paul Farley?"

"I knew of him." Paul Farley was one of the smartest people ever to graduate from Vegas High. "He graduated way before me."

"His partner went to Yale. Interesting, how many bright, talented young people, such as yourself, come back here after college. It's a good sign when youth believes in a place." He stood up and paced. "Twenty years from now, Las Vegas is going to be the fastest growing city in the country. It's all about land

and location. And in this town, the gold isn't in the casinos; it's in real estate. Wide, open spaces, and human nature to fill them. You'll never regret moving back here, Rebecca." His eyes gleamed. "I'll show you some of our current projects." He thumbed through a stack of blueprints and pulled out a sketch. "This is a rendering of an Episcopal Church on Maryland Parkway. Reverend Smith wanted modern. I suggested A-frame."

"Woodsy. Reminds me of Northern California."

"Exactly. The Reverend's delightful, but I couldn't believe his board." He raised his eyebrows. "I'd expected them to be more open-minded. After all, this is Las Vegas."

I smiled. "Most Las Vegans are very provincial."

"As I'm discovering." He handed me another sketch. "This is an Italian restaurant—going up between the Sands and the Flamingo."

"Very glamorous. It reminds me of the Sunset Strip."

He beamed at me. "Nina, come on out for a moment. And bring Carlo. I want you both to meet Rebecca Plotnik. Perhaps she can explain the disparity between the locals and the tourists."

Looking harried, Nina filled her coffee mug from the pot near the desk. Carlo leaned against the doorframe. He smiled, nodded. Dark, mustached, muscular, handsome in white Bermuda shorts, thongs and a bright green T-shirt. After an awkward silence, I realized they were waiting for me to speak.

"Well, I hate it when people say there's less hypocrisy in Las Vegas than in most places because everything's out in the open. Most of the locals are either Catholic or Mormon. You probably know that Mormons don't gamble, or drink, and they don't believe in divorce, but they sure do believe in money—they run most of the respectable businesses in town, and a chunk of their profits goes to the church. Of course, there wouldn't be any profits if it weren't for a handful of Jewish gangsters who put this town on the map, but they ignore that. They act like it doesn't exist, as do the Episcopalians, and the Methodists, and all the rest. If that isn't hypocrisy, I don't know what is." At first, I thought their silence meant I'd gone too far. Then, I realized I'd impressed the hell out of them.

"Rebecca, as far as I'm concerned, if you want the job it's yours." Nina smiled. Carlo shook my hand vigorously. "If possible, I'd like you to start tomorrow."

"The problem is, I don't have a car of my own." I was embarrassed to say more, but what else could I do? "My mother can drop me off, but I need a ride home."

"I'd be happy to drive you," Quent said, standing next to Nina. "I hardly need mention, Nina's from jolly old England," He clearly enjoyed teasing her, but she didn't seem amused. "Carlo came to us from Chicago, via Brazil."

Carlo shook my hand again, mumbling, "My pleasure is to meet you, Miss Plotsney."

"Plot-nik," Quent corrected him. "Back to work, you two." They seemed happy to leave. I'd thought they liked me. Now, I wasn't sure. "They have a five o'clock deadline," Quent explained, hurrying to answer the phone. "See you in the morning."

15.

After the thing with Billy Roberts, Sadie and I had reached a kind of truce. I'd said I was sorry for staying out all night and I wouldn't do it again; she'd apologized for calling me a tramp. There were still hard feelings on both sides, but I wasn't prepared for the venom on her face when I walked in, happy and exhilarated after the job interview with Quent. She handed me a letter. Postmark: New York. No return address, but she obviously knew it was Joey. As I read it in the bathroom, I noticed it wasn't his typewriter. It had all its g's.

Dear Beck, Sorry it's taken so long to write. I didn't want to burden you— you have enough troubles of your own—but I knew you'd worry not hearing. First of all, I got a letter from my draft board. Seems my life isn't mine anymore. It's theirs. I'm living with Alice, a dancer who studied with the New York City Ballet. We met in June, about the time you last wrote, and we've been together since. Alice works for the War Resisters' League. She's helped me think things through. I can't stay in a country that supports the draft, especially now that everybody says we're on the verge of a real war. Alice and I are moving to Spain—she has relatives in Valencia. I've told her about you. I hope we can all be friends. To be honest, I love you, and want to be with you, but you have other priorities, namely working out a lot of shit with your parents. I've known that since that night at the Catholic school, but I refused to admit it until you changed your mind about coming in June.

All I ever wanted was to act and make enough money for a roof over my head, but now I'm an anti-war activist. I'm giving up my career for my principles, which is the hardest thing I've ever had to do, especially now that my career is taking off. The off-Broadway show was a huge hit, and I'm getting calls from casting agencies. Too bad the army thinks I should be killing people instead. My dad calls me a traitor, but my mom gives me money behind his back. I wouldn't be surprised if they split. He's never been much of a father anyway. I'm just sorry for my mom.

I feel far from this country already. Far from our dreams about Plotnik&Goldman, and seeing our names in lights on Broadway. I have no idea how you are, or even who you are by now. I hope you're okay, and that you're closer to leaving your mother's room. You're incredibly talented, Beck. Never doubt that. Never give up. Write, but only if you want to. Don't know how long I'll be at this address. I'll try to keep you posted. I think about you often, and with love. J.

"You were in there a such a long time I thought you fell in." Sadie sat at the kitchen table, picking at her Sara Lee coffeecake. I went to the stove and put the kettle on. "Must have been a long letter."

"It's really over, Mom." My voice caught. Eyes

filled. "He has a girlfriend."

"He threw you over? Good riddance."

I whirled around. "Oh, for God's sake! Why wouldn't he have somebody? He couldn't wait forever."

"It's time you got over him. There are much better fish in the sea."

"Not only does he have a girlfriend," I got a carton of cottage cheese from the fridge, "he's leaving the country because of the draft." Stood there, holding it, sobbing, with the door open. "He's going to Spain, for God's sake. Now are you happy?"

"Oy! I hate to think what would have happened if you'd married him. You'd be a traitor."

"Jesus, Mother!" I blew my nose in a napkin, wiped my eyes. "He's not a traitor. He just doesn't believe in war."

"I bet he could get twenty years."

"Stop!" I got a mug from the cupboard. Slammed the door. "God!"

"Your father never served, either. He lied. Told them he had to take care of his mother. The army might have made a man out of him."

The kettle whistled. "World War II was different." I sipped my coffee at the counter with my back to her. Taking deep breaths. Trying to be calm.

"They say the communists will take over the whole world if we don't stop them. It's just like Hitler. If we'd stopped him earlier, millions of Jews would still be alive."

I yelled. "It's not at all like Hitler. Jesus, can't you show some compassion? Joey is giving up his hopes, his dreams, his career because he can't do something he doesn't believe in. Maybe you don't agree, but you have to respect him for…"

Not her. She was shaking her head. A monument

to patriotism, a mind wrapped in barbed wire.

16.

Driving to class, I realized I'd forgotten my notebook, but I wasn't about to go back for it. After fighting with Sadie about Joey, I'd shut myself in the bedroom and cried all afternoon. Spain seemed like the remotest place on earth. I hated Alice for taking Joey away, but I wished I had her courage and her principles. Joey would want me to go to New York on my own, but I didn't even like to go to movies by myself. Shit! All of our dreams had been shot down by the United States government. It seemed so unfair. I tried telling myself that my troubles were nothing on the scale of human suffering, but that only made me feel worse. I skipped dinner with Sadie and Izzy, and probably would have skipped the class, but I had to get away from them. I pulled into the university lot an hour early and checked my wallet. Three dollars. Enough for a notebook and coffee.

The university consisted of half a dozen two-story classrooms; an administration building, a round, ultra-modern library and a gym, all connected by cement walks. Neo-box architecture, I'd heard a guy say at registration. The bookstore was a small room in the administration building. I searched the faces in the hall praying I'd see somebody I knew, somebody I could talk to. More than ever, I needed and missed my friends.

The students didn't look like the ones at Arizona State. Most of them were older; even the ones my age weren't dressed like college kids. I recognized couple of former Vegas High hoods in spiffy suits chatting with a middle-aged man holding a clipboard and wearing a string-tie. There was a girl in high-heeled sandals and short-shorts I knew from somewhere, but not well enough to say hello. The one really interesting-looking person was a blonde woman in black at the end of the hall. She had on high-heeled black boots that came up just past her ankles, and a sleeveless turtleneck dress that barely reached her knees. She smoked a thin cigar in a holder. She wasn't tall, but there was something regal about her. Her boyfriend's iridescent blue shirt topped his skin-tight jeans. I wondered if he were as sexy from the front as he was from behind. If so, they were a perfect match. He turned.

Alex Harmon! Even in the midst of my heartbreak over Joey, I felt goose bumps. I hadn't seen him since graduation. He'd won a scholarship to a famous art school back east. I'd never expected to see him again. Senior year, at the yearbook signing party, Alex and I had sat on the lawn in front of the high school discussing <u>Waiting For Godot</u>. We decided Las Vegas was the ideal setting for the play and cast Andy Warhol and Truman Capote as Didi and Gogo. I'd memorized what he wrote in my yearbook: *Dear Beckett, I insist on calling you Beckett because Rebecca doesn't suit you. Too old fashioned. In you I see a soulful modernist, a shy iconoclast. Like Sam Beckett, you have a profound appreciation for the absurd.*

It was by far my most interesting autograph ever. I shuddered at the thought of mine to him: I'd really like to get to know you better. *Loads of luck in art school. Love 'n hugs, Becky P.*

He must have thought I was insipid. I hadn't

dared let him know how much I liked him. He'd belonged to GiGi. Beautiful GiGi. And now, it appeared he belonged to someone even more ravishing. They were walking toward me, ignoring the fact that people stared in awe after them.

"Beckett?" He stopped short. Took off his shades. "Is it really you?"

"Hi, Alex." We hugged, and squeezed hands, and I breathed in the musky odor of his after-shave. "Love your mustache. It's very Errol Flynn."

He put his shades back on. "God, it's been ages." His girl lagged behind. "You're so grown up and glamorous. Where the hell have you been, anyway? Last time I saw GiGi, she said, 'Arizona.'"

Out of the corner of my eye, I studied his friend. Stunning. Sensuous mouth, fabulous lower lip. Sapphires for eyes. Older than I'd thought. Thirty, maybe.

"I lived in Scottsdale for a while after I got my BA. Decided to come home and save money. I had this dream of moving to New York and being an actress." For a moment, I thought I might break down, but I fought it off. "It was just a dream. How about you? Didn't you get a scholarship to somewhere back east?"

"Yep. Spent a week at Rhode Island School of Design, desperately trying to pretend I belonged. Then, in a fit of cowardice, I ran away. Joined the army, saw the world, and came home to dear old mom. By the way, have you met my mother?"

I hoped my face didn't look shocked. "I don't think so."

She moved alongside him. So, he didn't belong to her, at least not in the way I'd imagined.

"Dana, this is Becky Plotnik, a.k.a. Beckett. Another member of the infamous class of '57."

"Hi, Beckett." A deep, sexy, smoker's voice. We shook hands.

"Dana and I are taking a class together-The Novel."

"Great." My heart pounded. "So am I."

"We hear the professor is brilliant," Dana said, touching my arm.

"He's a local boy," Alex said. "Went to Harvard. Taught at UC Berkeley. Moved back here because of his wife's health. She had some respiratory thing. Died about five years ago. They say he's still in mourning."

"Leave it to Alex to know all the deep dark faculty secrets," Dana said. "We've been taking classes for a couple years. He's English, I'm history."

"That's so neat!" I said. "Wish I could get my mother out here."

"Of course, it's a little hard on the ego when your son gets A's in everything."

I barely heard what she said. Had Joey's letter proved once and for all that fate didn't want us to be together? Had I come home to find Alex?

"Calm down, dearie," he said, putting his arm around her, "it's hardly the Ivy League." He looked at her fondly—then at me. "Actually, the faculty here is surprisingly good."

"But you haven't given up painting, have you?" My despair about acting and New York heightened what I felt for Alex. "You were brilliant! Everyone thought so."

"Oh, I still dabble. Mostly photography."

"He's being modest," Dana said, touching my arm the same place as before. "You should see his photographs." Her face glowed.

"I'd love to!"

"I've been trying to get a show together, but

there's not much point in Vegas. You really have to go to LA, or New York, and I'm not ready for that."

Dana's expression told me differently.

Without thinking, I blurted, "You're too good for LA! You belong in New York!"

We belong in New York. Dana's eyes filled with such intensity I had a feeling she had read my thoughts. And she approved.

"Actually, I love LA," Alex grinned. "It's so superficial."

He was every bit as cynical as he'd been in high school. And I still had the feeling that only I could save him. Dana laughed, humoring him. I followed her lead.

"He's too much, isn't he?" Dana said. She clearly adored him, but there was something odd about their relationship. They seemed almost too close to be mother and son.

"Dana and I were about to dine on the patio," Alex said. "Á la vending machines. Why don't you join us?"

"I've already eaten, but I'd love coffee."

"You two grab a table," he said, going toward the machines. "How do you take it?"

"Regular; lots of sugar."

My head was spinning as I followed Dana though sliding glass doors to a small patio with half a dozen glass-topped tables trimmed in green wrought iron and matching chairs. They looked like they belonged around the Tropicana pool.

"Fantastic," she said, tossing her black leather shoulder bag on a table, "we have it all to ourselves. That's why I like coming here right from work. There's nobody around to bug you."

I couldn't believe she was old enough to be Alex's mother. Everything about her was so young and hip. "Where do you work?"

"The Dunes. I'm a cocktail waitress. It's a drag, but the tips are fabulous. Every other weekend I sing with an accompanist downtown at the Kit Kat Lounge. That's my real love."

I could see her, belting out torch songs in some smoky bar. "I sing, too, but strictly musical comedy, and I've never done it professionally."

"Tough way to make a living." She ran her fingers through her shoulder length blonde hair. It was exciting just to look at her. Like seeing Alex as a woman. "I end up working full time to support my singing."

"It's incredible you're getting a degree, with all the other things you're doing. I wish my mother would do something interesting. She spends her time watching soap operas and cleaning house."

"One of my biggest regrets," she said, putting out her cigar in the glass ashtray in the middle of the table, "was not going to college. At seventeen, I was all set to go to Hunter but I got married instead. A year later Alex was born and I was divorced. After that, going to school was the last thing on my mind." She squeezed my hand. "I'm not sorry I had Alex—don't get me wrong. He's the best thing that ever happened to me. Just the timing wasn't great."

"Hunter. Isn't that in New York?"

She nodded. "I grew up in Brooklyn."

"How did you end up here?"

"Came out here to get a divorce," she said, with a sad shrug, "and stayed. I'm afraid I have a lousy track record for living happily ever after. As of last Friday, I've been divorced six times. I keep promising myself I'll never fall for another sweet-talking guy as long as I live, but I've never been good at keeping promises."

So open and honest. I liked her enormously.

Alex approached with a cardboard tray. He was too good-looking.

"They were out of tuna. Had to get ham and cheese." He handed Dana a sandwich and sat by me.

I felt more than lust. As always, I sensed that he needed someone like me. So did his mother.

"Your mother was telling me you were born in New York."

"Call me Dana," she said, touching my shoulder same place as before.

"I was only there for a year when I was a kid," he said. "My great-grandparents owned property in the village, right off Washington Square. They were filthy rich. But when the market crashed, they crashed too. Down to their last hundred thousand."

My first impression of Dana had been accurate. Down on her luck, but royalty just the same.

"My father squandered that in no time," Dana lit up another cigar. "We went from being aristocrats to poor white trash. Poof." She snapped her fingers. "Just like that. My poor mother, who had never worked a day in her life, ended up scrubbing floors in houses like the one she grew up in." Her beautiful eyes glittered.

Alex grinned. "That's why Vegas feels like home. People go from rags to riches to rags on a daily basis."

"I know. My dad's a gambler."

We all looked at each other, and smiled knowingly.

"I've been back to New York so many times I consider it a second home," Alex said.

New York. His second home. Everything was falling into place.

"We moved around a lot," Dana said. "He never had a real home, until Vegas, poor kid. We've been here close to ten years."

"I didn't mind the moving," Alex said. "It was all those damn religions that got to me." He frowned at Dana, but with affection. "Every time you got a new husband, we'd convert. I've been everything from a Jew to a Southern Baptist. Hope you're not shocked. Our family is a bit on the bizarre side."

"Oh, no. Mine is just as bizarre."

"Do tell," they said in unison.

I shrugged. "The saga of Sadie and Izzy. I call them Sadie and Izzy in my head, but I could never do that in real life. She's Republican; very conservative. He's a compulsive gambler, and never around. When he is home, all they do is fight. She hasn't slept with him in years. She sleeps with me."

They roared. I felt utterly at ease with them. Like I could say anything.

"I love it!" Dana said.

"At least we've never gone that far," he said, looking at her. Then at me. "That's what I love about Vegas. You think you've got it bad 'till you talk to somebody else."

"I shouldn't be living at home," I said. "If I had the money I'd leave."

"You can move in with us." Dana arched an eyebrow.

My God! She meant it.

"Of course," he added, "you'd have to share a room with my ten year old sister, and put up with three adolescent boys banging on the bathroom door, but what the hell? The more the merrier."

"For some reason, I thought you were an only child," I said.

"I am. We all have different fathers."

No wonder he was cynical. Next to him, my childhood was normal. "I can't believe you have all those kids," I said to Dana.

"Sometimes I can't either." She smiled. "It's wild. Alex is eight years older than the others. He's the competent one in the family. Takes care of everybody, including me. I can't tell you how many times I end up crying on his shoulder about some man or other. Without him, I don't know what I'd do." All at once, tears poured down her cheeks. "Shit!"

"Pull yourself together, love," Alex said, handing her a napkin. He was tender, like a big brother. "It's time for class. She's fine," he said to me. "She always gets weepy first week after a divorce. Give her a vodka martini on the rocks and she'll be dancing on the ceiling in no time, right, love?"

Dana took a mirror compact from her bag and dabbed at her eyes. "You wouldn't happen to have mascara, would you?"

I shook my head. "It's barely smudged. " I squeezed her hand. "You look great. Don't worry."

"Put on your shades, dear," Alex said, gently. "That's what they're for."

17.

Alex and Dana kept their shades on in class. We chose to sit next to each other, with me in the middle. I felt protected. At the same time, I had an overwhelming urge to protect them. Joey had wanted to protect me, and I'd felt useless. With Alex, I had a purpose. My own ambitions had never mattered enough, but the thought of helping someone else realize his thrilled me. I wouldn't have to give up New York! We'd move there together—Alex, Dana, me, the children. They needed me! Maybe that's what real love was? Being needed.

There were about twenty people in the classroom. I smiled back at a guy I'd gone out with in high school whose name I'd forgotten, and thought of Joey. An hour ago he had been the love of my life.

"Beckett, what's wrong?" Dana asked, touching my arm. "You look like you're in pain."

"It's nothing," I said, as if I'd been caught with the Mint payroll in my purse. "I just have that kind of face."

I would have said more but a man with wire glasses and a short, thick beard walked to the desk in front of the blackboard. He wore a navy blue U C Berkeley sweatshirt with sleeves ripped off at the elbows.

"Good evening," he scowled, "I'm Professor Milligan." He was really saying, *I'm the most brilliant person in Las Vegas—maybe on earth.* If Alex hadn't told me about his wife dying, I'd have hated him. "As you know, this is a seminar. We will meet every Wednesday for three hours, tonight's one-hour class being the only exception. In addition to a term paper, due at the end of the semester, I have assigned an essay every week, the first of which is due Monday. I'll be handing out a reading list/assignment sheet at the end of class. You may either mail your essays or drop them off at my office."

He sat at his desk and started lecturing on Faulkner and Hemingway. I drifted off, imagining myself ten pounds thinner, in a pale blue chiffon strapless gown with Alex, in a white tux, dancing to: *Heaven, I'm in heaven, and my heart beats so that I can hardly speak*... Milligan was a fly buzzing outside a window, until I heard him say, "I would like you to list at least five novels that have made an impact on you in the last five years."

Everybody was writing. Except me. Damn! I'd forgotten to buy a notebook. I rummaged through my purse. No pen, either. Should I ask Alex for help? No! I didn't want him to think I was disorganized.

"Dana," I whispered, leaning toward her. She didn't look up. I said it louder and touched her arm.

"Surely you don't need help from your friends."

I thought Milligan was talking to someone else, but there he was in the aisle, glaring at me.

"Unless you haven't read anything in the last five years," he snapped, "in which case, you shouldn't be taking this course."

Nervous laughter rippled across the room. I stared at my desktop where somebody had carved "Life Sucks." How could he do this to me in front of them? He was daring me to say something in my defense.

I blurted out: " The Catcher in the Rye."

"What was it you liked about it?" he asked, bored already.

"I didn't just like it," I said, hating him. "It was up there with 1984, and Camus' The Stranger, and Ginsberg's Howl, because it was about somebody who's persecuted for being honest. Books like those, you don't just *like*."

He gave me a shitty little smile. "It appears that Salinger's spoiled, self-absorbed, whiney adolescent has become the standard bearer for a whole generation of *rebels without a cause*."

I was on my feet. "Not only did you not understand the book, you didn't get the movie. Your generation has nothing worth passing on. All you care about is respectability and money! You define your-selves by your jobs and your possessions. We don't want to be like you, and you hate us for it!"

The whole class stared. I was too furious to care. "Thank you for your comments, Miss…?"

"Plotnik," I said, shivering at the sound of it, wishing I hadn't been so fucking emotional.

"Would anyone care to add to Miss Plotnik's list of provocative contemporary novels—the kind that, in her words, *we don't just like*?"

His wife must have died to get away from him. Nobody said a word. Milligan returned to his desk. Some guy by the wall came up with The Grapes of Wrath and started talking about Steinbeck. A few others piped in. I couldn't concentrate. I avoided looking at Alex or Dana. Anyway, with their shades on, I couldn't have known what they were thinking. The buzzer sounded as Milligan handed out his reading-list-slash-assignment-sheet. I stuffed it in my purse and followed Dana from the room, with Alex behind.

It was chilly out, the way the desert gets

sometimes at night. I wrapped my arms around my shoulders, leaned against the wall near the door, and stared at my feet while people passed. I was developing a blister on the inside of my big toe where my sandal rubbed against it.

"You were great, honey, " Dana said. "I'd never have the guts to say what you did."

Alex touched my shoulder. "I had a feeling there was passion beneath that timid exterior."

A little voice sang: "They love me!" Of course, they were going overboard and the whole Milligan thing never would have happened if I'd remembered my stupid notebook, but...*Passion beneath that timid exterior*...I stared at Alex's dark glasses, trying to imagine his eyes.

"I have to work tonight or I'd buy you both a drink," Dana said, checking her watch, "but how about Friday night?"

"Great." Sadie had banned me from going out after the Billy Roberts all-nighter. I'd beg her to let me go. I'd move out if I had to.

"We'd better run," she said, taking Alex's arm.

I was about to follow them down the stairs when I heard, "Miss Plotnik?" I froze.

"I'm sorry to have made you the brunt of my bad humor," Milligan said, as I turned. "You handled it very well. Better than I'd have done in your place."

"I was asking Dana if I could borrow a pen," I said, one hand on the railing.

"No need to explain." He came closer. He looked thinner. Sadder. "It was obvious, not only to me but to everyone, that you were a thoughtful, intelligent student." I couldn't help glowing. "Even if that weren't the case, I had no business humiliating you. This is a bad day. Tough day. My wife..." He looked away. "She died five years ago, in September. At any rate, I'd be happy to apologize to you publicly next class."

"I think we should forget it. I'm sorry about your wife."

He grimaced. "I'd like to think we could be friends."

Was that a pause before "friends?" He extended his hand. I expected a two-second shake, but he held on. "Good night, Miss Plotnik."

"Rebecca." Damn! It sounded like a come-on.

"A heroine's name. Suits you." He gave my hand a little squeeze. *Oh, God, what's happening here?* I could hear Sadie*: You must have led him on!*

"Thanks, Professor Milligan." I started down the stairs.

"Lawrence," lodged like a bullet in my back. "Wait. I'll buy you coffee."

18.

We sat on the patio—same table as with Alex and Dana. I had chosen Alex's chair. I blew on my coffee. I felt trapped.

"So, Rebecca," Milligan smiled, benevolently. "What brings you to the University?"

"I like to read." Did he think I was attracted to him? Talk about conceited! He had to be close to forty! "I like to be around people who think."

He ran his thumb back and forth along his beard, staring at me the whole time. "You're a writer, aren't you?"

I wanted to laugh. He was so convinced he was right. "No. I'm an actress." Did I detect disappointment? Disdain? "At least I was. It's been a while since I've done anything."

"We have a budding theater department," he said, with too much enthusiasm—probably to cover up for being wrong. "We recently hired a new director/playwright whom I hear is quite talented. You should audition for the fall play."

"I don't think so." Head-shots of Alex and Dana floated through my mind. "I don't want to get too involved. I might be moving to New York."

A frown. "New York?" His hands sliced the air. "You could act here. At the University. You could direct, write, teach. Opportunities are endless."

"Here? You've got to be kidding." Now I was

waving *my* arms. "New York is the center of theater in America. There's The Actor's Studio, Stella Adler, Broadway…"

"It's a tough profession. As I'm sure you know, very few make a living. At least, with a teaching degree, you'd have something to fall back on."

Oh, great. Another Sadie. But she was my mother. He had no right to boss me around. "Is that why you teach? For security?" He flushed. I finished my coffee and crushed the cup.

Milligan blinked, took off his glasses, cleaned them with a napkin. "Teaching can be deeply satisfying, on many levels. It's true, it can displace other ambitions," he cleared his throat, "but it's much less compromising than, say, business. And it leaves me free to write."

So, *he* was the writer. "What are you writing?"

"Various things. Some scholarly projects. Some poetry." He brought his coffee to his lips, then put it down without drinking. "Fiction."

"I've always wanted to write about growing up here." I thought about all the half-written stories in a box on my closet shelf. "But theater's what I love most. It's one of the main reasons I want to live in New York—to see great actors in great plays instead of the Lido de Paris." He actually looked sympathetic. "You grew up here, too, didn't you?"

"Yes. But I spent ten years back east. Then I taught at Berkeley."

"Why'd you come back?"

"My parents are getting older." He averted his gaze. "My wife was ill. Here, I had fewer academic responsibilities, could spend more time with her. After she died I realized I'd come home."

Home? I stared at the patch of desert between

us and the new grass in front of the next building. "You must have a different relationship with this town. My father's a gambler. Dirt and casinos depress me."

"That's understandable, with a gambler father." He finished his coffee. Wiped his lips with his napkin before stuffing it in his cup. "Fellow I met in Cambridge—brilliant, doctorate in physics from MIT, prominent Boston family—gave up a lucrative career for a teaching position, here. Needless to say, the University was thrilled, but little by little he began to regress—stopped showing up for class, looked as if he hadn't slept in days—and, eventually, he disappeared. His family went so far as to hire a private detective to find him. One of our students spotted him downtown, dealing cards—deathly pale, thin. He'd been eating only enough to stay alive. By the time his parents came to take him back to Boston, he was no longer the son they knew. Gambling had literally consumed him."

I pictured my dad after a gambling binge—thin, haggard, with that musty smell people get from sleeping in their clothes. "My mother says my father would be like that if she weren't around to take care of him."

Once again, his hands were slicing the air. "For me, the desert isn't casinos, Rebecca; it isn't the Strip. It's Red Rock Canyon, it's the Valley of Fire—it's space, solitude. Balzac's old soldier, in <u>Passion in the Desert</u>, says it better than I: '… in the desert there is all—and yet nothing…God is there, and man is not.'"

He was really beginning to bug me. "Beautiful quote, but I can't relate to it. The architect I work for says all that space is going to disappear someday. It's human nature to want to fill it."

"I don't think so. Las Vegas has already expanded way beyond its capacity. But if it should come to that, I'll move. The Oregon coast has always appealed to me. That's one of the advantages of teaching. Along with security, and..."

"Next to compromise, security's the ugliest word I know."

For a moment he was silent. I thought he was going to tell me off—God knows I'd been asking for it. But he smiled. "I admire your spirit, Rebecca." His eyes were too intense. Time to leave!

"It's late. I'd better be going. I borrowed my parents' car." I stood half-way up.

"First, you have to tell me why you feel your generation has been betrayed by mine."

"Oh, that." I sat. Squirmed. "Actually, I was thinking more of my parents' generation, but yours isn't so hot, either." Why did I say that? Now, I'd have stay even longer.

He leaned forward, bug-eyed. "How so? Give me examples."

"What is this, a test?"

"My generation's on trial. I'd like to know why."

He asked for it! "Okay. In four years of college, you—especially you English teachers-taught us to hate war, despise conformity, and reject our parents' values. You neglected to prepare us for boring, dead-end jobs that suck the life out of you. You didn't tell us that speaking up would get us fired."

His eyes gleamed. "We turn you into idealists, then throw you to the wolves."

"My boyfriend was suspended from Arizona State for quitting ROTC because he didn't believe in war. And now, he's leaving the country to escape the draft."

Milligan winced. "I understand your frustration, Rebecca. But we haven't abandoned you. Many of us are with you all the way. I'm organizing a chapter of War Resisters. Perhaps you'll join?"

At first I thought of Joey—then Alex. It seemed my loyalties had shifted. "I would, but, as I mentioned, I may be moving to New York."

"I hope you stay, Rebecca. The university needs people like you." Such loneliness in his eyes, I almost felt guilty. "By the way, next Friday, we're launching a new film series with Fellini's 8 1/2. Will you come?"

For a second, I was tempted. But I wasn't about to do anything to encourage him. "I love Fellini, but— I'm going out with friends."

His eyes were warm, wistful. "Well, maybe next time."

19.

Quent handed me an electric coffeepot. "Your first official responsibility. I'm expecting clients, and Nina and Carlo are addicted to the stuff." He'd had the office vacuumed. He wore a tan summer suit, and Canoe. "Love your dress. Red's my favorite color."

"Thanks. Mine, too," I said, adding, "That's a great tie," then wondering if I should have. After Milligan, I wanted to be sure I wasn't giving anybody the wrong impression.

"It's a Gucci." He showed me the label. "As you'll learn in this business, appearance isn't everything, but it's a close second." He chuckled. I liked his honesty.

On my way to the hall bathroom to fill the pot, Carlo smiled. Nina wiggled her fingers. Finally a place where I liked everybody. I checked my makeup in the mirror above the sink. Tomorrow I'd be going out with Alex and Dana. If I skipped dinner tonight and tomorrow I could probably get into my size ten bell-bottoms. Surprisingly, Sadie had approved when I asked if I could go. "I remember that Alex," she'd said. "The good-looking one with the sunglasses and the tight pants who won all those art awards. Unlike you, he had stick-to-it-iveness. Too bad he's not Jewish—he might be good for you." *Good for you*, like I was some kind of mental case. I wondered how Alex would respond when I told him how I felt about him. But if I didn't stop daydreaming, I'd lose this job.

Voices in the hall. I peeked. A dark-haired woman in a white linen suit and very high heels close to a tall man in beige. Another man, short, stocky, wrinkled pale-orange suit next to Quent. They all stared as I approached.

"Here comes our newest addition," Quent said, beaming like a proud father. "My secretary, Rebecca Plotnik." He put his arm around me.

The short man, whose mustache looked penciled on, jiggled his thick eyebrows and stared straight at my boobs. "Hello, sunshine."

I was so unnerved, I forgot their names the minute Quent uttered them. We filed into the office.

"Pastries?" Quent offered a tray. The short man grabbed a jelly doughnut. The couple said they'd wait for coffee. I was searching for an outlet when the phone rang. "Just say, 'Dreams Unlimited,' and take a message." Quent handed me a pink While You Were Out pad and took the coffeepot. The caller was Paul Farley, his lawyer, reminding him of a luncheon appointment. As I was hanging up, Nina brought sketches to the woman in white.

"I love the marquee," the woman said, resting her red fingernails on the tall man's shoulder. "Reminds me of that place on the Sunset Strip—remember, Brian?" Quent winked at me. Brian said, "Yeah, I like it." The short man stood to look, dripping doughnut jelly on his pants.

"Classy," he said. I handed him a napkin.

"Nina's still working on your motel, Morty," Quent said. "But, we have a problem with the wishing-well. Doesn't fit with your concept of a drive-up wedding chapel with nuptials conducted via speakers on the car windows. Wishing-wells suggest quaint." The woman in white giggled. So did I. "I noticed a sign for wishing-well weddings the other day, but in a more traditional setting."

"I think it needs some sort of unifying theme," Nina said, helping herself to a bearclaw. "Perhaps we could model it after those drive-in cinemas you Americans fancy, with rooms made to resemble automobiles."

Nina and I exchanged smirks. Carlos laughed from the other side of the wall. Morty still insisted on a wishing well, the coffee perked, the phone rang—this time, about the church on Maryland Parkway.

"Fetch the cups and napkins, will you, Rebecca? You pour; I'll pass the pastries." Quent said.

Carlo yelled for Nina to get him a powder doughnut.

"How's about we split a doughnut, sweetheart?" Morty asked as I poured.

"No, thanks," I said, eyeing a cheese Danish, "I don't like doughnuts." I hurried to get the next call, a prospective client planning a motel on the Tonapah Highway.

"We'd better get a move on," said Brian, looking at his watch and getting out his checkbook, "Betty and I have a meeting with our contractor."

"Take the sketches." Quent took the check, helping Betty from her chair. "You'll want to go over them with your contractor. Tell him to call if he has any questions."

Morty handed Quent a wad of bills and leered at my boobs. "See ya later, sunshine."

He kept his eyes on the goods as he backed out the door.

"Off we go to the bank," Quent said, instructing Nina to answer the phone. "Rebecca, after today, you can take the car to make deposits." I liked that he held my arm as we walked down the hall and the stairs—made me feel protected. "I'll show you how to put the top up on the convertible. I know how women are about their hair. By the way, I hope you didn't take offense at Morty Gold. He's a little on the crude side, but not a bad sort, really. Looks a bit like Lou Costello, don't you think?"

"Actually, he reminds me of my father."

"You must take after your mother." He grinned, which made him look boyish, adding to his charm. On the way to the drive-up bank across from the Sahara, Quent turned on the radio. Tony Bennett belted *From Rags to Riches.*

"You mentioned your father had worked for Bugsy Siegel," he said, turning down the radio. "I know he was a killer-for-hire, but no one can deny the man was a visionary. There was nothing here but barren desert and a couple of rustic hotels, but he saw gold. And ultimately, died for it. I must admit I'm one of his biggest fans."

I jumped at the chance to impress him. "He used to bounce me on his knee and give me silver dollars for my piggy bank."

His eyes were as big as silver dollars. "You don't say!"

"My mother thought he was the most charming man she'd ever met. I think she had a crush on him. She was always saying, 'Why can't your father be more like Benjamin? He's so refined.'"

He chuckled.

"Of course, she didn't know he'd murdered thirty or forty people," I continued. "My dad must have, but people close their eyes a lot around here."

"If you don't mind my asking, what did your father do for Siegel?"

"He was his personal accountant."

"My God!"

I hesitated, then plunged. "He was in charge of, well, skimming off the top at the Flamingo."

Quent's eyebrows shot up. "My, my, my."

"When I was about five, I heard my mother say it on the phone. I pictured my father in a big chef's hat, skimming the layer of cream off the top of the milk with a little butter knife."

Quent laughed so hard he shook. "That's wonderful, Rebecca. Absolutely wonderful." Still laughing, he wiped a tear from his eye and pulled into the drive-up bank window. He handed the teller cash and checks for deposit, introducing us. As soon as she was out of earshot, he said: "Was it hard for your father to find work after Siegel was murdered?"

"Very. People were afraid to hire anybody associated with Bugsy. Finally, one of his former bosses at the Flamingo gave him a job dealing cards at the Nugget, but he never got another chance at the big time. For years, he was a cashier. Now, he's a lowly bookkeeper."

"What a shame."

"Not really. In a town like this, it's better to be a nobody. It's safer."

"Poor old Bugsy learned that the hard way." He pulled into a space in the front lot facing the Sahara, and turned off the radio. "We have some time before meeting Paul at the El Cortez," he explained. A dozen or so tourists, all wearing Bermuda shorts and straw hats, stood under the Sahara canopy, waiting for cabs. "I find it odd that most tourists assume Vegas is only the Strip and the casinos on Fremont Street."

"Oh, God, I hate that. They're always saying 'I didn't know people lived in Las Vegas.' Drives me crazy."

His face was full of sympathy. "I don't blame you. They're unaware that Las Vegas is a real town, with kids, neighborhoods, schools—and social classes. Not the same ones most of us grew up with, but from what I gather, every bit as exclusive."

A Cadillac convertible whizzed by on the way to the drive-up lane. My God! Tammy Anderson, in a bikini, with a sugar daddy.

"Someone you know?" Quent asked.

I nodded. "We were in Home Ec. together, back when she had braces and brown hair." Quent snickered. Driving out, the old guy flashed a wad of bills, peeled one off, and tucked it in Tammy's cleavage. She pecked him on the cheek.

"In Las Vegas, nobody cares how you got your money," I said. I turned around in my seat so I could face him. "Well, almost nobody. Friday nights, at Temple, the mobsters would parade their shiksa mistresses down the aisle in minks and diamonds, and if the Rabbi disapproved, he was out. Needless to say, there was a huge turn-over of Rabbis."

Quent roared. "I imagine they would have to accept a loose interpretation of the Ten Commandments, especially 'Thou shalt not kill.'" His face turned serious. "Amazing they've never been able to pin Siegel's murder on Lansky. Everyone seems to think he gave the order."

"My dad says lots of people wanted Bugsy dead. The El Rancho mob threatened to kill him if he didn't leave town, and then he goes and builds the Flamingo."

He looked at me as if he were seeing me for the first time. "You really love this town, don't you Rebecca?"

I felt my face heat up. "Well, I... Yes, I guess I do

in a way." I turned away, embarrassed that he knew something about me even I didn't know. "I love the hotels, except for the Stardust, and the shows—it's incredible, you can see Ella Fitzgerald, at the Sands lounge for the price of a drink, and Carol Channing in the showroom at the Trop—her Marlene Dietrich imitation is one of the most brilliant things I've ever— and Peggy Lee's just so amazing, and Milton Berle who I never liked on T.V. but on stage he's—and Danny Kaye, one of the greatest performers... It's not as cheap as it used to be, but you can still go almost every night, if you want to!" I paused to catch my breath. I remembered the Mint, the slot machines. Sammy's Race Book. The sleaze of Fremont Street. "But it's hard to grow up here when your father's a gambler."

"It must have been." His eyes were full of compassion.

I stared at the Sahara. My parents took me and Leanne there for my thirteenth birthday. We had frozen eclairs. I felt like a princess. "But the shows—they almost make up for it."

20.

"I've never been to a real bar," I said.

Outside, the Kit Kat Lounge was all black except for two painted white cats that framed the door.

"They don't get any more real than this," Alex said. He and Dana smirked.

"Stand back, darlings. I'm about to make an entrance." As Alex opened the door, Dana undid her top three buttons, struck a pose in the doorway, removed her shades. The piano player switched from *Scotch and Soda* to *Satin Doll.*

"It's her song," Alex whispered. He seemed blasé, but I could tell he was proud.

Several patrons waved, a few raised their drinks, a fat guy in a Hawaiian shirt applauded wildly as Dana swished in, then stopped. It was like the scene in *The Barefoot Contessa* when Ava Gardner flings off her robe on the deck of some millionaire's yacht and everyone stares at her bathing suit.

"Drinks are on me," Dana said. "Order me a vodka martini on the rocks."

She sauntered over to the piano. The piano player handed her a mike on a long cord. His hand lingered on hers. She seemed to like it. Were they lovers? In any case, they were very close. Her throaty voice was imitation June Christy. It didn't matter. In cowboy boots, tight jeans and a white blouse unbuttoned to her bra, she was the Queen of the Kit Kat

Lounge.

"Martini?" Alex asked.

A cocktail waitress in a black mask with whiskers took our order. As she left I noticed her pink satin leotard had a long black tail. The room was dimly lit, thick with cigarette smoke. Two wooden cats, one painted pink, one black, hovered over a fish tank that occupied most of one wall. The clientele reminded me of the gamblers at the Mint: women with dyed hair and drawn faces, men who hadn't slept in days.

Alex offered me a Marlboro.

"No thanks. It's amazing I don't smoke. I'm so oral."

He laughed. "You're much too honest."

The waitress served our drinks. Alex tucked his shades in the left pocket of his white long-sleeved shirt. Those eyes! Sapphires like Dana's.

"How's the martini?" he asked. Without his shades, he wasn't merely handsome. He was Art. He seemed uneasy without his cover. But I sensed he expected people to stare and, on some level, thrived on it.

"It's great." I ravished the pimento in my olive. "I've always had them with gin."

"Vodka's more interesting, with fewer calories."

"I'm not much of a drinker. Can't stand feeling light-headed—being out of control."

"But that's the best part! Anything can happen." He grinned. "And does. Who was it that said bars are closer to God than churches? Maybe I said it. I was probably too drunk to plagiarize."

He was pretending to be shallow, but his eyes were full of pain. His hand trembled as he reached in his pocket for another cigarette.

"Love your hair down, by the way," he said. "It's

more flattering than the ponytail and straight bangs you wore in high school."

"Oh, God. My Debbie Reynolds phase. I was so weird."

"No you weren't. You just didn't fit in with the cretins. You had the best cheekbones of the class of '57. GiGi and I were horribly jealous."

Of me? I was so ordinary next to them. As usual, I felt jealous of GiGi, and wondered if he still had feelings for her.

"I'd love to photograph you," he said. My heart pounded.

"Any time."

He ordered another round of drinks.

"I was surprised when Dana mentioned you were a photographer. I loved your paintings. So many people hate modern art—they don't understand it, they find it disturbing—but that's why I like it. It jolts you. Makes you think." I was trying to impress him, but I meant it, too.

"I suspected you were a rebel at heart." He smiled. I loved his mustache. Like an extra top lip. "I love photography." His eyes lit up. "I took it up in Europe—became obsessed. The camera is a lens to the imagination. Nothing is what it seems, not that ashtray, or this martini glass." He held up his glass. His long, tanned, elegant fingers curled around the stem. I wanted to be that stem. "Unfortunately, I don't have the money to pursue it. The University is paying me to do photographs for the yearbook. A pittance, but at least I can cut back on construction work. My ex-stepfather is a contractor."

It broke my heart that someone as talented as Alex couldn't afford to do what he loved when people were out there throwing money away on gambling.

"I'll bet Quent knows him—the architect I work for. He's only been here two months but he knows practically everybody. Remember Paul Farley from high school?"

"Red hair? Tacky dresser? Harvard?"

"Quent's lawyer. We had lunch with him Monday. Paul says if anybody can make a fortune in Vegas without going near a casino, it's Quent. He's a great guy, too. Nicest boss I've ever had."

"I hope this doesn't mean you've given up acting?" His eyes burned into me. "I thought you had a better chance at success than anybody in our class."

"You're much more talented than I am. Actresses are a dime a dozen."

"You're far from ordinary, Beckett." He smiled. This time, it wasn't for an audience. It was only for me. "You're a brilliant actress, and witty as hell. I loved your column in the Desert Breeze." He leaned back in his chair, as if to see me from a better angle. "In high school, you were the idealist. Caring too much about other people—not enough about yourself. That's probably why your name isn't in lights by now."

"That's very kind, but the main reason I'm not acting is I don't have the guts to go to New York." Maybe this was the time to let him know my feelings? "I do think love is more important than anything, so in that sense maybe you're right."

"Speaking of love, I think our professor's quite taken with you."

Play dumb! "He is?"

"Why else would he have attacked you in class? Men like Milligan hate being out of control. He's attracted to you, and it terrifies him."

"I don't think so."

"My dear, I'm an expert."

152

All those divorces, he would be. "But he's so old. He must be close to forty."

Alex grinned. "Reminds me of 'September Song.' *And these few precious days, I'll spend with you...*"

My face was on fire. "I'm not interested in Milligan. I'm in love with somebody else."

He arched an eyebrow, puckered his lips, leaned in. "Tell me about him."

The second round of drinks arrived. He offered his olive. I sucked it off the toothpick.

"What's that song?" I asked. "The lyrics are incredible."

"'Lush Life,'" he said, savoring the L's. "The ultimate bar song." He sang along with Dana. *I thought for a while that your poignant smile was tinged with the sadness, of a true love for me. Alas I was wrong. Again I was wrong...*

Not about me, Alex. I'll never let you down.

"Dana has a thing for maudlin songs." He smirked. It seemed to be his favorite expression. We stared at Dana. It may have been the light, but I thought I saw tears in her eyes.

"When Dana was about twelve, her father left the house to buy a paper and never bothered to come back. Since then she's been looking for someone to take his place. Only once she finds them, she drives them away."

The father she told me about, who squandered the last of the family money. "That's so sad."

Alex turned toward the bar. A young guy in a Madras shirt that accentuated his tan had ordered drinks on the house for everybody. He'd had a big win at the Nugget. He stared at Dana, inch by inch. She stared back, singing, *I'd like to get you, on a slow boat to China.* "You mentioned seeing Gigi," I said, to the back of

Alex's head. I had to know how he felt about her. "I thought she was in Reno, living with her boyfriend. She didn't answer my last letter. That was way over a year ago."

Alex turned. "She's back." His face was hard. "I see her as little as possible. She's been a lush since her boyfriend threw her over for a rich girl with political connections."

"Oh, my God." My stomach clenched. I knew it was crazy, but I felt responsible. I'd always envied GiGi more than I'd loved her. "Why didn't she tell me? I'll call her. Did she move back with her parents?"

"You don't want to see her, believe me. She married a slot-machine mechanic who can barely speak in sentences. She must weigh two hundred pounds. They do nothing but drink beer and eat Twinkies."

"Oh, Jesus." I tried, but couldn't stop the tears. Alex seemed oblivious. I knew better. He'd cared enough to keep seeing her. "She was so beautiful. Witty. Full of life." I thought of Libby Coleman, old before her time at the employment office. And Darlene. But, Gigi was my friend. "I guess it can happen to anyone."

"Not to me. I could never take love that seriously. If I've learned anything from dear old Mom," he glanced back at Dana and the guy in the Madras shirt, "it's that nobody's irreplaceable."

A chill slithered down my back. But, why wouldn't he think that after all he'd been through? My love would change him.

He finished his drink. "You'd think Dana would know better after all these years of ending up alone, and broke." He gave me a hard look. "Don't throw yourself away for love, Beckett. Unless there's something in it for you, something real, it's not worth it."

Was he warning me against loving him? He called the waitress for more drinks. I almost told him not to order for me, but after what he'd said about Gigi, about love, I needed it.

"What is it they say about cynics?" I smiled, gently. "That they're failed romantics?"

"Not so much failed," he lit another cigarette, "as liberated."

Again, a chill down my back. Was there anyone in his life who hadn't let him down? "Do you ever see your real father?"

"When I was seventeen, I ran away from home to see him. It didn't go well. He's Jewish, a lawyer in New York. Very bourgeois. We had nothing in common. Dana married him right out of high school. They split when she was pregnant. She cut off all ties."

Great! A Jewish father. Sadie would like that. "What about your brothers and sister? Do they see their fathers?"

"God, yes. We've spent countless Christmases with assorted daddies, mommies and kiddies. It's all one big happy family until someone says something ugly, and all hell breaks loose." He exhaled a thin stream of smoke and grinned. "I consider myself fortunate to be fatherless." He put out his cigarette. "Enough about me. How was Arizona? I hear Scottsdale's a happening place."

Obviously, he didn't like talking about his family any more than I did about mine. "It's better than Vegas, but it's still the desert. I've had it with the desert."

"What about LA?"

"Too phony. I've never really wanted to live anywhere but New York."

"So why don't you?"

"I don't know. It's so far away, and such a big

city. I'd be all by myself. I was supposed to join somebody there but it didn't work out." I had tried not to tell him about Joey, but I suspected my face had just said volumes.

He leaned toward me. "That mystery man you mentioned before?"

"No. Just an ex-boyfriend—an actor. He's moving to Spain. Even if he weren't, it just wasn't meant to be. He's always had everything. He doesn't understand what it's like to worry about money, or respectability." Our eyes met. I'd never have to explain anything to him.

"If he wants to spend his money on you, marry him. I would."

"I could never marry for money."

"It's different for those of us whose families had money, and blew it. We think we're entitled to it." His smile wasn't so much bitter as sad. I felt such a connection with him. I sensed it was reciprocal. "As for respectability, Vegas is probably the only place in America where it's for sale. No questions asked." He smiled. Our fingers touched as he passed me his olive. "Remember Penny Kramer?" He raised an eyebrow.

"Red hair? Red convertible? Pixie haircut, Class of '55?"

"Everybody knew how she got the money for that convertible. Profligate Penny. Any other high school she would have been persona non gratis, but we all admired her business skills."

I sipped my drink, resisting the temptation to say something preachy about money.

"That's our home town," he said. The best looking, best-dressed, classiest women are call-girls, and the contenders for Father of the Year are murderers." He downed most of his drink. "Why wouldn't we be warped? I'll drink to that."

I hated to admit it, but he had a point. He finished his vodka, ordered another and turned his attention to Dana, who was wrapping up "Slow Boat to China." Her lips, her body, her throaty voice reached out for the guy at the bar who leaned toward her, grinning, eyes hot. The piano player announced he was taking a break and watched, amused, as Dana joined her admirer.

Alex frowned. "Here we go again. She can't go without a man for more than a couple weeks. This one's barely old enough to drink. Next thing I know, she'll be chasing after schoolboys."

"She looks about twenty-five," I said, then wished I hadn't. I didn't want him thinking I was on her side, but he was acting like her parent.

"I keep hoping she'll develop crow's feet and permanent bags under her eyes, but she never does." He sounded angry, and bitter. His drink arrived. He took a swig.

I'd thought he and Dana were best friends—not at all like Sadie and me—but they obviously had their issues. The young guy put his arm around Dana's shoulder and whispered in her ear. She whispered back. She laughed. He moved his arm from her shoulder to her waist. Pulled her close. Kissed her ear. Alex smoked. Drank. Scowled. I couldn't stand the silence.

"It must be hard, having a beautiful mother," I said. "I always criticize my mother for being conventional, but I guess I wouldn't like it very much if she weren't. I guess there are problems either way." He didn't seem to be listening. His face was twisted, almost ugly. "In a way, you have to understand her side." My voice sounded hollow. "She's just gone through another divorce. She's lonely. Depressed. I'd be embarrassed, too, and concerned, but we have to see them as people, not just our mothers." God, Beck, you're making things worse! You insipid, patronizing jerk!

Dana slid off the barstool, car keys dangling from one finger, and came over to us. "Hank is going to give me a ride home." She dropped her keys in front of Alex. "Take my car, okay? Better take Beckett home soon. We wouldn't want her mother to get a bad impression."

"Yes, Mother," he said, for everyone to hear, "anything you say, Mother." His wild face scared me, but Dana acted as if everything were fine.

"See you later, honey." Dana squeezed my shoulder, ignoring Alex. She went back to Hank, with everyone looking, slid her arms around his neck, rubbed it, kissed his lips. She had a right to her own life, but flaunting it in front of her son was cruel. All but Alex watched as they strolled out of the bar, her arm around his shoulder, his around her waist.

Alex downed his drink and held the glass. I thought he would throw it. People cast nervous, curious glances at us. I sensed this wasn't the first time Dana and Alex had performed before this audience.

"Let's get out of here," he said.

Things were blurry from too much vodka when I stood. I followed Alex in a daze. Outside, the piano player leaned against one of the cats, smoking. He smiled as if he knew me. I smiled back. Alex pulled me into the glare of neon from Fremont Street a block away. Pink KENO tickets covered the sidewalk. I stopped, scooped a handful, let them go. "Vegas confetti." I felt like crying. Not just for Alex, and Dana, and GiGi. For all the sad, lonely people in bars and casinos.

Alex grabbed my arm, hurrying me to the car. He shifted into first. My arm was red from his fingers. We drove past Sammy's Racebook. Unbearable silence. Hands tight on the steering wheel. I didn't dare speak until we reached the abandoned sofa on Paradise Road.

"My favorite landmark."

"What?" Voice like a switchblade.

"The couch, the rocking chair. In the middle of nowhere. My favorite landmark."

His lips formed a half-smile. "I wanted to use it for the cover of the yearbook, but the faculty thought it was depressing."

"So what? It's funny. It's warped. It's Vegas."

His eyes gleamed. "I've always wanted to do a series of living-room shots." The tension left his hands. "You know, typical American family on couch, dog, cat, parakeet, watching TV in the middle of the desert."

"I love it."

He turned on my street, pulled up in front of the apartment, lit a cigarette. Exhaled. "Sorry for the tantrum at the bar."

"It's okay. Really. I understand."

"Too many vodka martinis." He rolled down the window. Warm, heavy air replaced the air-conditioning. "It's hard to watch somebody fuck up their lives, and yours, over and over. She's a slave to her emotions. Never thinks about practical things, like food and rent and alimony." He flicked ashes out of the window. "At least she got the house when Buddy left. One of the few times she's come out ahead."

I tried, but couldn't stop myself from saying: "It's refreshing to hear that somebody in this town cares more about relationships than money."

He took a long drag on his cigarette and stared at the smoke as he exhaled. "From what I've seen, money lasts longer than love." The smoke trembled in the air.

"I don't believe that."

He smiled, ran his fingers along the side of my face. "Such passionate innocence." It wasn't love I saw in his eyes. More respect. Or envy. "Amazing you've kept it all these years, while the rest of us have become more and more jaded." He studied my face, as if memorizing it. "I meant what I said about photographing you. You have marvelous bones. With your eyes half closed the way they are now, in this light, you could pass for Dietrich."

I didn't say anything, hoping he would kiss me. He stared and smoked.

I summoned all my courage. "Remember in the bar when we were talking about Milligan and I said I was in love with somebody else?" His eyes were huge. "I was talking about you."

YOU, in red neon.

"Well," he said, finally, putting his cigarette out in the ashtray. "When did all this start?"

"In high school, but I wasn't fully aware of it until Wednesday, when I saw you again."

"You don't know what you're getting into."

"I'll take my chances."

"Look," he said, taking my hand, stroking it, "I'm not exactly the most stable person in the world. You'd be much better off with somebody else—like Milligan."

"I told you before, I'm not interested in him."

He squeezed my hand so hard it hurt. "I'm fucked up, Beckett. Royally."

"So am I. We're perfect for each other."

He laughed. "God." He shook his head. "You are too much." He stared at me. I could tell he was impressed. "You're determined, aren't you?"

"Yes. And once I get this way I don't give up."

"I'm flattered." He kissed my hand. "I really am." Kissed it again, palm up. He looked at me, my eyes, as if he were making sure I was real. "Who knows? You may be my salvation." He tilted my chin and kissed me, gently.

"I'd like to be more than that."

We kissed again, but not as gently. "We'd better get you in," he said, in a whisper. "It's past one."

We got out on his side, his arm around my waist.

"When can we see each other again?" I asked, amazed at my nerve.

"Next weekend, maybe."

"Couldn't it be sooner?"

"Better not to rush things."

But then he kissed my mouth—a long, wet kiss—and held my breasts. "Goodnight then, Beckett, with the soulful eyes."

21.

The entire time between that night and Milligan's seminar on Wednesday, I thought I would die of longing. I hovered over the phone. Not that I expected Alex to call, and I wasn't about to call him—I'd been way too forward already. Sadie knew something was going on. *So how was the date? You smelled like liquor. Did you go to a bar? Did you make another date? Next time don't go to a bar.* I insisted we were just friends. I didn't want her spoiling this one. Her suspicions were more than confirmed Wednesday night when I changed my outfit five times before class and left the house without eating.

"Beckett! We were just talking about you," Dana said, smiling. She and Alex stood shoulder-to-shoulder against the second floor balcony railing, waiting for Milligan to arrive. I couldn't help resenting her, though she clearly approved as Alex slipped his arm around my shoulder. My whole body tingled. "We were worried about your mother," she said.

"Hope she didn't mind your coming home late Friday night," Alex said, caressing my shoulder.

Loved his touch. But his shades were back on, and his breath smelled of booze. Dana'd had a few, too. They seemed to be buddies again—as if the bar had never happened. She wore a suede skirt and jacket. Rust silk blouse. His silky shirt was from the first class.

Did they clothes-shop together?

"Oh, no. It was fine. She took a sleeping pill. She was asleep when I got home."

"Good." Dana's eyes and lips smiled seductively. "Wouldn't want her to think I was a bad influence."

Alex laughed. "But that's what makes you so charming, dear heart."

Were they playing a little game, or was it just the booze talking? Whatever it was, I didn't like it. He put his free arm around her.

"We'd love to have you for dinner Saturday," Dana said.

Alex raised an elegant eyebrow. "If you can stand all those children. Actually, Dana has them so well trained, people mistake them for hired help."

Dana giggled and poked him in the ribs.

I felt like smacking her hand. "As far as I know I'm free."

Milligan came up the stairs, glancing our way as he reached the balcony.

"We'd better go in before our professor starts suspecting things," Alex said, exchanging veiled looks with Dana, who grinned. "Wouldn't want to put him in a jealous rage."

So that was what they were discussing: Milligan and me. Shit! Not only did their behavior feel creepy, I wondered if it was Alex's way of telling me he wasn't interested.

"Forgive us for being such voyeurs," Dana said, as we took our seats. She winked as Milligan handed back our written assignment from the week before. I forced a smile.

Alex whispered something to Dana; they smirked. I seethed, especially when I saw B/C on my paper and a note to see him after class about my grade.

To make matters worse, Milligan kept calling on me. Each time, Alex and Dana would look at each other. I was furious when Alex whispered, "Have fun," on their way out to gossip over vodka martinis at the K.K. Lounge. I glared at Milligan, who was shuffling through the piles of papers on his desk.

"Why don't you sit up front?" He was wearing his Berkeley sweatshirt. Third time. Was he short on clothes? "Hope I haven't intruded on your evening."

"Oh, no." I didn't even pretend to be sincere.

His smile was crooked. "Good. I want to discuss your work."

"Fine." I'd done a half-assed job on the Hemingway essay. So what? Milligan's class was hardly the most important thing in my life. He came around to the front of his desk and sat, mole-brown eyes burrowing into me.

"After we had coffee last week, I re-read your paper—the one I used to screen for the class. It was the best of the lot. But your first essay disappointed me."

"Look, Professor Milligan," I said, daring him to pull that 'Call-me-Lawrence' shit, "I appreciate your interest, but I'm not in the mood. Let's just say I'm an underachiever and call it a day, okay?"

"Not okay. One of my colleagues, Frank Sweeny, taught American history at Vegas High. He saw us having coffee and asked after you. He said you were a talented actress, and a brilliant student, but your work was inconsistent. Every time you excelled, you pulled back. He suspected there was something going on at home."

Good old Mr. Sweeny. He used to keep me after school, his big brown eyes full of phony concern. Like Milligan's. "I have a screwed-up family, okay? My overbearing mother hates my compulsive-gambler father and sleeps in my room. Now, can I go?"

Milligan didn't bat an eye. "I like you, Rebecca. Your spirit. Your spark. I'd hate like hell to see you blow it."

"What do you mean, blow it?"

His eyes: headlights. "I happen to think you're at risk."

"Why? Because I handed in a shitty paper?"

"Call it professional instinct."

"I don't know what it is with teachers. My journalism professor in college blew up at me because he said I wasn't living up to my potential. Maybe I just didn't like journalism? Or maybe you all think I'm smarter than I really am?"

"You may have done your best to turn in a shitty paper, as you called it, but your writing still showed promise—a series of brilliant starts that went nowhere. I suspect that's a metaphor for your life."

"How the hell can you say that? You've only known me a week."

"You go out of your way to sabotage yourself, Rebecca. Why?"

"Since you seem to know everything about me, why don't you tell me?" I tore at a chip in my thumbnail. "Why are you so obsessed about one little essay? I told you I didn't want to be a writer." His annoying eyes stared while I squirmed. "Everything I write falls short of my expectations, so why bother?"

"Is that true of acting as well?"

"Sometimes. I hold back too much."

"Why?"

"Fear, mostly."

"Of failure?"

"Jesus! I feel like I'm on trial!" I took a deep breath. "Success. They'll expect more."

"They?"

"People who judge." I glared at him. "Like you."

He frowned, emphasizing the gash between his thick eyebrows. "How do your parents feel about your ambitions?"

"He doesn't give a damn. She says I don't have enough drive to be successful. Not just at acting. At anything." I crossed my arms and sunk down into my seat, wishing I had the guts to leave. "Back in high school, Mr. Sweeny tried to get me to talk about my family, and I told him what I'm going to tell you. Fuck off! Only, in those days, I didn't say fuck." I was shaking. I'd never talked like that to anybody, especially a teacher.

Milligan didn't have that smug, know-it-all face anymore. "Your lack of direction has to come from somewhere, Rebecca, and I'm betting it's home." For the first time, his voice wasn't abrasive—it was gentle. "As much as I love this town, it can take a toll on children. As the daughter of a gambler, I'm sure you can attest to that."

"I shouldn't have told you about my father. I always say more than I should."

He smiled. "Don't worry, Rebecca. It won't go any farther."

"That's hard to believe when you and Sweeny have already picked me apart." I stared at my hands. They were trembling. Damn him!

"Why is it so hard for you to believe that people care about you?"

"Because most of the time they have ulterior motives." I thought of Alex and Dana, whispering, snickering, gossiping. "I'll tell you right now, I'm not sleeping with you."

He chuckled. "I may be a curmudgeon, Rebecca.

But, I'm not a lecher." His face turned serious. "I had an ethics professor at Harvard who believed one should discriminate, but vertically, not horizontally. Judge each person according to his actions, not the group. I'd like to think that applies to men, as well as minorities."

"Words to live by." I smiled. I still wasn't sure I liked him, but I was beginning to believe him. "About that essay, I'll try to make up for it next time. I actually enjoy your class. I like being around books, and people who love them. It's inspiring, especially in a town where good books aren't valued as much as a good tan."

Milligan offered his hand. "Friends?" I hesitated. But, I took it. This time he didn't hold on. "Okay with you if we meet again next week?"

"As long as we don't talk about my family." I grabbed my stuff. I started for the door, but turned back. "If you see Professor Sweeney, tell him he was one of the best teachers I've ever had. I'm sorry I gave him a hard time."

22.

"Las Vegas is America's ultimate resort, Chet," Quent said, smiling.

We sat in a leather booth at the Riviera Lounge that squeaked when anybody moved. Chet reminded me of Quent—same crisp white cotton shirt, same silver hair. He was smoking Marlboros and asked if I minded. He was much classier than his companions, who wore open, polyester shirts. Hairy chests. Cold eyes-emotionless, like the goons at the Mint.

"We're talking about a sizable investment on our part at a time when tourism is experiencing a slump," Chet said. "My partners are inclined to be cautious."

"A temporary decline in tourism may have the mobsters worried," Quent said, "but it's the best climate for acquiring property. I predict, over the next ten to twenty years the population will explode. Think about it. No state tax. Affordable housing. Minimal govern-ment, mild winters. And, potentially, more job opportunities than anywhere in the country. Hotels, the entertainment industry, casinos, construction. All the space in the world. It's human nature to want to fill it up."

"Let me ask you this, okay?" said the one with a gold cross peeking out from his curly black chest hair. "We pay for your design. When we use it we have to pay again, like a royalty on a book, right?" He smiled, but he didn't mean it. He and his fat friend with the bald head scared me. I had a hunch they were gangsters.

"Very good analogy, Harry," said Quent, "Exactly like a book."

"We're talking big money," Fatty said, his eyes menacing.

"We're talking about a design that has everything, Chet." Quent ignored Fatty. "A five-room house that stands out, but fits in. Different, but not too different. And affordable. That's key. Affordable."

Why was I here? I felt uncomfortable, especially with Chet staring at me. I should have brought a notebook and pretended to take notes. The waitress, in a strapless cowgirl outfit with toy guns in the holster, brought the drinks: Bud for the boys—for us, tonic and ice tea.

"I'll be right back with your salad, honey," she said to me, "and your sandwich, sir."

"Take all the time you need—just don't shoot," Quent said, hands in the air. She must have been desperate for humor. She laughed so hard she dropped her tray. Except for Quent, none of the men even smiled. Maybe it was too close to home? I asked Chet for the sugar.

"Sure you don't mind the smoke?" he whispered.

"Oh, no." He certainly was polite. Maybe he was just a front man, and the other two did the dirty work? I pretended not to notice he was staring at me while Quent talked circles around the hairy chests. Like Izzy, they complained of too many hotels, the decline of downtown, new people running the show. But unlike Izzy, they seemed quite capable of doing something about it. Something violent. Out of the corner of my eye,

I noticed a willowy blonde, about my age, in a low-cut evening gown and heels. She had to be close to six feet. Exquisite face. Probably a showgirl. Shaky on her feet. Glassy-eyed. Was she drunk? Drugged? A squat man, in a dark blue suit led her by the wrist to a table near the stage. Three men in suits followed.

"Rumor is, the Frontier's folding," Chet said.

"They're handing out free champagne during happy hour," Harry added. "That's a bad sign."

The woman collapsed into a swivel chair and her head fell to the back of it. Huge eyes, staring at nothing.

"The Landmark Tower bunch lost their financing," Chet continued. "It's sitting out there half-built."

"Looks like somebody's fuck'n dick stick'n up," Harry said.

Chet glared at Harry.

"Sorry, Miss Plotnik."

"No problem."

I wished he would stop apologizing. And staring! It was giving me the creeps. The squat man at the table near the stage yelled for a waitress. The woman continued to stare. She was heavily made up. Glamorous, rather than cheap. Voluptuous mouth, high cheekbones. I turned back into the conversation.

"Nobody's moving here right now," Fatty said. "Land hasn't been this cheap in ten years."

"My point, gentlemen," Quent said. "The time to build is now. Apartments are springing up between Flamingo Road and McCarren Airport. Ninety dollars a month, pool, air-conditioning, two beds, two baths. Families are crowding in. Growing families. Why? Not enough houses. Our houses will be three beds, wall-to-wall, yard, patio. All that for a mortgage no higher than rent. They'll sell, gentlemen. In fact, there'll be a waiting list a mile long. If we play it right, these things will be paid for before they're even built. Details, gentlemen. It's all in the details."

I'd told him all that stuff about my parents' apartment last week! He was good!

"If the hotels fold…" Fatty began,

"…the suckers will stop coming." Harry concluded.

"The hotels won't fold," Quent said, calmly squeezing lime into his second tonic. "They'll bail each other out. I hear the Sands is taking over the Frontier. I predict in the '70s and '80s, our houses will be selling for three times as much."

I drifted off again. Why was that staring woman there, poor thing? They paid no attention to her. She was like a pet. I thought of the gold woman in the Lido show, tied to a post. And Marilyn Monroe. Being beautiful didn't make them powerful. It made them victims.

"It's normal for a boom town to experience a few slumps. We have to think long range, Harry," Quent said. "The 'Wall Street Journal' just had an article about the rising trend toward retirement communities due to the population increase of people over sixty-five. Think about it, gentlemen. Vegas has all the space in the world. In thirty years, it'll be the fastest growing city in the US."

"There's no fuck'n water," Harry protested. "What're they going to drink? Dirt?"

My throat was parched. Couldn't stop looking at the woman. The four ugly men. I sipped iced tea, wanting to leave. Wanting to take her with me. Jesus! After they got drunk, they would take turns with her.

"Gentlemen," Chet said, without taking his eyes

171

off me. "I have another meeting at three. We need to come to a decision."

"No, no, no." Quent waved his hand. "We needn't decide now." He turned to me and said, quietly: "Rebecca, remind me to call our Del Webb contact in California." I played along with him. The others strained to listen.

By the time Quent had removed the toothpick from his sandwich, the hairy men had gone through a bowl of chips and finished their beers. Chet sipped his drink, winked at me a couple of times for no reason. The squat man called for more booze. The blonde woman closed her eyes. Her lips were open.

"Time is money," Fatty said, grabbing one of my rolls from the basket. He wore a pinky ring with a huge safire surrounded by diamonds. I wondered how many people he'd murdered to get it.

"Take it easy, Herbie," Chet said.

"All I need at this point is a non-refundable deposit," Quent said.

Chet said, "No problem," and ordered another round of drinks. I thought he'd said he had another meeting at three? Liar! I had to warn Quent about these people. He didn't know Las Vegas the way I did.

When the waitress came with the bill, Chet insisted on paying. By then, Harry and Herbie were shaking hands with Quent, patting him on the back, telling him to be patient, they just weren't used to dealing with architects. Because they were killers! Sliding out of the booth, I dropped my purse. Chet bumped his head on the table getting it for me. I glanced at the blonde woman. Her eyes were closed.

"Well," Chet said, shaking my hand, "nice meeting you."

"What did you think?" Quent asked, in the car

on the way back to the office.

My instincts told me to keep my mouth shut about Chet and the boys until I had proof. "Chet seemed sold from the beginning, but he needed you to convince his partners. They probably had the money and he had the finesse. Only, why was he so nervous around me? He kept staring at me. Did he think I knew something?"

"Always take an attractive woman along," Quent said. "It puts the men off-balance."

My stomach churned. "What do you mean?"

He smiled. "Human nature. They can't help wondering if she's part of the deal."

Tall blonde woman with empty eyes, men in suits taking turns with her... Izzy, showing me off... Want to see a good-looking girl? She's part of the deal ...

"Rebecca? What's wrong? You're white as a sheet." He pulled into the driveway and stopped.

"I... there was... in the lounge, this woman, with these awful men in suits. She was—she was what you said. Part of the deal." I was shaking.

"Forgive me, Rebecca. I didn't realize how sensitive..." He held my hand, which calmed me, but didn't relieve my embarrassment.

"You must think I'm incredibly naïve."

"I think you're much too intelligent to allow yourself to be taken in by men like them. Besides, I'll never let them near you." He squeezed my hand. He had no idea how dangerous they were, not only to me, but to him. "By the way, you did a terrific job on that report you typed up for Paul. I suspect you were being modest about your secretarial skills."

"I just never had a job that I cared about." I could tell from his face that he knew what I really cared about. What he didn't know was how much. "It makes all the difference."

23.

Izzy was watching David Brinkley when I walked in from work, and didn't even bother to turn around. I wished I were back in the car, with Quent.

"Your mother's sick."

My stomach went crazy. "Where is she?"

"Playing canasta. Fanny Sweet picked her up."

Thank God. I'd imagined her at Southern Nevada Memorial. Still queasy, I dropped my purse on the rug and sat on the couch. Izzy's belt was undone. His shoes and socks were off. If Sadie were home she'd be yelling about his stinky feet.

"Doctor says it's her gall-bladder." His eyes stayed on the TV. "They have to cut it out."

"She hasn't said a word to me."

"She says you don't give a damn about her."

"Where did she get that idea?"

"How the hell should I know?" He reached over to his special drawer, took out his Golden Nugget nail clippers and began clipping his toenails. "She don't trust the doctors here. Wants to go to Cincinnati, but she's afraid to leave me and you alone."

"Why? We're old enough to take care of ourselves."

"Damn right. That's what I told her."

I stared at the pile of toenails collecting in front of him. "I could make your TV dinners, pick you up from work." My God! I suddenly realized that in my entire life we'd never been alone more than a few hours. Without thinking, I said, "We could even go out for dinner—see a show."

"She says I'll gamble and you'll stay out all night with goyem." He looked up. I thought I detected residual anger from my Billy Roberts all-nighter, but it faded fast. He knew damn well that of the two of us, he was more likely to be the repeat offender.

"She's crazy, Dad. I'll talk to her."

"Yeah. You talk to her." He dropped his nail clippers in the drawer, took out a bag of M&M's, and turned back to the TV.

"You know, Dad, if I can talk Mom into going, we should take advantage. We can have a good time together. It's impossible when she's around."

"Yeah." He continued to stare into the television.

I thought again of Quent—how easy it was to talk to him, how he made me feel interesting, and competent. And important.

"You know, Dad, I borrowed one of your books the other night when I couldn't sleep—one of the Ellery Queen mysteries—and I really liked it. Know who you would like? Dashiel Hammet, who wrote <u>The Maltese Falcon</u>."

"The Sam Spade guy."

He still wouldn't look at me, but at least he was paying attention.

"Yeah. That's the one. He's a terrific writer. When I get paid, I'll buy it for you."

"Nah. Don't waste your money."

"I can afford it—don't worry."

"I got too many books already."

The little bookcase by the TV contained the extent of his library: an Ellery Queen collection and an eight volume pictorial history of World War II atrocities.

"You have room for one more—a gift from your daughter. You don't even have to read it—only if you want to."

"You should spend the money on yourself."

My stomach clenched. Poor Izzy. He probably thought he wasn't worth it. Why wouldn't he? The way Sadie treated him.

"C'mon, Dad. You're worth it. Tell you what— when Mom goes to Cincinnati, I'll treat you to a dinner show—my way of thanking you for all the shows you took us to when I was little—every weekend until I was nine or ten and the price went up. It's because of you that I fell in love with performing. Remember how I used to mimic all the comedians when we got home? How I made you laugh?"

Until I said it, I hadn't realized it was true. No kid in America had had a better education in stand-up comedy. It was a gift he had never meant to give me. And he had no idea what I was talking about; not really. But I owed him just the same. And I was pretty sure he was smiling for me, now, not David Brinkley.

"Remember my twelfth birthday, when you took me to see Phil Spitalny's All-Girl Orchestra at the Last Frontier and Mom got me Evelyn and Her Magic Violin paper dolls, and Meg from <u>Little Women</u>, the Madame Alexander doll I wanted, even though she said I was too old for dolls, and we had frozen chocolate éclairs? My best birthday ever."

He turned all the way around to look at me. "Shirley Temples." He giggled, rubbing his hands like a little kid. "You loved Shirley Temples."

"Yeah, and I always ate the orange off the toothpick and gave you the cherry."

He kept on giggling. "You hated cherries."

"I was such a picky eater."

"Shirley Temples—they were your favorite fruit."

It used to drive me crazy when he used the wrong word, but not now. My God! Maybe that was why he wasn't a talker. He didn't think his English was good enough.

"Yep. Now, I eat everything. Maybe I was better off before? Huh, Dad?"

We stared at each other without speaking. Yes, it was awkward, but there was hope. We'd actually had a conversation and the newness, the strangeness of it had hit us. I wanted to get us over the hump, but the best I could come up with was, "Sure did love those Shirley Temples."

A car door slammed and Sadie hollered goodbye to Fanny Sweet. Izzy stopped smiling, put his M&M's back in the drawer, switched off the TV. The minute we heard her start up the stairs he went off to his room, leaving shoes, socks and toenails behind.

24.

I couldn't help wishing Quent were my father instead of my boss. Unlike Izzy, he made me feel that he cared. Plus he was cultured, intelligent-and he had integrity! When we were having lunch at the El Cortez, Paul Farley asked Quent if he'd heard the latest rumors about JFK, Bobby Kennedy and Marilyn Monroe. Supposedly, the Sands had a special room reserved for their threesomes.

Quent looked stern—almost angry. "I have nothing but contempt for politicians who abuse their power by exploiting women."

If he hadn't been so old, I'd have kissed him!

I would do just about anything to protect Quent. The more I thought about Chet, the more I was convinced that he was a front man, and Harry and Herbie were mobsters. I even said as much to Quent, but he just laughed, and assured me he could take care of himself. He was thrilled to have them as clients. Why wouldn't he be? The housing development would put Dreams, Inc. on the map. But what if something went wrong? What if Quent needed more money? Or Harry and Herbie didn't like the model home? Gangsters are not known for patience. They go crazy and start killing people. Benjamin Siegel wasn't called *Bugsy* because he looked like a bug! But the contract signing was set for Saturday at Paul Farley's office, and there was nothing I could do to stop it.

On Friday, Quent asked me to drop off some sketches at Chet's office. He wouldn't be needing the car since Chet and the boys were picking him up for lunch.

"Nina and I have made some changes to the model home," Quent said, handing me the sketches as well as the car keys. "Chet won't object. They're minor, and won't cost a cent more. I just want him to have a look before he signs on the dotted line." Quent leaned across the desk and lowered his voice. "Harry and Herbie are a different story. I don't want them involved. They tend to be a bit..." He paused.

"Paranoid?" I filled in the blank.

He smiled. Patted my arm. "Construction is set for Monday. I don't want any delays." Wink.

Driving to Chet's office, I tried to think of a way to convince Quent to pull out of the project before Saturday. Quent had told me that Chet had given his staff a couple days off before construction began. The office would be empty! I could poke around to see if anything looked fishy. I could go through the files—see if any of Chet's clients were shady. I knew a lot of gangster's names from my dad. Quent wouldn't want to be associated with known criminals. Better still, I could try to find something on Harry and Herbie. An incriminating letter in a desk drawer. Something that connected them to the mob. Quent wouldn't want to be paid in blood money. It was a long shot, but it was all I had.

Donovan Contracting was on west Main, north of Fremont—a mostly residential neighborhood, with a corner store and cottonwood trees. Chet had told us it was so safe he never had to lock up, but that didn't make it respectable. The houses across the street were old and dilapidated. with more than a few ladies in bathrobes, cigarettes dangling from their lips, staring out of the windows. Even though there was parking in front, I decided to park in the alley across from the Richfield Truck Stop. Since I might be there for a while, I didn't want anybody to see Quent's car out front. I was probably being paranoid. Chet and the boys would be with Quent for at least an hour-maybe two. There was very little chance they'd catch me snooping around. Still, getting out of the car, I felt so queasy I had to hold onto the door. What if Chet came back early and found me going through his files? He'd probably think Quent put me up to it. He'd pull out of the deal. Quent would have to fire me! Jesus! What if Chet made a pass at me? Maybe I should forget about being Nancy Drew? But, if I did, and anything happened to Quent, I'd never forgive myself.

The office was a one story warehouse, made of some flimsy kind of metal, with a sign over the door that said Donovan Contracting and Development. I'd expected something fancier, but I remembered Quent saying that there weren't many developers in town, and most were just starting out. A "closed" sign dangled from the door knob. I peered over my shoulder. All clear. The door squeaked as I opened it. The lights were out, the Venetian blinds closed. I decided not to turn on the lights. Why risk calling attention to myself when I could see well enough without them? The minute I closed the door I had a sneezing fit. The place reeked of sawdust. Men's shoe prints covered the floor. To my right, was a large window, and an office area with a long counter containing small metal objects, such as hinges, and small pieces of different kinds of wood. Samples, probably. There was a large, wooden desk behind the counter which I took to be Chet's, and a sloped drawing table, like Nina's at Dreams, Inc. I deposited the sketches in the middle of the desk where I thought Chet would find them, and opened the middle drawer. My hands were shaking. No incriminating letters. Just a pack of Lucky Strikes, matches from strip hotels, paper clips, pennies. The side drawers were just as mundane: documents, work-related magazines, a few Playboys—Miss September had lopsided boobs. But I jumped when I saw what was in the bottom right drawer. A gun! I backed away. I'd never even seen one except in movies! This was exactly what I was looking for. So Chet wasn't just a front man. I couldn't wait to tell Quent. I closed the drawer with my foot and started for the door. Wait a minute, Beck. Lots of people own guns for their own protection. It's not like it's a machine gun. It's perfectly legal in this state. In no way does it prove that Chet is part of the mob. Damn!

I looked around for the file cabinets, but I didn't see any. Maybe they were in the workshop in the back of the room? It occurred to me that my high heel footprints from the front door to the desk were okay, but beyond that Chet might find them suspicious. I crammed my heels in my purse but my stocking prints looked just as suspect, so I erased them with my left foot as I went along, which wasn't a great solution, but the best I could come up with given the circumstances. The workshop was kind of interesting: machines, saws, piles of sawdust, barrels full of nails. But how anybody could work there with that sawdust smell was beyond me. I noticed a wooden ladder that led to an opening in the ceiling. An attic? Why would Chet need an attic? For things he didn't want his customers to see! I'd take a peek after I went through the file cabinet, which I finally spotted against the back wall, next to a small, square safe. I glanced behind me at the clock on the wall. I had about thirty minutes before I needed to leave. Damn! It could take me that long just to go through the files. Luckily, there wasn't a lot to go through—bills, contracts, letters from clients, a thick file on Dreams, Inc. All respectable as far as I could tell. I wished I could get into that safe. That's probably where Chet would keep anything incriminating. Shit! It seemed like I had risked my job for nothing. Then I remembered the attic.

I hung my purse around my neck and started to climb. The ladder seemed flimsy for a man Chet's size. It had obviously been made in the workshop—the rungs were rough and uneven and hurt my feet, the sides unfinished. I'd have to watch out for splinters. Worst of all, the ladder creaked as if it were about to break. I was tempted to turn back, but if it could hold Chet, it could hold me. Slowly, carefully, I continued until I was eye level with the opening. I couldn't see a thing past a few feet. I wasn't going in there if I couldn't see. There could be mice! Or spiders! And, how could I find anything without a flashlight? Anyway I was almost out of time. I hated to go back to the office empty handed, but I had no choice.

I started down the ladder, trying to ignore the creaking, making sure to place my feet securely on the rungs. If I fell, I could break an arm, a leg, my neck! I had just about reached the bottom when I heard something outside. My hands tightened on the ladder. It sounded like a car pulling up in front. Chet? My heart pounded. Not now. Too early. A car door slammed. Then another. He wasn't alone! Footsteps on the pavement. Men's voices. Coming closer. Oh, Jesus! Without thinking about the ladder, about falling, about mice, I scrambled all the way up and crawled inside. I sat, clutching my shoes like weapons. The door creaked. I bit my lip.

"Chet?" Somebody yelled.

"Told youse he wouldn't be here, yet."

It was them. Harry and Herbie. The gangsters, the murderers, the enemy! I couldn't let them find me! Somebody switched on a light. I knew they couldn't see me but I scooted in further until I was entirely in the dark, surrounded by boxes. The dust was worse than downstairs. Plus, I felt like I had bugs crawling all over me, but I didn't care. I just wanted to get out of there in one piece! Harry and Herbie went on arguing about Chet, and who had told whom he wouldn't be there yet. I heard them come closer, talking the whole time about the casinos, gambling, stuff I had no interest in. I had to be absolutely quiet—couldn't cough, or whimper, or sneeze. Oh, God! I felt a tickle inside my nose. It was just a matter of time before I sneezed. I pinched my nose, which seemed to work. Maybe, when Chet showed they'd all leave and I could leave, but if they stayed I'd have to stay, no matter how long. Quent would wonder what happened to me, and his car. Oh, God! He'd probably call the police. My teeth were beginning to chatter.

"I dunno about De Remis. I don't trust him."

"He better not take us for a ride."

"Or we'll take him for a fuck'n ride, and he won't come back."

He laughed. The other one joined him.

I may not have found anything in the office, but I had just overheard exactly what I was looking for! I had to tell Quent. But first I had to get out of here, and the sneeze was coming again, and it felt like it wasn't going to be one of those dainty, lady-like sneezes, the ones you can barely hear. Oh, no. It was going to be huge! There was no way they wouldn't hear it. And they would figure out where it came from. And they would come and get me. Thank God I was wearing a full skirt! I flipped it over my head and buried my face in it. And prayed. But this time, there was no stopping it.

25.

It was teeny. The smallest sneeze ever. I barely heard it myself. Harry and Herbie finally gave up on Chet, and left. In the car, I wracked my brains trying to think of something to say when Quent asked where I'd been, but when I got back to the office he was still out. The phone rang. Nina came out to answer and stared at my head, grinning.

"Better go to the loo and check the mirror, love," she said. "I'll get the phone. Might as well. Been doing it all day." She winked, so I knew she wasn't peeved.

The top of my head looked like a bird's nest made of dust clumps and spider webs. It must have happened when I stood up in the attic just before I climbed down. I had no idea what Nina thought I'd been up to. Whatever it was, I'd let her keep right on thinking it.

Quent didn't return until almost five. He took the car keys, told Carlo to drive me home, and dashed out to a meeting with a new client. I didn't have a chance to tell him what I'd overheard. I'd have called him, but I didn't have his home phone number, which was unlisted, and I had no idea where he lived. I would just have to let the contract signing happen, and construction begin, and pray that nothing terrible would come of it.

26.

"I guess half a Jew is better than nothing," Sadie said, as I dressed to go to dinner at Alex's. At least we were making progress. When I'd first told her Alex had a Jewish father, she'd said it didn't count unless it was the mother.

"You've always had a way with words, Mom." I stared in the dresser mirror. The weather had turned cool. I wore red wool and Fire and Ice lipstick. "Could you get the thingie at the top of my dress?" I bent my head while she fastened me. "I'm glad you decided to go to Cincinnati to have your gall-bladder out. You seem a lot more relaxed."

"I would be, if I didn't have to worry about the two of you."

"Don't worry. I'll see that he doesn't stay out all night. You can count on me."

"About him, I don't care anymore." She tucked in the label at the back of my dress. "At least 'New Jersey's left the country. Where did you say he is?"

I combed my hair in front of the mirror, pretending not to feel the knots in my stomach. "Spain. Valencia, Spain. Let's not talk about him, okay?"

I turned for the bathroom.

Sadie planted herself in the doorway before I could lock the door. "Tell me the truth. Which one is it? Joey or Alex?"

Her intensity caught me off guard. I blurted,

"Alex, Mom."

She nodded her head. "We could do worse. A lot worse."

Alex had said to look for a boring tract home with little white rocks instead of grass. Right away, I knew which one was his. Modern art sculptures and cactus plants with bright pink flowers poked out from the rocks. At one side of the door stood a kind of totem pole with snakes curling around it. Arty! Alex answered the bell, barefoot in tight, faded blue denims and a navy blue sweater. I could see him collecting seashells on a foggy California beach.

"The lady in red." He took my wine, kissed my cheek. My face tingled.

Framed photographs covered the wall of a long entry hall.

"Yours?"

"Ran out of wall space in my room. Dana insisted on putting them up."

"I can see why. They're incredible."

Faces, and full portraits, mostly in black-and-white, filled the wall: a woman in curlers, bathrobe and bunny slippers playing a slot machine; a thin, grim-acing man in a skimpy bikini trying to clear a wooden bar while doing the Limbo at The Nevada Club; a cowboy in a ten gallon hat with zombie-eyes and lips crusted white from too much sun; several color close-ups of a man's sun-ravaged face; a heavily made-up, bleach blonde in a gold lame bikini that barely covered her boobs, and three-inch gold heels, standing in front of Woolworth's, cigarette in one hand, shopping-bag in the other.

"You've captured Las Vegas—people who live here. We locals get so used to being around bizarre things we don't even notice them. But, you notice them. You notice everything."

Alex's eyes gleamed. "If only the local critics were as hip as you."

"You're brilliant, Alex. You don't need the stupid, local critics. You're going to be famous, but not until you leave this town. You have to go to New York."

He started to say something, frowned, took my hand and led me to a couch in the livingroom. "Should this be chilled?" He held up the wine.

"The man at the wine store said to keep it in the fridge. It's Liebfraumilch."

"Lovely," he said, looking back on his way to the kitchen. "We adore German wines."

We, as if he and Dana were married. Why was he so conflicted after I complimented him? It had to have something to do with her—with leaving her. I sat on the couch, a thin cushion on a platform with the wall and three big pillows for a back. The burnt-orange fabric clashed with my dress. Opposite the couch, the wall was covered with Alex's paintings, including my favorite from high school—a cubist self-portrait in shades of green. The furniture was orange except for two black butterfly chairs. The wall on the far side of the room was all shelves filled with books, records and art objects, including a gargoyle with a real cigarette in its mouth. In my entire house we didn't have anything that cool. The coffee table was a slab of glass held up by a huge chunk of driftwood. On top were art books, the latest issue of <u>Vogue</u>. Dana had left her car keys on a stack of <u>Horizons</u>.

"Sorry the couch isn't all that comfy," Alex said, entering with a tray of cheese, crackers, and two glasses of red wine. He sat next to me. "I made it out of a door and foam rubber. Our old couch was the one piece of furniture Stepfather Number Six refused to part with."

I thought of Sadie's brocade furniture with the plastic over it. "I love it!"

"Except for the butterfly chairs, Number Six and I made most of the furniture. He's Buddy, the contractor I told you about. He added on four bedrooms, a new kitchen. He could build just about anything, but couldn't keep his marriage from falling apart."

There was irony in his expression, but sadness, too. He was letting me see so much more. Trusting me. He held my hand. Looked in my eyes.

"Beckett!"

I jumped.

"When did you get here?" Dana called, from the doorway of her bedroom at the far end of the hall.

Alex let go of my hand. His mask was back in place.

"I was in the shower. Didn't hear you come in. Love your dress."

I smiled a thank-you. She sauntered in, wearing jeans and a tee-shirt with an orange towel around her head like a turban—stunning, even without makeup.

"We're fine without you, love," Alex said, as if it were a line from a movie. He waved her away. "Go put on your face."

"Pour me a glass of wine, will you, darling?" Another movie. "I'll just be a minute." "Guess I over-dressed." I stared at my heels.

He took my hand as I was about to grab some cheese. He kissed it. "Don't worry. You're charming."

I was so in love I forgot about eating.

"Hey, you! Don't stand there gaping. Come and be introduced."

An adorable young girl in jeans and a man's

white long-sleeved shirt entered from the hall with three teenage boys behind her. She held a fat black cat.

"This is Adrienne, better known as Addie."

She sank into a butterfly chair, cat on lap.

"Hi. I'm Becky."

Two of the boys sprawled on the rug by the coffee table and helped themselves to hors-d'oeuvres. Dark hair, sullen expressions, acne. One was a head taller. A third boy, younger, much more appealing, sat cross-legged on the floor by Addie. Blond, blue eyes, braces.

"Your brother calls me Beckett," I said.

"Wow. Neat name," said the blond boy.

"That's Craig," Alex said, moving the cheese away from the others, "and these ill- mannered brats are Brett and Tyler. Time for kitchen duty," Alex said to them. "I'll get Mother's wine."

They slouched behind him to the kitchen. I took a cracker and a giant piece of cheese, moving the tray toward Addie and Craig. "What grade are you guys in?"

"Fifth." Addie combed her long blonde hair with her fingers. She had Alex's eyes. "He's in Seventh. I'm the only kid in this family who's gone to the same school all their life. Alex says I'm almost normal, except for my father's a creep. He won't pay for braces which is why I don't smile."

"Braces are a pain," said Craig. "You don't know how lucky you are."

"His father's rich. He gets more stuff than the rest of us," Addie said.

Craig blushed. Stared at the floor. For the first time in my life I was glad to be an only child with both parents.

"I hope they haven't been telling family secrets," Alex said, re-entering with Dana's wine. He sat close to me. Addie and Craig glanced at each other—they seemed a bit intimidated by him—as if he were more of a father than a big brother.

"Oh, no," I said. "We've just been talking about school, movies, stuff like that."

Addie smiled with her mouth shut.

"Voila!" Dana posed in her doorway, arms in the air; a repeat of her entrance at the Kit Kat, but this time she was a showgirl modeling a red velvet, floor-length gown with a hood—the kind you see in loungewear ads. Her hair was piled on top of her head. Long, rhinestone earrings dangled from her ears.

"Darling, you look marvelous." Alex danced her into the living room.

"Don't mind them," Addie whispered. "They always act like that."

"They're great," I said, while Frankie Lane sang in my head: *Jealousy, why is it you torture me*? "So bohemian."

"Gets pretty boring after a while," Craig said, eating a cracker. I felt like hugging him.

Alex and Dana waltzed around the room singing *Shall We Dance*? Finally, he deposited her on an orange chair, fetched her wine, and sat on the floor, head against her leg. They made a great magazine cover. Decadent Living.

"Love your outfit," I said. Was she wearing red because of me?

Breathing hard, she managed to flash a smile. When she crossed her legs I glimpsed gold sandals with tiny heels and red toenails.

"Yeah, Mom," said Craig, and Addie was right on cue with, "You look great."

"Thanks, sweeties." Dana adjusted a few loose hairpins. "It's the only way I know to get rid of the blues."

Addie leaned toward me. "She's been waiting three days for a call from her new boyfriend."

Dana and Alex glared at her. Probably the guy in the Madras shirt, from the bar.

"Spaghetti's ready," somebody yelled from the kitchen.

Alex took Dana's arm and mine. We glided into the dining room, which I enjoyed in spite of myself.

"How elegant," I said, as Dana took her place at the head of a long teak table with dark blue place mats, white plates and pale green candles. She smiled. Alex and I sat at either side of her. The kids scurried back and forth while we waited like royalty. One of the older boys dimmed the lights. Addie and Craig lit candles.

"Craig, honey," said Dana, as he placed a basket of bread before her, "you did a great job on the silverware, but the knives are facing the wrong way." She winked at me, as if she and I were homemaker queens.

"Told you she had them trained." Alex held out his wineglass to be filled by the tall kid.

"Oh, stop," Dana laughed, as she ladled a small portion of spaghetti and sauce onto a plate and handed it to Addie, who served me. "With five children I had to do something to survive."

"Smells delicious," I said, taking garlic bread as the basket came around. The cat rubbed my leg. I reached down to pet it.

"She cooks it for two whole days," said Addie. She sat beside me.

"She learned how from my father," the tall kid said from the end of the table.

They all glared at him.

"And that, my dears, was the full extent of his

contribution to this family," Alex said, looking at Dana who rolled her eyes. "Aside from fathering another child."

"Remember the time he and Mom got in a fight and he broke all our glasses?" asked Addie.

The tall kid gave her a dirty look.

"There was like an inch of glass all over the kitchen floor," Craig said, waving his fork. Why didn't Dana steer the conversation away from her ex-husbands? From the look on her face, you'd have thought we were discussing great books.

"Ah, yes," Alex said to me, trying to affect boredom, but the pain in his eyes burned through me, "that was the day one of the grownups knocked over the Christmas tree, but we won't go into that."

I remembered what he'd said at the bar, about things turning ugly with all the ex-husbands and their families. God, he needed me. They all did. But what could I do?

"All those lovely ornaments my mother brought over from Germany," Dana said. In a matter of seconds, her face had turned pale, eyes sad and lost. I thought of the little girl whose mother scrubbed floors on her hands and knees. "Smashed in a million pieces."

"Hey, Addie," the tall kid said. "Remember when your father ripped the kitchen phone off the wall?"

"Shut up, Brett." Addie pushed her plate away.

"God, was he a creep," Brett muttered.

Dana sipped her wine like a robot. Addie chewed her fingernails, refusing to touch her dinner. Craig shifted nervously in his chair. Brett and the other boy stared at nothing. Alex smiled, as if he and I were above it all, his hand trembling as he sipped wine. Except for silverware clinking against plates, the rest of the meal was silent. Addie finally gave in and ate a piece of bread. Alex was the first to put down his napkin.

"Anyone for seconds?" Dana's voice was gratingly cheerful. "There's a teense left." Mine was the only clean plate. The kids shook their heads in unison. A row of solemn faces.

"Dana's famous for her miniscule portions," Alex said. "That's how she keeps her girlish figure. Trouble is, we all have to starve with her."

Dana laughed. "Oh, Alex." She turned to me. "The one thing we always have plenty of is wine."

I smiled out of politeness. She refilled my glass, her hand trembling, like Alex's. The kids cleared the dishes and disappeared into the kitchen. I wanted to scream. Or cry.

"I guess we're not exactly your typical all-American family," Alex said.

Dead silence. He and Dana looked at each other and burst out laughing. I pictured Sadie screaming at Izzy, food drowning in ketchup. I laughed, too. Alex's lips were purple inside. So were Dana's. I supposed mine were. I didn't give a shit. I laughed and laughed until I hurt.

"That's what I love about Vegas," Dana said, squeezing my hand. "It's not all puffed-up and phony like other places where everybody pretends to be respectable. You can be yourself, and nobody can say anything because we're all in it together."

Somewhere in the back of my fuzzy mind I didn't really agree, but I held my glass up for more. The kids in the kitchen were singing a Kingston Trio song: *Tell the captain ashore I wanna go home…* I loved this family. I was one of them.

"I would love a cigar right now," Dana said, in a husky voice. She reached over and caressed Alex's cheek. "Baby, be an angel and get me one." Her hand rested on his neck.

I stopped drinking. This wasn't dancing in the living room. This was sick.

"Why of course, dearest," Alex took her hand from his neck and kissed it, staring languidly into her eyes, "but only if I can have one, too."

"Of course, my love."

Palm to palm, their hands slid slowly apart. He smiled back at us as he left. At the bar, he'd acted like her parent, but now he seemed more like a lover filling in between husbands. And she was orchestrating it.

"I'm glad you could come tonight," Dana said.

I couldn't stand to look at her.

"You're good for Alex." She touched my hand.

My God! Was she trying to seduce me, too?

"I trust you, Beckett." Her voice cracked.

I turned toward her. My head was spinning from the wine.

Tears glittered in her eyes. "He needs somebody who will be there for him no matter what." Her face pleaded with me. To do what? Be the mother she couldn't? "Shouldn't have left him with the kids while I went away. Two, three days at a time. He was just a kid himself." She sobbed, steadied herself, finished her wine, poured more. "Sorry. I'm getting drunk. That's why I smoke. Slows down the drinking." She dabbed at her tears. Held up her glass. Stared at it. "Men don't like women who can't hold their liquor."

Daddy went out to get a paper. Never came back. Oh, Dana. Oh, God. "I'm getting drunk, too," I said, gently. How could I hate her after all she'd been through? "And I don't smoke."

"Nasty habit," she smiled, "but it makes a great prop." She took some wine in her mouth, let it sit, then swallowed. "How the hell do people get through life without booze?" She laughed way back in her throat. "Too much reality would do me in."

"All those divorces. All those children." My eyes filled.

She touched my face. "Oh, baby. You have so much love to give. Don't waste it, Beckett. Don't waste it, like me."

We both looked up. Alex stood in the doorway, cigar in his teeth. He took out a matchbook, closed the cover over the tip of a match, and pulled. It hissed, flaming up for a moment. He lit the cigar, inhaled, flicked the match away. Make love to me, now, on the rug, please, Alex, oh, please on the floor, the dining-room table.

"He's too much, isn't he?" Dana said, caressing my arm.

"He's incredible." I put my hand on hers. Alex strode over, stood behind her chair, handed her the cigar. He placed his hand on ours. The phone rang. Hands jumped.

"It's for you, Mom," Addie said, poking her head in from the kitchen. "Some guy."

Dana flushed. Stood. "Be right back." Handed the cigar to Alex. Closed the kitchen door. Alex smoked, grim-faced at the other side of the table. The candles had burned down. Sapphire eyes, glowing in the dim light. It took all my courage to stay put.

"The end of a perfect evening." Alex inhaled. Blew smoke, slowly. His hand shaking. "You might want to leave before things get really ugly."

I shook my head. "I'm staying."

"Why are you so fucking nice? It's getting on my nerves."

My face stung. He was testing me. "I'm

determined. Remember?"

I jumped as the kitchen door swung open.

"That was Hank." Dana fussed with her hair. "He's at a bar on Flamingo Road. He's coming over."

"In case you're wondering, Hank is the sweet young thing she picked up at the bar the other night."

"Stop it, Alex." She glowered at him, smiled at me. "I'm making coffee." Turning to Alex. "I think it might be a good idea if you had some." She started for the kitchen.

"Why, Mother?" He was trembling—his whole body. "Afraid I'll say something to embarrass you in my drunken state? God knows, you never give a thought to embarrassing me."

Dana paused, hand on the door. Jesus! It was like a Tennessee Williams play. If I were home, I'd run to the bathroom and lock the door, but I was trapped. She left. I let out my breath.

Alex shoved his chair away from the table. I followed him to the living room, keeping my distance. He leaned against the bookcase, smoking. She said I should be there for him, no matter what. The gargoyle with the cigarette glowered from the shelf above his head. He needs somebody he can depend on. Addie sat in a butterfly chair, reading a magazine, black cat on her lap. Waiting. A car door slammed. Addie looked up. Alex began pacing. The doorbell startled the cat. It jumped off Addie's lap. Alex froze. He's hurt, desperately hurt. Hank and Dana at the door, talking, laughing. She ignored us as they passed by the living room. Hank glanced over, embarrassed. Shrugged, as if he had no choice but to follow as she led him by the hand to her bedroom and locked the door. Alex grabbed Dana's keys from the coffee table. He ran outside.

"Don't!" I had to stop him. He wanted to hurt

himself to get back at her, to punish her.

I stumbled after him in my high heels, but by the time I got there, he was in the car.

"Take me with you!" The door was locked. I pounded the window.

He shifted into reverse. Gravel sprayed from the driveway, pricking my legs as the car screeched off. Addie came out of the house holding the cat. The two older boys hunched over sharing a cigarette by the streetlight. They put it out when they caught me staring.

"Don't worry, Beckett." Addie smiled her funny smile. "He always comes back."

27.

I drove past a sign for Mount Charleston. What was I doing? Driving without thinking, without direction. I made a U-turn back toward town. I knew I should go home, but I couldn't. I had to find Alex—but where? The Kit Kat Lounge. That's where he'd be— getting stinking drunk before smashing up Dana's car. I had to stop him. It's crazy to hurt yourself because of them, Alex. In the end, you're the one who pays—they get off easy.

My eyes burned entering the dark, smoky bar. Two couples and an old man sat around the piano, singing along to *Misty*. The old guy was loud. Tone deaf. Very drunk. The place wasn't crowded like the other night. Alex wasn't at the tables. A cocktail waitress told me, "Sit anywhere."

"I'm looking for somebody." I said, glancing toward the bar. "Supposed to meet them."

A thin guy with a goatee gave me the once-over as I searched faces. At the far end of the bar, three strangers hunched over their drinks. My head hurt; my feet felt worse. I had to sit down. The piano player wrapped up *Misty*, nodding as our eyes met. The two couples headed for the bar. The old guy rested his head on the piano. The piano player twisted to switch off the light over his sheet music. Our eyes locked for an instant. He stared at the piano keys.

"I'm looking for Alex Harmon."

I sat on the chair nearest him, wiggling my heels out of my shoes so they dangled from my toes.

"Haven't seen him." He kept his eyes focused on the keyboard. "He only comes in with her."

A few strands of fine, blond hair fell on his forehead. He pulled a comb from his shirt pocket. Ran it through.

"I—I've got to find him. Do you know where he hangs out?"

He smoothed his hair, put his comb away, smiled. "I just provide the music." He struck a few minor chords. "I stay out of their lives." He looked at me—really looked at me. "Maybe you should too." He shifted his gaze to the piano and began to play *Lush Life*.

I slipped on my shoes.

28.

"I thought I could beat you to class," I said, catching my breath after racing up the stairs—happy and relieved to see Alex there, on the balcony. My first impulse was to throw my arms around him, but on the way home from work I'd poured my heart out to Quent. He'd advised me to be cool. Let Alex take the lead.

He flicked his cigarette over the rail, put his hands on my shoulders and drew me near. His kiss was gentle, and lingering. He hadn't shaved. He had on the same blue sweater and faded denims. The scent of English leather was strong. Had he been home at all? "I was hoping you'd come early."

"Where's Dana?" Of all the things I felt about her, jealousy bothered me the most.

"She's not coming. Too much going on in her life. She dropped the class."

"That's too bad. I'll miss her." She wants me to take her place! Bless you, Dana!

He removed his shades. His eyes were bloodshot. Surprised he would let me see. He put his arm around my waist. I nodded at a professor passing by, smiled at a girl from class. Alex ignored them. His hand pressed against my ribs.

"Are you okay?"

"Yeah," he said, his voice scratchy. "I'm all right. Sorry I left Saturday without saying good-bye."

"I was worried."

He let go of me to light a cigarette, hand trembling. "Dana's the one to worry about. I'll survive. I'm too selfish not to."

"No you're not. Now that I've met your family, I understand you better. You do what you have to do. All of you. Especially Dana."

He smirked. "Yeah. We do what we have to do." He rubbed my shoulder. Smoked.

"Hope you don't mind my saying this, but I think Dana needs help. Anybody would, with all she's been through."

"She's been to shrinks." His eyes gleamed. "She and Buddy went to a marriage counselor. Made things worse." He flicked his ashes over the railing. "You've never experienced poverty, have you?" It wasn't an accusation. Just a statement. He spoke before I could answer. "I was about ten. The year we couldn't afford socks. Dana was between marriages. She had a boyfriend who bit the tops off beer cans and spat them across the room. We lived in Jersey, in a building that reeked of urine. People called us white trash behind our backs." He ground his cigarette out on the railing. "I'll never live like that again." I wanted to comfort him, but he wouldn't like it.

"We've been poor on and off," I said, "but not like that. I guess it's easier with one child. But, I don't care about money. I just want enough to support myself and have some left over for books and movies." Joey's words. It felt strange to be borrowing them. As if he were present.

"That's not enough for me." His smile wasn't about greed—it was about addiction. "I love the feel of expensive clothes—silk against skin, real gold jewelry. A fat wallet."

"You can't count on money. You can have it one

minute and lose it the next. That's something I've learned from living here." I remembered what he said at the bar, about money lasting longer than love. "Have you ever been in love?"

He turned away. "Not really."

"What about GiGi?"

"That was lust. Her parents were in Tahoe for a couple weeks. We fucked in every room of their house, even the broom closet. We wrote to each other when I was in Germany, and she was on the verge of getting engaged. Before he dumped her." He kissed my fingertips, one by one. "The rest you know."

"I was terribly jealous of her in high school. Because of you."

"Wish I'd known." His eyes tired, old. "You might have changed my life."

"It's not too late."

He wanted desperately to believe me—I could see it in his eyes. We jumped as Milligan passed, books tucked under his arm.

Alex laughed. "Caught in the act."

"Guess we'd better get to class."

Alex took both of my hands, searching my face as if he wanted to confide something but didn't know if he could trust me.

"What is it? Tell me."

He let go of my hands, then closed his eyes and shook his head. "It's nothing. Too much booze, not enough sleep."

"There's so much I don't know about you," I said, still wondering where he'd gone last Saturday. I heard Addie saying, *Don't worry, Beckett, he always comes back.*

He put on his shades. "If you really knew me I would bore the hell out of you." He pulled me close.

Kissed me. Long and deep. "I'm taking pictures for the yearbook, Saturday. Pick you up around noon?" Kissed me again. "Better freshen your lipstick."

After class, Milligan sat on his desk. Smiled. "Good job, Rebecca. You put a lot more into this essay."

I chose a seat in the third row to put some distance between us. "So why the B plus?"

"Because you write like it's a chore."

I started to argue, but caught myself. With Alex to look forward to on Saturday, nothing Milligan could say would get to me. "You're right. The only thing that really matters to me right now is going to New York, and it might be sooner than I thought."

He leaned forward and looked me in the eye. "Would you go by yourself?"

He knew damn well I wouldn't. He'd seen me kissing Alex. "There's somebody I know—we might go together. Pool our resources. But, it's still in the planning stage. I figure it doesn't really matter what I do—I can get any old job."

"So, you'll go to New York with this somebody, and get a dead-end job that sucks the life out of you— your words, by the way. That's the plan?"

As usual, he made me feel like a child. "Sort of. But this person is incredibly talented."

Milligan got up. Paced. "As opposed to you." He shook his head angrily. "And you'll live through him?" I didn't respond. He was right, and I hated him for it. He frowned so hard his eyebrows almost met. "Christ, Rebecca! What's it going to take for you to believe in yourself?"

"I thought we were going to discuss my writing, not my life!"

"You can change locales, Rebecca, but you can't

change who you are. Put a million miles between you and your family, you'll still be you."

"Jesus! You sound like my mother! Just what I need—somebody else telling me I'm hopeless. I came home from Arizona because I couldn't keep a job. I gave up on myself. But, now I'm working, and taking this class, and planning my future. I'm not going to give up on New York. Not this time."

"Whether you go or stay, you have to start taking yourself seriously, Rebecca."

"What do you mean?"

"No holding back. Right now you think you've got a lot more time than you really have." His wife. I got a lump in my throat. He pointed at me. "Yes, you!" Shook his finger. "A bad choice could cost you years."

Was he referring to Alex, New York, or both? "You're right. That's why I should get out of this town before it's too late."

He looked at me. Long, and hard. "You can do just about anything you set your mind to, Rebecca." He meant it. I was stunned. But, then he added, "If you stay here."

I was on my feet. "Why in the hell would I?" I said, at the top of my voice. "All my friends are gone. My mom is threatening to blow her brains out. My father's addicted to gambling. And I don't care what you say about the solitude of the desert, Las Vegas is about gambling. It's about getting people to throw away money. It doesn't matter whether you're a professor or a blackjack dealer at the Nugget, you can't live in this town and not be affected by all the crap that goes on. When somebody blows their life's savings and drops dead at a roulette table, we're part of it. We support it by living here." My voice cracked. Milligan started to speak. I wouldn't let him. "New York may be a cold, hard city with people who will mow you down on their way to the top, but there's music, art, theater, museums. Why wouldn't I want to be around that instead of this?" I sat down. Breathless. Exhilarated.

Milligan stroked his beard. "You assume that there's nothing here for people who think, people with talent and imagination. No doubt you think I'm crazy to teach here when I could have tenure at some Ivy League college." He stood, eyes suddenly gleaming, passionate. "What if I told you that some of the most brilliant people I have ever met have sat right here in this room?" He gestured at the seats. "A handful, but they stood out. They were unique." He began to pace, the way he did when lecturing in class. "My first week at Harvard, I discovered there were thousands like me, which was devastating for an arrogant son-of-a-bitch like myself. My small town arrogance was nothing compared to East Coast intellectuals." He paused to look straight at me. "And New Yorkers are the worst. They think their precious little universe is the only one that counts. The rest of us don't even exist." He sat on his desk and leaned toward me. "I'm not denying New York has a lot to offer, Rebecca, but at its core, it's all about making money, and in that sense it's not any different than your hometown." He smiled. "Don't turn your back on Las Vegas, Rebecca. Growing up here has shaped your character—made you unique. No matter what the bastards say, be proud of it." He lowered his voice, as if he were telling me a secret. "I know you won't believe this, but anyone can be a New Yorker."

Anyone can be a New Yorker. What a shitty thing to say! I was beginning to hate him all over again! But how could I hate him when he really believed New York was a bad choice? He cared! He really cared! Jesus! Maybe Alex and Dana were right? Maybe he cared too much?

I stood, legs wobbly, heart pounding. "Look, Professor Milligan, I really appreciate your concern, and maybe I am expecting too much of New York, but the point is, you've been there. I've never really been anywhere. If I don't go to New York I'll always feel I missed out on something, even if it turns out to be the biggest disappointment of my life. I'll always be ashamed that I didn't have the guts to go—which is not going to help me believe in myself."

He had lost, and he knew it. It was all over his face. "Go. Get it out of your system. But promise you won't give up on yourself if it doesn't work out." His eyes glistened. "Remember that you have other options. And there are people rooting for you back home." His smile was so warm that I smiled back in spite of myself. He went to his chair, sat, shuffled some papers, adjusted his glasses. He had become the professor again, and I was his student. "As your teacher, I'd like to see you work on something meaningful for your term paper. Have you chosen a novel, yet?

"No. But I love D.H. Lawrence. What about Women In Love?"

He nodded. "Yes, do read Women In Love, but take a look at George Eliot's Middlemarch." He smiled, as if recalling something. "I think Dorothea Brooke would intrigue you."

I thought of Alex, and Dana at the Kit Kat Lounge. "I don't know if anything literary could intrigue me right now. My life's too crazy."

"Never underestimate the power of words."

29.

"Becky's told me so much about you," Sadie gushed, playing with the buttons on her stylish pink-and-orange smock. Alex had arrived ten minutes early, in tinted green aviator glasses and a sexy black leather jacket. "And your mother."

"See ya, Mom." I grabbed my purse.

"How about coffee before you go?" Her eyes darted from Alex to me. "A cold drink?"

"Coffee's great." Alex steered me, unwilling, toward the kitchen. "We have time."

"I saw your paintings at the bank," Sadie said, putting the kettle on and piling a plate with Oreos and Lorna Doones. "I don't usually like modern art, but I recognize talent when I see it. They say I have a good eye." I stifled a groan. She put the cookies on the table, sat, snatched an Oreo. "Now that she's been to college, Becky thinks I'm uncultured."

"Oh, Mom!"

"Moving here was very hard for me. In Cincinnati, where I grew up, they had everything. Museums. Music. My brothers are very cultural, especially my brother Jake, the surgeon. He's on the board of the Opera at the Zoo. It's very well known."

"Yeah," I said, "in Cincinnati." She glared.

Alex smiled. "I'd forgotten about those paintings. I've been concentrating on photography the past couple years."

"I know a lot about photography," she said. "Edward Weston, Stieglitz."

Name-dropper! I made a face at her as I got up to get mugs, spoons and Maxwell House.

"I used to go to the Chicago Art Institute with my cousin Dorothy. She was a genius. You remember her, Becky?"

I handed her a mug and rolled my eyes.

"Always reading. Used to recite her poetry in cafes. Very bohemian. I went once, but it was Greek to me, if you know what I mean. She started a bookstore, but it folded. Wasted her life, Dorothy. Dreaming in the bathroom."

The kettle whistled. She went to the stove. I ate a Lorna Doone as she filled our mugs.

"My cousin painted that." She pointed at a still-life of a vase and flowers on the wall of the dining area. "My cousin Florence."

"Very nice," Alex said. Couldn't tell if he meant it.

"You may have heard of her." She got her half-and-half from the fridge. "Florence Cohen Black?" She sat. "She does mostly still-lifes. She's had exhibits all over the South. Son's a math prodigy. Never fit in. A recluse. A brain like his is a mixed blessing." She stirred her mug. Dunked an Oreo. "Like I keep telling Becky, it isn't talent that counts, it's character. Self-discipline. Without it, you can't get to the corner. My brothers would study all night and work all day. I was lazy. Becky takes after me."

"Gee, thanks, Mom." I gulped down my coffee. Looked at Alex. "We should get going."

"We should," he said, standing. "Thanks for the coffee, Mrs. Plotnik."

"Sadie," she beamed as she stood, waving even

before we opened the door.

"I didn't know you had a truck."

Alex helped me up the step. "Belongs to Buddy, the contractor."

"Is that his furniture in back?"

"It's mostly junk I found in the desert around our house." He smiled and waved at Sadie who watched like a hawk from the balcony. "I'll be using it in some shoots. The faculty advisor finally relented about our favorite landmark. I'm going to create that living room in the desert we talked about. Not today, though." He looked at me as he turned onto Flamingo Road. "Today, I'd like to photograph you."

"Oh, God, I wish I'd worn something else." I had on a beige bulky sweater and jeans.

"You're fine. You can wear my jacket. Women are sexy in men's clothes."

"I've never posed for anybody."

"It's like acting. You'll love it."

We crossed the Strip.

"Sorry about my mother. She can be a real pain."

"She's charming, in her own way."

"You don't have to say that. Really."

"She seems lonely, out of place. She must have been stunning when she was younger."

"Life sort of did her in."

"It happens. Especially to women."

His compassion shamed me. It was probably the result of putting up with Dana. Still, it convinced me I should be with him, not Joey. I hated to admit it, but it felt great to be going out with somebody Sadie approved of. It felt real.

We pulled into Denny's 24 hour Coffee Shop

near the Dunes. On our way in, the cashier called: "Alex! Haven't seen you in ages."

He blew her a kiss and led me to a corner booth, waving at a man with prominent cheekbones and blue eye shadow two booths down. "He's a dancer in the lounge show. I used to hang around the Dunes when Dana worked nights. Got to know everybody. "

He called the waitress by her first name and ordered BLT clubs.

Two tall, tanned, voluptuous women, a blonde and a redhead, in skintight slacks with low- cut halter tops, squealed, "Alex darling!" as they came in the door. "Where have you been?"

Two pairs of high-heels clicked across the floor. "We miss you!" Iridescent pink lipstick, false eyelashes, foreign accents. German, maybe?

Alex stood halfway up. The blonde bent down. They kissed on both cheeks. She stepped aside to give the redhead her turn.

"Lottie and Ingrid, this is Beckett."

They barely acknowledged me. I chewed the shaved ice from my water, hating my clothes, my body, my bourgeois upbringing.

"Come see the new show," Ingrid said, her arm around Lottie's waist. "Fairy tales. For adults only!" She winked. They giggled. "<u>Snow White and the Seven Dwarves</u>."

"I'm Droopy," Lottie said, touching Alex's shoulder. "Can you believe it, darling?" She jiggled her boobs. "Droopy!"

"And that's the eyes," Ingrid said, touching Alex's hand. "You should see the mouth!"

They howled. Alex smirked. Oh, my God!

"Alex, come swim with us." Lottie said. "We miss you. They made us stop going topless. Can you imagine?"

I imagined Alex, in a pool surrounded by siliconed boobs.

"Did you read?" Ingrid looked at us, eyelashes fluttering. "It was in the paper, darlings. Front page. Such hypocrites in America."

Our BLTs arrived.

"Ciao!" said Ingrid and Lottie, kissing our cheeks. "Call us!

I said, "Bye." And, even worse, "Nice meeting you."

"Darling!" They joined the man in blue eye shadow.

"They're delightful," I said, biting into a wedge of BLT, trying to convince him, and myself, that I wasn't jealous.

"They're as comfortable nude as most people are in haute couture. Americans are such prudes. We're all naked under our clothes."

"Not me. I've got underwear laminated on."

"Liar." He laughed, reaching with his napkin to wipe mayonnaise off my chin. "I can see the real you. An elegant barbarian, tearing apart a carcass of beef, with manicured nails, in a floor-length black velvet gown. By Dior."

"Only if it's kosher."

"You hide behind your wit."

"You hide behind your shades. We're a perfect match."

I held onto the dashboard as the truck bounced along the dirt road behind the Dunes. "Someday I want to live around millions of trees," I yelled, over the racket.

"Trees are overrated," he yelled back. "The

desert is a canvas. None of this," he waved his hand at the hotels, "will last. If nothing's permanent, anything's possible." He stopped the truck. "C'mon. I'll show you how to read the light meter." He hoisted his tripod from the back of the truck.

We tramped around the desert behind the hotels, shooting mountains, sky, dirt, rocks, snake holes, the wooden supports under billboards, garbage cans, beer cans, broken bottles, rusty old car parts, neon signs. And, every so often, a reluctant me. It was exciting to watch him work—to try to see things through his eyes. To learn from him.

"I can't believe how ugly the hotels are from the back," I said, watching him shoot the Dunes sign from his knees.

"Ugliness doesn't bother me," he said. "It's real. You can trust it. Beauty's more insidious."

"I thought beauty was truth."

"Maybe on a Grecian urn, but not on the Strip." He stood to reload his camera. "From here, the Dunes sign looks like a giant phallus." The camera whirred. He put his eye to the viewer. "The desert's what I like best about Vegas," he said, stalking a lizard skittering on the rocks.

I kept my distance.

"Cover it with grass, parking lots, hotels, but it's still here," he said. "It'll be around long after we've turned to dust."

"I wish I had your photographer's eye. All I see is dirt. At least, in Arizona, the ground had some color, and saguaros. Here, nothing grows. It's depressing."

"Not at all. It's exhilarating—space, sky, mountains. Your mother must have brainwashed you into hating it."

"I'm not like my mother!" I kicked a beer can. It

flew. The lizard went crazy. Alex laughed, tracking it with his camera. "She cares what other people think."

He spun around, camera poised. "Great!" Click. "Don't stop!" Click. Click. "You're brilliant when you're pissed!"

"I'm not pissed!" Click. I turned my back on him, kicking the dirt. "You love it here because there's no competition. You can be a star without trying—without sticking your neck out." I faced him. He had that amused, detached look. "You just pretend to be cynical because you don't want anybody to know how vulnerable you are. It's pride that keeps you here."

"Is that what keeps *you* here?"

"We're not talking about me. You know I'm right."

He blinked. "What I don't know is, why you care."

I put my arms around his neck and brushed my lips across his. He held my face still and kissed me, over and over until all my lipstick was gone.

Joey… saguaros… how long ago that was… how adolescent.

"Want to come out to the house for a drink?" he asked, back in the truck. "Dana's out until dinner. The kids are at Buddy's."

"Love to." I wanted to be beautiful for him. I got out my Fire and Ice.

He grinned, eyes wicked. "Let me do that for you." He held my chin, "Close your eyes," painting my top lip in short, premeditated bursts. "Red's a great color for you, with your pale skin."

For the bottom lip, he changed his technique. He cruised. Back and forth. Cool, sticky lipstick. I touched the tip of it with my tongue. I could feel his warm breath on my mouth. I saw us naked, entwined.

Chills. I opened my eyes.

"I love the taste of fresh Revlon," he said. He didn't touch me with his hands. Just lips, playing with my lipstick, slowly licking it off, leaving a faint trace of red on his mustache.

"We still have some of your Liebfraumilch from the other night," Alex said, opening the fridge. He poured two glasses. "Means 'mother's milk' in German. Sexy, don't you think?"

Why did I buy that wine? "I'm dying to see the rest of your photographs."

"The ones in my bedroom?"

He took my hand, leading me down a hall of bedrooms. The door to Addie's room was open. All pink, with the cat curled up in the middle of her unmade bed. Alex's room was the last in the hall, the farthest from Dana's.

"Wow. Your room is so sensual—all the wood, the colors. I love it," I said, inhaling English Leather, taking in a mahogany double bed with a carved headboard, covered by an antique gold spread with matching fringe; a small, gold-leaf end table containing an oversized glass ashtray, matches, and a pack of Marlboros; a teak desk with a stack of novels from class and a small camera; an Art Nouveau standing lamp with a green stained-glass shade. Photographs, unframed and held up with thumbtacks, covered wood walls. "These are different than the others. More provocative. Scary."

"They wouldn't be here if they weren't."

I smiled, sipping my wine, studying the photographs, wondering if I'd have the guts to know what he knew. "Where did you find these people?"

"They're mostly two-bit performers from tacky

downtown shows. The guy in the Zorro costume actually paid me to photograph him. He needed publicity shots."

"Who is he?" I pointed to an emaciated man in his sixties, or older, sitting on a bed in a seedy hotel room, wearing a tutu and tights. His mouth was smeared with lipstick. His eyes were desperate. He was reaching out. "His hand looks like it could grab you."

"He used to be a female impersonator. Now neither sex will claim him." Alex folded back the bedspread, sat, took off his boots and put his feet up, leaning back against the headboard while I looked at the rest of the photographs.

"They're brilliant. Disturbing, but so what? They take your breath away. I love the stripper with the boa constrictor."

"She was a fun girl. Used to do a routine with a Great Dane, but it was too dirty, even for the Savoy Lounge, so she switched to snakes."

"Wild! Reminds me of that song from *Gypsy*. *You gotta have a gimmick...*

He finished the line. "*...if you want to get ahead*. Love that show."

"Me too." I stood by the bed gazing down at him. The light streaming from the window gave him an aura. Fallen angel. "Maybe we can see it together someday. On Broadway."

"Maybe." He sat up, slipped his hand under my sweater and tugged at my bra. "Come on down."

"What if the kids come home?"

"They know enough to stay away when the door is closed."

Dana, leading Hank to her room, like prey. He scooted over. I thought of Ingrid and Lottie. I pulled my sweater over my head and threw it on the floor.

"Let me get that," he said undoing my bra, and cupping his hands under my breasts. "Warm, soft Miss Plotnik."

"Beckett. Plotnik's too ethnic."

He unbuttoned my pants, pulled down the zipper. I kicked them out of the way and took off my panties. What would Dana think? And Sadie? This has nothing to do with them. He got out of bed. I watched him undo his shirt, button by button, twirl it, then tie it behind his waist, like Billy Roberts in his green apron; like my dream with the mirrors on the ceiling, only now I wasn't afraid. At least, not in the same way.

He reached under his Levi's, undid his fly, peeled his Levi's off. Flipped up his shirt. Grinned. Wow! No underwear! On my feet, I threw my arms around him. He lowered me onto the bed, rolled on top of me for a moment, backed off, then slowly swept down, as if he were a plane and I his runway. I wanted him so much I moaned. This time would be different. Love would make it different. He laughed. I closed my eyes. Please, God, make it different and I'll believe in you again.

"In France," he whispered, "they open their eyes the whole time."

I watched. He moved. Writhing, slithering, touching, never lingering, eyes open, never seeing, never connecting. As if he were performing for a hidden camera. I was entranced. Consumed with desire. But alone. Abandoned. Like the old man with his hand, reaching out.

"Don't go!"

I wrapped my arms and legs around him, knowing, but not wanting to admit that his elusiveness thrilled me. Made me want him more. He slid into me. My body pulsed and shivered. I clung to him. He pulled out, just before he came. Way before I was ready to let him go. He reached for a cigarette, struck a match.

"We're quite a pair. The daughter of a gambler, and the son of a divorcee. It's so Vegas."

"Yeah." My voice was flat. "I guess it is."

"Sit on your knees. There, near the base of the bed." He draped his jacket over my shoulders, leaning back against the headboard to have a look. "A bit full around the upper thighs. But other than that, stunning." His photographer's face glowed. He grabbed the camera off his desk. Click. Click. Click. "Absolutely stunning." Above the bed, I noticed a framed photograph of Dana, singing into a microphone at the Kit Kat Lounge. Her eyes stared straight at me, as if she knew I'd become part of what went on in that house behind closed doors.

30.

"Are you always this quiet after sex?" Alex ground his cigarette into the glass ashtray by the bed. I lay on my side, facing the wall. I didn't want him to know I was disappointed. At least, I wasn't dead inside—I could feel pleasure, passion—just not the kind I'd dreamed of. It wasn't like Lady Chatterley and Mellors. Not yet.

"Just thinking."

"Next time we'll have to get condoms."

He had almost read my mind. At that moment it meant almost as much as a declaration of love. I rolled over, kissed his neck. We leaned against the headboard, shoulders touching. Dana staring down at us. Photographs of people with empty eyes—freaks—staring.

"Alex?"

"Hmm?"

I sat up. Stared at the window blind. "I wish we didn't live with our mothers."

"Ah, but we're being kept." He ran his finger down my spine. "It would be foolish to give that up."

I turned to face him. "We could live together. There's nobody I'd rather be with."

His face tightened. "That's because you don't see me that often."

"If you love somebody, there's never enough time."

He moved to the edge of the bed. "I'm barely

saving any money as it is, and that's without paying rent."

I touched his arm. Rubbed it. "I could support us until you graduate. I can make a lot of money selling real estate, you could go to school full time, and in a year and a half we could move to New York."

He shook another cigarette out of the pack. Pulled on his jeans. Smiled, but his eyes were distant. "You've thought it all out, haven't you?"

"I'm not saying we should get married or anything. I have no interest in getting married or having children." My hands pleaded. "We could just live together."

He lit a match. It didn't take. He flung the matchbook. "I'm not the struggling artist type."

"But—I'll support us in New York, too."

"What about acting?"

"I'll put it on hold."

His face was hard. "The woman behind the man. It's so fifties." He got up. Found his matches. Came back to bed and lit up. "I'd never let you throw away your career for me. The only way I'd accept your help is if I pay you back. Most of my stepfathers were pricks. I refuse to sink to their level." I was stunned, especially after what he'd said about being kept. "Dana's a different matter." He'd read my mind again. "She owes me." He ground out his cigarette in the ashtray on his night table, and faced me.

I took his hands. "You said I might be your salvation. Well, I am. And you're mine."

"Beckett with the soulful eyes." He held my face, and kissed me. "But why New York? I know you don't like LA, but it's really happening there." He stroked my hair. "Next time I go, I should take you along."

"LA's too close." I paused. Moved away from

him. Leaned against the headboard. "You've got to get out of here, Alex." His face open, curious. Should I chance it? I had to. "You have to get away from this house." My chest tightened; I took a breath. "And all that's happened here." His face told me nothing. "I like Dana. She's an amazing person—but the two of you are so close it's like you're fused. When she comes apart, so do you." His face was ice. "I've seen it, Alex. After dinner, when you ran away. At the bar. It's destroying you, I know it, I feel it in my bones, because my mother is destroying me." I was trembling. "We have to get as far away from them as we can before they pull us down with them."

His eyes stared at nothing. "An angel come to save me." He stared at me. "You really mean it, don't you?"

"Yes, but I'm no angel. I want to go to New York more than anything, but I'd never have the guts to do it on my own. With you, I feel like I can do anything."

He ran his finger across his mustache. Smiled. "Living in sin has never appealed to me. It's so— common." His eyes gleamed. "Let's get married. We can always get a divorce."

I was stunned. "But it's so conventional."

A big wicked smile. "How about a five-minute ceremony on the Strip? The Chapel of the White Stars? You can wear my leather jacket and a Maidenform bra."

I laughed. "Are you serious?" I jumped out of bed. Twirled around the room. "*I dreamed I got married in my Maidenform bra.* Carrying a bouquet of plastic roses. That I'd consider!" I got back in bed. Threw my arms around him, laughing. "After a few vodka martinis!"

"You're warped." He played with my hair, pushing it behind one ear, pulling it forward over my eye. "I love that about you."

"Let's do it around Christmas. My birthday's December twenty-third."

"Speaking of Christ, your mother will expect a Jewish wedding."

"No way. The Chapel of the White Stars is perfect."

"Why break her heart? Besides, I like weddings. God knows I've been to enough of them." His laugh was bitter.

"Couldn't we just elope?"

"Why? Think of all the wedding gifts."

"The Hadassah group would probably give me a shower. I'd rather die."

He got out of bed. "Dana's been through a Jewish wedding. She knows the ropes." He step-together-stepped, as if coming down the aisle. "Instead of being the bride, for once," he grabbed the sheet off the bed, wrapped it around him, toga style, "she can be the matron of honor. In a dumpy taffeta gown with a gardenia pinned on her shoulder strap." He pulled me to my feet and bowed. "Upstaged by the blushing bride."

"I can't do it. Marriage scares the hell out of me. The most I could handle would be the Chapel of the White Stars, because it's not real."

His eyes narrowed. "I'm moving to New York for you."

In his eyes, his face, I saw a little boy, all those weddings. "Okay. I'll do it. For you."

"That's my girl."

"But first, tell me where you went Saturday night." I couldn't believe I'd had the nerve to ask. He frowned. Looked away. "Addie said you make a habit of disappearing."

"One bar's the same as another. I don't keep track." He grinned. "Don't worry. I'll mend my wicked ways after the wedding."

31.

"I'm getting married."

Sadie dropped an egg on the kitchen floor. "Who?" She stepped in it. "Alex?"

She took off her shoe and wiped it off, over the sink, with a sponge.

"In December."

She clutched her stomach and ran to the bathroom. "I haven't even met the mother."

I yelled through the door. "Alex suggested a Jewish wedding. It was entirely his idea."

"I'll talk to the cantor." She was silent. Thinking. "I hope he's circumcised."

"He is."

"Why does it have to be so soon? You're not—"

"No, I'm not, Mom, but you're on the right track. After he graduates we're moving to New York."

"Pipe dreams. He's sensible. He'll talk you out of it."

At dinner she told Izzy. "Plotnik, your daughter's getting married."

He stopped eating his meat loaf. "What the hell does she want to do that for?"

"He's hopeless," Sadie said to me. "Thank God you have one normal parent."

That night I dreamed that Alex and I were naked, making love on the abandoned couch off Paradise Road. The TV was on. Sadie was a contestant on *Queen for a Day*. Out of the corner of my eye I saw Dana in the rocking chair wearing a leather jacket. She turned into Tony Perkins as Norman Bates in *Psycho*. "Help!" I yelled to Alex, who floated several feet above me. "Come back," I pleaded, but he kept going until he was just a dot in the sky. I looked at the rocking chair. Norman was gone. The leather jacket lay crumpled on the seat. I ran over to put it on, but there was blood all over it. I woke up. It was only five in the morning. I couldn't go back to sleep.

I spent most of Sunday in bed, dozing off and working on my essay for Milligan: D. H. Lawrence on marriage, as expressed in <u>Women in Love</u>. I'd found a subject to be passionate about. No holding back. I underlined passages that applied to Alex and me: "Two pure beings, each constituting the freedom of the other, balancing each other like two poles of one force." Instead of a Tuna-Casserole-Marriage, ours would be a creative partnership based on respect, trust, freedom. I longed to be independent, aloof, like Gudrun. I suspected I was really more like Ursula, who craved "unspeakable intimacies." But for Alex I would change. And he would change for me. He would mend his wicked ways.

"I was just talking to Fanny Sweet," Sadie said, poking her head in the bedroom. "Her cousin Florence is married to a photographer. He does very well. Specializes in weddings and bar mitzvahs."

"Alex is an artist, Mother. Artists don't do bar mitzvahs."

"We'll see."

"What about matchbooks with 'Alex and Becky' on the cover for the wedding dinner?" Sadie asked, serving Izzy burnt brisket. It was Wednesday, before

225

class. "Fannie Sweet says his name should come first, because it's alphabetical. I think it should be yours. After all, we're paying for it."

"Who's paying for it?" Izzy ate a piece of charred meat, then poured a sea of ketchup on the rest.

"You, Plotnik," Sadie said.

"Like hell I am. Why don't they get married by whatsisname at the courthouse?"

"Great idea, Dad." I poured ketchup on my cottage cheese. "Or maybe we could have the ceremony at the casino of your choice so you wouldn't even have to leave your poker game."

"What's she talking about?"

"She's being sarcastic. Don't you know anything?" Sadie pushed her plate away. "If worse comes to worse I'll ask my brothers for the money. My only child is not going to a justice of the peace."

"Let's just forget about the damn wedding," I said, giving up on eating.

"See what you've done, Plotnik? She doesn't want to get married anymore."

"Shuddup!" Izzy banged his hand on the table. All the plates jumped.

"I've had it. I'm going to class."

Sadie followed me to the door. "Tell Alex I want to meet his mother. Before I leave for Cincinnati. Or the wedding's off."

I drove to Payless Drugs, bought a Milky Way and a Heath Bar and ate them in the store. The first chocolate, other than Oreos, I'd had since that binge with Sadie over my job at the Mint. I'd get so fat, Alex would cancel the stupid wedding with the printed matchbook covers and the fights about money and the relatives looking down their noses. Damn them all to hell!

Alex wasn't waiting outside of class which didn't surprise me, since I was late, but he wasn't in his seat, either. We were supposed to go out after. I felt queasy all over. Maybe he'd had an accident… stretched out on the road in a pool of blood. I told myself to stop being melodramatic; he was probably just working late.

Milligan looked at Alex's empty seat, then at me. As he handed back my essay on Women in Love, he smiled. In red, at the top of my paper, was "Bravo! The writer in you has finally taken over. But Lawrence's ruminations on marriage don't translate well into reality. I think he expected more, esp. of women, than is humanly possible, or practical. Or even desirable. What about Middlemarch? Speak to me after class."

I bolted out the door. I drove aimlessly. Where was Alex? Had he changed his mind about us? Was he avoiding me? He'd sounded okay, Sunday, when he called. "Told Dana about us. She's not thrilled about my moving out, but she adores you. Thinks you'll be a good influence." Monday I had called him. "I still think we should elope. I'm afraid my mother will spoil the wedding. And my father's embarrassing in public. He's used to being with gangsters." He'd said not to worry; we'd talk about it Wednesday after class. Maybe he was sick. He should have called. He knew I'd worry. I pulled into a Mobil station on the Strip and dialed his number.

"Alex went out last night and didn't come back," Addie said. "You know how he is. Do you want to talk to my mom?"

I felt like I was back in the dream with Dana in the rocking chair and Sadie on TV. "Don't leave me," I said to Alex, but he drifted higher and higher, until he was just a dot in the sky.

"It's okay. Just tell him I called."

No, Addie, I don't know how he is, where he goes, what he does. Maybe he always comes back, but that's not good enough for me. I drove past the Dunes where he used to hang around when Dana worked nights. No point looking there. Those women at Denny's, the blonde and the redhead, hadn't seen him in ages. I couldn't go home. Not yet. I'd told Sadie I was going out with Alex, and not to wait up. She'd ask me what happened. I didn't want her to know. So I headed for the Kit Kat Lounge. Maybe the piano player knew more than he was letting on?

The piano was dark. I asked a cocktail waitress what time the music started.

"Around nine," she said. "You're a half hour early."

I sat at a table near the piano—ordered a cherry Seven-Up. And another. A few customers wandered in and sat at the bar. The piano player came in slightly before nine. I motioned for him to join me.

"Looking for your friend again?" he asked, pulling out a chair. "Or picking up his bad habits?" He nodded at my drink.

"Seven-Up. I'm not much of a drinker. Alex and I are taking a class at the University. He didn't show. We were supposed to go out. When I called, his sister said he didn't come home last night."

"Why are you here?" He unbuttoned the cuffs of his white long sleeved shirt and rolled them up.

"I had time to kill. And, I thought you might point me in the right direction."

He flexed his fingers. "Told you before, I'm just a piano man."

"Dana's been coming here for years. You've seen things. Heard things. I'll bet she confides in you."

He laughed. Shook his head. "You're as hard to shake as a bill collector."

"That scene the other night, when Dana left with that guy and Alex blew up—it's happened before, hasn't it?"

He shrugged. "You could say it's part of their repertoire. Variations on a theme."

"Was it different when Buddy was around?"

"Her ex?"

I nodded.

"They had some pretty big rows. The kid never took sides."

"He's been through hell because of her, and she's worried about him." I searched his face, his eyes. Nothing. "Does she have reason to worry?"

"Stop playing Sam Spade." He stood. "Go home, before you get in over your head." He sat on the piano bench and switched on the light. Played a few bars of *The Man That Got Away*.

"Alex and I are getting married."

He stopped playing—stared at the piano keys.

"So I guess I'm already over my head."

"Take my advice. Don't go looking for him." He played a few more bars. "Dana's the one who can fill in the blanks." He gave me a crooked smile. "Ask her. She'll tell you everything you don't want to know."

The following night, Sadie had left to pick up Izzy. The radio was playing a medley of Sinatra tunes—*make it one for my baby, and one more for the road*—when the doorbell rang. "Alex. Oh, my God!" His face and arms were bruised and cut. His left hand was wrapped in gauze. I reached out to touch, then drew back. Afraid I'd hurt him. "Are you okay? What ...?

"Too many beers after work. I smashed up

Dana's car." He grimaced. "Hit a caution sign. Thought you'd appreciate the irony." He leaned against the wrought-iron railing, trying to be blasé. "Spent Tuesday night in the ER at Southern Memorial."

"First thing I thought when you weren't in class was an accident."

He put his shades in his back pocket. His left eye was swollen. "I knew you'd worry. I borrowed Buddy's truck to come over here. Didn't want your mother to see me like this. I knew she picked up your dad around now, so I parked—waited till she left."

"Can I—can I touch you?"

He opened his arms. His body was hot under his tee-shirt. "It looks worse than it is. A few cuts. Sprained wrist." He smoothed the back of my hair. Kissed my forehead. "You should see the car. Dana was great about it. Went right out and rented a Chevy convertible. Fire engine red. Milligan gave me an extension on my essay since I can't type for a week."

I clung to him. "I knew you'd smash up the car and hurt yourself."

"Don't worry. If I ever kill myself I'll do it with pills. I'm too vain to fuck up my looks."

"Thank God you're okay."

"I'm a survivor, remember?" His lips melted into mine, again and again, until I was breathless. I kissed his bruised face. Snuggled my head against his chest. His body tensed. "I better go before your mom comes."

I blurted, "She insists on meeting Dana before she leaves for her gall-bladder thing. Maybe we could all go out to dinner this weekend. If you're up to it."

"This weekend's impossible. Ex-husband Number Three is camping out on our living- room floor with his tacky wife and her three obnoxious children. How about the first Friday in October?"

"That's only two days before she leaves, but sure—it's fine. I hate to put you through this, but she won't agree to the wedding before she meets your mom."

"Don't worry. We'll be on our best behavior."

"Don't bother. My parents are incapable of behaving."

He glanced toward the street. I didn't want him to go. Not yet. Not ever.

"Maybe we could see a show this weekend? Have you heard of Barbra Streisand? She's the opening act at the Riviera, but people are crowding in just to see her. They say she's brilliant. We could get seats. My dad knows the maitre d'."

His jaw tensed. "Can't. I don't want to be around when Dana's guests arrive, so I'm moving in with Buddy. He's behind-schedule on a job. Promised I'd help him out, which means getting up at dawn for five days and working until dark."

"You mean I won't see you for…" Damn! I was showing how much I needed him. He didn't like it—I could tell.

"It's only five days." He touched my face but he wasn't all there. "I'd much rather be with you, you know that. But Buddy's a source of income." He brushed my hair out of my eyes. "Be patient, darling. We have to save our pennies for New York."

"You're right. I'm sorry. I was being selfish."

"You're incapable of being selfish." He kissed me again, but cut it short. "Gotta go. See you Wednesday." I watched him walk to the truck without looking back.

If Milligan was giving him an extension because he couldn't type, how could he do construction?

32.

"I'm turning in," Izzy said, shuffling off to his room after *Have Gun Will Travel*.

Sadie had unfastened her bra. It was sticking up out of her robe. Her nylons were rolled down to her ankles. Stiff with Spraynet, a giant silver clip across her bangs, her hair looked like a wig. She made me think of a female impersonator between acts.

"So what are you and your fie-antz up to this weekend?" she said, eyes on the TV. I hated her tone of voice; the way she pronounced, fiancé. *Gunsmoke* had replaced *Have Gun*; Miss Kitty was talking to Marshal Dillon outside the saloon.

"He's working." I didn't sound convinced; I wasn't. I knew she'd pick up on it.

"The whole weekend?"

"Five days straight."

"You just got engaged, for chrissake. Couldn't he ask for a night off?"

"His boss is behind schedule."

"Boss. You mean the ex-stepfather? I can't believe he wouldn't let him go. What's a few hours? You should have insisted. It doesn't pay to give them too much freedom, especially at this stage of the game."

"It's not a game. It just so happens that we trust each other." Liar! "If we didn't, we wouldn't be getting married."

"Flossie Sedway used to let her husband play

cards every Wednesday. Turned out he had a tootsie at the Union Hotel." She gave me her worldly look: eyes half-closed, nostrils flared, lips smug.

"C'mon, Mom." I looked her in the eye. "Besides being a bitch, Flossie Sedway is one of the ugliest women in the universe. Be honest. You don't even like her."

There was a hint of a twinkle in her eye, and a trace of a catty smile. "She looks like Woody Woodpecker, with all that henna on her hair."

I giggled.

She laughed, too, pleased with herself. "To tell the truth, if I was him I'd have a tootsie every day of the week." We both giggled. "And he's no bargain either. God did us all a favor by making them childless." We both broke up again.

This was the side of Sadie I missed. I put my arm around her. I wanted us to be friends, especially now that I was leaving the nest for good. "So, do you need any help getting ready for Cincinnati, Mom? Maybe I could drop off your dry cleaning?"

"Nah. I took care of it already."

Until now, I hadn't really noticed the dark circles under her eyes. I felt pangs of guilt. I hadn't paid much attention to her in weeks, even though I knew she was sick.

"Why don't I do your eyebrows? We can't let you go to Cincinnati with bushy eyebrows."

A tentative smile. "Well, okay."

"I'll get the tweezers."

Sadie hadn't cleaned the medicine cabinet in years. I had to take out a whole row of creams and pills to find the tweezers. They were stuck to the glass shelf, covered with something sticky like Mercurochrome. I pried them loose and rinsed them in hot water.

Sadie taught me to do my eyebrows when I was fourteen. Back when we owned the house on North Ninth Street and she and I were close. "Do it fast. It'll hurt less. And always take from the bottom." When I mastered my own eyebrows, she let me do hers. She was too nearsighted. I felt like an artist, shaping her brows into thin, elegant curves with a peak in the middle. After that she always asked me to do them. I didn't mind. It was a chance to have her all to myself. By the time I was sixteen, we had grown apart. When she asked me to do her eyebrows, I made excuses, except for the Jewish holidays and Mother's Day. I considered it a chore.

The TV was off. Sadie sat resting her head on the back of the couch near the end table with the big lamp, her eyes closed. She held her glasses in her lap, chin trembling.

"I'm glad I suggested this," I said, sitting next to her, smoothing down her eyebrow with my finger. "It's been a long time since I've had a chance to be nice to you." I turned her face slightly toward me to get a better angle. It made me think of Alex putting on my lipstick in the desert.

"Once in a while, I have them done at the beauty school. But they don't know what they're doing and it hurts like hell."

"I don't know why you go there."

"It's cheap. Doesn't matter where I go. I still come out looking like an old bag."

"What an attitude! I was just thinking how young you look."

She didn't respond. I knew she was pleased. I put the tweezers down and massaged her temples. "I used to love your hair. It was always so stylish. I remember when you wore it in a pageboy, like Joan Fontaine. You remind me a little of her."

"Believe it or not, they used to say I looked like Marilyn Miller, the Ziegfield girl. Except for the nose."

"I'm surprised you never wanted to be an actress."

"I was too shy to get up on stage. But, I loved to clown around. They called me Silly Sadie. My brothers would tell me jokes, and I would figure out how to make them funnier. In my day, nice girls weren't supposed to tell jokes, especially dirty ones, but that didn't stop me."

"My friends used to love your stories, and those funny little dance routines, and the Yiddish songs. Nobody knew what the words meant, but it didn't matter. You had us in the palm of your hand."

"I took after my father. My mother was serious—a bookworm. My brothers took after her. I used to get in so much trouble. My poor father would shake his head and say, 'In a normal family, it's the boys who cause problems—in this family, my daughter is the one who gets expelled.' But, I always knew he was proud of me. I think he felt closer to me than the boys."

"Guess I take after you, eh?"

"I was worse. My brothers were the best students. I found other ways to get attention. But, boys were scared to death of me. That's why I was an old maid. Until your father came along."

I picked up the tweezers and started in again. "Remember that story you told me about the night before your wedding? How you tried to back out, but your mother wouldn't let you because people were coming all the way from Chicago and Louisville?"

"He repulsed me. He was short, bald, uneducated. He didn't have any manners. She said, 'Go on the honeymoon and come home.' I didn't have to let him touch me. We'd get it annulled."

"And he got on his knees and begged you to stay."

"He said I'd never have to work, we'd be rich. I was embarrassed to be living with my parents. I hated my job. So I gave in. At a certain age, a woman can't afford to be choosy."

"I can understand staying with him for a while, but thirty years?"

She fussed with her robe. "When we were on our honeymoon I wouldn't let him touch me. He slept on the couch. Then, the last night, I felt sorry for him." She looked at her wedding ring, rubbed it, gazed up at the ceiling. "He was so happy he cried. I thought I wouldn't like it, the sex." She smiled. Not a big smile. A little, sheepish one. "But I did." She shrugged. "So I stayed."

Jesus! I felt like strangling her with her bra! All those years of making me feel guilty about sex. What a hypocrite. Now I knew why she liked reading Harold Robbins. Now I knew why she took him back after we lost the house. I almost liked it better thinking she had married him for his bankroll. I laughed. It was all I could do.

"Oh, God," I said, my head on the back of the couch. "Mother, Mother, Mother."

"What's so funny?"

"It's just such a joke. I mean, all these years I was convinced you were sort of a Jewish nun, you know? And all the time you had this hot thing going with my father. Boy, did you have me fooled."

Her jaw tensed up. "I shouldn't have told you."

"What were you afraid of? I'd turn into a

nymphomaniac or something?"

"I wanted to protect you."

"From what?"

"From marrying the wrong man."

"Oh, God. Oh, Mom." I turned the tweezers around in my hand. "I'd better finish your eyebrows. It's getting late."

"Don't bother. I'll go to the beauty school." Her face, all pride and self-pity.

"It's not a bother, Mom. I want to do it. It'll only take another five minutes or so." Her eyes stared straight ahead as if I didn't exist. I touched her shoulder. "C'mon, Mom. Then we can go to bed."

She sighed. Closed her eyes. I moved to her other side. Neither of us talked while I worked. She winced a couple of times. "Sorry." I stood up to get a better angle. Her eyebrows looked pretty much the same; admirable, under the circumstances. I could have sent her off to Cincinnati lopsided.

"Okay, Mom. Done."

She opened her eyes, ran her fingers across her eyebrows to make sure they were still there, sat up, put on her glasses. Her chin was tied in a little knot. She stared at the silent TV, refusing to have anything to do with me. After tonight's revelation, I wondered what else I didn't know about her.

"If you liked having sex with my father, why did you move into my room?" It was an impulsive question. Almost wished I hadn't asked. I thought she would ignore it, but she looked right at me. No more anger or defensiveness in her face. There was nothing but a horrible kind of boredom.

"He cashed in my General Motors stock without asking. Lost the whole damn thing. I couldn't take it anymore." I'd heard bits and pieces of this before, never appreciating how hard it must have been for her.

I sat down, put my arm around her. "You should have left Las Vegas right after Bugsy Siegel died."

She fiddled with her ring. "He didn't want to leave."

"Why didn't you make him get a job that had nothing to do with gambling? Things could have been a lot better in California, or some place." I rubbed her shoulder. "Maybe you wouldn't have ended up sleeping with me instead of him."

"Nobody would hire him."

"A math-whiz like him? I don't believe that."

She clutched at the top of her robe so that it covered her bra. "He had a record."

"A what?"

"Before I met him, he took a rap for Benny. Served some time. After that nobody legitimate would hire him."

I moved away from her. "Jesus! That's awful."

"It wasn't such a big deal. Everybody did it in those days. Benny was very good to him after that. He made him his personal accountant."

"It's bad enough he worked for the mob, but a record?"

"Your father thought it was an honor to go to jail for Benny."

"Goddamit, why didn't anybody tell me this before?" I got up and kicked the newspaper around the rug. "And you have the nerve to say it's not a big deal. It is a big deal! Maybe not for you, but for me! I'll never get out of this town. Where can I go? An ex-con's daughter."

"Shuddup!" Izzy's voice rang out from down the hall. "I'm trying to sleep!"

His voice! As if he'd been right there in the

room with us the whole time. My father the gambler, the jailbird. Sadie's secret lover. I closed my eyes and sobbed.

Sadie stood up, close to tears herself. She put her arms around me. "Don't cry, honey. It's not worth it."

"Oh, Mom. It's just all so depressing."

It was comforting to rest my head on her shoulder.

"I know, baby," she said, rubbing my back, "I know. C'mon. Let's go to bed."

33.

Chet raised his plastic cup. "To the model home, the first of many collaborations with Dreams, Inc.!"

"Hear, hear!" Quent said, eyes full of twice as many stars as usual.

"Cheers," said Herbie and Harry, gulping down their drinks. Their hairy chests no longer bulged out of their shirts. Thank God for cool weather. I'd never told Quent what I'd overheard that day in Chet's office. I couldn't see the point. The contract had been signed, construction had started. It was too late to back out. He'd probably have insisted they were joking, anyway. I knew better. The model home had gone up without a hitch, but if the houses didn't attract buyers, Harry and Herbie wouldn't be toasting Quent's health.

"Hope you can accompany us next time, Miss Plotnik," Chet said. "I'd like your feedback. We missed you." He made *missed you* sound dirty.

"Love to," I said, forcing a smile while holding the cheese tray for Herbie and Harry, who substituted grunts for thank-you's. Nina replenished their drinks.

"Couldn't spare her last week," Quent said, arms around Herbie and Harry. "With Nina and Carlo setting up the home site, somebody had to mind the store. Everybody's been working overtime. I'm glad you gave the construction crew time off. They earned it!"

Herbie belched. Chet reddened.

"Quent tells me you're interested in the real

estate end of the business," he said, closing in on the desk where I leaned, sipping champagne. He wore way too much after-shave.

"I've signed up for a six-week course at the university. Starts mid-October."

"Real estate's my area of expertise. Perhaps I can help," he smiled, wrinkled his nose, "over dinner." He thought he was being charming. I thought about the gun in his desk drawer.

"It's nice of you to offer, but my fiancé might object. He's the jealous type."

His eyes were panting. "I would be, too, if I were in his shoes." He slid his cowboy boot close to my foot, blocking me from slipping away. I felt like kneeing him in the balls.

Out of the corner of my eye, I saw Quent watching us. Making good on his promise to keep the wolves at bay, he took center stage. "I have an announcement to make. Rebecca's getting married in December." He held up his glass and everyone followed suit, Chet included. "To Rebecca and Alex." I whispered *thank you* as Quent hugged me. "Rebecca, you and Nina tidy up while I deliver these landscape designs to the Ogdens." He pulled Chet along as they followed Harry out the door.

Chet blushed as I caught him staring. "Good-bye, Miss Plotnik."

Nina and I began collecting garbage. "I'd say that one's definitely a breast man," she said. "The other blokes are keen on legs. Their beady little eyes bulge out of their sockets whenever I wear a miniskirt."

Today she wore a red corduroy smock and turtleneck, with black tights and clogs. Very Scandinavian.

"At least Quent keeps them in line." I held the

wastebasket while she emptied ashtrays. "God! The place reeks of cigars and Brill Cream."

Nina laughed.

"Any champagne left?" Carlo asked, from the doorway to the adjoining room.

"Help yourself, love," Nina said, handing him a bottle. She spread cheese on a Ritz cracker and poured herself a drink. "You've earned it, all the bloody hours you've put in, and so have I."

"I'll drink to that." Carlo went back to his office with the bottle. He managed to find blues on the radio. *Every mornin hear me moanin, Yes Lord.*

I got the broom and dustpan from the closet. Nina was friendly, but private. She seldom left her drawing board except to cover the phones or warm her coffee.

"Do you like working for Quent?" I asked, getting the broom and dustpan from the closet.

"He's all right." She put down her drink and held the dustpan for me. "Bit of a slave driver. At least he keeps his hands to himself."

"He's the best boss I've ever had," I said, tempted to confide in her about Harry and Herbie. "Sometimes, I think he's too nice, especially to clients like Chet. Las Vegas can be dangerous. Certain types of people—well, you just have to avoid them."

"You can't mean Chet. I've seen him with his construction crew. He's completely legitimate."

I shushed her. I didn't want Carlo to hear. "I think Chet's a front man. Like Wilbur Clark at the Desert Inn. Harry and Herbie are mobsters. Believe me, I know what these people are like."

I could tell she wasn't convinced. We finished sweeping, folded up the tables and put away the extra chairs. Nina went back to her champagne. I poured myself half a glass. Nina smiled and put her arm around me.

"Don't worry about Quent, love. He has all three of them in the palm of his hand. Harry and Herbie are uncommonly stupid. They're no match for someone like him." She finished her drink and poured another. "And even if what you say is true, it's too bloody late to do anything about it." She winked.

Clearly, she didn't care about Quent the way I did. I could have told her what I'd overheard at Chet's office, but I doubted it would change her mind. I stuffed a Ritz and cheese in my mouth and poured myself more champagne, thinking how much I missed having girlfriends. "You doing anything tonight?" I asked. "We could take in a lounge show."

"Love to, but Quent gave me time off for working the weekend. I'm off to LA with friends. Back on Thursday."

A horrible, sinking feeling. The champagne bottle slipped out of my hand. It didn't break, but made a nasty spill on the floor.

"You all right?" Nina asked, going to the closet for paper towels.

I couldn't bear spending another evening with Sadie and Izzy, thinking only of Alex, wondering if he'd lied.

"Don't worry. I'm fine. Just tired."

Together we wiped up the spill.

34.

"Beckett! I've been meaning to call you for the longest time."

"Me too. I finally just said to myself, call Dana." *She can tell you everything you don't want to know.*

"This—this is all so new to me. The mother-in-law thing, I mean. It's hard for me to think of Alex— well, you know—leaving and all that." She choked up on leaving. I'd thought she was okay about the marriage. "Don't get me wrong. It think it's great, it's just... it took me by surprise. It's so soon."

"Well, we realize it's kind of soon, but we feel like we're too old to be living with our parents, so... I mean, it's not like we're leaving town right away. New York's a long way off."

A long, awkward pause.

"I'm looking forward to meeting your parents. Alex said next Friday."

"They're looking forward to meeting you, too. I thought it might be good for the two of us to get together before then. Maybe have a drink or something?"

"How about tonight? I'm working the night-shift for a friend, but we could meet before, say around seven. The Dunes has a great bar."

"Fine. I'm pretty sure I can get the car." I hesitated. "Alex wouldn't happen to be around, would he?"

"He's staying with Buddy for a few days. He said you knew."

"I did. Just couldn't imagine how he was going to work with a sore wrist. I mean, he said he couldn't type."

"Guess he can still hold a nail in place with his good hand. Buddy likes having Alex around. He's the closest thing to a father Alex ever had."

He hadn't lied. I was relieved. But it wasn't enough.

"Well, see you tonight, at the Dunes."

"Beckett!" Dana waved from the far end of the long bar near the entrance to the lounge. We kissed cheeks with tense faces. I settled into a plush leather chair that swiveled.

"Vodka martini?"

"Sure."

Her empty glass and her breath told me she was at least one ahead of me. She called the bartender by name.

"I like this bar, especially early. It's private. The slots are far enough away that they don't drown you out." She wore black slacks and a sleeveless white turtleneck. Hair over one eye like Veronica Lake. I was still intimidated by her glamour.

"It's nice." I took a sip of vodka, wondering where, how to begin. "I'd really like to meet Buddy. He's so much a part of Alex's life."

"He'll be at the wedding. I'm sure he's not thrilled about seeing me. We're not exactly on speaking terms."

"Oh, God. I hate to put you through…"

"I can handle it. With six ex-husbands, I've been through worse." Her eyes turned hard, bitter. "Much worse."

With a last name, I could get Buddy's address from the phone book. I could go there.

"Alex told me his last name but I've forgotten it."

"O'Conner. Bud O'Conner." She let out her breath. "Still hurts to say his name."

"I'm sorry. Shouldn't have brought it up."

"It's okay." She called for another drink. Squeezed my hand and looked me in the eye. "He lives six blocks from me, Beckett. And another martini is not going to make him go away." She ate her olive, tossed the toothpick in the glass ashtray. "It just dulls the pain."

Steer the conversation back to Alex, Beck. Remember why you're here.

"You know, the last time I was at the Dunes I was a sophomore in college. My girlfriend tried to order a drink but they asked for an ID. Alex said he used to hang around here when you worked nights."

"Yeah." she sighed. "Probably shouldn't have let him, since he was a minor, but he looked older." She tossed her hair back out of her eyes. "So nobody said anything. They adored him. Everybody. Especially the dancers in the lounge."

"I met some of them when we were at Denny's." I took a deep breath. "They were... delightful."

"Alex loved watching them rehearse. He learned all their routines. The choreographer—he's one of the best in the country—said Alex had talent, but Alex is like me. School was more important." She downed her drink. "Some people would think I'm a terrible mother, letting my son run around with strippers."

"Oh, no! I don't think you... I mean, they seemed really nice, and..."

"They're European," she made big gestures with her hands, "so of course they're more open-minded about things. What's wrong with that?" She called the bartender and ordered another drink. I got out my wallet. She pushed my hand away and paid. "The dancers here, once you get to know them, are the sweetest, most generous ... Not greedy and materialistic, and—and hypocritical, like Americans." The bartender brought her martini and removed the empty glass. She looked at me while she drank. Her hand trembled. "It's just so easy to judge people, isn't it?" She shook her head, her eyes, more weary than angry. "So fucking easy."

Was all this Europe versus America stuff really about meeting my parents? She obviously knew Sadie would judge her, and possibly Izzy, but did she think I took after them?

"You know what it is?" I said. "It's values. My grandmother's generation was different. They didn't care about keeping up with the Joneses. They were immigrants, and proud of it. But my mother's is all about competition. And respectability. And you're right. They're hypocrites. Very materialistic, very conservative, which I sort of bought into until college." I took a couple swallows of vodka. "Then, I started thinking, questioning. Stopped believing in God, religion. Which totally screwed things up with my mom."

"She's not going to approve of me, is she?"

I avoided her eyes. "She—she adores Alex. Thinks he's good for me."

She touched my arm. "It doesn't matter what she thinks, as long as you approve of me."

I had to look at her. Oh, damn. Her eyes were filling.

"Approve... I-I mean, it's such an obnoxious...

Who am I to approve of... of anyone? We're all in it together."

I'd quoted her from that night at her house. I didn't think she noticed.

"You know what my papa would say when he liked somebody? He'd say-you're people. His English wasn't that good—he was already grown when he came over from Sicily—so it sounded like jou peeppala. But we knew what he meant." She gripped my hand. Her smile, her chin trembled. "He wasn't really my papa, Beckett. My real father, he, he abandoned..." She took a deep breath. "So Mama couldn't marry again. But Papa, he was more of a father than that sonofabitch, that sonofabitch ever..." She bent over, as if her gut was tearing her apart.

"Oh, Dana." I put my arm around her. "Oh, Dana." She was still holding my other hand. So tight.

"You, you're people, Beckett." She let go of my hand and touched my face. "And I want you to know, no matter what happens, if—if you and Alex are broke, or you have a fight, or if he walks out on you, you have a home with me." I let go of her shoulder and reached in my purse for Kleenex, offering her some. Wiping my eyes. "A roof. Somewhere to go. I mean it, baby. I mean it." She squeezed my shoulder. "I mean it."

"I know you do."

"I know."

"I mean it."

The bartender asked if she was okay. I nodded. Slipped him money for her last drink plus a big tip.

"You know, I really want you to meet my boss."

She looked incredulous—like I had spoken in a foreign language.

"He's a great guy—very smart, successful, both feet on the ground. I think the two of you might really hit it off."

"Oh." She laughed. "You mean, you want to fix me up with your boss? Is that what you mean?"

"Well, I… It's just… you've had such a hard life, and it's not your fault. None of it is really your fault. I just wish there was something I could do to make it better."

"Oh, baby." She touched my cheek. "I don't know if there's anything anybody can do to make it better. Too much water under the bridge, you know?" Her world-weary eyes said it all. She looked at her watch. "Oh, shit. I better have some coffee. Sober up. Change. The show must go on, right?"

"Are you sure you're okay?"

"Honey," she took her arm off my shoulder and straightened up, "I have never missed a day, or night, of work. You'd never know it to look at me, but I'm tough. I am one helluva tough broad." She held onto the bar while she stood. Wobbled a little. Steadied herself with the chair. "Would you mind handing me my bag." She pointed to a navy blue TWA bag at the base of her chair.

"I'll carry it for you."

She unzipped a side pocket and pulled out her shades.

"Join me for coffee?"

"I better get home. But I'll walk with you."

Arm in arm, we crossed the casino like sisters.

I looked up Buddy's address at a Chevron station. I drove as far as Alex's house, wondering if I'd have the guts to go the whole way. I had no plan. Just wanted to see, touch him. Believe he was real. He'd probably feel I was coming on too strong. Men don't like needy women. It drives them away. But we were engaged. I had a right. I trembled all over when I saw the house. Passed by. Circled around. Passed by again. And again. Parked on the opposite side of the street. What now, Beck? What now?

The house was part of the same tract as Dana's, but fancier, on a brand new road. It sprawled for a quarter of a block, with oleanders against the front and roses along the outside of a white brick wall. The living-room was lit up. Country music blared from a stereo. I got out of the car. Leaned against it. Breathed. What the hell would I say? I'm looking for Alex Harmon. I'm his fiancé. D.H. Lawrence would probably call this a breach of faith, a violation of boundaries. But, as Milligan pointed out, Lawrence demanded too much of people, especially women.

Knees shaking, heart banging against my ribs, I walked down the cement path to the door. Why are you here, Beck? What's the deal? This is really stupid. A man, belly hanging out of his jeans, dirt-caked workman's boots with laces undone, beer bottle in hand, lay on the well-tended lawn, staring vacantly at the sky. I pretended not to see him, not to hear the voice in my head repeating *stupid, stupid*. I climbed three steps to a door with gold lanterns at either side. Rang the bell. You're getting married. You have every right to be here, Beck. Every right. Except it's stupid. It will only cause problems.

Somebody yelled over the music, the laughing, the rough voices, "Answer the fucking door."

A thin, red-bearded man with a bald spot and bloodshot blue eyes asked, "Hi doll, who're you?" One of his front teeth was missing. Sounded like a crowd inside. I glimpsed a few apes guzzling beer.

"I'm looking for Alex." My voice so soft I couldn't hear it. "Huh?"

The bearded man made way for a young guy

with blond curly hair and no shirt. "Hey, baby. Let's party."

"Is Alex Harmon here?" I felt like I was ten and asking if Alex could come out and play.

The bearded man turned and yelled, "Hey! Where's Harmon?"

Somebody yelled back, "How the hell should I know?"

"He don't usually attend our little parties," the beard said. The blond lost interest and wandered off. "You want to speak to Buddy?" Beard asked. He turned his back to me without waiting for an answer. "Hey, where's Buddy?"

Somebody said they thought he was in the kitchen. Somebody else said he'd gone to get more booze.

"Musta gone to the store. Why dontcha come in and wait? Buddy might know somethin."

"Oh, no. That's okay. I should get home."

I was almost relieved Alex wasn't there with those apes. And at least I'd had the guts to ring the bell. But where was he? Everybody adored him, especially the dancers. Maybe he was with the dancers. Skinny-dipping in their swimming pool. Three-way sex. Orgies. He was still single. He had a right.

"Old Alex," the Beard grinned, "he has a way of disappearin, don't he?"

"Yeah. Guess he does."

35.

"Your hair's very sexy like that," Alex said, before class. Brilliant in a black turtleneck and jeans, he flicked his cigarette over the balcony rail and slipped his arm around my waist. I put my arm around his. For a moment, it was enough to be touching, looking, loving without speaking. Without thinking. His blond hair shimmered under the lights. He was still bruised, and scratched, and his wrist was taped, but it only made him look sexier. His hand left my waist and held my chin. He smiled. "I love the way you can change your looks completely. The actress in you. Dana said you had a drink together Monday."

"You'd told me she was feeling blue about you. Us. I thought it might help."

"Whatever you did worked. She says you're the best thing that ever happened to me." He stroked my chin. "She's right."

"I hope so." I had what I'd wanted—his trust, hers—but I felt undeserving. Should I tell him about going to Buddy's? The guys were probably too drunk to remember me. Should I ask where he was? "How was your week?"

"Construction workers are hardly my idea of scintillating."

"Do you have to hang around with them after work?"

"It goes with the job."

"So you go to their parties and stuff?"

"Buddy'd be pissed if I didn't. He has no one else to talk to."

He was lying. Oh, Christ! Why? "He must be the closest thing to a father you ever had."

"He's okay. I talked to him about us. We can have one of his apartments rent-free if I manage the unit. With you working, we can live off our savings for five or six months when we get to New York. Maybe more. If we're good." He squeezed me closer. He looked happy, hopeful, completely unlike himself. "First Sunday, we'll splurge, dress to the teeth, have cocktails at the Plaza. There's a brilliant cabaret downstairs. 'The Julius Monk Revue.' The kind of comedy you should be doing. You will be doing. It's just a matter of time."

I didn't care where he'd been, or that he'd lied. There was nothing he could do that would make me stop loving him. "What about a musical? On Broadway?"

"Orchestra seats. But after that it will be job hunting, bargain matinees, and hounding the galleries, and auditions." He let go of me. Lit a cigarette. "God, this is crazy. We should be looking for a patron."

"We don't need anybody. There's no way you won't be famous. You're the real thing."

For once, he didn't protest. He ran his fingertip along my cheek. Lovingly. "I told Dana to keep Friday open for dinner with her in-laws. She's worried your mother won't approve of her."

"She won't. So what else is new?"

"Here comes our professor." Milligan walked past without looking. "What do you think? Should we invite him to the wedding?" He kissed my neck. "Or would that be cruel and unusual?"

"Who cares? Can we go for a drink after class?"

"I would, but Dana needs the rental car."

Smile, like it doesn't matter "Oh, well. We'll see each other Friday."

"By the way, the pictures I took of you are astounding. I'll show them to you next week. Not only are you incredibly photogenic," he tilted my chin, kissed my forehead, "and beautiful," he kissed the tip of my nose, "you're the least demanding woman I've ever known."

"So, Rebecca, how's it going?" Milligan had accepted my excuse for missing our meeting last Wednesday. I'd blamed it on some stomach thing, but I was sure he knew it was some Alex thing. We sipped coffee outside on the small patio adjacent to the administration building. I reminded myself I was there to talk about books-not family, not Alex-books.

"I started <u>Middlemarch</u>."

His eyebrows went up. "What do you think?"

I added even more sugar to my coffee. "The wrong man can really screw up your life."

He laughed. "I guess women of your generation can still identify with Dorothea. That's good."

He didn't know a damn thing about women my age. "Why wouldn't we? She's intelligent, sensitive, aware. She should be doing something worthwhile instead of wasting her life on a man who doesn't deserve her."

His eyes zeroed in. "How do you define a wasted life?"

Clearly, he didn't think I had the vaguest idea. "I had a friend in high school who had everything—looks, talent, brains. Now she's a fat alcoholic married to a slot machine mechanic. I'd say that's a wasted life, wouldn't you?" He started to speak, but I cut him off. "My mother's another one. She grew up thinking she was stupid compared to her brothers. She could have been a teacher, or even a lawyer like her brother, if she'd believed in herself. Instead, she married my father so she could quit her boring job and leave home, and all she has to show for it is me."

"She chose security over love, and over independence as well." His head bobbed. He chewed his lip. "Maybe, for her, that was more important."

If he was trying to annoy me, he was succeeding. "She blew it! Love is much more important. Without it, life's not worth it."

He pointed a finger. "Hence, your fixation on Lawrence. I thoroughly enjoyed your paper on <u>Women In Love</u>. Clearly, the subject of marriage inspired you. I'm glad, though, that you've let Eliot in."

I didn't have the heart to tell him I was only reading Eliot because he'd asked me to. "Eliot's probably more realistic. But she's so predictable. She has brilliant Dr. Lydgate, falling for this blonde bimbo just because she fits his dream-wife fantasy, and Dorothea's hung up on horrible, ugly Casaubon because of his intellect, not realizing he's a total wind-bag. You just know Lydgate and Dorothea will end up together in the end."

He looked pleased. "We'll talk some more about Eliot's predictability, but after you've finished the book."

"Oh, I see. Eliot's teasing us with a Hollywood ending that she has no intention of delivering. That's not fair."

Big grin. He was having a great time at my expense. "Read on."

"I still think Lawrence is more-I don't know-modern. He thinks marriage should liberate people instead of trapping them."

"Do you think Eliot is championing traditional marriage?" He pointed his finger again, the way he always did in class. "Do you think she wants you to take Dorothea as a model? Or is this a cautionary tale?"

"This is starting to feel like a test."

He chuckled. "Force of habit."

"I should probably save my opinions until after I've finished the book, but so far I think Eliot might be restricted by her time. Women didn't have many options in her day. But Lawrence is more like us."

"Us?"

"My generation. At least, those of us without children. It's bad enough to be stuck in a traditional marriage, but children limit your choices even more." His brow wrinkled like he was deep in thought. "My mother would have been much better off if she hadn't had me." I remembered that ugly scene a few weeks ago, when I defended Izzy, and she hit me.

"Are you saying you ruined her life?"

"She left my father at one point—only went back to have a child. On her own, she might have made something of herself, but she felt she had to experience motherhood or her life wouldn't be complete. I don't know what it is with women. My dad didn't want me. She ended up raising me by herself. She used to say to me, 'My life is over; only yours matters.' What kind of a life is that?"

"For many people, having children is not merely an option, it's a privilege—and being a parent—a good parent—can be more fulfilling than seeing one's name on a marquee." There were sparks of anger in his eyes. This wasn't about literature—this was about losing his wife.

"Look, I really like children—I was everybody's

favorite baby sitter. It's just, I haven't been exposed to very many happy families, at least not the kind I'd want. And I doubt that I'd make a good parent. I don't know how. D.H. Lawrence and Frieda never had children together."

"And you want to be like the Lawrences? You and Alex Harmon?"

I felt like slapping his arrogant face. "That's not a literary question. That's personal."

He put up his hand. "I retract it." He leaned toward me. I moved back. "It's none of my business, but I think you may be in over your head."

First the piano player, now him. "You're right. It's none of your business."

"As a friend, I'm expressing concern, that's all. Harmon and his mother have been the subject of many a faculty coffee klatch. They're extremely attractive, bright. Alex, in fact, is brilliant. But—keep in mind that, however genuine or earnest, love is not a panacea."

I collected my books and stood. "Why is it I keep having to remind you that you're my teacher, not my parent? And for your information, Alex would never allow me to sacrifice myself. He cares more about my future than I do!"

Milligan just smiled, as if he'd heard it all before.

"From now on, let's stick to novels, okay?"

"To quote one of my favorite contemporary writers, 'the wrong man can really screw up your life.'" His eyes sparkled. "See you next Wednesday."

36.

"So where are they?" Sadie looked at her watch. She wore a powder-blue knit dress and fake pearls. She looked almost stylish. She'd lost weight since she'd been sick.

"Give them time. We're early. Dad's not even here yet."

We stood by the door to Lucy's Restaurant: carved, polished mahogany with a brass handle.

"I hope they don't expect us to pay for them."

"I'm sure they don't."

"Your father will have a fit. You know how he was about the wedding."

"Don't worry, Mom. It'll be fine."

She'd been on edge for days—probably worried about her trip. Or maybe she was anxious about making a good impression on Dana? If so, she'd never admit it. I glanced toward Fremont. Izzy shuffled around the corner, a newspaper under his arm. Probably a racing form. Directly behind him were Dana and elegant Alex. My insides swirled. Pale blue sweater, gray slacks. I started to wave. Too corny. They saw us, quickened their pace, passing Izzy by. Under different circumstances I'd have thought it was funny.

"Here they come," I said. Sadie peered around me for a look. Dana wore a rust suede suit. Her hair was in a chignon. Her alligator shoes matched her handbag. Not only was she stunning, nobody ever looked more respectable.

"For a cocktail waitress, she certainly makes a good impression," Sadie whispered.

"Jesus, Mother!" I felt queasy. I'd forgotten how great they looked together.

"Becky, darling." Dana leaned to kiss my cheek. "What a charming dress."

"Thanks. You look smashing!"

My other cheek tingled as Alex kissed it. "Hi, gorgeous."

English Leather. In my haste to kiss him back I stepped on his foot and smeared lipstick on his ear.

"Mrs. Plotnik." Dana extended her manicured fingers like royalty. She didn't appear nervous, but I knew better. Loved her for it. "Delighted to meet you at last."

Sadie shook her hand too vigorously. "Likewise, I'm sure."

What was going on? I'd never heard Sadie say that before—it was right out of *Guys and Dolls*. Could it be that a mere cocktail waitress had made the queen of respectability feel coarse—so she had acted accordingly? Izzy, the outcast, stood by the curb.

"Dad," I waved him over, "Come meet everybody."

Dana and Alex seemed surprised, even shocked at Izzy's appearance. His sweater was missing several buttons; there was a hole where a pocket should have been; his shoes were scuffed and worn; he had a five o'clock shadow. But he wasn't as embarrassing as Sadie, fuming and snorting at the door because he was getting all the attention.

"How do," he mumbled, shaking Alex's hand and nodding at Dana.

"Let's go in already," Sadie bellowed.

My feelings gushed out on my face. I wanted to whisper apologies to Dana, but she had followed Sadie inside. I took Alex's arm. "She's on her worst behavior. Told you it would be an ordeal."

He smiled, whispering, "Don't worry," as he held the door, but I sensed he was nervous. Why anyone would be intimidated by my parents was beyond me. Especially him. We entered a long, narrow bar that became a restaurant further back. I cringed when Sadie marched up to the hostess and announced: "Plotnik, party of five."

The Old West motif at Lucy's wasn't subtle: brass spittoons and fixtures, wood paneling, oversized paintings of scenes from the Golden West in gilt frames. At least it was one of the few places in town where waitresses wore black dresses and white aprons instead of skimpy costumes. The hostess led us to a dark red horseshoe-shaped booth near the back. Dana and Alex sat at one end, Sadie and Izzy at the other, me in the middle. I moved my place-setting closer to Alex's.

"Order me the spaghetti," Izzy said, disappearing into his racing form.

Sadie took it away. "Order it yourself."

Alex's smile was reassuring. It didn't help.

"Anything from the bar?" the cocktail waitress asked. Unlike the regular waitresses, she wore a long red dress trimmed in black lace with black feathers and sequins in her hair. To the right of her top lip, a beauty mark had been drawn on with eyebrow pencil.

"We don't drink," Sadie said, as Dana and Alex asked for vodka martinis on the rocks. The waitress looked confused.

"I'll have one, too," I said, to spite Sadie.

A regular waitress came by with a basket of rolls. I half-expected Sadie to slip a few in her purse, but she controlled herself.

"We haven't been here in ages," Dana said. "I'm so glad you suggested it, Mrs. Plotnik."

"Call me Sadie."

Their lips smiled; their eyes anything but friendly.

"Mind if I smoke?" Alex asked Sadie.

"Not at all." You'd think he'd asked her on a date the way she batted her eyes. She lost the glow when she looked at Dana. "Becky tells me you have a big family."

Dana's smile was tentative. "I assume you mean my five children."

She was good! The cocktail waitress brought our martinis. Sadie's eyes snatched mine from my hand. I gulped it.

"Five children. Never know it to look at you. You have such a lovely figure." She smiled at Dana, then me, like she expected a medal.

"How sweet of you to say so."

What a pro! Nobody else talked. It was like a prizefight. We were there to watch the two of them duke it out. I was rooting for Dana, but Sadie could deliver a mean punch. Alex fed me his olive. He was wearing a ring. A gold zigzag, with an emerald at the point.

"Hey, toots," Izzy said, waving at a waitress with a tray of dirty dishes on her arm, "how's about taking our order? We've been here an hour, for Christ's sake."

Sadie jabbed him with her elbow. "Behave yourself, Plotnik."

At least he didn't know any better. She was going out of her way to be a cartoon.

"May I take your order?" another waitress asked, placing a bowl of black olives, celery and carrot sticks in the center of the table. Izzy grabbed a handful of carrots.

"I can't have anything but the fish," Sadie told the waitress. "I'm having my gall-bladder removed. Not here. I wouldn't trust these quacks. I'm going to the Jewish Hospital in Cincinnati. My brother Jake is a doctor on the staff." She glanced at Dana to see if she were impressed. "I'm leaving Sunday."

The waitress smiled, straining to be polite.

"Spaghetti," Izzy said, "and make it snappy." He broke open a roll and buttered it, leaving a pile of crumbs on the tablecloth.

Alex put the napkin to his mouth and snickered, "They're too much."

He and Dana ordered steak sandwiches. His cashmere sweater brushed against my arm as he turned toward her, whispering something. She giggled. My shoulders stiffened. I saw dinner at their house, the cigar passing from his lips to hers. I asked for a chef's salad without onions.

"Sorry you're ill, Sadie," Dana said.

"Oy!" She said, to remind them they weren't really Jewish. "What I've been through. And on top of everything they want to get married in December. I haven't had a chance to make the arrangements. She'll have to do it while I'm gone, but if I know her it'll never get done."

Damn her! Did she have to say that in front of them? Izzy chomped celery. The sound was deafening.

"Can I help?" Dana looked at me.

I glared at Sadie. "Don't worry. I'll take care of it."

"I don't see why they have to get married now," Sadie said. "I think they should wait until he graduates, don't you?"

"We don't want to wait," I said. Defying her was reason enough to do anything.

"The other alternative would be to live in sin." Alex directed a charming smile toward Sadie. "We didn't think that was fair to all of you."

I squeezed his hand. He squeezed back. Sadie looked dyspeptic.

"We have to face it, Sadie," Dana said, her smile charming as Alex's, "they're old enough to make their own decisions."

Yay, Dana.

"I still make her bed and do her wash." What the hell was she doing? My face burned. "How's she going to manage?"

I remembered her scowling when I was five and couldn't tie my shoes. *You're hopeless. You'll never be able to dress yourself.*

"I was like that before I married," Dana said, still smiling. "It's amazing how fast you learn."

Bless you, Dana. I hoped Sadie would back off. Instead, she rolled her eyes.

"Who's going to pay the bills while he's in school? She's never kept a job more than three months."

I thought she approved of this marriage! It seemed like she was doing everything she could to jinx it.

"Leave the kid alone, Sadie."

I'd almost forgotten Izzy was at the table. I was stunned. So was Sadie. It was all over her face. He'd never defended me in his life. I tried to catch his eye but he was hiding behind his racing form.

"You underestimate your daughter, Sadie," Dana said, taking Izzy's lead. "I think she can do just about anything she puts her mind to." She smiled at me with so much respect.

Oh, my God! I thought of Joey, that time he spoke up for me, only Dana was my future mother-in-law and I had no problem accepting the complement. Alex slipped his arm around me. He and Dana were my family. And Izzy. Sadie's lips wrinkled up like they'd been sewn shut.

The waitress arrived with our food, serving Izzy first. He tucked his napkin under his chin and began eating before anyone else was served. Sadie smacked his arm. I wanted to shake her. So what if he was crude? He cared about me. She made me feel like a piece of junk she was ashamed to sell.

Alex ordered another round of drinks. I had a terrific urge to pee, but I didn't want to leave Dana and him alone with Sadie. I'd hold it until after we ate. I poured a gravy boat of Thousand Island dressing with little pieces of hard boiled egg in it on my salad. My favorite dressing. Halfway through my lettuce, I noticed Alex eating his sandwich. Such small bites. Elegant. Even the way he chewed! A lifetime wouldn't be long enough with this man. Izzy belched.

"Shut up, Plotnik. You're embarrassing me." Sadie moved away from him and focused on Dana. "Becky says you work at the Dunes."

"That's right." Dana's chin went up ever so slightly. She pushed her plate away, placed her napkin to one side. "I'm a cocktail waitress."

"How interesting." Sadie's smile was laced with venom.

Izzy was the only person at the table who didn't seem tense. Far from it. He was snoring. Dana lit a cigarette. The smoke drifted right over to Sadie. Bette Davis couldn't have done it better. "As a matter of fact, it's boring and demeaning. But it pays well and I have children to support."

I wanted to applaud. Sadie's face blended with the red booth. The waitress cleared the table and asked if we wanted dessert.

"Just coffee," Sadie said. She'd lost her appetite.

It seemed like a good time to go to the bathroom. Sadie appeared to have exhausted her repertoire, and Izzy was half-asleep. I wasn't about to wet my pants in addition to all the other humiliations I'd suffered.

"Ladies' room," I whispered to Alex. He and Dana slid out of the booth so I could make my exit, which was surprisingly graceful, considering. Once in the ladies' room I tore through the powder room to the toilets. Thank God I was alone.

There is something consoling about sitting on the toilet with the door locked. Wonderfully private. I wished I could stay indefinitely. Spending another night next to Sadie was unbearable. At least she was leaving for Cincinnati in two days. I almost wished she'd die and I'd never have to see her again. Horrible thoughts. I'd loved it when Dana blew smoke in her face. Why couldn't she be more like Dana? Like Dana? My God, had I forgotten this was the woman who treated her eldest son, my fiancé, like a lover, and abandoned her kids to run off and have affairs, and paraded her boyfriends in front of her ten-year-old daughter? ...*As long as you approve of me*... Dammit! How could I? She was a terrible influence on Alex, on everyone, including me, but, oh shit! How could I judge her when she had been so good to me, trusted me, said I was *people*?

The door to the bathroom creaked open. Somebody entered the next stall. Chanel. Alligator shoes. Dana! To be thinking such intimate thoughts about a person and then she's peeing next door... I rushed out. Didn't even wash my hands.

I stopped midway to the door. She must have known I was next to her. I couldn't just leave. The least I could do was thank her for what she'd said. No matter how I felt about her as a mother, she was my friend.

A large gilt-framed mirror ran the length of a long marble counter with tissues, hand lotion, and a small dish for tips. I sat on a vanity chair covered in peach velvet that matched the flocked wallpaper, imagining Dana beside me. Two women exchanging pleasantries while applying makeup in front of a gilded mirror.

I had just covered my top lip with Fire and Ice, when she entered the powder room. I smiled in the mirror as she approached. She smiled back, sat in the next chair, and removed a gold compact from her purse.

"Thanks for saying what you did at dinner." My voice was thick with emotion. I rubbed my lips together and blotted them on a Kleenex. "To my mother, I mean. I was," I let out my breath, "I was so humiliated by what she said. I'm sorry for putting you through this."

"She doesn't want to lose you," Dana said, powdering her nose, her face impassive.

"Really? She has a funny way of showing it." I got out my comb and teased my hair.

"You're all she's got."

Wow. That took class! Defending Sadie when she knew Sadie wouldn't do the same for her. And she was probably right. Yes, Sadie had pushed me to find a husband, but when it came right down to it she didn't want me to leave her. And though she denied it, she knew we wouldn't be staying in Las Vegas forever. I stared in the mirror as Dana applied lipstick, a frosted orange that blended brilliantly with her rust suit. Her hand trembled.

"It must be hard, spending practically your whole life raising children just to see them leave," I said. "I don't understand why women do it."

She blotted her lips on a tissue, crumpled it, turned slowly toward me. "There's nothing like the love you feel for a child." Her eyes filled. "Especially your firstborn."

I felt Dana's pain like a knot in my chest. I handed her the tissue box.

She dabbed at her eyes. "Forgive me."

I touched her shoulder. "It's fine. Really."

The door swung open. Dana turned her face to the wall. I half expected Sadie to barge in, but it was a young woman with a little girl in a starched pinafore. The child kept pulling away. Her mother had to drag her along, screaming. I felt a strong connection with the little girl. Even at her age, she was practicing to leave her mother.

Dana powdered underneath her eyes where her mascara had smudged, her hand still trembling. I got out my comb again.

Dana touched up her bottom lashes with mascara. "Alex can be difficult. Of course, he's an artist, but it's not just that." She put away her mascara and turned to me. The faint lines on her forehead deepened. "Maybe if our lives had been less hectic, he wouldn't have to…" She seemed to be searching.

The bathroom door opened. The little girl noticed the hand lotion on the counter and asked to use it, but her mother guided her firmly toward the door. If only they hadn't come in. Dana had been on the verge of confiding something, but the moment had passed. She gathered her comb, lipstick and compact.

"You were saying, about Alex, he…"

"We'd better go." She rose, smiling as if we'd been talking about the weather.

I got up, shaken. She touched my cheek. "Dear, sweet Beckett," she said, a far-off look in her eyes, "so kind and forgiving."

Suddenly we were embracing, both of us clutching our purses in one hand. It looked charming in the mirror, but I had the same uneasy feeling I'd had when Alex said I was the least demanding woman he knew.

On the way back to the table, Dana slipped her arm around my waist. Sadie drank us in like cyanide. As we settled into the booth, Alex was asking Izzy about Bugsy Siegel and the Flamingo. They seemed to be hitting it off. Izzy was actually responding in sentences rather than monosyllables. Sadie wasn't butting in for a change. The waitress had left the bill on a little brown tray in the center of the table. Izzy took it and began checking for mistakes, the way he always did at restaurants.

"Why don't we just split it down the middle?" Dana took out her wallet.

I caught Sadie's eye. She scowled. The cocktail waitress collected the martini glasses. Her beauty mark had worn off.

"It's on me," Izzy said, warding off Dana's money with his hand.

"Don't be such a big shot. Take it," Sadie said, grabbing his hand in midair.

"I insist." Dana handed him a ten.

Sadie frowned. Ten wasn't enough for her?

"We should be going," Dana said, finishing her coffee. "Alex has to get up early and I have to work the night shift. Let's do this again sometime, after Sadie gets back."

My heart fluttered wildly. I wasn't ready for them to leave. I'd pictured a prolonged good-bye on the sidewalk.

"See you after your mom leaves," Alex whispered in my ear, his hand hiding his face as his tongue traced my earlobe. I shivered with pleasure, scooting out to let him by. We kissed cheeks.

"Good-bye, Becky darling." I met Dana halfway as we kissed, very lightly so as not to leave lipstick.

I climbed back in the booth. Izzy and Sadie remained glued to their seats. "So glad we had a chance to meet," Dana said, shaking hands with Izzy.

"At least we got a good look at each other before the wedding," Sadie said, squishing poor Izzy to shake hands with Dana and then Alex.

They smiled back at me as they left. It was all I could do to keep from running after them.

"They drink a lot, the gentiles," Sadie said, when they were out of earshot.

I slapped her with my eyes. The waitress fetched the bill.

"Keep the change." Izzy took a Golden Nugget matchbook from an ashtray and began flossing his teeth with the cover.

Sadie didn't seem to be in a hurry to leave, either. She lay back against the booth and closed her eyes.

"So what did you think of Alex, Dad?" I leaned forward, smiling.

He tossed the matches back on the table and shrugged. "Looks just like his mother."

37.

Izzy switched on the TV to catch the end of *77 Sunset Strip*. Sadie dropped her purse and plopped on the couch. I headed for the bedroom.

"What's the matter? Can't stand to be in the same room? I'm leaving Sunday. The plane could crash."

"I'm tired." I closed the bedroom door and collapsed on the bed. The door flew open.

"After the way you treated me at the restaurant," she said, sticking out her chin, "I should be the one who's mad." She slammed the door behind her.

I sat up, staring in disbelief. "What are you talking about?"

She clutched at her pearls. "You made me feel like a frump."

Oh, God! This was all about her fucking vanity. "Jesus, Mother!"

"You acted like you wished she was your mother instead of me."

"Why wouldn't I?" I stood. "You treated me like I was a two-year-old. 'She doesn't make her bed, she can't keep a job, she...'"

"Who the hell does she think she is?" she paced, waving her arms. "My family wouldn't spit on her. Cocktail waitress. The lowest of the low."

"Your family came from Russia without a cent to their name. Hers lost their fortune in the Depression, so how dare you say they're not good enough. Your husband has a record, remember? You're just jealous because she's young, and better-looking, and she's doing something with her life."

"What's so wonderful about her life? All those men, and she drinks like a fish."

"At least she loved the men she married."

She shoved me toward the door. I banged my ankle against her suitcase. The pain shot up my leg.

"Go on!" She shoved me again. "Get out! Go live with her!"

"I wish I did live with her. You say you love me, but all you do is criticize." The minute I said *criticize* my eyes filled. I turned away.

"What do you want me to do? Lie?"

Her words cut into me. I faced her. "I know what you were doing at dinner. You were trying to scare him away. You don't care about my happiness. All you care about is yourself. Goddamit, I hope you stay in Cincinnati! I hope you never come back!"

She turned ghostly pale. *Don't apologize, even if she has a gall-bladder attack.* She went to her side of the dresser and opened the top drawer, flinging gloves, scarves, nylons on the bed, everything she hadn't already packed for her trip. Slammed the drawer, opened the next. A perfume bottle rolled off the dresser without its cap. The room smelled of Tweed.

"It would serve you right if I stayed in Cincinnati. You and your father." Father, as if it were a dirty word.

"Don't you dare criticize him!"

"You deserve each other!"

"He believes in me! You don't."

"I should have moved a long time ago!"

Bras, slips, girdles flew. She grabbed her biggest

suitcase from the closet, slammed it on the bed, stuffed it with dresses, hangers and all.

"You think we'll fall apart without you, but we won't."

Sadie froze. Her chin quivered. "At least in Cincinnati they appreciate me. In Cincinnati, I'm some-body."

Most of her lipstick had worn away. Her mouth was lined with tiny red stitches. She looked so small. Small, and sick, and old. She finished packing her suitcase, snapped it shut, dragged it off the bed, taking part of the bedspread. It hit the rug with a thud. She'd left a girdle in the middle of the bed, the kind with thick elastic around the top and garters dangling.

"I'll come back for the wedding."

Her voice broke on wedding. I could see her, huddled in a corner at the back of the temple, a black shawl over her head. The uninvited guest. A tear trickled down my cheek.

"Mom?" My voice, so young it startled me. "I didn't mean it... about wishing she was my mother." I stared at the girdle. It sucked my breath away. "I'm sorry I said it. Don't stay in Cincinnati. Please? I want you to come home."

"I've already packed the big suitcase."

"I'll unpack it for you after you leave. Don't worry. I'll put everything away. I love you, Mom."

She bent down and retrieved her nightgown from the suitcase.

The clock radio said 5:37 A.M.

"Becky? You awake?"

"Woke up about an hour ago. Couldn't go back to sleep."

"I haven't slept at all."

"Jesus, Mom. I apologized. What more do you want?"

"I was thinking about what you said. How I embarrassed you. I don't know why I said those things. Maybe you're right. Maybe I really don't want you to leave."

"It's okay, Mom. Dana told me she's having a hard time with it, too. I guess it's part of being a mother." I paused before adding, "You're just a bit more extreme than most."

She was silent. Probably mad about the postscript, and for mentioning Dana.

"It's hard to be a good mother."

"Don't worry about it, Mom. I understand. Go to sleep."

"In case something happens, Sunday, with the plane, there's something—something I should tell you."

"Oh, Mom. Nothing's going to happen."

"I know. But just in case. It's not a big deal, now that you're getting married. I just want to get it off my chest."

"Go on." I yawned. "Is it about my dad?"

"No. It's about your former boyfriend."

"Former boy-?" I sat up, wide-awake. "Joey?"

"You got a letter."

"A letter? When? Where is it?"

"I—I don't have it."

"What do you mean? Jesus! You didn't read it, did you?" The Kotex box. My letters. Queasy feelings in my gut. "Where is it? Give it to me."

"Lower your voice."

"Give me my letter!"

"Shhh. You'll wake your father."

I got up and turned on the light. "Why in hell didn't you give it to me when it came?"

She was sitting up in bed, wild-eyed. "I did what any mother would do. Someday you'll understand."

"What are you talking about?"

"I burned it."

"You did what?" She was lying. It was all over her face. She just didn't want me to look for it. "Oh, Jesus. Joey's letter. Oh, my God, Mother." I bumped into the dresser, walls, holding my aching, angry head. "Why did you keep it from me?"

"I didn't want you getting confused."

"You did a terrible thing."

"I did the right thing. He was bad news. His kind never holds a job. You'd end up supporting him, you who can't even type. I didn't want you changing your mind."

"Oh, Mom." My knees gave in. I sat on the bed; hot, angry tears. "Oh, Mom. How could you?"

"I did it to protect my daughter. I'm proud of it. He was worse than I thought. You were an angel next to him."

I spun around. "What in God's name?"

"You said he was so principled and moral. He wouldn't do this, he wouldn't do that. I knew better."

"What are you saying? Did you read it? Did you read my letter?"

"I did what I had to do."

"Oh, Joey." I rocked, arms folded across my stomach. Gasping. "Oh, boy." Sucking in air. "Oh, God."

"I'm glad it's out in the open. Now we can let sleeping dogs lie."

"Oh, no. No we can't." My chest, so tight I could hardly breathe. "I'll never forgive you."

"He's the one you shouldn't forgive. He lied. He told you he was giving up his career for his principles. He didn't give up a damn thing."

"What do you mean lied—are you saying he never left—he never went to Spain?" Jesus! Now, it made sense. That night Sadie grilled me—*which one is it, Joey or Alex?*—and when I said Alex, *We could do a lot worse*. She knew that Joey didn't go to Spain. She didn't want me running off with him, so she settled for Alex. She had no right to decide for me! I got up, started for the door. Remembered my nightie. Threw on my coat.

"Where are you going in the middle of the night?"

"It's morning." I sat on the floor. "I have to get away from you." Put on my shoes. "So I can breathe."

"You're crazy. Come back to bed."

Her purse was where she'd left it, by the couch. I opened it, felt for her car keys.

"What are you doing with my pocketbook?" She stood outside the bedroom door, Joey's letter in her hand. Did she really think she could bribe me?

"What does it look like?" I jingled the keys. Threw her purse on the couch.

She came toward me with the letter. "Here."

My hand froze in mid-air. I felt incredibly stirred up at the thought of seeing Joey again. I thought of Alex. How much he needed me. "You can't bribe me, Mother. I'm getting married, remember? I don't want to read it."

Her jaw dropped.

I started for the door.

"You can't have the car. Your father... how will I take him to work?" She blocked the door.

"I'll be back by then."

"You're not leaving."

"Get out of the way, Mother." I grabbed the knob. She held my wrist. "Let me go!"

"Shuddup!" Izzy stood outside his room, hands

in the air. "What's the matter with you?"

"Go back to bed, Plotnik."

Distracted, Sadie let go. I pushed past her. Cold wind whipped my face. Grasping my unbuttoned coat, I started down the stairs. Sadie followed, sideways, holding the rail with both hands, still clutching the letter. "Come back!" Her nightcap fell off. She might as well have been naked in her thin nightgown, her pathetic terry-cloth slippers.

"Mom! What are you doing? Go back inside. The neighbors. Oh, God! Oh Jesus!"

Second stair from the bottom, she grabbed my coat sleeve, dropping Joey's letter. "Come back in the house."

"No!" I pulled away from her, backed down the cement walk that led to the neighbors' apartment.

"What did I do that was so wrong?" She came after me, arms everywhere. "I tried to protect you. Is that a sin?"

"Leave me alone." My arms kept us apart.

"What kind of a sin is that? I didn't want you to get hurt."

I kept backing away. "Let me go, Mom. Please, please, let me go."

"When you were little, and wanted to run in the street..."

"I'm not a child!" I brushed her arms off me. "I don't need you anymore. Jesus!"

"I didn't want you to end up like me." Her teeth were chattering. "That's the worst thing for a mother." Her nose was running. "To see her baby make the same mistakes."

"Oh, God. You're shivering." I opened my coat, trying to cover her. "Look at you!" Out of the corner of my eye, the neighbors, peering through their curtains.

She touched my face. "You were such a beautiful child. A movie star. Everybody loved you." We held each other. "But then, they broke your heart."

"It's okay, Mom."

"All the relatives, they said, 'What happened? She used to be so pretty.'"

"It's okay."

"And I said, 'she's still pretty,' but they wouldn't listen."

"I'm a lot older, Mom. I can handle it."

"It's not that I don't think you're talented. I saw what it did to you. I don't want you to get hurt like that again."

"I know." I patted her back. "I know." We rocked back and forth, sobbing.

"Everything I did was for you."

After Sadie was asleep, I crept outside, retrieved Joey's letter, and hid it in the Kotex box on the closet shelf. Better not to read it until after the wedding. Less confusing. Anyway, I was too exhausted to deal with it.

38.

Saturday, I did everything I could to avoid being around Sadie. I convinced her to drop me off at the University library when she took Izzy to work, and spent all day working on my term paper. The more I thought about the pre-nuptial dinner debacle and it's B-movie aftermath, the more I looked forward to her leaving. Maybe that was why she was in such a bad mood on the morning of her flight. She knew damn well she wouldn't be missed.

Izzy and I packed the car. He loaded her winter coat and regular suitcase. I took her extra pocketbooks and the little blue overnight case she'd bought with Green Stamps. When Izzy asked about the big suitcase by the bedroom closet she looked at me.

Maybe I was fed up with her craziness, but that didn't mean I wanted her to stay in Cincinnati. "You don't need it, Mom," I smiled, "it's only two weeks."

"Leave it," she told him.

On the way to the airport, Sadie reminded us she had stocked the freezer with TV dinners. "I don't expect perfection. All I want is for you to clean up after yourselves. I don't want to come home to a mess after surgery."

Izzy turned on the radio for the first time in years. A mixed chorus sang, *KLAS, LasVegas, with studios at Wilbur Clark's Deh-eh-zert Inn*, followed by a weather report.

"Great weather for flying, Mom."

There were only about a dozen people checking in at TWA. As usual, I wondered why the airport was so small—and uninspiring. With slot machines filling in the gaps between the basics, it looked like a casino in disguise. The nicest feature was a coffee shop-dining area at the far end, where you could watch planes take off. While Sadie checked in, Izzy and I went to the magazine stand. He bought her <u>Life</u> magazine and a pack of Wrigley's spearmint gum.

"For the trip," he said, holding out the magazine.

She responded with a cold stare. Any other time he would have sulked off to the slots.

"C'mon" he jerked his head. "Let's have coffee."

"Don't want any," Sadie said, but she tagged along.

We chose a table next to the windows with a ringside view. The tablecloth was white linen, with matching napkins. A touch of elegance. I settled back in my chair, pretending I was flying to New York with Alex. Izzy ordered two coffee regulars.

"Maybe I'll have some of yours," Sadie said to me, instructing the waitress to bring her some half-and-half.

"Why are you nervous?" The little lights in Izzy's eyes danced. "It's safer than a car."

"Yeah, Mom. Nobody crashes these days, especially TWA."

"It's not just the plane." She drew an arc with her chin, and froze for effect. "In case you forgot, I'm having an operation."

"Ehh," Izzy said, waving his hand, "you'll be fine."

Sadie hissed and waved hers.

"C'mon, Mom. The other night, when Uncle Jake called, he said it was routine, and not to worry." I attempted to hold hands.

She moved hers away and began picking at a chip in her nail. The waitress brought our coffee and a saucer of plastic cream cups.

Sadie stared at the planes. "I'll call after I get in," she said, without looking at us. "Don't call me. It's too much money."

"I'm working." I blew on my coffee. "I'll pay for it." My voice had more of an edge than I'd intended.

"Save your money," Sadie said, in that flat, mean way of hers. "You'll need it after you get married."

I started to say I'd call if I felt like it, but Izzy wrinkled his nose and winked. I winked back. We were a team. We didn't have to wait to go to a dinner show, we could do it tonight. I'd dress up. Might even talk him into dancing, the way we used to when I was little. Me, with a big pink bow in my hair, watching my Mary Janes while Izzy pumped my arm to the music. *The bells are ringing, for me and my gal*… Even at that age I knew he'd rather be off with his cronies in the casino. But we were adults now. We could be friends.

The waitress refilled our coffee.

"Want some, Mom?" I pushed the cup toward her.

"A little." She added cream just as her flight was announced.

I felt a twinge of guilt. Izzy, too. Saw it in his eyes. Sadie spilled her coffee as we got up. A big brown stain on white linen.

It was chilly out. There were fifty or so passengers milling around the plane. They weren't saying good-bye to anybody. Tourists. My teeth chattered as Izzy kissed Sadie's cheek. The steward took her heavy coat.

"Take it easy, toots," Izzy yelled above the roar of the engines. He patted the shoulder of her jacket.

Sadie's eyes bored into him as if she were remembering every cent he'd lost the past twenty years. "Behave yourself."

"Don't worry," he said, dismissing her with a wave of his hand.

"Bye, Mom." I kissed her quickly, so we wouldn't hold up the line, patting her shoulder where Izzy had. "We'll be fine."

There was panic in her eyes. She grabbed my arm, looking at Izzy, standing off by himself near the wing. "I shouldn't be doing this," she yelled at the steward and the woman passenger whose way she was blocking. "Why did I let them talk me into it?"

The woman pushed ahead angrily, as did the other passengers. The steward shrugged, waiting for a signal from me.

"She's nervous," I yelled. "Go on, Mom." I spoke right into her ear, taking her hand from my shoulder and holding it. "Nothing's going to happen. It's only two weeks."

The steward gave me a knowing look and took her arm. "Come on, now, Mrs...?"

"Plotnik," I shouted, as he guided her up the steps.

She kept glancing back at me and Izzy, who was swaying back and forth with his head bowed, as if he were praying in temple.

"For a minute I thought she was going to change her mind," I said, as we cut through the desert to the parking lot in front of the airport. He walked so fast I had to run to keep up. "Didn't you?"

The wind blew dust in my eyes. I clutched my

sweater with one hand, shielding my face with the other. It would have been easier to go through the building, but he'd chosen not to. Maybe he thought we should suffer for sending her away.

"Nah." He zipped his windbreaker, tucking his hands under his armpits. "I knew she'd go."

"I think she's afraid we won't be able to get along without her."

"Yeah."

"Where does she get all those crazy ideas?"

"Beats me."

We reached the parking lot. There was nothing but desert around us. The middle of nowhere, as Sadie would say. Izzy unlocked the car. Sadie's seat smelled like White Shoulders and Spraynet.

"Hard to believe she's gone." I warmed my hands between the legs of my corduroy pants.

Izzy's lips twitched. He turned left on Paradise Road. It felt like a first date when you're searching for things to talk about while he's driving.

"Two whole weeks!"

It was tacky to show so much enthusiasm, but I knew he felt the same. Why wouldn't he talk? I'd thought it would be different, especially after the night when we'd reminisced about floorshows and Shirley Temples. And last night, when he'd defended me. The silence made me nervous. Maybe that was why Sadie babbled incessantly. I didn't want to be like her. We drove past the university. I saw the library, the building where class met. I imagined Alex on the balcony in his black turtleneck.

"I'm going downtown for a while," Izzy said. "You take the car."

"Sure."

I wondered if he'd heard the hurt in my voice.

Probably not. He was never going to be a father. Not that I'd expected him to spend the whole day with me, but he could have put off gambling an hour or two. Stop judging. He's celebrating his freedom. It has nothing to do with you. He's so used to getting the cold-shoulder from Sadie, he doesn't expect affection from anybody.

"I've been meaning to thank you for standing up for me at dinner. It meant a lot. I know I always took her side when I was a kid, about the gambling, I mean. But now that I'm older I can see it was more complicated."

His lips pressed and relaxed.

"Gambling was all you had, especially after I came along. I got all her attention. It was natural for you to resent me. But now I'd like us to be close." I moved closer. "Why don't we go out to dinner tonight—and a show?"

His eyebrows went up.

"Remember, we talked about it? That night when Mom was out playing canasta? Me treating you to a dinner show the way you used to take me? First night on our own, we should celebrate, don't you think?"

He wrinkled his nose. "It's too much money. I'll pay."

"Oh, no. It's my turn. There's nobody I'd rather be with tonight than you, Dad. Not even Alex. I mean it."

He blushed, from head to chin.

"So, how's about it?"

His head bobbed up and down. It wasn't yes; more like maybe.

"Last time I remember doing something without her was at the Grand Canyon when I was eight and you took me to the coffee shop at the lodge for BLTs. If she'd known we were eating bacon she'd have died."

He smiled. "Best sandwich in the world's a BLT Club."

"Nothing like a BLT," I said.

We turned onto Flamingo Road. He sniffed, made clicking sounds in his throat. I read the Flamingo marquee.

"Tony Martin and Cyd Charisse. You like them, don't you? Why don't I make reservations?"

"Save your money for a rainy day." He made a right onto the Strip.

Boundaries. Lines. "Okay, Dad. If you insist on paying, fine—the important thing is being together. It'll be a chance for us to get to know each other. As adults. There's so much I've been dying to ask you. About Russia and coming to America in the early 1900's. You were only ten, right? It must have been hard. How did you meet all those gangsters? Dutch Schultz, Meyer Lansky, Benny? My own father, and I know so little about you."

We drove past the Desert Inn. On the other side of the street, the Silver Slipper sign tilted up and down. They'd replaced the missing lights in the shoe.

"You know, Dad, I'm glad I grew up here." I said it to bring us closer.

It worked. Izzy smiled, wrinkling his chin. In a way, I really was glad. I might have been happier growing up somewhere else, but it sure wouldn't have been as colorful. Or as unique. Milligan was right about that.

We stopped at the light across from Wolfie's Deli. I liked their Monte Cristo sandwiches better than BLTs, but I'd never tell him.

"I mean it. If it hadn't been for you I'd probably have grown up someplace boring, like Cincinnati."

"Cincy ain't so bad."

"Oh, come on, Dad. It's so conservative. I could never live there."

Izzy stopped at a red light by Sill's Drive-In.

"Wow. Sill's is practically empty. In high school, you could never get a parking space, especially on weekends. Everybody hung out there. Eating burgers in their parents' cars. Or making out in the back seat. Don't worry. I was a good girl."

Izzy turned off the car heater, rolled his window halfway down. "I met Sadie in Cincy. She was just a kid, but she had class."

I remembered a black-and-white photo of Sadie in her teens, her sultry Theda Bara eyes. Middy-blouse. Bobbed hair. Bangs.

"Did you ever think you'd marry her?"

He made a left on First Street. "Nah. Never thought she'd get mixed up with somebody like me. She was too respectable."

"How long did it take you to change her mind?"

"Fifteen, twenty years. She came to California on a trip. Looked me up. She was in her thirties. I was working at a track near San Diego doing some jobs for Benny across the border. I showed her a good time."

"So you swept her off her feet."

"Nah. She just wasn't so picky no more."

He'd never thought he was good enough. Sad. We drove past the Union Hotel, where Sadie claimed Flossie Sedway's husband had had a tootsie when he was supposed to be playing cards. Open window, third floor. Torn curtain, fluttering in the wind. What a hole, as Sadie would say.

"If you had it to do again, would you have married her?"

I surprised myself. Such an intimate question. If he minded, it didn't show.

"She was quite a dish, your mother." He sucked his bottom lip. "We had some good times. It all went to hell when Benny got knocked off." It broke my heart to see the pain on his face. "Everything went to hell."

He pulled the car over near the Hotel Sal Sagev sign. Growing up, I'd seen it a million times. Until I read an article in <u>Colliers</u>, I'd never realized it was Las Vegas spelled backwards.

"Should I pick you up here," I asked, "or somewhere else?"

"Nah. I'll take the bus."

"Why should you take the bus? I'm not doing anything."

"It's too much trouble." He opened the door.

"Trouble! You don't know how much I'm looking forward to this."

He looked back at me, then quickly shifted his gaze to the dashboard.

"I love you, Dad." My heart was beating as if I'd had ten cups of coffee. I touched his hand. It jumped, but didn't move. "I want us to make up for lost time. I'm getting married. Moving away. If we don't do it now, we might never have another chance."

He nodded without looking at me.

"And tonight's just the beginning. We've got two whole weeks."

"Yeah. We'll have a good time." He slipped his hand away and touched my shoulder. "Gotta go, honey. See you later."

"What time will you be home?"

He was halfway out of the car.

"Seven? Seven-thirty?"

"Yeah. Seven-thirty." He closed the door.

"The show's not 'till eight. We'll have plenty of time."

"Yeah." He wrinkled his nose and winked. I moved to the driver's seat and watched him walk down Fremont and disappear into the California Club.

With Sadie gone I felt like a stranger in the apartment. Things stood out like I'd never seen them. The knickknacks from our house on North Ninth, when Sadie decorated in Chinese Modern; the plastic covers on the cream-colored brocade couch and chairs she'd bought when we moved; the heavy ornate lamps on the end tables; the small square table near the TV with Izzy's special drawer full of souvenirs and candy. All the furniture had been bought with gambling winnings. There was a crystal vase on the coffee table. I'd given it to Sadie for her birthday when I was in high school. It was the only thing she hadn't thrown at Izzy.

I tossed my sweater and purse on the couch and went to the kitchen. Sadie had left an open package of Lorna Doones on the counter. I bit into one, then spat in the garbage. No food until dinner. I had to be beautiful for my dad.

I woke up to the phone. Six o'clock. Must have fallen asleep on the couch reading <u>Middlemarch</u>. It rang and rang. Sadie. Nobody else would be that persistent.

"Hi, Mom... How was the plane? ...Yes, I'll change our sheets before you get home... Yes, I'll do the dishes... He went out for orange juice... I know it costs too much for me to call you. You already told me. I'll wait for you to call. Tuesday night, after surgery. Love you."

It was almost time for Izzy to come home. I hurried to the bedroom. Sadie's killer girdle glared at me from her open suitcase. I snapped the lid and kicked it out of the way.

I decided to give the black sweater and skirt I'd worn with Milton Sweet another chance. Red lipstick, lots of mascara. A half-hour later I was still in my slip. It had taken all that time to do my nails and hair. "Please, don't come early," I said, pulling my sweater on. Had to do my bangs over.

I curled my eyelashes, applied two coats of mascara, checked my teeth for lipstick and put on my highest heels. They hurt right away. One must suffer to be beautiful, as Sadie would say. Seven-thirty. He was late, thank God. I dabbed Chanel behind my ears and at my wrists, having read somewhere that pulse points were the best place to put perfume, packed my purse with lipstick, eye shadow, eyebrow pencil, took out my black coat, stuffed Kleenex in the pockets. Seven-forty-five. In three minutes we'd be late. I looked out the window. No sign of him. Was he standing me up? Terrible feeling in the pit of my stomach. He wouldn't do that, would he? Not after I'd poured my heart out.

At eight o'clock I called the Flamingo. If we came while the dancers were on they'd still seat us, but not after Tony and Cyd made their entrance. Maybe I should meet him at the bus stop a block away?

Driving to the bus I realized I should have arranged to pick him up at the bus stop from the beginning. I could see the headlights as I pulled up to the corner. We could still make the show with five minutes to spare. I wouldn't blow up when I saw him, the way Sadie would. I'd wink and say, "Get in." The bus stopped. A woman with a bag of groceries stepped out.

Shit! The next bus wasn't due for twenty minutes. Damn him and his stupid gambling! I turned the car around. Why was I crying? He wasn't worth it. He'd probably call with some lame excuse. I'd let him have it. He was my father. Why couldn't he act like it? I wiped my nose on my sleeve. No wonder Sadie threw things. I felt like doing it, too. He probably wouldn't have the guts to call. He'd come sneaking home in the middle of the night, expecting me to be asleep, but I'd yell and scream. Loud enough to wake the dead, as Sadie would say. I ran over the curb when I parked, slammed the car door. Mrs. Reilly from downstairs poked her head through the curtains. Mind your own business.

"Damn him!" I kicked off my shoes, threw my coat on the floor. "He said he was coming home. He lied!" My throat burned from screaming. I stormed around the room. "C'mon, Beck. Laugh it off. He's just your father. What if he were your husband? He must have stood Sadie up a million times to your one. But she didn't love him, and you did. She'd be on her way downtown by now, trying to stop him before he lost the rent money."

I ran to the bathroom for Kleenex. Mascara and green eyeshadow smudged around my eyes, loose eyelashes hanging down like stalactites. I'd spent a goddam hour putting on makeup, only to be thrown over for a lousy poker game.

39.

There's this movie with Sinatra, *The Man With the Golden Arm*. He's a jazz musician, fresh out of prison, trying to go straight, but his invalid wife, Eleanor Parker, tears him down. He goes back to dealing poker to pay for heroin, but Kim Novak falls in love with him and helps him kick the habit once and for all. I could see Izzy as the dope addict, Sadie as the sadistic wife, but I wasn't sure I had what it takes to be Kim Novak. In a way, she had it easy. All she had to do was lock him in a room and stay with him while he went through withdrawal. It's harder with a gambler. You have to convince him he's a winner, even if he's old and broke, his wife treats him like garbage, and the only job he can get is the lowest of the low. But first you have to convince yourself that love is a bigger draw than money.

Before I left the apartment I changed to flats and stuffed my coat pockets with Hershey's Kisses. My legs look better with heels, but I didn't want to deal with sore feet on top of everything else. As I drove, I remembered being ten and seeing Izzy playing cards with a bunch of half-dead gamblers in the back of a smoky casino. It was summer. I'd been standing outside the Savoy, waiting for Sadie. Hot. Lonely. I went in. A man in a green apron steered me toward the door.

"No minors allowed."

On my way out I looked back and saw Sadie

bending over Izzy. "You sonofabitch!" She smacked him in the head with her purse. I waited outside, refusing to cry until a woman with a New York accent asked if I were lost.

Twelve years later, I was in Sadie's role. I had no intention of playing it the way she had. I wouldn't speak when I found him. I'd say it all with my face. If he refused to budge, I'd pull up a chair. Not too close. Izzy had often said women were bad luck at card games. When the game broke up, I'd go over to him, smiling at his friends like I approved, and was just there to give him a ride. I'd touch his shoulder. "Let's go, Dad." In the car, I'd tell him I'd been hurt when he stood me up, but I'd realized he couldn't help it. He didn't have to apologize or feel guilty. We'd have dinner another time. If he needed money to pay off a stack of I.O.U.s, I'd chip in. What's a daughter for? But he had to promise to stop gambling. Of course he couldn't go cold turkey. I'd understand that. We'd work on it together. Over time.

Holding the steering wheel with one hand, I tore the silver wrapper off a Hershey's Kiss and put it in my mouth, sucking my fingers clean. I turned left at Sill's Drive-In and made a right onto Main. It was dark and deserted until the Union Hotel, when I saw the lights from the casinos. I switched on the radio. The Four Aces singing *Shaboom, Shaboom* as if they didn't have a brain between them; Johnny Mathis crooning *Chances Are*; Patti Page recalling the night she lost her true love while dancing to the *Tennessee Waltz*. I switched it off. I was not going to cry over a stupid Patti Page song.

I made a right on Fremont. The neon stung my eyes. I knew from Sadie, Izzy's pattern was to go from casino to casino, especially when he was losing. Going through all of them could take all night. My stomach cringed as I drove past the Mint. I'd promised myself I'd never go in there again as long as I lived. I glimpsed the Horseshoe, where I'd lost my eight dollars. Izzy wouldn't be there. He'd always complained their cards were stacked against him. The Nugget was one of his favorite haunts. Billy Roberts worked there, which made me want to puke, but the night shift didn't start until eleven.

No spaces on Fremont. I turned at the Nugget; found one near Lucy's. I ate the rest of the candy. Hard to believe only twenty-four hours had passed since the prenuptial dinner. I'd been so preoccupied with Izzy I'd forgotten Alex. He'd probably be home from work. But I wouldn't call. This was between me and Izzy.

Once I left the car, I was cold, even in my coat. My goddam knees were shaking. This was crazy. Who did I think I was, Joan of Arc? Izzy would show up eventually. I reached in my pocket for the keys, but something inside me said *find him.*

If I'd parked on Fremont, I would have tried the California Club first, but the Nugget was right in front of me. Inside it resembled a saloon. All gilt and mahogany. Carved nudes. Dark, crowded, noisy. My stomach hurt. I walked through the slot machines to the tables. The dealers were young. They all reminded me of Billy. The air was thick with seduction and after shave.

"Looking for someone?"

A hand on my shoulder. A chill down my back. Shit! Billy wasn't supposed to be here. Not yet. His hand slid slowly down my arm. His breath was on my neck. He tugged at my sleeve. I turned, like an obedient child.

"Want to go for a drink?" His eyes toured my body. He still reminded me of James Dean. "I switched to the day shift. I'm off at ten."

His lips puckered in a kiss. A tease. A taunt. He was performing, for his buddies behind the green felt tables. I was just another piece of ass, come to the Nugget begging for more.

"Go fuck yourself." I flipped a bird at him. And at his friends.

His smile faded. I would have enjoyed it if I hadn't been shaking so hard. I hurried past smirks and stares and slot machines into the bright lights of the street, crossing Fremont against traffic and blaring horns. I couldn't go back. Not even for Izzy. The California Club was a block down on the other side of the street. I didn't know anybody there. I'd be invisible.

Izzy had worked at the California Club, but this was my first time inside. There was no attempt at decor. If the Nugget had cost a million, this joint must have cost a thousand. The customers were middle-aged. Depressed. A man in a wide-brimmed hat out of a '40s movie hit a jackpot. Didn't even crack a smile. Some of the employees looked familiar, like long-lost relatives. I probably recognized them from back when I was a kid, at Temple Beth Shalom.

There were three card games going on in the back. Lots of cigar smoke. No sign of Izzy, but I had a feeling the players were pals of his. They reminded me of the guys at Sammy's. Old-timers who'd been in Vegas forever. Maybe they could tell me where to find him. I didn't have the guts to interrupt. Nobody talked except to bet. The only sounds were cards being shuffled, chips moving across the tables, slot machines grinding from up front. Jesus, Beck, what are you afraid of? This isn't *Gunsmoke*. They won't plug you for lousing up a win. Worst they can do is tell you to beat it.

"Anybody here know Izzy Plotnik?"

Nobody said a word. I started to leave.

"You his daughter?" Asked a man in a pink fluorescent baseball cap, with a voice out of a Dristan commercial.

"Yeah. Know where he is? I'm supposed to pick him up."

I was amazed he knew about me. Maybe Izzy had bragged a little. "My daughter, she's a looker, college graduate." I smiled, though it gave me the creeps.

"Try the Nevada Club," a fat man with a cigar piped in from the middle table. "He likes the Nevada Club."

So much for being invisible. Like it or not, I was one of the family.

The Nevada Club was a couple doors down. I'd been there once to see a show. They had entertainment, if you could call it that. Strange offbeat performers you'd never see anywhere else—like a troupe of skinny male dancers in sequined bikinis who did the limbo five inches from the floor, and a three-hundred-pound man with a spoon who played show tunes on water glasses. This time, first thing I noticed about the casino was the smell. Perfume, hairspray, cigarettes. There were more women at the slot machines. Customers were younger. Soft, flattering lighting, more bar than casino. A cocktail waitress in a black turtleneck leotard and net stockings asked if I'd like a drink on the house. She was about my age, slim, pretty, long platinum-blonde hair. Made me think of Dana. I smiled. "No thanks."

My heart was beating harder, faster. I sensed Izzy was in the room. It didn't seem like his kind of place, but there was a lot I didn't know about him. I wandered through the slot machines, past the tables, taking in the faces, dodging customers with drinks in their hands, cocktail waitresses with empty trays.

You could usually see the floor show from the roulette tables. Tonight, too many people crowded behind the velvet ropes. I heard a piano. The audience was laughing. Somebody was singing, *A pretty girl, is like a melody*, in a raspy voice. Couldn't tell if it was a man or a woman. Close up, I realized the words had been changed. I couldn't hear well enough to understand the joke. I knew I should find Izzy and leave, but I was drawn to the show.

I noticed a gap in the crowd by the side entrance and moved in. There must have been fifty tables jammed right up to the platform where a singer was seated at a piano, backed up by a drummer, a bass, and an electric guitar. The piano was positioned so I could see her clearly. Her face, even her body, reminded me of a bulldog. Chartreuse eyelids, pomegranate cheeks, cherry lips, and orange hair. She was stuffed into an emerald-green satin gown, strapless, with a slit up the side. Never again would I think I had the worst legs in town. Shimmying to her feet, she kicked the piano bench to one side, grabbed the mike off the stand and barked: *A pretty girl is just like a pretty boy*... which brought down the house. I cheered. Great deadpan! She bowed, blew kisses, tried to leave. We begged for more. She resumed her position at the piano and launched into, *I Ain't Got No—Body*... I'd never seen a show, or an audience, like this. A few gorgeous women here and there, but everybody else was male. Beautiful young men, arms draped around each other; Brando imitators in leather; old men with menacing eyes and lascivious grins; flamboyant men in eyeshadow, shirts open to the navel, skintight pants. I was scared. Fascinated.

An old man sat near center stage under the

lights. He was right out of <u>Tales From the Crypt</u> comics—completely bald, blotchy skin. Thin black eyebrows that looked drawn on, bulging eyes. A gold cross rested on his chest, just above the V of his royal blue sweater. He wore rings on all of his long, thin fingers, drawing attention to his fingernails, so long, they curved down, like claws. Next to him, close to the stage, sat a young man whose face was turned toward the show, but his blond hair glowed like a halo. I shuddered as the old man kissed his long, elegant neck, licked his ear, traced his perfect cheekbone, ran his nasty fingers through his hair, put his arms around him, as if he owned him.

Why would he let a man like that touch him? Probably a male prostitute. Disgusting. The song ended. The young man reached for his drink. My God! He was so much like Alex they could have been brothers. The same arrogant eyebrows, bored blue eyes, thin mustache. The way his lips lingered on his glass. Just like Alex. I felt like I was falling. Down, down, into nothing. No! It's not Alex. It can't be Alex. We're getting married. I tried, but couldn't stop my eyes from staring. He must have felt them, must have known he was being watched, because he stood. Face pale. Horrified. His arm, reaching. Fingers, reaching.

"Beckett!"

I ran! Pushing, shoving.

"Beckett! Wait!"

I didn't look back. I would die if I saw him. I would die if he said anything to me, touched me. I pushed my way through the crowd on the sidewalk. A man with a lewd gap between his teeth leered from a doorway. I crossed the street. In front of the casinos, dealers in green aprons puckered their lips. Under the Mint sign, a woman who could have been Darlene, in a white blouse, black skirt, face thin, gaunt. Like a skull. I ran the other way, toward the railroad station; the sidewalk, a blur of lights, faces, sounds. Colors. The orange flame as Alex lit Dana's cigar, passing it from his mouth to hers. His sapphire eyes. *Don't worry, Beckett. He always comes back*... Dana, in the ladies' room at Lucy's, *If our lives had been less hectic he wouldn't have to*... You can fill in the blanks now, Beckett. Where he goes. What he does at night... *Dear, sweet Beckett. So kind, forgiving*...

"Beckett?" His hand on the back of my coat. I staggered deep into the crowd. People, cursing me. "Watch where you're going!" Didn't know where I was going. Crossed the street. Away from the lights. Down a side street with pink Keno tickets on the sidewalk... *He needs someone like you, Beckett. Someone he can count on*... Dizzy. Out of breath. I leaned against a door. Sammy's Race Book. Oh, Christ. Why here? Of all places, why here? Can't run anymore. Throat dry. Chest full of pins. No more running.

"Beckett?" He stood at the edge of the sidewalk, face flushed, breathing hard. Eyes, pleading. "Never meant you to see me with—never dreamed you'd—why were you...?"

"Father... I was looking for my father."

"Oh, Christ!" He came to me, took my hands.

I pulled them away. Covered my face. Both of us, breathing hard.

"Look, darling, I know how you must feel, but you're taking it too seriously." *Making love in his bed, my fallen angel, blond hair gleaming like a halo.* That man, that thing with claws, touching, kissing him. "That man doesn't have a thing to do with us." He stroked my hair. "He's just a silly old letch who likes to buy me things." The ring with an emerald at the point. "I was going to stop seeing him after we were married. Beckett? Why won't you look at me?" He took my hands down. Lifted my chin. I jerked it away. "I'm not a fag, if that's what you're thinking. That's it, isn't it? You think I'm a fag."

I shook my head.

"Believe me, I don't have a thing for dirty old men. It's strictly for money. I don't roll over for anybody." I gasped. "Poor darling, did I shock you?" A low, cynical laugh. "I keep forgetting how innocent you are."

I rolled my head against the door, side to side. "You lied to me." My whole body sobbed. "You lied."

He held my face. Made me look at him. "I lied because I didn't want to lose you." He didn't let go until I stopped shaking. He reached in his pocket for a cigarette. Lit a match with trembling fingers. "I didn't think you would want to know about my sordid little affairs. That's all they are, Becket. I fill their emptiness. They fill my pockets. And after a few drinks, it all seems like a bad dream." One eyebrow raised. "Told you from the beginning I was fucked up. You didn't believe me." He took a long drag on his cigarette and exhaled. We both watched the smoke disappear. "But I believed you." He gripped my shoulders. "Hey. You're my salvation, remember? I love you, Beckett. I really do."

The tears that streamed down my face were as much for Alex as they were for me. "I'm sorry, Alex. I can't save you." My voice, a whisper. "I can't save anybody. You're too far gone. Like my dad." I left the door, backing away from him.

He took my place at the door. Smoked. Eyes hurt. Lost. Angry. "Guess I overestimated you." He flicked ashes on the sidewalk.

"Yeah. Guess I'm just a bourgeois little Jewish

girl, after all."

40.

The door to Izzy's room was closed. Like him. Dirty fingerprints, smudges around the knob. Sadie cleaned ours with Ajax. I hadn't been in his room since she'd moved into mine. I needed something of him. Candy. I would eat his candy. But first I needed a drink. The Manischewitz, in the linen closet behind the sheets, hadn't been opened in years. I drank from the bottle, hoping the dust would kill me. I found a bag of peanut M&Ms in Izzy's special drawer by the TV. He didn't deserve them. I ate them outside his door, washing them down with wine.

I switched on the light. The room smelled of dirty socks, stale air. Blond wood night tables and dresser from our house on North Ninth; the big bed with its curved Art Deco headboard. I'd slept in that bed, next to her silky nightgown, long ago when I had nightmares. Holding her warm, soft hand, listening to him click his throat in his sleep, hating him for making Mommy cry when he stayed out all night, losing our money.

My insides knotted up, seeing his miserable, one-track, outcast life. Blue-and-white-striped pajamas, rumpled sheets, a torn chenille spread the color of face powder. On the rug, more pajamas, boxer shorts, black socks, undershirts, newspapers, racing forms.

Sadie told me I was wasting my time on him. Why didn't I listen? He didn't even want to have me.

Little girl with a pink bow, dancing with Daddy at the Flamingo. Daddy's heart belongs to the poker game in the back room. He doesn't have a soul. He sold it for money. Like Alex. I'd gone out of my way to find somebody different from Izzy and ended up with someone just like him. I held myself to keep from screaming. I had to sit on the bed. The dirty, contaminated bed.

The table to the right of the bed had pennies on top; an empty, soft plastic eyeglass case with Prudential Insurance in gold letters; half a roll of lifesavers. Pineapple was next in line, or I'd have eaten it. Inside the drawer, loose change, a folded piece of paper, probably an IOU; souvenir nail clippers, matches, money clips, a Golden Nugget lead pencil, cleaning powder for false teeth, hard candy. I popped a few lemon balls in my mouth. Dropped the wrappers on the beige carpet.

I went to the table on the other side. It had a pair of shorts on top; inside out so I could see the stain. I hated him for that. For being a slob. I opened the drawer. Took a Cadbury bar with hazelnuts and a bag of M&Ms. I ate the Cadbury bar first. Then the M&Ms. One by one. Drank more wine. It backed up in my throat. I spat it on the spread. Izzy and Alex. I'd thought they had nothing in common, but I was wrong. They were both addicted to money. "Damn them!" I screamed at the white walls without pictures. "Damn them both!" I screamed, cried, threw Izzy's shoes and dirty clothes at the wall, just like her. Just like Sadie. I am Sadie. Oh, Christ! I needed more candy. Where would he hide it?

I slid open the closet door. Clothes piled high in a corner. Old shirts. Filthy underwear. Kicked it. My shoe touched something hard. I moved the clothes away with my foot. Cigar boxes. Stacks of cigar boxes.

Garcia Y Vegas. Spanish dancer. Red lips. Izzy didn't smoke. I opened one on top. Silver dollars. Ten, twenty, maybe thirty boxes of silver dollars. Izzy'd always said silver would be worth a fortune when they stopped making it. Sadie'd called it a pipe dream. My God! I'd found his nest egg. His savings account. Hidden from her, like my Kotex box, but all I had was letters. Hundreds of sliver dollars, probably worth a fortune. He had watched her scrimp and save and borrow, with all that money in the closet. But he wasn't saving for a rainy day. Not him. He'd gamble it away at some casino. I shoved the door so hard it came off the track.

I turned on the water and poured in Joy liquid detergent. More bubbles than any other brand. Scooted down in the tub. Disappeared in a million bubbles. Natalie Wood went crazy in the bathtub in *Splendor in the Grass*. Tried to drown herself, but they put her away. People like me don't commit suicide; we would rather suffer. First time I'd been able to take a bath without Sadie banging on the door. Almost missed her. The mother I treated like shit. Only person who really cared. Poor Mom. Now I knew how it felt to be a gambler's wife. I leaned over the side of the tub. Grabbed the wine. Let it dribble down my chin as I drank. If I'd married Alex, I might have ended up bitter, angry, empty. Alone. Like her.

It's not your fault, Alex. None of it is your fault. It's mine. I made it happen. You warned me. I wouldn't listen. But you listened. I'm sorry, Alex. So sorry. Never should have offered hope where there was none. Never should have promised I'd be there... no... matter... what.

I turned on the Hot full blast. Sweat poured down my face. Good-bye Alex. I've burned all that was left of you out of me. All but a tight little knot of pain. I pulled the plug. Let some of the water drain out. Let the drain suck my fingers. Another man down the drain. New York City down the drain.

Joey! Forgot all about him. About the letter. Maybe… No! Can't go running back to Joey just because Alex didn't work out. Can't use him, like Sadie used Izzy. Broke up with him twice already. Three times you're out. Plus there's the money, Beck. He has it; you don't. You'd be a leech. Joey's not an option. Joey's a dream. Plotnik & Goldman. An impossible dream. My stomach groaned. Cried. Took another swig of wine. But I'd been saving the letter until after the wedding. No more wedding. I held on to the side of the tub with both hands and climbed out, grabbed a pink towel and left the bathroom, half-staggering, bumping into the dresser, on my way to the closet. Reaching for the Kotex box I knocked down Sadie's hatbox, filled to the brim with old photographs. There she was on her honeymoon in a cloche hat and a coat with a fur collar, feeding a bear at Yellowstone National Park. Izzy probably took the picture. Before or after she decided to stay married to him? I didn't give a shit. I sat on the bed and read:

> New York, Sept. '62
> Dear Beck, I didn't go to Spain. It was the right and moral thing to do but my mom bribed a doctor to give me a heart murmur. My precious career came first, as always. You never asked how I could afford Stella's class on my meager earnings. I get a big, fat check from Mommy every month. I was ashamed to tell you. As you once said, it's easy not to care about money when you've got it. By the way, Alice dumped

me. She said I was gutless. The rest of my life I'll have to live with the fact that I copped out, and no amount of time working for War Resisters will make me less of a coward. Since I'm feeling shitty about myself right now, might as well tell you about my sordid sex life. I used to sneak off to Nogales every chance I got when I was at Arizona State. Beautiful Mexican ladies of the night, passed out on peyote in alleys that smelled of piss. I was relieved when you didn't want to have sex. Scared I'd give you the clap. So, if either of us is a saint, it's you, Beck. Sorry for stringing you along, letting you put me on a pedestal. I liked the view. But the only thing that was real was my love for you. To quote your letters of contrition, write, but if you don't I'll understand. J.

Joey... Part of me wanted to forget about the money, the lies... Part of me longed to see him, touch him... But, I was right that night at the Catholic school—he wasn't talking to me, *Atta baby, atta girl*, he was talking to his Mexican whores, in alleys that smelled of piss. Great line. Didn't sound like him. He probably stole it from Kerouac. Damn you Joey! Why didn't you tell me? Things might have been different, even with my parents across the street. My whole life might have been different. All this time I blamed myself. You blew it, Joey. I guess I never really knew you.

41.

"Have you read all of those?"

Milligan's desk was cluttered with Hemingway, Faulkner, Thomas Wolfe, Fitzgerald. He leaned back in his swivel chair.

"Many times. You still haven't told me what was so urgent that it couldn't wait until Wednesday after class." He took out a tobacco pouch. Filled his pipe. Pointed it at me. "You look like hell, by the way."

"I've been sick." It sounded like a lie, but I didn't care. From the expression on his face, neither did he. "Stayed home from work today."

"Coffee?" To his left was a hot plate on a cart. Glass coffee maker. Maxwell House. Tea bags. Mugs.

"Tea, actually."

He got up to heat the water. From the window behind his desk I could see grass, desert, mountains.

"Nice view."

He had his back to me. "I held out for a second story office."

"You were right about Alex, by the way. It's over."

He turned. Smiled, but there was sympathy in it. "Good you called things off before New York." He handed me tea in a brown mug. "Now that you've chosen not to be the woman behind the man, what's next?"

I blew on my tea, avoiding his eyes. "I don't

have the money or the guts to go to New York by myself. I'll stay here. Look for an apartment. Thank God I have a job I like, and once I have my real estate license I can buy a car. I'm depressed about Alex, but as you said, it's good it happened now." I took a sip of tea. "Do you have any sugar?"

He handed me a small blue ceramic bowl with a sunflower on the lid. If he was pleased about New York, about Alex, he didn't show it.

"I finished Middlemarch, by the way. I guess Eliot preferred irony to romance."

"And you?"

"In real life, or in novels?"

"Take your pick."

"I've got irony written all over me."

His brown eyes were moist, kind. "You can always revise."

In spite of myself, I smiled. "Did you ever read Marjorie Morningstar, by Herman Wouk?"

He raised his eyebrows. "I did. Many of Wouk's critics found it reactionary. I imagine you would agree."

"I hated it, especially the ending. But it's a lot like Middlemarch. Marjorie gives up her dreams of being an actress and becomes a respectable Jewish housewife. Dorothea defies society by marrying a man without money, they leave Middlemarch, move to London, but she ends up being a housewife. A nobody."

He leaned forward. "But Wouk wants us to approve. Elliot's ending is..."

"Infuriating."

He sat back. Puffed on his pipe. "How so?"

"She has her heroine fall passionately in love and devote herself to her man, but unlike Wouk, she wants us to think, 'There goes another brilliant woman down the drain.'"

He smiled. "I thought it might rile you."

I looked away, flushing. "I think Eliot was really bitter about being a woman. Why wouldn't she be? She had to change her name from Marian to George to get published. But, then she has her narrator tell us it's okay for Dorothea to give up her identity to be a wife and mother, because giving is what makes women like Dorothea happy. What a hypocrite!" Milligan looked like he wanted to laugh. I glared at him. "<u>Middlemarch</u> was just about the worst book I could have read right now. It's a highbrow version of <u>Marjorie Morningstar</u>."

He stopped smiling, but I could tell he was still amused. "But, Marjorie and Dorothea married men worthy of their love. I should think you'd approve. Didn't you tell me that without love, life isn't worth it?"

"Yes, but I don't want to end up like them! How the hell are women my age supposed to know what's best for them? Even if I did know, I'd probably fuck up, given my track record. God! I sound like Dana Harmon. Now there's somebody who never should have married. And she never, ever should have had children."

He got up to replenish my tea. "Perhaps Eliot is saying there are no easy answers?"

"Whatever she's saying, it's depressing. Everything's depressing." I felt anger, frustration, pain pour out of me as our eyes met.

"Why don't you disregard the next essay assignment and take a look at Balzac's <u>Passion in the Desert</u>."

"I won't be coming to class anymore."

"Alex?"

I nodded, handing him a manila envelope. "I brought you everything I've written so far, on Lawrence, and <u>Middlemarch</u>. It's not finished, but there's enough to prove I took it seriously."

"You can continue to work on it outside of class."

"I can't. Not right now."

He tried not to show any emotion, but I could tell he was disappointed.

"Are you officially withdrawing?"

"I was hoping you could do that for me. You've spent a lot of time trying to help me and I don't want to let you down, but…"

He leaned against his desk. "Let's make a deal. I don't want you to disappear on me. Promise to send me your work, promise to read the Balzac and talk with me about it, I'll turn a grade in for you. I'll give you my home number-it's unlisted. I'll miss you in class, but under the circumstances…"

I stood and gathered my things. "Okay. I promise. But it might not be for a while."

"Within a semester."

"I'll try. But don't bet on it, okay? You might lose."

"But I might win." His eyes gleamed. "Both of us might win."

"I don't care about winning. All I want right now is to survive."

42.

"This is Dr. Cohen. I'm answering my page."

"Uncle Jake. Hi. It's Becky. How's my mom?"

"I was just in her room, checking on her. Thanks to Miltown, she's sleeping like a baby. If you're worried about tomorrow's procedure, don't give it another thought. We'll be sending her back to you good as new."

"Actually, I've been thinking she should stay in Cincinnati. Permanently. Don't say anything to her, but my father's on a gambling binge. He hasn't been home since she left." Silence. Awkward silence. "She'd be much better off with you."

"Your mother knew what she was getting into when she married him, Rebecca."

"That's not fair, Uncle Jake. She didn't know. You have to live with a gambler to know what it's like."

"She'd be out of place here. She'd be bored. She's better off in Las Vegas. She has her women friends, her Haddasah group, her routines."

They didn't want her. The brothers she worshipped. She'd be out of place.

"But I still think ..."

"Don't worry. We'll continue sending her monthly checks. I'll give you a ring tomorrow, after the surgery. I'll tell her you called."

"Tell her... tell her I love her."

"I think she knows that already."

"Tell her anyway, okay?"

43.

I needed to go to work more than anything—to see Quent, talk to him, pour my heart out. Quent would understand—he would comfort and advise me. But, even after twenty-four hours I was still hung-over. And late. Quent wasn't at his desk. Nina wasn't bent over her drawing board. Carlo's radio wasn't blasting. I peeked in. All their things were gone: the radio, Nina's orange cup where she kept her pencils and paint brushes, her cactus plant; Carlo's collection of tiny, grotesque creatures he called "Little Horribles"; his Marilyn Monroe calendar. We weren't supposed to move for another two weeks. When I left work last Friday they had been complaining about having to come in over the weekend. But they wouldn't quit without notice—one of them, maybe, but not both.

At least Quent's office seemed intact. He'd started packing. There was a row of boxes behind his desk. His red coffee mug by the phone was half full. He was the fussy type; he wouldn't leave a dirty mug overnight. He'd been here and left in a hurry. I hoped I hadn't missed something important; I was only a half-hour late. The phone rang.

"Morning, gorgeous."

"Sorry, Morty. Quent's not in."

"Don't want him, sweetheart, I want you. How's about joining me for drinks at the Sahara? I got a couple of investors from LA. They want to meet you."

A wave of nausea. "Little early for drinks, Morty. Besides, I'm working, remember?"

"Your boss won't mind. It's good for business."

"Being polite to letches is part of my job, Morty. But I don't go anywhere without Quent."

"Your loss, sweetheart."

He'd treated me like a call-girl. Quent would be furious. My head throbbed. So did my feet from my high heels. There was a bottle of aspirin next to the stapler. I went across the hall for water. Checked my makeup in the mirror. Except for puffy eyes my face looked fine. The killer girdle I'd squeezed into so I could wear that red dress the clients liked was killing me. At least the damn thing worked. Nothing jiggled or sagged. I hobbled back to the office to answer the phone.

"Where's Quent? It's Betty Ogden. Brian and I were supposed to meet him at our lawyer's first thing this morning, but he hasn't showed."

My stomach trembled. Had I forgotten to go over his appointments with him? Oh, God. Maybe my worst fears had been realized? Maybe Harry and Herbie had taken him for that little ride in the desert? "Something urgent must have come up. Why don't I take your number and have him call as soon as…"

"Never mind."

She'd sounded annoyed. Quent's disappearance probably had nothing to do with Harry and Herbie. More likely, it was me. I stared at the boxes against the wall, trying to remember if the missed appointment was my fault or Quent's. The move. It all came back to me. Most of Friday, I'd made arrangements for the reception, talked to caterers, ordered flowers, champagne, mailed invitations. Everything had to be mailed that day to give people two weeks' notice.

What else? Money. I took a lot of money out of the bank. I remembered being nervous with all that cash in my purse. A hundred thousand dollars in tens and twenties. Quent needed it to close a deal. He didn't even count it when I handed it over. He said he trusted me more than anybody. Oh, God. I hoped I hadn't done anything to change his mind. The phone rang again.

"Hello, beautiful." Chet? But he always called me *Miss Plotnik.* "How's about joining me for breakfast in bed?"

He had to be joking. I'd play along.

"I'm sorry, Mr. De Remis designs buildings, not beds. You must have the wrong number."

"Stop playing games. We've been making eyes at each other since the first time we met. It was just a matter of time before we bedded down."

"Go to hell!"

I slammed down the receiver. What was going on? First the empty room, then Morty, then Chet. I'd thought my job was the only stable thing in my life. I pictured myself running down Fremont, only it wasn't Alex closing in on me, it was a crowd of men with their chests hanging out and gold chains.

I turned to the row of diplomas and awards on the wall. I had to be careful not to confuse Quent with Alex and Izzy. If anybody in this world was real, it was Quent. I'd overreacted to a couple of crude phone calls. Understandable, given what I'd been through, but the nightmare was over. I took out my purse, touched up my eyes. Any minute now, Quent would walk in, looking like an ad for <u>Gentleman's Quarterly</u>. I didn't want him to catch me without my war paint, as Sadie would say.

Sure enough, I heard footsteps. Quent wasn't alone; a woman laughed. I got out my notebook, to look busy. She laughed again. It was more of a giggle. An annoying giggle.

"Morning, Rebecca," he smiled. By his side a young, gorgeous blonde in a floor-length red gown with his blue blazer around her shoulders.

My cheeks burned. Who the hell was she?

"Good morning, Quent," I smiled.

Up close she looked even more gorgeous. Creamy complexion, powder-blue eyes with thick dark lashes by Maybelline. The gown was a bit showy for ten in the morning, even by Vegas standards. I searched her head for black roots.

"Lanie, this is my secretary, Rebecca Plotnik."

Lanie framed her perfect teeth in a red smile. "Lanie Lamarr," she said, presenting her hand as if she expected me to kiss it. "A pleasure to meet you."

Her face made it clear she regarded me as only slightly more interesting than the furniture. The way she enunciated each word, she had to be an actress. Corny stage name. Heddy Lamarr had to be turning over in her grave, and I wasn't even sure she was dead yet.

"I'll get a chair," Quent said, scurrying over to the folding chairs against the wall. He kept looking back. Afraid she'd disappear? "I was at the Greyhound station this morning, dropping off a client, when I noticed Lanie."

She sat. He stood, feasting his eyes on her cleavage. So unlike him!

"She was hard to miss, sitting on a bench in that gown with her overnight case in her lap, especially since she was crying her eyes out."

Lanie sighed and kicked off her heels, bending over to rub her feet.

"I asked if I could help. It turned out her boyfriend had gambled away all their vacation money and left her stranded. Poor thing had to sell her clothes for a bus ticket back to Phoenix."

I clicked my tongue. "Another tale of greed and lust in the town without pity."

He chuckled, but there were sparks of anger in his eyes. "Right then and there, I offered her a job."

My heart joined my stomach in a clinch.

"And I accepted." Lanie giggled.

"We'll need another receptionist in the new office." Quent paced. "Twice as many calls, twice as many clients, especially if we have twice as many beautiful women." Wink. "The first thing they'll see is you," he pointed to me, "and Lanie. I'm thinking of replacing the front windows with a sheet of glass. Appearance may not be everything in this business—"

"But it's a close second." I finished the sentence with him, finally understanding its full meaning. What I didn't understand was what had come over him. "By the way, you had a message from Betty and Brian while you were out." I thought that would bring him back to reality, and his senses, but his expression was deadpan. "Something about an appointment with their lawyer?"

"Oh, that." He returned to Lanie's side. "You're not cold anymore, are you, dear?" She shook her head, fluttering her false eyelashes while he took his blazer from her shoulders and hung it on the coat tree by the door. "Don't worry, Rebecca, I've already taken care of it." He stood in the middle of the room, like an emcee. "I don't know about you ladies but I could use some coffee and a Danish."

He didn't even sound like himself!

"Mmm," said Lanie Lamar.

"Rebecca," Quent said, handing me his keys and slipping me a five, "why don't you pick up some pastries from Wolfie's? I'll make coffee."

I was tempted to give back his money and tell him I'd lost my taste for Danish, and Dreams, Inc., but I had to believe he'd see through her eventually. He was too smart not to. I put on my coat and took the coffee pot from the closet, my hands shaking,

"You just relax, Quent," Lanie said, grabbing the pot, "while your new receptionist makes coffee."

I took out my anger on the car, slamming the door, grinding the ignition, screeching around the corner. So what if they heard? I didn't give a damn. How could he offer her a job on the spot like that? He didn't know the first thing about her. At least he'd interviewed me, and twenty-five others before me! I had a bite of Danish on the way back to the office, leaving crumbs all over the seat. Would have eaten more but my girdle pinched. I switched on the radio. Patti Page singing, *How Much Is That Doggie in the Window*? Was she following me? First the *Tennessee Waltz*, now this.

Back in the office, Lanie sipped coffee and inspected her nails. Quent was on the phone, his back to us. I took the napkins out of the file drawer.

"Danish?" I asked, offering her a napkin.

"No thanks." She looked at me like she knew everything I'd eaten in the last twenty-four hours. "I never touch sweets."

"Bad news, ladies." Quent swiveled around to face us. "I thought we'd have a chance to relax, but I have to dash off to a meeting." He grabbed a Danish on his way to the file cabinet. "Lanie," he said, rummaging through the drawers, "I'll get you a room at the Sahara until we can find you an apartment."

"Oh, Quent. How can I ever thank you? It's my favorite hotel," Lanie said, stepping into her shoes and shimmying her gown into place. She pulled a compact out of a little red purse and stepped into the hall to freshen her makeup.

"Rebecca, you stay here and take calls. Say I'll get back to them tomorrow. I'm tied up all day."

"Are Nina and Carlo coming in?"

For a second, he looked as if he'd never heard their names, like in a Hitchcock movie. "The model home," he said, turning back to the files. "They're organizing things out there." He stuffed a bunch of files in his briefcase, snapped it shut, looked at me. "Keys?" He held out his hand.

Why would they be at the model home? And what happened to all of their things?

"KEYS Rebecca!"

I jumped. This wasn't Quent. He would never yell at me. I hurried to the coat tree and fetched the car keys from my coat, heart pounding, thinking of Izzy and how I used to hide in the closet when he lost his temper.

"I didn't mean to snap at you," Quent said, as I handed him the keys. "Forgive me, Rebecca. It's just that I'm under pressure to close a deal." He gave my shoulder a pat. "Be back around two."

I was confused. One minute he was an ill-tempered letch, the next he was warm, fatherly, my old boss. But my old boss wouldn't have made a fool of himself over Lanie Lamarr. She could be a doggie in the window. I was not for sale. I'd tell him that to his face. Without thinking, I grabbed a Danish, opened my mouth, realized what I was doing and dropped it in the trash. Throw out the rest before you change your mind. I held the plate over the trash, allowing myself to lick my fingers as I dropped the pastries, one by one. I had just done away with the last bearclaw, following it with the contents of the ashtray in case I weakened, when a door slammed.

"What the hell did you do with my car?" It was Quent, red-faced, eyes burning.

"I parked it in the lot."

He looked like he wanted to hit me. "Well, it's not there now."

"I—I don't understand." I stammered. He'd never sworn before, or yelled. This had to be a dream—a nightmare.

Quent paced. Lanie glared from the door.

"It was there when I came back with the pastries." Maybe I forgot to put on the emergency brake and it rolled away? "Maybe somebody stole it!"

"Dammit, I don't have time for this. Call a taxi. Tell them we'll be downstairs at the back entrance."

I wiped my sticky fingers with Kleenex and called Red Cab. My hand was shaking as I hung up the phone. I raised the venetian blinds so I had a clear view of the parking lot. Only a few cars. Quent's blue convertible wasn't one of them.

Somebody must have stolen it. I still felt I was somehow to blame. He should have called the police.

The phone rang.

"Your boss in yet?" It was Brian, of the missed appointment.

"He's out for the day."

"Tell him he can kiss this account good-bye."

He hung up. Quent had said he'd taken care of it. Maybe he'd patched things up with Betty and she hadn't told Brian. That didn't make sense. Nothing made sense. Nina and Carlo, the phone calls, Lanie, the missing car. I had to do something.

"Is this an emergency?" The receptionist asked.

"I want to report a stolen car."

She transferred the call to an officer.

"Blue Chevy convertible, brand new, don't know the license plate, belongs to my boss. I'll spell the name…"

My head throbbed. I reached for aspirin; even though less than four hours had passed since my last dose. Washed them down with Quent's cold coffee. The officer had said the car would be hard to trace without a license number, but they would check into it. I was sure I had told him more than he wanted to hear—about Lanie Lamarr, Morty, Chet. I even reported Nina and Carlo missing. But I thought it was important for him to know there was more going on here than a stolen car. He'd probably thought I was making it up. So what? Soon as Quent came back I was quitting. The old Beck would have given him the benefit of the doubt, but not after what I'd been through with Izzy. I'd write a letter of resignation. The hell with his stupid phone calls. That was Lanie's job, now.

I got out the letterhead stationery. The phone rang. I ignored it and continued writing. When it stopped, I took the receiver off the hook. Still couldn't concentrate. After a dozen or so botched attempts ended up in the trash, I closed my eyes. When I opened them again I was slumped over the desk. I'd fallen asleep. I saw the crumpled letters in the wastebasket; remembered Quent had said he'd be back around two. The clock over the door said quarter till. I didn't want to see him, or that woman. He had betrayed me, like every other man in my life. In my letter I told him I objected to being used as an enticement to clinch a deal and being displayed in a glass case to attract new clients. I asked that he send a check for the entire month of October to my home address.

I put on my coat and was half out the door

when I felt weak in the knees. I leaned against the door frame. Home. Ten to one Izzy wouldn't show until Sadie got back. I would be alone in that apartment for twelve nights and eleven days. Without a fiancé, or a father, or a job. Without friends! The floor didn't feel strong enough to hold me.

I went back to the desk, shaking all over like a kid scared to be alone while her parents are out. I took the Kleenex box from the bottom drawer, blew my nose, tried to tell myself it wasn't that bad, I had TV, books, two weeks of frozen dinners. But I'd go crazy if I went back there. My job was gone. I'd counted on having somewhere to go Monday through Friday.

I was so distraught that when Quent came in I didn't care. Just stared, as if he were a mirage. His tie was undone, his shirt unbuttoned at the neck. He walked slowly toward me, carrying his blazer.

"Don't cry, Rebecca." He looked directly into my eyes. "I'm back." His voice was soothing. He came around the desk and stood behind me, gently massaging the back of my neck with his warm, smooth fingers.

44.

The Riviera lounge was empty. We sat in a booth watching a piano player dressed like a blackjack dealer sing, *It was just one of those things*. He was no Sinatra.

"I'm sorry about this morning, Rebecca." Quent's eyes were old. "I behaved like a fool. When you first arrive in this town, you see things clearly, but after a while you find yourself dazzled by the same chunk of neon as everyone else."

"I wrote you a letter of resignation." I stared at the piano player. "I don't want to work with Lanie Lamarr."

"No reason why you should. It was a middle-aged fantasy. She wouldn't have fit in."

He was saying all the right things, sounding like himself again. Still, I didn't trust him. The cocktail waitress arrived with our drinks. Quent had ordered Scotch. Out of habit, I'd asked for a vodka martini on the rocks.

"I really shouldn't have this on an empty stomach." I ate my olive.

Quent called the waitress. They weren't serving lunch any longer but she'd bring us some pretzels and chips. I sipped my martini.

"When I took Lanie to the Sahara, she ran into a young man she knew from Phoenix. She introduced him as a friend, but he was more. I could see it in her eyes. She took me aside, patted my cheek, thanked me for my kindness. I reminded her of her father." He moved closer. "Forgive me for going on about myself. Let's talk about you." He put his arm around me. It wasn't threatening—it was comforting. "How's your young man? You said last week you were introducing him to the family."

"The wedding's off." I hadn't expected to blurt it out. It was all I could do to keep from burying my face in his chest and sobbing.

"I'm so sorry, Rebecca."

"It wouldn't have worked." My face was burning. Please, please, please, Beck! Don't tell him any more.

The waitress brought a basket of chips and pretzels. Quent ordered me another martini. He was still nursing his Scotch.

"But I remember how excited you were about the wedding." His hand gently guided my head to his shoulder and then stroked my hair. "My poor little girl."

It meant so much to have somebody to talk to, somebody who cared. I closed my eyes.

"When I walked in and saw you crying, I knew it had to be Alex."

"I'd rather not talk about it." One martini and I was floating. I needed an anchor. "Could I have a potato chip?"

Quent fed me a potato chip, then another. His finger sent a chill down my back when it touched my bottom lip. The last thing I wanted was to be attracted to him.

"I need to sit up."

"You need another drink." He took his arm from my shoulder and handed me a fresh martini.

I ate my olive, sucked the toothpick.

"You and I have had quite a day, haven't we?" He smiled, sadly. The little lines around his eyes closed and opened, like a wink.

"Quite a day." I repeated it several times.

He took my hand, studied it, traced each vein with his thumb. "If only I'd met someone like you when I had 'world enough and time.'"

"Andrew Marvel, 'To His Coy Mistress.' Memorized it in high school." I finished my martini and ate the ice, struggling to keep my eyes open.

"They are not long, the days of wine and roses..." he said.

I attempted to finish the line. "*Out of a dream...Out of a misty dream... emerges, closes...*"

"You have the loveliest voice. It's more than just tone and timbre; it's sensitivity, intelligence, depth. The first time I met you I knew you were... Did I ever mention I was engaged to a Jewish girl?"

"Family never accepted you."

He finished his Scotch. The waitress brought my martini, asked if Quent wanted another. He waved her away. "You remind me of her." Such a pained expression, I was afraid he would cry. "Of course, you're very fair-skinned and your features are more delicate, but there's something in the eyes. Compassion, soulfulness. Women like Lanie are irresistible at first, but that kind of beauty doesn't hold up over time. It's only skin deep, if you'll forgive the cliché." He handed me my drink.

I ate the olive.

"I'd better take you home before I say something I shouldn't."

"I misjudged you." I patted his hand. "You're the nicest boss I ever had. You made a food, a fool of yourself over Lanie, but so did I." I nodded my head. It was heavy. "I did too. Over Alex. Over my father. Oh, God. I'm so very drunk."

"You're charming."

"Thank you. I'll keep the job. Forget the letter, okay?" The police. Better tell him I called. Nah. Tell him later. Too tired.

Quent paid the check and took my arm, trying to pull me along as he slid out of the booth.

"I think I had a little too much to drink," I said, slumping onto the booth. "I'll just take a little nap."

Quent's laugh sounded as if it were coming from underwater. I felt his hands grip my shoulders and pull. I remember leaning against him, stumbling, taking off my shoes, giggling when he put them in his pockets. He was half-carrying me by the time we reached the parking lot. He had rented a red Cadillac with white leather seats.

When I opened my eyes, we were parked in front of a small house with little white rocks instead of a lawn, like Alex's, but not arty or interesting. It had a big sign in front, "Dreams Unlimited," and some names I didn't recognize. The houses around it were only half built.

"Hello, sleepyhead." Quent was smiling. He had a bunch of keys in his hand.

"This isn't my house."

"I wanted you to see the model home before I drop you off."

I slid all the way down to the seat. "Just want to sleep."

I heard him laugh, get out of the car, open the passenger door. "Come on. Fresh air will do you good."

I was only half-aware that he pulled me out of the car and hoisted me over his shoulder.

"You're heavier than I thought."

Inside the house, he took off my coat, deposited me on a mustard-yellow couch, put my purse on the coffee table, said he'd be right back. I watched him go off to the bathroom. I lay on my back. Saw an ugly light fixture in the middle of the ceiling, like Lifesavers stuck together with chewing gum. Made me want to puke. I rolled onto my stomach as Quent closed the bathroom door.

"Could I go home pretty soon? I'm not feeling well."

The couch shifted as he sat down beside me. "You don't really want to go home," he turned me on my back, "do you darling?" He unzipped his pants and put my hand inside.

For a second I didn't realize what was happening. "Oh, my God. Don't!"

He tightened his grip. I tried to sit up. Fell back. The room was spinning. All those years ago. Frosty Ryan. But this was Quent!

"I thought-but you were-a father-protected me-not-"

"Shhh!" His finger on my lip.

"I want to go home. Please take me home. Please."

He let go of my hand and got on top of me, his face a smiling blur. "Not until I make you happy."

"You're not going to make me happy." I put my hands on his shoulders and pushed. He wouldn't budge. "You're going to make me depressed." I couldn't move.

He was kissing my neck. I tried to push his head away. He grabbed my wrist. "If I get any more depressed..." He was licking my ear. "I'll have a nervous breakdown." He kissed my mouth. I clenched my teeth so he couldn't get his tongue in.

"Come on, darling. Relax!" He was pulling up my

dress.

"No. Stop!"

"Enjoy it."

"I don't want it!"

"Ah, but you do, my sweet. Now close your eyes." My dress was up to my waist. "Stop, goddam you!"

I dug my fingernails into his hand. Pulled his hair. He wouldn't stop. I felt as if I were falling, head first.

"What in the hell are you wearing—a chastity belt?"

He rolled off me. I tried to sit up. He shoved me down, straddled me on his knees, forced his fingers inside the waistband and yanked.

"Goddam girdle! Take it off!"

"No!"

"Yes!" He grunted like a pig, pulled until he was red in the face. "Jesus H. Christ!"

Sadie was the only other person I knew who said that. Must be a generational thing. He stood up. "You fucking little Jewish cunt! You goddam prick-tease!" He kicked the coffee table, hurt his toe, jumped around holding his foot in one hand, shoes in the other, yelling, "Shit!"

I grabbed the back of the couch, pulled myself to a sitting position. My head was beginning to clear.

"I called the police." He was too busy limping and cursing to hear me, so I yelled. "I CALLED THE POLICE."

"What?" He froze.

I recognized the look on his face. Guilt. Fear. I didn't know what he'd done, but I knew I had him. "I called the police. Told them how clients were propositioning me on the phone and how your car disappeared from the parking lot."

"No!" He backed away from me, shaking his head.

My head cleared even more. I was beginning to enjoy watching him squirm. Go on, Beck. Play it for all it's worth. Make up stuff. "I told them I thought Dreams Unlimited was a front for a prostitution ring."

He believed me—I could see it on his face, so I lied some more.

"They said they'd check into it."

"This isn't real. It's a dream." He smacked his head. "A fucking dream." Laughing, but not really laughing. "She wouldn't call the cops, not her. Shit! She wouldn't have the sense."

"Oh, yes she would!"

He reminded me of *Rumpelstiltskin* when the Queen guesses his name and he goes crazy. He smacked his head a few more times, grabbed his jacket from a chair, ran out the door carrying his shoes, yelling and cursing, just like in the fairy tale.

I hurried to the door, fell against it, turned the lock, fastened the chain. "Go to hell, you bastard! Oh, God, were you lucky, Beck!"

I leaned against the door, half-laughing, half-crying.

45.

I would have gone straight to bed the minute I got home, but first I had to call Sadie and pretend nothing had changed, when everything had changed. I reached in my purse and took out my girdle. I had survived the worst three days of my life because of luck, (I hugged my girdle), and perseverance. Not only had I fended off Quent's advances after three martinis on an empty stomach, I had crossed the desert at night with no idea where I was going. If I hadn't pulled a knife on the bus driver, maybe I would still be sitting on a bench in the middle of nowhere. Now, I had to decide where to go from here.

"Sorry to call so late, Mom. I just got home."

"I'm groggy. They gave me a sedative."

"I was worried it was too late, but I talked to Uncle Jake a few minutes ago. He said to go ahead. I'm glad everything went okay."

"Pain everywhere, every time I move. They said I was a good patient. Very brave."

"You are brave, Mom. I've been thinking about that since you've been gone. You put up with a lot, not only from my father. From me. I've realized how strong you are, to be married to a gambler. It hasn't been easy for you. Ever! I want you to know that I've been thinking and, well, you were right about a lot of things, it's just, I couldn't listen because you're my mother, but

I'm finally ready to take your advice and forget about being an actress. Like Natalie Wood in <u>Marjorie Morningstar</u>."

"Morning what? Who?"

"The movie, Mom. The one where Natalie Wood changes her last name from Morganstern to Morningstar because she thinks she wants to be an actress but she really wants to be a housewife. I'm more like her than I thought which you knew all along but I had to learn the hard way. I'm human. I need security. I need to know what's going to happen tomorrow and next week and next year. Dreams aren't enough for me, Mom. Mom? Are you there? Mom?"

"Dreams. My mother told me: follow your dreams. I was your age. Shoulda listened."

"What? Grandma Rosie said what?"

"Shoulda gone to Chicago. Write novels. Be a bohemian. Like my cousin Dorothy with the genius I.Q. My mother said: follow your dreams."

"But, Mom, you're not listening. I'm finally admitting I'm just like everybody else. I'm growing up, dammit! I thought you'd be proud of me."

"Shoulda gone to Chicago."

"But-but you're going back on everything you've ever said. You can't do that, Mother! Not now. It's too late."

"Late. You called too late."

"Mom?"

"Next time, call early."

Click.

46.

The cab pulled into the parking lot behind the Dreams, Inc., office building. A police car was parked by the outside stairs, with a gold Chevrolet Manza next to it. I'd seen the Manza somewhere before. Couldn't think where. Thank God Quent's rented Cadillac wasn't around. At least I wouldn't have to deal with him. Yesterday, I'd parked my car on the other side of the lot, next to a pickup truck from the flower shop on the first floor. I took out my keys and started toward it, knees wobbly. My feet hurt. At Sunrise Hospital, the doctor had bandaged my feet and said I should try to stay off of them for a week or so, but what could I do? I needed the car.

"Rebecca?"

I froze. The voice coming from the stairs sounded familiar. I turned, slowly, telling myself to stop shaking. A policeman and two men in suits were hurrying toward me. So what if I was wearing mukluks? That didn't make me a criminal. I knew the guy with red hair: Quent's attorney, Paul Farley, in plaid pants with a striped jacket. That's where I'd seen the gold Manza.

"Hi, Rebecca." Paul squeezed my hand. "We just tried to call you. This is Lieutenant Kolb. He's a special investigator."

"Special investigator?" This had to be about Chet and his boys. Good! I'd love to see them all go to jail!

"You did us a favor by reporting that missing vehicle, Miss Plotnik." A heavyset man with a thick black mustache shook my hand. I saw a shoulder holster under his jacket. His sidekick looked like a regular cop—about my age, with a gold front tooth. "Turned out it wasn't stolen. It was repossessed."

"Repossessed? But Quent wouldn't…"

"Quent hadn't bothered to make his payments," Paul said. "Why should he? He had no intention of keeping the car for more than a few months."

"I don't understand."

The lieutenant took a small notepad and pen from his jacket. Tough, smart, professional. He reminded me of Bogart in "The Enforcer."

"Your former boss is one of the slickest con-artists in the business. He's wanted in seven states. Even passed himself off as an M.D., back east. Got away with it for close to a year."

"You—you mean he wasn't an architect?"

Paul patted my shoulder. "I'm afraid not, Rebecca."

I felt dizzy, so dizzy I staggered. It was one thing, finding out he was a letch, but— "But all those degrees on the wall?"

"All bogus," Paul said.

"Oh, my God." I felt cold. What a fool I'd been. I'd thought Chet was just pretending to be respectable, but Quent? Never in a million years.

"No reason to be embarrassed, Rebecca. You're not the only one who was taken in," Paul said. "My partner and I were completely fooled. So were his clients. He took Donovan Contracting for over a hundred grand. All told, we think he got away with close to half a million."

Jesus! Chet was a victim. Like me.

"Would have been a lot more, if it hadn't been for you." Lieutenant Kolb pointed his pen at me, smiling.

"Me?"

"If you'd confined your report to the car, we wouldn't have put it together, but the raunchy phone calls, the missing employees, the high-class call-girl fit this individual's pattern. About the time he moves in for the kill, he tends to show his true colors. First by getting rid of any employees who are on to him, paying them off if he has to; then the women. This guy once ran a million-dollar prostitution ring."

"Oh, my God." Prostitution ring: my very words, at the model home, right before Quent did his Rumpelstiltskin routine. But then I thought I was making it up. And Nina and Carlo. Had he paid them off? Or were they in on it the whole time? I felt sick. I took a few steps back, forgot that my feet were hurt, stumbled.

"Are you all right?" In a flash, Paul was at my side, holding my arm. He must have thought I was going to faint. My head was spinning.

"I'm fine," I said, taking my arm back. "It's just a shock, that's all. I've got to sit down." I turned my back on them and started toward my car, my mukluks flapping on the asphalt.

"Just a minute, Miss Plotnik," Lieutenant Kolb said.

I kept going, like a robot.

"I have a few questions."

"Miss Plotnik is obviously too distraught to answer questions at this time," I heard Paul say. He was acting like I'd appointed him as my attorney, which bugged the hell out of me.

"It's okay," I said, unlocking the car. "I'd rather get it over with."

Before I could open the door, Paul crowded in front of me.

"Maybe you shouldn't drive. I'd be happy to give you a lift." He had his arm on my hand again.

"I'm FINE!"

Paul backed off, shocked. I opened the door and got behind the wheel.

Lieutenant Kolb moved in with his notebook. "When was the last time you saw De Remis, Miss Plotnik?"

"Yesterday." Oh, Christ. Yesterday. The model home.

"What time?"

He had to be wondering why I had left my car in the lot. "I—I'm not sure. After I reported the car, Mr. De Remis came back. I told him I was quitting."

"We saw your letter on his desk."

Don't say any more than you have to! It's none of their business. "He was upset, didn't want me to quit. Insisted on going out for a drink. We went to the Riviera lounge and..." Lying was out; the cocktail waitress had witnessed the whole thing. "I'm afraid I had too much to drink."

Kolb's face was impassive. Mine was red. He got the picture.

"He had to drive me home." I looked at the keys in my lap, glanced at Kolb then back at the keys. "He tried to..." I put my head on the steering wheel. This was not lying; this was Method acting. The emotion was real. So were the tears. The facts were altered slightly to protect the innocent.

"Okay, guys, let's call it a morning. I have your phone number, Miss Plotnik. I'll let you know what happens with De Remis."

"Thanks." I got a Kleenex from my purse. Blew my nose.

Paul was still by the car. "Listen," he said, "I'll call you for lunch, later in the week. There's so much for us to…"

"No, there isn't." I shifted into reverse.

47.

All I could think of was food. I drove to the Safeway near the Huntridge Theater, floating down the aisles as if I were dreaming. I bought a six-pack of Tab and eight dollars' worth of Pay Days, peanut M&Ms, Milk Duds, Tootsie Rolls, Nestle's Semi-Sweet Morsels, Milky Ways, Mars Bars, Hershey's with and without almonds, and Snickers.

"Having a party?" the cashier asked. "Say, don't I know you? Aren't you Becky Plotnik, Class of '57?"

"Never heard of her."

I drove to the black rocking chair on Paradise Road. Alex had obviously been there. The stuff he'd collected in the back of Buddy's truck had been carefully arranged for a photo shoot: the TV with a smashed screen now rested on little stand in front of the couch which sported a green and white throw with cavorting scotties and Home Sweet Home printed across its middle, beer cans and <u>True Crime</u> magazines had been strewn about. I sat on the rocking chair, Safeway bag on my lap, opened a can of Tab and took a swig. Shivered. Buttoned my coat to the chin. Didn't help. The wind blew dust in my eyes. It hurt. Everything hurt. I felt horribly empty. Any minute I could blow away. Needed something to hold me down, an anchor. I crammed a whole Milky Way in my mouth, but it felt like trying to swallow a chocolate fist. I spat it out, crumpled the wrapper, threw it. Shit! Now I'm crying. Every part of me. Guts, brain, even my hair. Tears pouring out like rain, but nothing green or hopeful will come of it. Not in this fucking desert. Oh, God, I hate this desert. I hate it!

I felt in my pockets for Kleenex. Both of them had holes. I wiped my face on my sleeve.

Quent De Remis. Damn him, I thought he was real. De Remis. Say it fast and it sounds like Dreams. Maybe it's all a dream. *Shaboom, shaboom, life could be a dream, sweetheart...* I opened another Tab and sang... *All day I paced the barren waste without a taste of water. Cooool water... Oh, give me land, lots of land with the prairie skies above, don't fence me in...* Used to sing those songs on car trips with Sadie and Izzy when I was a kid. Cowboy songs. All the way to LA. *Don't bury me in this prairie, take me where the cement grows...* All the way to Del Mar where Izzy blew our vacation money at a racetrack... I should have known better than to bet on Izzy being real, but I never doubted Quent. Bogus. Everything about him. Even his name. I'd thought I was the actress. He was acting the whole time. I could see him saying, "Rebecca, you're a breath of fresh air in a city of con artists." I guess you would know, Quent, if anybody would.

First night at The Mint, Darlene had said, *You can make lots of money around here if you know how.* And I'd said, *But that's stealing.* That same night I'd filched two quarters from the rolls. Fifty fucking cents. I was so guilty I couldn't sleep! Not even with foil on the windows. What a fool I'd been. A push-over. Quent knew me for a push-over the minute he saw me. All that crap about <u>The Forsyte Saga</u>, when he'd probably never read it. Everything he said was calculated to seduce suckers. Like me! The stuff about the Kennedy's and

Marilyn Monroe—he knew I would eat it up. Jesus! He'd told me I was too intelligent to be taken advantage of by men like Chet and his pals, knowing he was far worse than any of them! Oh, God! I'd even wanted him to be my father-in-law. He must have laughed his head off at that one. She wouldn't call the cops. Not her. Hah! Guess who just had the last laugh? Fucker!

Yeah, Beck, but you get a big, fat F for flop when it comes to judging character. You fell for the bogus architect and doubted the trustworthy professor. You wouldn't listen when Sadie said Izzy didn't give a damn about you. You convinced yourself that fate had picked Alex to be the love of your life. You even convinced him, you goddam fool! I reached for another Milky Way. My hand froze. There was Grandma Rosie, way up in the flamingo pink sky, floating headfirst in my direction, clearly unaware she was just a figment of my imagination. And, she was singing. At first I couldn't make out the words, but as she came closer I heard: Snickers, PayDay, and Mars Bars. After a charming little somersault, she landed on her feet, took my hands, and pulled me out of the rocking chair. "Let's cut a rug," she said. Not only did we dance, we sang:

> Farewell to Snickers
> Adios, PayDays,
> M&M's and Mars Bars
> I'm throwing you away.
> With or without almonds
> Hershey's gotta go,
> Milky Way you're so passé
> Don't need you any mo' – O…

Our performance was all the more remarkable for its stylish choreography and clever harmonies reminiscent of the Andrews Sisters minus Laverne. Grandma Rosie was quite the belter. I did a little soft-shoe. Rosie showed some leg. After three or four sets, she turned to me and said, "Enough. You don't need candy any more, and you don't need me either." She disappeared in a cloud of fairy dust. I carried the Safeway bag to a spot near the TV. On my knees I tore at the hard crust of the earth. It hurt my fingers, but the pain spurred me on. I dug until I had made a small grave. I stood up, turned the Safeway bag upside down, held it high, watched the candy bars drop in, covered them with dirt, and vowed never to binge on chocolate again because it made me feel worse when I deserved to feel better.

Milligan yawned. I wasn't insulted. I'd been talking forever, pouring my heart out about Izzy, Alex, and especially Quent.

"Sorry for going on and on, but it's terrible to think you know somebody and find out they don't exist. Like being in an earthquake. You think you're standing on something solid, then it caves in. Makes you wonder if anything's real."

Milligan's big yellow dog padded in and plopped at his feet, whining, drooling. Pleading eyes, the same brown as his. "Hey, Emma," he said. She licked the hand he offered.

"You're real," I said. "Emma's real."

"That's why you're here." He smiled. "Want something to eat?"

I shuddered. "The last thing I want right now is food."

"Suit yourself, but I'm starving." He rummaged in the fridge, taking out an open package of hot dogs, tearing one in half and throwing it. Emma lunged, caught it in midair.

I stared at the basket of fruit in the middle of the wooden table Milligan had made with his own hands.

"You've got a great place here. Off by yourself with a view of Sunrise Mountain, and all the books in the world. And a fireplace. I don't know anybody else who has a fireplace."

"I like it. <u>A Room of One's Own</u>. Another book you should read if you haven't already."

"A room of my own. I've forgotten what that's like. Which brings up the subject of my roommate. I thought I knew everything about my mother, but lately she's been dropping these little bombshells. The other night on the phone she confessed that when she was my age she wanted to move to Chicago to be a writer. Her mother told her to follow her dreams, but she didn't have the guts. Now she wishes she had. This, from the woman who told me dreaming would get me nowhere. Of course, if I called her right now she probably wouldn't remember a thing. Even if she did, she'd deny it."

"You never had an inkling that your mother wanted to be a writer?"

"She never talked about her ambitions, so I assumed she didn't have any. Her brothers were the achievers. She once told me any woman in her right mind would be a man if she had the choice. Great thing to tell your daughter."

"So, as her daughter, where does that leave you?"

"With more options than she ever had. But, as I told her on the phone, I'm finally admitting that I need security. Going off to New York to be an actress, without a penny to my name, would be like jumping off a cliff."

Milligan went back to the fridge for a jar of hot peppers, Tabasco sauce and beer. He put the stuff on the table. "The first time we talked, you said next to compromise, security was the ugliest word you knew."

"Yeah, well, that was bullshit. I probably need security more than anything, having never had it." I felt Emma's wet nose on my leg. I stroked her head. "And you were right. Las Vegas is an opportunity, not a dead-end. Only I can't bear to live with my parents any longer—especially now, with my dad, but I don't have the money to move." I took a deep breath. "I don't even have a job." Emma must have sensed I was upset, because she licked my hand. It helped.

"That's a tough one." He speared half a dog and two peppers with a skinny fork and sprinkled Tabasco on it. I made a face. He shrugged. Grinned. "You can send the boy to Harvard but... Sure you're not hungry?"

"Even if I were, it wouldn't be for that."

"Bachelor food."

Loneliness in his eyes. Just a trace, but enough to snap me out of my self-pity. My problems were nothing compared to losing his wife. Oh my God—I hoped I hadn't given him the impression that I wanted to move in with him. Jesus, maybe I did? Jo, in <u>Little Women</u>, fell in love with a professor who was a lot older than she. Yeah, but I was so depressed when she married him that it ruined the whole book. It was time to leave.

I stood. "Well, there's not much I can do about my situation until I've saved some money, so I'll check out the want ads in tomorrow's paper. Actually, now that acting is out of the picture, I can pursue other things. I was good at journalism in college. My advertising professor said I was a whiz at copy writing—best in the class."

Milligan tilted his head from side to side, stroked his beard, frowned.

Please oh please don't try to rescue me. You can't, and I can't rescue you.

"One of my colleagues is looking for a nanny. Live-in job. Two kids. You said you were everybody's favorite babysitter. Nice little squirts. Nice house."

I let out my breath.

"Your own room," he added.

"Being a nanny?" I sat down again. "I don't know. I've never considered…"

"You'd have room and board, salary, plenty of time to take classes-toward your master's."

"My master's?"

"Why not? Christ, Rebecca, we have freedom."

"We just don't take it."

"Words to live by." I sucked my lip until it squeaked. "Joey and I used to collect words to live by."

He gave me a hard look. "You liked this guy, this Joey?" Milligan loaded his fork again, without taking his eyes off me.

"Yeah. He's an actor—lives in New York. But it's complicated."

"Sure that's not just an excuse?"

"Godammit, I hate it when you say things like that!" Emma stood, whimpered, ears cocked. "Sorry, Emma. I didn't mean to scare you." I patted her head, partially to avoid looking at Milligan. She snuggled it in my lap. "It's just—money's a problem. He has it, I don't. Or, rather, his mother has it. It just wouldn't work."

"So. Shall I call Thompson about the nanny job?"

"Yes." Queasy feelings. "Call him."

He reached for the wall phone.

I stopped seeing Joey in my head and saw me, lecturing to a class. They respected me; were even scared of me. Rebecca Plotnik, M.A., Ph.D. "Actually, it's perfect. I won't have to live with my parents. It would solve all my problems."

He dialed.

"I'd like teaching English. Maybe I could teach theater, as well? I'd love that. I really would."

My stomach flip-flopped.

"Read your notes on Lawrence and <u>Middlemarch</u>, by the way. Great job. Basically, it's there. All you need's a conclusion."

"Okay. Here's my conclusion: At the end of <u>Middlemarch</u>, Elliot marries Dorothea off, gives her a couple of kids, and tells the reader to bear in mind that in her heroine's day women didn't have many options. <u>Middlemarch</u> is depressing. Lawrence, on the other hand, is inspiring! He makes the reader believe that life's worth living if you have the courage to live and love with passion. <u>Lady Chatterley's Lover</u> is one fucking great book!"

Milligan hung up the phone. Chuckled. "After all you've been through, you're still a romantic at heart."

"But, I'm not a fool—not any more. I couldn't wait to give up everything for Alex. Never again."

"So, I assume you want me to keep trying to reach my colleague about the nanny job? Unless, you're serious about selling real estate?"

"Keep calling." I felt a little quiver of doubt, but ignored it. "After my last job, I refuse to sell dirt, even if I could make a fortune at it. Teaching is as real as it gets."

He smiled, as if pleased things had gone his way. "You won't regret it." He dialed. "Your actor friend, Joey Goldman, sounds interesting."

"More than interesting. He's incredibly talented, but ruthlessly ambitious. Unlike me." My stomach twisted. "We had an act—Plotnik & Goldman. We were good—really good. He wanted me to quit college and move to New York." I took a breath. "But, I wasn't ready."

"Still no answer. But, I expect they'll be home any minute." We stared at each other. The hardwood floor creaked as I shifted weight from side to side. "Something wrong?"

I avoided his eyes. "I don't know. I guess I'm feeling a little uneasy—about the nanny job."

He looked annoyed. "You said yourself it's the perfect solution to all of your problems."

"I know. And I don't want to sound ungrateful." I stared at the clock, the ceiling, the floor. "It just feels like I'm rushing into it."

Milligan actually smiled. "Go home and think about it. You can call me in the morning before ten."

It felt like my feet were glued to the floor. "I can't go home. Not yet. It's too depressing. I need to force myself to make a decision. Waiting until tomorrow will only make it harder."

Milligan's face was a rock. "For once in your life, you have to face reality, Rebecca. Without money, your only choice is to stay here and make the best of it. New York is out of the question. It's a dream."

"I just—I just wish I had more options."

"But, you don't." Milligan went to the sink. Splashed water on his face. Glanced back at me like he wished I'd disappear.

"You can't expect me to feel good about staying here when so many bad things have happened—not only to me, to my family, my friends." He didn't respond, but there was a trace of sympathy in his eyes. "How can I forgive this fucking town?"

"I can see why you would want to leave,

Rebecca, given what you've been through. But, that's the past." He glanced at the phone. "I can help you change all that."

I sat down at the kitchen table. I tried to tell him to make the call, but the words stuck in my throat. I closed my eyes. Until that moment, I had never thought about Izzy's nest-egg. I could see the cigar boxes stacked against his closet wall, five-six thousand dollars, maybe more—enough to move to New York— enough to support me for a year—even two, if I worked part-time. Money Izzy would just gamble away. Why shouldn't I take it? It wouldn't be stealing. Izzy had never been a father. He'd never given me anything. He owed me!

I stood, holding onto the chair with one hand. "Okay. I've made a decision." I swallowed—took a deep breath. "I'm going to New York."

"What? But, how-?"

"I have the money. All I need is the guts to take it."

"Ten minutes ago you were broke and unemployed. Now, you're asking me to believe that everything's changed?"

"The money is real. I wish you'd stop looking at me like that. I'm not crazy." Emma trotted over and licked my hand. I bent down to pet her without taking my eyes off of him. "You know something? Your dog is too good for you."

Milligan laughed, in spite of himself. "Big realization. Big, important realization."

"No. The big, important realization is, that I'm finally ready to go to New York." I took a deep breath. "My mother didn't have the courage to follow her dreams, but I do. And I don't need anybody to make my decisions for me—not my parents, not Joey. Not even you."

"Well," he said, "this certainly is an unexpected turn of events." He smiled. "I agree about making your own decisions. It's your life. The rest of us can only advise. I may disagree with your choices, but I admire your spirit. Always have." He went to the fridge, started to open it, then looked at me. "I hope whatever it is you're planning to do won't get you arrested. I'd hate to have to bail you out."

"Don't worry. I'm not going to take anything that doesn't belong to me. But, I appreciate your concern." I continued petting Emma. "You're the only thing I'll miss about Las Vegas. You and Emma." I wanted to hug him, but hugged Emma instead.

Milligan went into the living room and came back carrying my things. He didn't say a word as he helped me with my coat, but at the door he took my hand.

"Keep in touch. I'll be rooting for you."

48.

The bus driver dimmed the lights. Our bus was next in line to leave the station. On train trips to Cincinnati with Sadie, she would always pack little treats in our suitcases. Hard candy. Mrs. See's chocolates. Crumbled Lorna Doones in Tupperware. She loved the dining car. The waiters in long white aprons, the hot chocolate in little silver pots. She especially loved chatting with strangers in the ladies' room while we waited to brush our teeth. "You meet the nicest people on the train," she'd say. Over and over. Which is why I was on the bus.

"Where are you going, dear?"

The woman sitting next to me was about sixty. Plump, in a pink angora sweater and gray wool skirt with accordion pleats on the sides. Vaselined lips. Glasses on a chain. Her name was Doris, she'd told me, but everybody called her Dorrie. On her lap, a tin with an old-fashioned Santa Claus and his reindeer on the lid. Chocolate chip cookies. She'd offered me one; I'd declined.

"New York City. How about you?"

"Oklahoma City." She was sucking a Lifesaver. Whistling through her teeth. "See you've got your mukluks on. I brought mine along, too. I'll change into them right before I go to sleep. Want a Lifesaver? They're practically no calories."

I shook my head. "I hurt my feet. Doctor wants

me to wear slippers for a week or so."

"How did you do that?"

"Oh, you know." I shrugged. "Those shoes with high heels and pointy toes."

She shook her head with disgust on her face. "You girls! Why on earth do you wear those things? They ruin your feet."

"I guess we're just slaves to fashion." My stomach growled. "Maybe I will have a Lifesaver. Anything but pineapple."

"The next one's cherry."

"Cherries are good." I chuckled, remembering how the slots ate all my nickels at the Horseshoe Club. "Think cherries." I popped it in my mouth.

"I was only in New York once, but I'll never forget those skyscrapers. You feel so small and unimportant. Everybody's in a hurry. Is this a vacation?"

I shook my head. "I'm moving there."

"Moving to New York City! Well, aren't you brave!"

"My boyfriend lives in the Village. He's going to help me get settled." *Joey was sweet on the phone. Insisted on meeting me at the Port of Authority. Funny name for a bus station.* "I won a scholarship to study acting with Stella Adler. The Israel Plotnik Performing Arts Award."

"Well, isn't that exciting! My son's in show business too. Runs the lights at the Tropicana. He and his wife have a lovely apartment off Flamingo Road— swimming pool, air conditioner. Never get a place like that in Oklahoma. For the money."

"My parents have a place like that. Swimming pool. Wall-to-wall carpets." I'd destroyed most of a sponge getting wine stains out of that carpet. Yesterday.

Seemed like years.

"They must be proud of their little girl. Bet they're busting their buttons."

Dear Mom, I know how hard it is going to be for you with me gone, but this is something I have to do, and on some level I know you'll understand. If you divorce my father, I'll be a hundred and fifty percent behind you! Throw the bum out! You deserve to be happy!!!

"They are. Especially my dad. He sort of gave me that extra little push."

"Makes such a difference if your family's behind you." She clicked her tongue. "Nothing like family."

"For years he saved all his silver dollars for me. If I succeed," I took a breath, "it will be because of him." Didn't leave a note for Izzy. One look in his closet, he'd know.

The lights came back on as the bus driver revved the engine and backed out of the Greyhound Station driveway.

"Leaving home is hard, isn't it, dear?"

"Yeah, but growing up in Las Vegas prepares you for just about anything." I got out a Kleenex and blew my nose.

Dorrie patted my shoulder. "So many girls want to be actresses these days, but very few succeed. Don't be too disappointed if things don't work out. Just remember, you have a home to come back to."

"The thing is, I have an added incentive: my mother. Her mom told her to follow her dreams when she was my age, but she didn't have the money. Now, she wishes she'd done it anyway. So, I can't go home until I've made both our dreams come true."

"Well, aren't you the sweetest thing?"

I stood and reached up to the rack where I put my over-night case and a paper bag with books for the trip.

"What's that you're reading, dear?"

"Oh, a book my professor gave me—<u>Emma</u>, by Jane Austin. I think he has a crush on me, but he's too old." I winked.

Dorie puckered her lips as if she'd tasted something sour, and got out her knitting.

The bus picked up speed once it reached the highway. I thought about turning around to take one last look. Instead, I turned the page.

About the Author

Marilyn grew up in Las Vegas, where Bugsy Siegel bounced her on his knee and gave her silver dollars for her piggy bank. She spent her formative years acting in theater companies in Connecticut and Massachusetts, and went on to write and direct the show TIME PLAY, which won both the National Endowment for the Humanities and the National Endowment for the Arts grant. She also acted in one of the most widely viewed sex education films in the US, DEAR DIARY (much to her children's dismay). She has written extensively for print and theater and maintains a vintage Vegas blog at www.neondreamsthebook.com. Neon Dreams is her first full length novel.

She has three grown children and currently lives in Brookline, MA with her husband, Mike.

Made in the USA
San Bernardino, CA
18 January 2014